C000321272

SEDU[CTION]
by DESIGN

GLADYS
HOBSON

Seduction by Design
Gladys Hobson
Cover picture by Charles Davis

Printed by Direct-POD
www.direct-pod.com

Copyright © 2010 Magpies Nest Publishing
ISBN 978-0-9548885-3-4
Magpies Nest Publishing
seduction@magpiesnestpublishing.co.uk

May be ordered from bookshops or directly at
www.magpiesnestpublishing.co.uk

My thanks to all, family, friends and critics, who have
encouraged and supported me as an author .
A special mention to Simon Hobson for his valuable
contribution to the book's production.

Seduction By Design is a sequel to Awakening Love,
also published by Magpies Nest Publishing.

The third part of the trilogy is called Checkmate

Prologue

Spring 1959

Feeling hot and sticky from the day's activities, June took a quick shower before slipping into the exquisite white nightdress Rob had given her to try on. Just the feel of its silky smoothness clinging to her body, and the sight of peaked nipples peeping through the lacy top, changed her self-perception. She now felt herself to be a highly desirable woman.

Looking at herself in the mirror, she saw hazel eyes, bright with the surge of sexual pleasure, smiling back at her. Now brushing her dark curly hair, aglow with chestnut highlights, she was pleased to see her pleasant oval face had lost the ageing lines of emotional stress. The youth of her twenty-eight years had been regained — no, more than that, she felt, and looked, younger and more alive than she had done for several years.

She put down her brush and smoothed her hands over her full breasts and down the luxurious fabric to her hips. The strength of her sexuality began to rise even further. She knew Rob had given her the garment deliberately; he understood such things.

She was anxious to know if she was still attractive to him. For reassurance, nothing more. Nervously, she walked to the door, eager yet fearful to enter the bedroom knowing in the depth of her heart what the encounter might lead to.

Much to her surprise, Rob had changed into a black silk kimono, and was looking ruthlessly sexy. He turned and gazed at her. An appreciative smile curled his full lips and softened his chiselled features. In his usual manner when judging clothes, he rubbed a thumb into the deep hollow of his chin. But combined with the narrowing of his penetrating eyes under their heavy brows, the simple action conveyed to her a much deeper meaning.

'Beautiful,' was all he said. But the way that he said it quickened her heartbeat and brought colour to her cheeks.

She could see the effect she was having on him. He was so obviously aroused, and it thrilled her. He told her to turn around and show off the back of the nightdress. But she knew what he really wanted and her body tensed in anticipation. He came up close behind, pulling her to him and smoothing his hands over her body. Through the thin garment she could feel him hard against her. Then his mouth — so soft and moist — touched her neck and shoulders. Her spine tensed and curved as he continued to pleasure her.

'You are adorable,' he whispered in her ear.

She felt his fingers slip under the straps of the gown, and she trembled as it slithered to the floor... a soft silky pool around her ankles. Now his hands were fondling her breasts. Oh, yes, yes... sending her into phantom journeys of erotic delight.

'No more, no more,' she moaned unconvincingly.

He turned her to face him, sweeping his eyes down her tensed-up body. She felt them piercing into her sensitive flesh, causing her to shiver in expectation of what was to come.

'No more?' he whispered mockingly.

She caught her breath, knowing what he would do to her. Her body was aglow and she could not resist him. 'No more—' A sharp intake of breath silenced her pleading: 'Ahhh!'

He was mouthing her breasts, radiating sensations to the whole of her body. She heard herself panting as his tongue followed his fingers on a downward path. She longed to give in to hedonistic pleasure. Earthy passion was urging her: yes, oh, yes. But feelings of guilt told her to resist. She had never been unfaithful to her husband.

'No, don't. Please don't. I can't do this.'

She knew she was free to go; he wasn't holding her. But she was thrilled by what he was doing to her and she couldn't escape her desire for more. More. More. Oh, yes, more! Her back arched with the pleasure of it and she groaned in ecstasy. Her eyes closed to the intensity of the rapture.

She felt herself being lifted up. Conscience finally subdued by desire, she fell easily into his arms. There was no help for it: he could do with her as he pleased.

Chapter One

July 1969

Captain Charles Rogers sat in his Mercedes thinking about making love to his sister-in-law, June Rogers. Years of self-denial, at least as far as June was concerned, had never lessened his sexual urges every time he thought about her. But now that possession of her had become a possibility, his erotic thoughts of exploring her beautiful body had a habit of spilling over into orgasmic responses — even before his imagination could get as far as the ultimate penetration.

He had been driving for hours, and needed time to unwind and get his thoughts together before reaching his destination. Parking his silver Mercedes in the lay-by to eat his sandwiches had seemed like a good idea, but he was finding it hard to take his mind off what his body was crying out for.

He brought to memory June's reactions when he'd visited her a little while after his brother Arthur's funeral: her response to his touch, her expression of joy at seeing him again and her acceptance of his kiss. The ashes of a much earlier romance were certainly far from dead.

More than anything else he wanted to marry her, but he would accept anything she was willing to give. Could a love that flourished twenty years earlier burst into flame once more? She was still in her thirties, a brilliant designer, elegant and good-looking. For certain, he would not be the only one to desire her: as a wife, a business partner, or simply to get her into bed.

Such thoughts renewed his urgings. How on earth would he be able to cope with living so close to her? With his appetite for women, voluntary abstinence from the fairer sex whilst waiting for June was not going to be easy; neither would close contact with her look-alike daughter.

Sighing deeply, he put aside the remains of his sandwiches and screwed the top back onto his flask of tea. Time to move on and face the future so full of possibilities, whether pleasurable or disappointing. Deep in thought, he automatically put the car into gear and drove the last few miles to his new home — Bloomfield. On reaching the familiar avenue of mature lime trees, he turned into the drive and parked the Mercedes in front of the substantial brick-and-stone Victorian residence.

There she was at the open door, dressed in a youthful yellow-flowered dress. As he left the car, she came running down the steps to greet him, her rich brown hair bobbing around her bare shoulders, and her face flushed with excitement. As he bent over to kiss her, she threw her arms around his neck and fully responded. Even though it was only done in greeting, there was both warmth and desire in that embrace.

'Charlie, it's so lovely to see you,' she said, pulling a little away from him, as though afraid of her aroused emotions. 'Just bring your small bags for now. We can get the rest of your things later.'

As she turned to his car to reach for a bag, he tenderly caught her arm. 'Are you sure you want an old sea-dog cluttering up your place?'

'Oh, Charlie, we all want you here. The boys are so excited that you're staying. And you know you're Rosie's favourite uncle.'

Charles framed June's face with his hands and looked down into her gold-flecked, hazel eyes, searching for her feelings about him. They were bright and shining, moist with happiness. How he longed to speak passionately of his love for her, to take her inside and consummate that love, but he knew that must wait.

'You know, you are still the girl I fell in love with,' he said tenderly. 'You look too young to be Rosie's mother. You haven't changed a bit since that night I took you dancing, and people stood and watched because you looked so beautiful.'

'They stood and watched because you were such a wonderful dancer. You even made me seem good. It was rather wonderful.'

He was thrilled that June remembered the night he had spoken of his love for her. He kissed her gently and gave her a hug.

'That was a real night to remember,' he said, releasing her. 'We must go dancing again sometime.'

'That will be lovely. I know it's what Arthur wanted,' she said, shying away from his concentrated gaze. 'Maybe in a few months' time. Now let's get you inside.'

He detected a sudden cooling of the situation. Hardly surprising: it was only five months since Arthur's funeral. Now he was feeling guilty of trespass, and no doubt June had her own conflicting emotions to contend with. No matter what Arthur had requested, in fact, begged of him, their personal grief would take time to heal and feelings of transgression were not easily abated.

They carried a few of the smaller items of luggage through the porch and into the large panelled hall. Like all the main rooms, it had a fine moulded ceiling and elaborate cornices. He looked around him, nostalgia tugging at his heart. Yes, most of the furniture had changed since he was a boy, but the grandfather clock was still ticking, keeping alive poignant memories of times happy and sad. His last visits, coming to see Arthur when he was dying and afterwards to visit June in her grief, seemed both far away and yet so near. Putting aside such powerful thoughts and feelings, he followed his dead brother's wife up the first flight of carpeted stairs and listened to her cheerful chatter.

'I've had the whole of the upper floor, apart from the storage rooms, converted into an apartment for you,' she said as they reached the landing and approached the door to the top floor. 'I hope you will like the furnishings. I designed the whole scheme myself. But perhaps I should have consulted you first.'

'Not at all,' he said, concerned at her self-doubt. 'Whatever you have done will be lovely. But you had that floor previously converted to workrooms for your design business. Do you have new premises?'

'No. I guess I let things go into decline when Arthur was ill. When he died, I lost interest. I seemed to lose it… the inspiration I mean. I had no heart for the work. I felt dead inside and it showed in my designs. Hardly surprising the business went into decline. Then my cutter-fitter landed a top job in London, and the rest of them went to work for Robert Watson. I have my studio and I still design fabrics for Rob. He doesn't know it yet, but Rosie has done most of the dress designing.'

'Good for her. Just like her mum, beautiful and gifted.'

June sighed as she opened the door to the stairs of his new apartment. 'Not any more as far as I'm concerned, but Rosie has a lot of talent.'

They reached the top floor hallway and put down the bags. He turned and held her shoulders, firmly but gently. 'It will come back, June. Once you get inspired, ideas will just flow from you. You need to get away from sad memories for a while and start to live again. You can't possibly lose such a precious gift. It just needs reawakening.'

She dropped her eyes. 'Start to live again? That's exactly what Rob wrote to me when Arthur died. "Start to live again, the door is open." When I left Watson's to marry Arthur, Robert told me that one day I would be back working for him. But I'm afraid, Charlie. Once I get really inspired I get carried away.'

He felt her body give a little shudder. Drawing her head to the firmness of his chest, he held her closely in his arms as though to protect her from all harm.

'Let go, June, it's better to live dangerously than to be dead to life. Arthur knew that. Didn't he encourage you to go on with your work even when you were prepared to give it up for love of him?'

'Yes. But he didn't want Robert Watson to take me over body and soul. Didn't he tell you, Charlie? He negotiated with Rob on my behalf. I guess Arthur knew me better than I knew myself.'

'Yes, I can believe that.'

But Robert Watson could be discussed later. His own relationship with June was far more important at that moment. 'Show me around this place,' he told her with sudden enthusiasm. 'If the rest of it is as good as the hall, I'll give this flat a five star rating!'

He put a hand on June's shoulder and they walked around his new home. The rooms had a masculine feel about them. He admired the green leather armchairs, cream-and-green carpeting, dark G-Plan furniture and built-in bookshelves in his large sitting room. The enlarged bathroom, with its white five-piece suite, had walls bright with mirrors and glossy black tiles; a thick brick-red carpet was covering the floor, and green towels and foliage added a sense of outdoor freshness. Everything was to his taste, including the luxurious fitted bedroom furnished in deep-blue and white with splashes of red. He looked at the king-size bed with longing in his heart. His wishful thinking didn't escape June's notice.

'One day, Charlie, it's what I want too. It's been well over a year since I had sex with Arthur. At least, full sex, if you know what I mean.' She sighed deeply. 'I must confess, I've missed it. Arthur always made it so good. Even when he became impotent, he did his best to make up for it.'

Tears glistened in June's eyes. Charles felt her pain in his own heart. He took her from the bedroom and suggested he made them a pot of tea.

'I'll do it, you finish looking around,' she told him, forcing a cheerful smile.

While she made the tea in the kitchen, he peeped into the huge attic storerooms filled with old furniture he recognised from his youth. Standing on a small mahogany table, was a model sailing ship he'd made when he was a boy. He picked it up and took it to the kitchen.

'Arthur helped me make this boat. He helped me with so many things in life. But how come it's so clean and polished?'

'When your parents moved out, Arthur found it in the attic. He brought it out, cleaned and mended it, and said it must always be there for you when you returned home. It's funny, as if Arthur knew you would be back here one day. He said something about bees to honey. I'm not sure what he meant though. I suppose the attraction of this place.'

Charles laughed. 'Not the place, June. The person in it! Father always said you were like honey... sweet and innocent. He was right. I guess he found you attractive himself. We old men still find youth attractive you know.'

'Come off it, Charlie! You're only fifty tomorrow.' She swept her eyes over him. 'And still as handsome as ever.'

'Flattery will get you everywhere!'

'Right, in that case....' She grinned and cocked her head coquettishly. 'Tall, broad shouldered and in good trim. Fantastic tan, and what a gorgeous smile. Such strong white teeth! Nicely shaped nose. Big mouth with lips ripe for kissing. Oh yes, and lovely dark bedroom eyes.'

Charles tried to pull his thoughts away from the picture her words had generated in his mind. 'I am indeed flattered.'

'And we must not forget that glossy dark hair, as seen in the best hair cream adverts. Even that tinge of grey is rather sexy!'

They both laughed. Charles had to rest the boat on the table. 'Well, with a testimonial like that I should win the Hunk of the Year competition!'

He sat down and picked up his cup of tea. 'Better drink this before it gets cold.' After a moment's reflection, he asked her, 'Are you going to walk through Robert Watson's door and start to live again?'

June sat down opposite him. She picked up her cup. He watched her closely as, deep in thought, she turned a finger around the golden rim.

'I don't think so. You see, Charlie, there's something you don't know about me and Rob. Yes, he could make me come alive again, but there's a dark side to him and that affects me too. Anyway, I have to see him. Sooner rather than later.'

'You mean about your youngest son, James?'

June looked at him wide-eyed. 'You know about Jimmy?'

'Arthur told me. When he asked me to take care of you, he thought it only fair I should know what I would be taking on.'

'You can still love me, knowing what happened?'

'Arthur never stopped loving you. In fact, he blamed himself for what happened. Heavens! Who am I to judge an angel like you? Me, former lecher, unfaithful husband of a faithless wife, and not short of the odd affair since I was divorced from Angela.'

'I'm no angel, and it wasn't Arthur's fault. I don't know what he told you but I must take all the blame. You have to know the truth — the real truth — of what happened.'

'June, if you want to tell me, I'm willing to listen, but I'm more inclined to believe my brother.'

'You may judge differently when you hear the facts,' she said, taking a sip of her tea and putting down the cup. Her finger again circled the cup's golden rim. She looked up and gave him a nervous smile. 'As you know, about the time Peter was born, your father was getting Arthur seriously involved in politics. That brought him into close contact with your father's secretary, Betty Butler. I knew Betty was in love with Arthur, even if Arthur refused to acknowledge it.'

'I remember Betty helping Arthur out sometimes, but she didn't seem the type to split up a marriage.'

'Betty didn't do anything, really, but she was always in the background. After Peter's birth, I became tired and depressed. Arthur made sure I had all the help I needed, but everything seemed an emotional burden. It all became a vicious circle. My work fell off and I lost some of my customers. I became even more depressed and inspiration failed me. Our lovemaking became less exciting and less frequent. I was constantly tired. The children got on my nerves. I felt I was a bad mother and an even worse wife. I lost interest in my work. In everything. And so it went on.'

Charles took hold of her hands to reassure her. 'I'm so sorry,' he said, sensing her pain. 'I should have realised at the time, but I guess I was too tied up with my own marital problems. I suppose Arthur felt powerless to help you.'

'He tried to be at home more, but he was under a lot of pressure at the time. He was going to give up the political work but I knew his thoughts were on Parliament. I wanted him to get there, Charlie. Arthur seemed so right for the work.'

'I guess he took after Father. I suppose that's where Betty came in. She was really good in politics and probably helped him quite a bit.'

'Yes, but Betty is only part of the story.' She glanced down, sighing. He gently squeezed her hand. She looked up again and gave him a forced smile. 'When my designing fell off, Rob could easily have ended our contract, but instead he asked me to design clothes for children. Since I was involved with children, he said it might inspire me to design for them.'

'So Robert Watson was close to you at that time?'

'Yes, but at a distance. His main concern has always been profitable business. Then he wanted me to get involved with a new line in lingerie. He asked me to go to London with him. I said that Arthur was away — in London, as it so happened — and I didn't want to leave the children. Rob said I was being ridiculous; a change would be good for all of us. He suggested I go and surprise Arthur by turning up to sleep with him at night. Rob has always believed sexual satisfaction helps creativity to flow. He should know... after all, he is a successful entrepreneur in the world of fashion with quite a reputation where women are concerned.'

'You said that once you get inspired, you get carried away. Is that what happened with Rob? Is that what you're afraid of now?'

She slowly nodded. 'Not without reason.' She rose from her chair and walked over to the window. A breeze had sprung up and the curtains — bright red and white check to match the red pots and utensils — were flapping wildly. She closed the window a little and sat down again. 'I went to London with Rob and we visited the shops and some of his contacts. It was wonderful. Rob refused to let me be weary or dull. He took me to Arthur's hotel, saying to stay the night. We were to have a business discussion the next day, but he said not to rush my time with Arthur.... I had never known Rob to be so considerate.'

Charles was aware that June was beginning to tremble, and he asked her if she really wanted to go on.

'Yes... I must. You have to know what happened.'

While he waited for her to continue, he poured them both another cup of tea. 'Take your time. There's no hurry.'

'Arthur was in his dressing gown when he opened his door. At first, he seemed pleasantly surprised, but suddenly he looked concerned. I soon found out why — Betty was sitting there! I can see her now, dressed in a pretty silk dressing gown. Then I noticed the wet hair.'

'Wet hair? They had showered and were relaxing in their dressing-gowns?'

'Said like that, it sounds so innocent. But you see, our lovemaking often started in the shower. Seeing Betty — a woman in love — dressed in that flimsy garment and with her hair wet through, made me think of only one thing. I ran off. I saw Rob in the hotel bar and begged him to take me away from there.'

'What did Rob think about it?'

'He was happy to take me to his hotel, but he said that I was being stupid about the whole thing. He said it was ridiculous for me not to expect Arthur to have a change occasionally, and that I should do the same thing.'

Charles nodded. 'I guess he was getting you prepared for just that.'

'Do you really think so? I must admit I hadn't thought of what happened that night as being premeditated by Rob.' She was thoughtful for a moment or two. 'Maybe you're right. Well, he shook me and told me to forget Arthur and concentrate on the job in hand. The lingerie we'd bought that day was spread around Rob's room. It was so pretty and feminine that my enthusiasm returned. After discussing possibilities for our own range, he approached me again about going back to work with him full time.'

'Give up your other work?'

'Yes. He was about to expand his business and it was all so exciting. I let go of Arthur... the children... my responsibilities, and just for a while contemplated being back in the swim of things.'

Even as June was speaking, her face lit up with remembered zeal for her design work. Clearly, it meant a lot to her. He must try and get her back into the fashion business. It was what Arthur would have wanted.

'It probably did you a lot of good, no matter what happened afterwards.'

'I don't know, Charlie. You had better hear the rest of the story.' She closed her eyes a moment as though to view the long-ago scene. 'Rob handed me a gorgeous silk-and-lace nightdress. He told me to try it on in his bathroom. I couldn't refuse. I was dying to see what it looked like on. It had been a hot day so I took a quick shower to freshen up. As I said, it was an expensive garment and I didn't want to soil it. Well, that is what I told myself. But, was that the real reason? I very much doubt that I was being honest with myself.'

'But June, we all have mixed motives for everything we do,' Charles told her, worried that she was about to accuse herself of premeditated adultery. 'Being complicated is what makes us human.'

She smiled. 'Dear Charlie, always ready to think the best of me. You'll see for yourself that I was not the good little wife you imagine me to be.'

'I'll take some convincing otherwise. It seems to me Rob set you up,' he told her with conviction. 'Anyway, I interrupted you. Please go on with the story.'

'When I put the nightdress on, I felt somehow different. It clung to my figure and was quite revealing. I felt myself to be a desirable woman, instead of a sexless creature.'

'Sexless? You were never that. Every time I visited your home, you always looked so lovely.'

'You might think that, but there were times when I hated myself for being selfish and always wanting Arthur to be with me, especially in our bed. I detested myself for not being the mother I ought to be, or the wife I should be. I thought myself ungrateful for having so much and yet wanting more. Hatred made me ugly.'

Charles squeezed her hand. 'You're too hard on yourself.'

She shook her head. 'Perhaps you only see in me, what you want to see. Anyway, after talking fashion with Rob I was lifted out of myself. And then putting on that nightdress and seeing myself in the mirror, well, I began to see a young alluring woman. Rob understands these things. It's what he tries to get in his designs. You know, clothes with sex appeal. Clothes that make women feel good about themselves. I guess he knew the effect the nightdress would have on me. I wanted to see if I was still attractive to him after eight years… sort of confirm what I could see in the mirror. I went back into his bedroom and found him stripped and wearing a kimono.'

'Watson certainly knew what he was doing. He trapped you when you were most vulnerable.'

'Maybe,' she said thoughtfully. 'But perhaps I wanted to be trapped.'

For a few moments she closed her eyes, as if reliving her feelings at that time.

'He looked so handsome and sexy in that black silk kimono. I can see him now, with his dark curly hair flopping over those smouldering eyes of his. It was so obvious that he was aroused. It thrilled me, Charlie, really thrilled me.' She ran a finger around the gold rim of her cup. 'And he knew it,' she added, nodding her head. 'He came behind me and I could feel him hard against my body. I wanted to pull away before things got too far, but part of me was desperate for love — torrid love.' She put her hands over her eyes and was silent for a moment.

'Would you like to stop now?'

She shook her head, and once again traced the cup's rim. 'He kissed my neck and smoothed his hands down my body, running his fingers all the way down my spine, and I mean *all* the way. That's something I find irresistible.'

Charles made a mental note for the future. He was finding it hard to stay detached. He could see the scene before his eyes and it was most disturbing.

'He slipped the straps of my gown over my shoulders. The nightdress slithered to the floor.'

She stopped again, her eyes far away, her breath becoming more rapid. 'He caressed my body with his mouth... if you know what I mean?'

'I certainly do,' he told her, his throat dry and his voice a little husky.

He watched her closely, his imagination working in tune with her memories. He realised he was being considerably aroused, and hoped she would soon finish her story before he had to rush to the bathroom.

'The point is, Charlie, I couldn't help myself. I was thrilled — ecstatic! I loved every moment of his love-play. Then Rob picked me up and put me on the bed. He didn't rape me, like he did on the factory floor all those years ago, because I was a willing partner. I wanted it, craved for it. But I felt as guilty as hell. I wanted his lovemaking to really hurt. You know, punish me for being wicked. But it didn't. It was terrific. Rob went on, harder and harder, until... well... you know.'

Charles was now sweating profusely. 'Yes, I know,' he said, loosening his tie and unbuttoning the neck of his shirt.

'When I got home, Arthur was already there and worried sick. He explained about Betty and I felt so ashamed. He was surprised that I wasn't angry and that I actually believed him. But then, of course, I had to tell him what had happened with Rob. Arthur was so understanding. He must have been badly hurt, but he hid his own feelings and said that he was as much to blame.'

Charles nodded in agreement. It was what Arthur had told him.

'Our lovemaking grew stronger and I was also happier with my designing. Rob kept his distance but we got on well with the lingerie range. In a way, Arthur was grateful to Rob for renewing my creativity, but he still hated him. He made sure that we met as little as possible and never alone. When James was born we hoped it was Arthur's child, but a blood test told us otherwise. I guess we knew it all along. Jimmy is so like Robert. He has a similar build, and that same determined chin with the deep hollow. Both have dark, thick unruly hair. If Robert ever saw him and knew his exact age, he would know that Jimmy is his son. What's more, with Robert getting more in the public eye, who knows what may be conjectured?'

'I can see the problem. Perhaps...'

Sounds of heavy footsteps and noisy chatter told Charles his first visitors had arrived.

'Uncle Charlie! Uncle Charlie!' James yelled, throwing his arms around Charles. 'Will you take us sailing?'

'Can we sail the Scottish lochs, Uncle?' Peter butted in.

David's deeper voice sounded above the others: 'No! Uncle Charlie said we could sail the Caribbean. He promised us.'

'Yes, David, I did promise. It was something I was planning with your father. It had to be cancelled, but we can do it next year. I'll talk it over with your mother.'

'A Caribbean trip will need a lot of planning,' June said. 'We were in the early stages when Arthur was taken ill. I'll have to think about it.'

The children started shouting all at once. Charles was about to quell them when June raised her voice.

'Downstairs, all of you. Let your uncle settle in.' She ushered them out, going downstairs with them. 'Get yourselves washed ready for dinner.'

Just as their protests faded, Rosie arrived at the top of the stairs. Charles had to catch his breath. With her summer tan, fresh complexion, bright hazel eyes and flowing dark hair, she looked so much like June had done at seventeen. But her clothes were certainly different. She was wearing the briefest of miniskirts below a red strapless top, showing off her comely breasts and gorgeous shapely legs to great advantage. Charles made a mental note not to walk up the stairs behind her. He stood up.

'Nice to see you again, Rosie.'

She came up to him, hands on hips and sweetly smiling. 'Hello, Charlie, it's good to see you,' she said in a silky voice. 'I hope you'll be happy here. If I can do anything — anything at all — to make you more comfortable, just let me know.'

'Thank you, Rosie, I'll keep that in mind,' he said, hoping the suggestive manner of her welcome was not a harbinger of trouble ahead. 'What a mature young woman stands before me. No longer that shy little girl I once knew.'

'I have never been a shy little girl. You must be thinking of my mother when she was young. Daddy used to tell me about my innocent, shy mother.' She looked him in the eye. 'He told me that you loved her too. Are you going to marry her?'

With her posing seductively by the kitchen cabinet just a few feet away, he was expecting her to throw her arms around him any second. He offered her a seat at the kitchen table. She slid herself into the chair and crossed her legs. He sat down opposite her. He felt safer with the table between them.

'I take it you would be happy with the idea,' he said, trying to ignore her exposed bare thighs.

'I know it's what Daddy wanted,' she said, squirming round in her seat to pick up a gold-rimmed red cup from the worktop. Charles closed his eyes — worried she was about to pop out of her clinging top. 'I think Mum wants it too, but I guess she's still too upset to think about marrying again.'

She poured milk into her cup and drained the pot of its stale tea. 'I think the boys need a father. Mum's too soft with them. The sooner you live with us for good, the better it will be.' Her eyes, with their long lashes, were peering at him quizzically over her cup of tea.

Charles rose from his chair, ostensibly to put the kettle on, but really to escape his discomfort. 'Well, it's nice to know I have your approval,' he said cheerfully.

Rosie slithered out of her chair. 'It will be nice to have you around the house, Charlie.'

Throwing her arms around his neck, she stretched up on her toes and kissed him full on the lips. He didn't want to push her away too abruptly and risk tantrums, but she was putting him into a sweat. After almost ten seconds, he gently pulled himself away. He foresaw problems looming. The last thing he wanted was finding Rosie slipping into his bed in the middle of the night.

'That was rather nice, young Rosie. But for my sake, perhaps we should keep any kissing to a peck on the cheek.' He said this firmly, but with a gentle smile.

'If you say so, but we both know you enjoyed it as much as I did,' she said, glancing downwards.

'Can't deny it, can I? I'm only a vulnerable horny male. But it's not good for either of us. I'm your father's brother. Sorry, my lovely niece, but it's not allowed, which is just as well, since I'm an old fogy who's in love with your mother.'

'I'm not proposing marriage, Uncle,' she said, looking at him from under her lashes. 'You have experience of many women. Everyone knows that. But, Uncle, you should get with it. Flower power is here to stay, and I'll be your Rosie-bud any day.'

'Now then, young lady, you're only trying to shock me. Or worse still, trying to see what you can do to my anatomy. So stop kidding me, woman, and go help your mother get my dinner.'

'Chauvinist piggy!'

Rosie disappeared down the stairs, leaving Charles sighing with relief and hoping she really was kidding him. Taking on Rosie, her demanding teenage brothers, and that particular problem concerning young James as part of a marriage package, was going to be quite an experience. Not only that, but June's relationship to Robert Watson was also a potential threat to future happiness. Well, he had dealt with worse things in the Navy — or had he?

Chapter Two

By the time dinner was ready, Charles had done all things needful, including showering and shaving for the second time that day. He had changed into his grey casual trousers and white open-necked shirt. Gone were the days when he was expected to dress formally for family meals, especially in the middle of summer. On the way downstairs, he nearly bumped into June's sister, Peggy. At least, he thought it was Peggy. She was wrapped in a pinny and carried a duster. Her dark hair was peeping below a scarf tied like a turban, her nose — too big for her face — was looking a little red and puffy as though she had been crying, and her hazel eyes looked at him through heavy make-up. She had neither June's good looks nor her elegance, but there was something about her that he recognised.

He stopped to greet her. 'Hello. Peggy, isn't it? June's sister. Used to be called Rose?'

Her eyes lit up with pleasure. 'Fancy you remembering that, Charlie. It's a long time since anyone called me Rose. When I got married, I became Margaret Rose Bush. I got sick of the jokes, and anyway my husband always called me Peggy. So, Peggy I am. I come in nearly every day to give June a hand. Didn't she tell you?'

'No, but we haven't had much chance to talk yet. Is June's housekeeper, Nanny Joyce, still here?'

'Joyce left two months ago. She wanted to go back to looking after young children. The older boys are at boarding school most of the year, and there's not so much work now that we don't have workgirls traipsing through the house. June can manage okay with me and Mrs Craven — the old soul still comes a few hours, most days. June still relies on her to keep the pantry and cupboards stocked, but I do most of the shopping. I like spending other people's money on things I can't afford myself.'

'Well, how are you? Last time I saw you must have been at Arthur's funeral. As I remember, you were busy then. I didn't see you when I was here three months ago.'

Peggy leaned on the banister as though in need of support. Charles sat on a stair and pulled her down next to him. 'Take the weight off your legs a minute or two, Peggy.'

She gave him a grateful smile. 'Thanks, Charlie. It's been a rough time for me as well as for June. My husband left me just before Christmas. Our twin sons have just gone in the army. They were always in trouble, so it's a bit of a relief, but I miss the few pounds they paid me. I've been looking after Mam since Dad died. She's gone funny in the head. That's what made Jerry go off, really. But she's in a home now. She got dangerous to herself and to others... nearly set the house on fire. It was hell. Poor old Mam.'

Charles gently placed a hand on her shoulder. 'I'm so sorry, Peggy.'

She beamed, as though the comforting gesture had given her new vigour. 'So, I'm fancy-free, Charlie. Which reminds me, would you like me to keep your rooms clean and tidy?'

'That would be quite splendid. Let me know the going rate.'

'Will do. I must get on.' She stood up. 'They'll be waiting for you in the dining room.'

Charles followed her down the rest of the stairs. 'Aren't you coming to join us?'

'No. I just come to help June with cleaning and laundry. We both decided it would be best to keep our lives separate. I need the work, you see. It's easy coming here.'

'I'll see you around then, Peggy.'

'You certainly will,' she said, lifting her duster. 'Cheers, Charlie. It'll be a pleasure to work for you.'

It was a noisy dinner. Apart from arguing, the boys were continually asking him questions, but giving him no chance to answer them. Eventually June told them to be quiet or they would be sent to their rooms. Finally, she turned to him. 'You tell them, Charles,' she said, desperation wrinkling her brow. 'They need a man's firm hand.'

Charles was pleased to receive her permission. He was used to a life of order and objected to poor discipline.

'That's enough, boys. I'll talk to you later, one at a time. Do as your mother tells you or you will answer to me.'

Charles heard James muttering something about him not being his dad.

'No, James, I am not your dad. I don't pretend to be.' His voice softened. 'I know you miss your father. It's hard for you youngsters. Please understand, all of you,' he said, casting his eyes over the boys: 'I am not here to replace him. But I am your uncle and godfather, and I take those responsibilities seriously. Your father expected it of me. Now, please be quiet.'

Arthur, who had been a major in the army, had used a similar moderated note of authority when he found it necessary to be strict with his sons. Charles had heard him on a number of occasions. He knew he sounded like their father and he hoped to get the same response. He did — silence!

'Now, in the Navy we do things by the book,' he told them. 'After supper, I want you to go to your rooms and think up some rules and regulations for us all to live by. I want your own ideas as to how we run this ship you call home.'

He had their attention. The boys were sitting up straight and looking interested.

'You had better be sensible with your suggestions. I don't want rules impossible to keep. We'll get together later to discuss them.' He ran his eyes over them. 'Well, men, what do you think of that?'

David said, 'Fair enough,' and the others nodded in agreement.

'Right, so finish this lovely meal your mother prepared,' Charles said, casting his eyes around the table with its plates of half-eaten food, 'and think about what I said. When I've had a chance to discuss things with your mother, we'll talk about that holiday I promised you. If your mother agrees, we'll spend this year getting ourselves into a team. We'll do the English Riviera for practice, ready for the big trip next year. The Caribbean will be great fun, but we don't want any shipmates going overboard. Right, men, eat up and clear those plates.'

The response was instant. June smiled at him. 'Don't let yours get cold either.'

'Since you were addressing the boys, does that mean I don't belong in this family any more?' Rosie said, sounding much aggrieved. 'Am I a nobody? I prepared most of the meal. I took the boys out so you could get a quiet start with mother. I even finished mother's print designs so she would have time for you.'

Charles splayed his hands apologetically. 'I'm so sorry, Rosie, I had no intention of missing you out. Of course I want some input from you.'

He touched her hand, but she snatched it away and grunted.

The tense situation built as the boys waited for his reaction. June looked embarrassed. 'Rosie, that's no way—'

Charles put up a hand to stop her. This was something between him and his niece. 'It's all right, June, Rosie has a right to be upset.'

He glanced at the boys and nodded for them to go on eating. Sighing within himself, he sat back in his chair and looked at the young woman toying with her food. What did he know about young females, how they thought, their loves and passions? Nothing! He decided to be open and honest.

'It's a long time since my sisters were young,' he said quietly. 'I know nothing about bringing up young women. I only know about training young men.' He tried to catch Rosie's eye, but her head was down as she stabbed at a piece of pastry, turning it to a mushy mess. 'Please forgive me, Rosie, I had no intention of ignoring anyone. I guess with working alongside men for so long, I feel awkward with young women.'

Rosie laughed derisively. 'Huh! From what Peggy told me, I should have thought you were quite used to young women, and know exactly what to do with them. What a disappointment! I guess I'll have to give you a little training. How to spank me when I'm naughty. How to make me better. My Paul knew how. I'll pass it on.'

June thumped the table. 'Rosie! Stop this at once! You've gone too far.'

'Really, mother? How far do you intend going? How soon before Charlie takes Daddy's place in your bed?'

'Enough!' June snapped. 'Apologise at once. You're being offensive and you know it!'

Rosie jumped up from her chair and ran out of the room, crying. The boys were agog but said nothing. June looked at Charles, totally embarrassed.

'Don't worry,' he told her, 'she doesn't realise what she's saying. I'll go to her.'

As Charles reached the landing at the top of the stairs, he saw Rosie disappear into her bedroom. He walked silently along the hallway and lightly knocked on her door. 'Rosie, may I come in?'

'Go away. I don't want you here. You don't love me. My dad loved me and he's dead!'

'Rosie, you're so wrong. I do love you.' There was no reply. 'I'm coming in, Rosie.'

He hesitated a moment before entering, wondering at the wisdom of being alone with her in her bedroom. But compassion and a shared grief overcame his natural caution. The room, with its poster-bedecked walls, and white furniture scattered with a young woman's bits and pieces, was bright with evening sunshine. But, drowned in her personal darkness, Rosie lay sobbing uncontrollably on the pretty cover of her bed. He went over to her and looked at her with an aching heart.

'Rosie, I've loved you ever since you were born. Each time I've visited, I've seen you growing into the beautiful person you are today.' He sat on the bed beside her. She was facing away from him, her head buried in her arms and a hand grasping a soggy corner of a sheet. He touched her shoulder. 'Can't we be friends? I'm not trying to replace your father, I just want to love and protect you all.'

He stayed beside her, silently sharing her grief. Eventually, she stopped crying — her body tremulous while she sniffed away her tears.

'Will you help me, Rosie? I don't want to fail your father. I loved him too, you know. When I was young, he was always there for me. He's been my friend throughout my life. Please, Rosie, please. Will you help me?' His throat tightened with emotion; the pain of Arthur's death was never far away.

Rosie turned to face him, clearly shocked at the grief he was unable to hide. She knelt on the bed and put her arms around him.

'I'm so sorry, I never thought of you being upset,' she said, between sniffs. 'You're always so strong and brave.'

Charles took her hands from around his neck and held on to them. 'I have news for you, young lady. Strong men grieve like anyone else, especially when we hurt the ones we love.'

Rosie hugged him, but he was afraid she was going to be passionate again. Gently pulling away from her, he kissed her on her forehead and asked her if she was going to be his Lieutenant Rosie Rogers and help him do his duty.

'Aye, aye, Captain!' Rosie answered, jumping off the bed and standing up straight. She gave him a smart salute.

He stood up and returned her salute. 'With you on board, Rosie, we'll run a tight ship. Keep those rascal recruits in shape!'

She grinned. 'Aye, aye, Captain!'

'I must go now and have a word with your brothers. We'll have another chat sometime. Okay?'

She visibly relaxed. 'Yes please, Uncle. Thank you. I'm glad you're here.'

As he was about to leave the room, he gave her another salute. 'Stand easy, Lieutenant.'

She laughed, and he laughed with her.

As he was about to go downstairs, he heard voices coming through the open door of David's bedroom. He glanced inside and saw Peter and David sprawled on the bed with chins cupped in hands. They seemed to be having a serious discussion. The deep-blue papered room, equipped with desk, cushioned chair and ash-veneered furniture, was orderly — a place for everything and everything in its place. Charles smiled. David was like Arthur in so many ways. He tapped on the door.

'Hi, there. Do you mind if I join you?'

'Of course not, Uncle,' said David, sitting up and offering him a chair close to the bed.

'Thanks,' said Charles, sitting down. 'Are you both okay?'

Peter frowned. 'I know Rosie was rude to you and Mum, but I don't know what all the fuss was about.'

'Oh, Peter!' said David impatiently. He turned to Charles. 'I've been trying to explain things. You know… sex and all that.'

'Really? I guess you're getting a bit of an expert on the subject.'

'Some of the boys at school were at it in the lavatories. You know, with other boys. They were nearly expelled. And a girl in the village got pregnant by a boy in the sixth form. There was a hell of a stink about it. He was an idiot, he should have used a raincoat.'

'Sounds as though you've had a bit of experience yourself.'

'I'll soon be sixteen. Dad went over it several times. You know, for when I'm older. He told me ways to make a girl feel good as well as myself. He wanted me to know about these things before he... he... he wasn't with us any more.' He stopped talking, his face twisting as he fought to control his emotions. Putting on a cheerful mask, he continued: 'I've kissed lots of girls though, and I like to look at them and, you know... well, feel them close to me. You know what I mean?'

'I certainly do.' David's openness had pleasantly surprised him. 'When I was a kid, your dad told me exactly the same things. He was eight years older than me and a wonderful big brother.'

'He gave us a book to read,' David informed him. 'It tells you everything. You know, about sex and all that. But Dad believed sex that made babies should wait until people marry. He said sometimes people get too excited and make mistakes. He told me what to do if I get strong urges hard to control. I was doing it anyway but it was good to know it was okay.'

'He did the same for me. Stick to what he told you. I wish I had. I know it isn't easy.' Charles thought, with his reputation, he was getting into deep water. 'Your dad was right, though. When two people are involved it's selfish to think only of yourself.'

'Can I ask you something, Uncle?' said Peter.

Charles did his best to answer everything put to him. It was a strange experience. He knew he was only reiterating what Arthur must have told his sons, but, of course, his experiences had been totally different from those of his brother.

David suddenly declared: 'I think Rosie's just jealous. She really likes you, Uncle Charlie. I bet she wants you in her bed.'

Charles was shocked to hear such words. The trouble was, he had a horrible suspicion they might be true!

He forced himself to stay relaxed. 'She's just upset and didn't realise what she was saying. You don't either, David. People don't make love with close relatives. I'm just an uncle who's naturally fond of her. No more so than either of you. Rosie knows that now. She was just upset because she felt left out. It was nothing more than that.'

Charles gave them another ten minutes and then went in search of James. He found him with his mother, taking a walk in the garden to look at the children's flower and vegetable patch. He asked them both if they would like a game of table tennis. James was keen, but June said she had to go and clear the dining table. Charles suspected she wanted him to have a chance to talk to her son alone.

'Well, let's see how good you are, young Jimmy.'

'I bet I can beat you. I beat all my school friends, and my cousins.'

'Really? Well, I can only do my best,' said Charles, admiring the young boy's confidence.

With James happily chatting, they went to the billiard room. The table had its flat wooden cover placed over it, ready for the children to play out their ping-pong battles. The net was already in place. Charles looked around him: billiard cues, scoreboard, cupboard stuffed with children's games, a cabinet filled with cups and trophies, the large ornate fireplace overhung with a huge heavy-framed mirror. He was overwhelmed with nostalgia. The last time he had been in that room was to play billiards with Arthur. The last time he had played table tennis had been with Arthur, June and his sister Clare... twenty years ago?

It was an exciting, hard-fought match. Charles conceded that James was a good player and nippy on his feet, but he had kept himself fit for the last twenty years and would have won the match easily had he not allowed the boy to have the edge on him. His nephew was ecstatic at winning.

'Told you, Uncle. I can beat anyone!'

'We'll see about that, young man. Now, it must be about your bedtime.'

Charles led the way out of the room.

'Will you read to me when I'm in bed?'

'Aren't you a bit big for having stories read to you?'

'Yes, I know. I do read myself. I've read Treasure Island lots of times, but it's nice to share a story. Mum sometimes reads to me. She says she likes reading my books. They're mostly about pirates.'

Charles gave him a friendly pat on the shoulder. 'Sounds my sort of thing, but not tonight, perhaps tomorrow sometime. I'm going to find your mother right now, I need to talk to her.'

'Okay. Thanks, Uncle Charlie.' James turned and slowly dragged his feet up the stairs. Halfway, he stopped and turned. 'See you tomorrow,' he called wearily.

'I look forward to it. Goodnight, young James. Sleep well.'

Charles found June busy in the kitchen. With her standing near the west window, the last of the golden light of a perfect sunset was filtering through the leaves of an Acer tree and playing on her rich brown hair. Love and deep appreciation of her beauty threatened to overwhelm him. He straightened his back and composed himself as she turned around.

'How did you get on with Rosie?' she asked, handing him a cup of coffee fresh from the pot.

'Poor kid. She really misses Arthur,' he told her, pouring cream into his cup. 'Thanks, this is delicious,' he added, taking a sip. He sat down at the large kitchen table already set for breakfast. He fiddled with a spoon, frowning at his thoughts. 'She's all mixed up. Longing for love but with her sexual desires misplaced.'

Ignoring a resolution to cut down on sweet things, he stirred a spoonful of sugar into his coffee. He sighed deeply. 'I have to admit that I'm concerned. She knows she stirs me up and plays on it. But I think we have things sorted now. I hope so, I don't want her to get hurt.'

June pulled out a chair and sat opposite him. 'I thought we might have a problem there. Not only has Rosie lost her father but her boyfriend, too. I know she finds you attractive, but then, girls always have, haven't they?'

Charles slowly nodded. It was quite true: throughout his whole life women of all ages flirted with him, embarrassingly so. 'Yes, but I didn't expect my own niece to come on to me, even if it was a big tease. Heavens, June, not only is Rosie my niece, she's just a kid and I'm an old man.'

June stretched an arm across the table and took his hand. 'I'm so sorry. Arthur asked too much of you. Perhaps it would be better for you to live elsewhere. How about you stay when the older boys are away at school and Rosie goes off to college?'

He appreciated her concern for him, but her suggestion was out of the question. He squeezed her hand reassuringly. 'I want you, June… and your family. I love those kids as if they were my own.' He sought for words to communicate his feelings and heartfelt desires. 'I've watched them growing up, wishing they were our children. Yours and mine. Angela never wanted children. I have to admit, I truly envied Arthur.'

June left her chair and came up behind him, wrapping her arms around his shoulders and pressing her cheek against his head. 'But, Charlie,' she whispered, 'we can still have your children. I'm not too old, you know.'

He could not believe what he was hearing. His beloved June, already a mother of four, was willing to give him children? He took her hands and pulled them to his lips. 'That is more than I ever hoped for.'

She kissed his cheek. 'I know Arthur would approve.'

He rose from his chair and swept her into his arms. He kissed her open lips and pulled her tightly to him. After so much heaviness and sorrow, he savoured her body coming to life with a fresh vitality. Ashes of an old love were being rekindled, and he felt the heat of them overcoming the resistance imposed by loyalty to her dead husband.

Her heavy breathing fuelled his own ardour. Years of self-restraint fell away. He kissed her as he'd done so many years before. She responded as she had done then — eagerly welcoming his passionate kisses.

Voices were heard coming in their direction and June pulled herself away from him. 'Let's go up to your place, we have things to discuss.'

Her voice, and the way she looked at him, suggested that action was going to come before talk.

Leaving the kitchen, June told David and Peter to get a drink and watch television in the sitting room. 'I have important things to discuss with your uncle. We don't want to be disturbed. Do you hear me?'

'Yes, Mum,' they said together.

Charles saw David look at Peter and give him a knowing wink. Peter grinned.

At the top of the stairs, Charles took June's hand and searched her face. 'Are you sure this is what you want?'

Although his body was crying out for her, there must be no pressure.

'Need you really ask?' she whispered, her face flushed and her breathing rapid.

He pulled open the door to the upper floor. Trying to quell his eagerness, he tremulously led the way up the next flight of stairs. They headed for the bedroom across the thickly carpeted hall and stood by the door, looking at each other, hardly daring to enter.

Shirt wet with sweat and clinging to his muscular chest, he pulled her hard against him. 'So, here we are then.'

Clearly, she had no intention of denying him. Trembling, she pulled away from him to turn the handle of the door.

June couldn't believe her eyes. Rosie was lying on Charlie's bed, reading a book!

'Why are you here, Rosie?' she demanded, her emotions in turmoil.

'I want to ask Charlie about something I'm reading.'

'You shouldn't come to your uncle's rooms without asking,' June told her, trying to quell the resentment and anger she was feeling towards her daughter. 'You must give him some privacy. We only discussed the matter last week. Have you forgotten already?'

'No. It's just that...'

Charles, obviously bemused by deflated expectations, was already picking up the book Rosie had been reading. June could see it was a guide to marital sexual expectations. It was a book Arthur had given her about the joy of sexual experience.

'I think your mother should help you with this. It's not fitting for me to advise you on such matters.'

Rosie sat up straight. 'Huh! I can see you're both too busy anyway. I'll go. Unless you want me to stay and learn?'

June felt tears of frustration about to flow. 'Rosie, why are you being so difficult? Don't you want me to be happy?'

Her daughter sprang off the bed and ran to the door. Charles caught hold of her. 'We don't want to do anything to make you unhappy, but please try to understand.' He turned Rosie to face him. 'What did you want to ask me that couldn't wait?'

'If you'd ever sodomised a woman, and if she liked it.'

'Rosie!' June yelled. 'Apologise at once!'

But Charles calmly put up a hand. 'It's all right, June. I don't mind answering the question.' He took a step back from his niece. Casually folding his arms, he leaned against the wall. 'No, I haven't, nor a man either for that matter. But apparently some women do enjoy it. Or so I've heard. Why do you ask?'

'It's why I fell out with Paul. He wanted to. He said I'd still be a virgin. But I wouldn't do it. Now I've lost him.' She wiped a hand across her wet eyes.

June was speechless. What an absurd situation! She sat on the bed and watched as Charles put his arm around her daughter's shoulders. He was so unruffled. Her admiration for him reached new heights.

'Let him go,' Charles told Rosie. 'He shouldn't ask you to do anything you don't want to do. That isn't love: it's manipulation.'

'But I love him. I just couldn't do it though. Shouldn't you do things for love even if you don't really want to?'

'If he truly loved you, Rosie, he would respect you. If he's walked out on you because he can't get his own way, then he doesn't deserve you. Try to forget him. There's a man somewhere out there, who's far more worthy of your love.'

Rosie glanced at June and then looked at Charles from under her dark lashes. 'I'm sorry I've messed things up for you both,' she muttered dolefully.

'Don't worry,' said Charles, squeezing her shoulders and then letting go — an end-of-conversation gesture. 'We'll have another chat about Paul, but not right now. I couldn't put my mind to it. Okay?'

'Thanks, I'd like that.'

June stood up, her feelings in total confusion. Was her daughter genuinely contrite or was she just playing up to Charlie for her own devious reasons? Rosie came over to her and gave her a hug. 'I love you, Mum. I didn't mean to be horrid and spoil things for you.'

'You're just unhappy,' June told her, now feeling bad at doubting her daughter's integrity. 'We'll have a heart-to-heart talk. Go along with your book now. I'll see you in your room shortly.'

June stood by Charles, watching Rosie go across the hall and down the stairs. They looked at each other and smiled forlornly.

'I guess it just wasn't meant to be, at least, not tonight.' She said wistfully. 'I wondered why they had split up. Poor Rosie. I wish she'd come to me about it. I'm sorry if she embarrassed you with her problem.'

'She did nothing of the sort. I understand her situation. It was the kind of sex that Angela wanted, plus a lot of masochistic stuff. I refused to oblige her. That's why she left me. She made me feel totally inadequate.'

'I'm so sorry, I had no idea. I guess Rosie has brought up memories you would rather forget.'

He shrugged it off. 'All part of life. But Rosie has dominated our lives today with her sexual problems. I hope things will soon be normal.'

June smiled at her thoughts. 'Normal? Have you forgotten your own youth?'

'Quite right,' he grinned. 'Now what about us?'

'I'm so sorry, Charlie. I just can't, at least, not tonight. I must go to Rosie.'

'Yes, of course you must. I quite understand.'

She looked at him, thinking how lucky she was to be loved by such a generous and kind-hearted man. She kissed him lightly on the lips. He didn't try to hold on to her.

'You're a lovely man, Charlie Rogers,' she said. 'I'll see you in the morning.'

Charles knew that Rosie and the others were always going to come first. Of course they should; they were her children, after all. But to get so far and no further, after all those years of loving her from afar — it was unbearable! He was frustrated, and his body ached with the strain of it. He watched her go and then went for a shower to freshen up. As he took off his clothes and caught sight of himself in the long mirror, he said with great feeling, 'Oh, June, what you do to me!'

Chapter Three

Charles woke up at his usual time of six-thirty. He found old disciplines hard to break.

It was his fiftieth birthday and he was now officially retired. Even so, he started the day as he had done for many years. He jumped out of bed, did some gentle exercises followed by more aggressive ones until, having worked up a good sweat, he took a shower. Shaved, and dressed in a pristine white vest and casual navy shorts, he went to his kitchen and prepared himself a light breakfast of scrambled eggs with toast and marmalade.

He was drinking his second cup of coffee when he heard a young voice calling up his stairs.

'Uncle Charlie, can I come up to see you please?'

It was young Jimmy. He went to the top of the stairs and told him to come up. Charles made a mental note to get both a bell and a lock fixed to the door leading up to his rooms.

James came running up the stairs. 'Happy birthday, Uncle Charlie!'

'Thanks, Jimmy. It looks like it's going to be a sunny one. Nice of you to visit me.'

James beamed. 'If you don't mind, Uncle Charlie, Mum would like you to come downstairs. We've got a present for you. Oh yes, and Mum sent up your paper. Here.'

Charles took the Telegraph and placed it on the small hall table. 'Thanks, I'll read it later. You say there's a present for me?'

'A birthday present. We all made it for you. It's a — oops! I nearly told you.'

'That is exciting. Does your mum want me to come now?'

'Yes please. You don't have to, but we're itching to see if you like it.'

'Okay. I'll be down in a minute. I'll get my jumper and go for a jog afterwards.'

James followed him. 'Can I come with you?'

'Why not? But I hope you like jogging. I'm going at least three miles.'

'Great! I hope you can keep up with me because I can jog really fast.'

By this time they were halfway down the stairs. At the bottom, the door was open. Peggy was standing waiting for them.

'Happy birthday, Charlie. Is it permitted to give you a birthday kiss?'

'Don't see why not. Put down those sheets, I'm ready and waiting.'

James groaned.

Peggy threw the sheets on the floor and went up to Charles with open arms. She put her arms around his waist and pulled him to her, pressing her lips to his. Her moist tongue was soon worming its way to link up with his. A bit too steamy for a mere birthday kiss! Charles concluded that Peggy, in her early forties, was a bit starved of affection since her husband moved out, and intended making the most of what she could get. He resisted the overture and pulled himself away.

James was getting tired of waiting. 'Come on, Uncle Charlie, you can kiss Peggy any time.'

'He certainly can!' Peggy said, smiling at Charles. 'Anytime at all. Here, or at my place.'

James took his hand and pulled him towards the stairs. 'Come on, Uncle.'

June, looking summery in a pink floral dress, was busy in the hall. When she saw him, she called the children to come and join her at the bottom of the stairs. They all sang a cheerful 'Happy Birthday.'

Charles smiled with delight. June came over to kiss him. Then she stopped, looking carefully at his face. 'I thought you'd cut yourself shaving. But no, I guess a female got to you before me.' She grinned. 'Could it have been my sister, by any chance?'

He wiped around his mouth with a hanky. 'Jealous? I hope so!'

June had kissed him quite lightly, but in the touch of her lips there had been a promise of better things to come. Rosie, looking perky in a short white skirt and sleeveless pinstriped blouse, also kissed him, lingering too long for his comfort.

He saw June looking a little worried. Obviously, the talk she'd had with her daughter the previous evening hadn't worked. Trying to make a joke of it, he shrugged his shoulders, splayed his hands and grinned. 'Can I help being attractive to women?'

Laughing, June led him to the sitting room and sat him down on the comfortable feather-cushioned sofa. She handed him a big pile of envelopes. 'These have been arriving here for the last couple of days. And this morning,' she added, looking around at her children. 'By the way, we're having a bit of a family get-together at lunchtime, I hope you don't mind.'

'Sounds great. Gosh, what a pile of cards.' He saw the boys waiting impatiently with a large, carefully-wrapped parcel. 'I'll look at them shortly. I'd better see my present first.'

Peter and David carefully put the parcel on the table in front of the sofa. James handed him a pair of scissors. 'Be careful, Uncle Charlie. Keep it that way up.'

All three were standing watching, their bodies tense with excitement, as Charles deliberately made a great fuss of opening his present slowly and with considerable care, making sure that even the paper was not torn. 'I like the striped paper, lads, I might want to use that again,' he teased.

The wrapping paper finally off, a cardboard box was revealed. He carefully lifted out an imposing model of a sailing ship made out of matchsticks. He was overcome by the amount of work the boys had put into it. 'It's great, fellers. Fantastic!'

James said, 'We started it ages ago. We were making it for Dad but we couldn't get it finished in time.' He looked down and blinked hard. When he looked up again, he was smiling. 'We all want you to have it, Uncle Charlie. It took us years to collect the matchsticks and build it. We only finished it last week.'

Charles looked round at their eager faces and was truly moved. Their gift was a significant step in their acceptance of the role he hoped to fulfil. 'It's quite wonderful. Brilliant workmanship. Thank you, boys.'

Rosie, uncharacteristically coy, came forward with her gift. Charles unpacked it to find a beautiful watercolour picture of a yacht at sea. He looked at the signature at the corner. 'Gosh, Rosie, I knew you could design, but I had no idea that you were such a good painter. This is quite splendid. What an artistic person you are.'

'I'm glad you like it,' she said, her face glowing. 'I painted it just for you.'

'I love it. I really do. It will remind me of you every time I look at it.'

'A cute little craft!' David said cheekily.

They all laughed.

'You don't get my present until this evening,' June told him. 'I hope you've nothing planned for tonight.'

'No. But I do have a few notions about what I'd like to do.'

June's eyes met his, a smile curling her lips. 'No doubt we'll be able to combine our ideas,' she said, picking up the wrapping paper and carefully folding it. 'But right now, I have work to do in the kitchen.'

Charles grinned at her coded message. 'Looks like a busy day ahead. I'd better go for my jog, unless you need some help in the house?'

'Work on your birthday? Definitely not!'

'Right, see you all later.' He turned to James. 'Do you still want to go with me, Jimmy?'

'Can I come too?' David cut in.

Before Charles could answer, Peter said he wanted to go as well.

'None of you is ready,' butted in Rosie. 'I'll keep Charlie company. I can help Mum when I get back.'

'We'll all go,' said Charles. 'I'll give you boys two minutes to get ready.' Being alone with Rosie was not what he wanted until their relationship was under better control.

It was a pleasant jog: cheerful company, perfect weather, leafy lanes, river sparkling in the sunlight, a few dog-walkers and anglers lifting their hands in friendly greeting — just what he needed to begin his new life. To have June's children sharing it with him augured well for the future. Life was great!

Eventually, he had to slow his usual pace for the others to keep up with him. That is, except for James. The boy was athletic in build and incredibly fit. Charles allowed him to get a little ahead and then caught up with him just before they arrived home, the others trailing not far behind.

'Well done, whippersnapper.'

'Told you I can run fast.' The boy wasn't even out of breath.

'You certainly did, and you were right.'

'That young mongrel outruns us every time,' puffed Rosie, as she arrived with David and Peter. 'Don't know where he gets it from.'

Thinking about young James, Charles ran up to his rooms to wash and change. How was the lad going to take it when he found out why he was so different to his brothers? Not that the other two were alike. David took after his father and grandmother: fair hair and blue eyes. Peter was like him and his grandfather's side of the family: tall with dark hair and brown eyes. Both David and Peter had inherited something of their mother too, particularly the determined chin.

But James had thick dark unruly hair with none of the chestnut highlights of his mother's crown of glory. His facial features — deep dimples in chin and cheeks, broad nose and jaw-line — set him apart from his brothers. His eyes too, with their heavy brows, had an earthy depth of brown that seemed to darken almost to indigo when he frowned. Of all the four children, James had the most powerful physique. A mongrel within that family maybe, but a handsome child nonetheless.

Before Charles went downstairs again, he decided to ring his young friend living in Bath. He wanted to confirm his availability for the family sailing holiday being planned for three weeks of August. He pictured Commander Richard Andrews in his mind, wondering how he would fit in with June's family. Perfectly well, of that he felt certain. Richard was an unattached good-looking man in his mid-thirties. Although he worked for the Ministry at Bath, yachting was his main passion. It was sailing that had brought them together in recent years. Charles cast his mind back to when they had first met up. Was it really so long ago since they were both engaged in underwater exploits? Richard was then a young sub-lieutenant who had proved himself both dependable and courageous. Ah, how time flew! Yes, he was the ideal person to accompany them. He only hoped there would be no problems with Rosie. At least it would take some pressure off him!

Richard didn't answer the phone. Charles wrote himself a note to ring him later. He made himself a coffee, and then sat at his kitchen table to read the headlines and features from his paper.

The crossword was almost completed when he heard, from the open window, cars arriving in the drive below. The last time his family had met was at Arthur's funeral. Of course, they would know he was staying at Bloomfield, but did they know he'd moved in? How would they take it?

He ran down both flights of stairs to meet the first arrivals in the hall. His youngest sister, Clare, was dressed in navy-blue and white and looking the smart businesswoman. She was talking to their sister Kate, and Kate's partner, Rachel. They all turned to greet him.

Clare gave him an enthusiastic hug. 'Happy birthday, big brother.'

'Thanks. Did you get the executive job you were after?'

She smiled cynically. 'Yes. I sort of bribed the Managing Director to clinch it though. What a randy swine!'

Kate was aghast. 'How could you, Clare? Men should not be allowed to get away with it. Arthur would never have allowed that to happen when he was in charge of the firm. You were obviously the right person for the job.'

'It wasn't so bad. He's got what it takes in that department.'

Charles wanted to say something, but it was Clare's business. Anyway, Kate had enough to say without him chipping in. The entrance door burst open and in ran Charlie's nephews, Michael and Bobby — George and Helen's sons. They both hurried past, pushing a parcel into his hands.

'Happy birthday, Uncle Charlie!' they said in unison, and ran off shouting for their cousins. It was going to be a noisy lunch.

George and Helen arrived in the hall, greeting those present. They came up to Charles, George offering his hand and Helen giving him a kiss on his cheek.

'I hope you get everything you wish for, Charlie. You deserve the best,' she said, pushing aside a lock of hair from her face with her elegant pearl-tipped fingers.

Charles looked at her admiringly. She was slim but with full breasts, long-legged, and a little above medium height. She was dressed in a cream linen miniskirt with high-heeled shoes to match, and a flame-coloured, low-cut fitted blouse with a brief peplum. With her long blonde hair touched up with platinum highlights, she looked an absolute stunner. It was hard to believe she was in her thirties. He recalled their first meeting. It was before her marriage but while he was still wedded to Angela, otherwise they might have got something going. 'Thanks, Helen,' he said. 'I must say, you're looking glamorous today.'

'Hello, hello, what's all this? Better keep your hands off my wife, Charlie,' said George. 'That's one present you won't be getting.' A hint of warning flashed in his eyes before he started laughing. Was George having problems with Helen?

Charles noticed Rachel smiling at the cheerful banter. She was a slim woman with a pleasant oval face, short dark hair, light make-up, and wearing a neat blue trouser-suit. 'Rachel, isn't it?' he asked, offering her his hand.

'Quite correct. It's nice to meet you again, Charles,' she responded warmly. 'You certainly don't look your age. Life treating you well?'

'Peter Pan, is what we all call him,' said George. 'And here comes Wendy!'

Charles turned to see June coming with a tray of appetisers. She looked at them puzzled.

'It's all right, June,' he said, smiling. 'George is observing the fact that you have kept your youth and beauty over the years. I'm sure we all agree with him.'

Out of the corner of his eye he saw Kate look at Rachel, smile, and wink. No need to guess where her affections resided. He could accept their lesbian relationship, but he did wish his sister, a good-looking woman of similar build to June, would dress a little less masculine. But then, if she desired to make some kind of statement through her motorcycling gear, it was her business.

After lunch, the adults sat in the roomy lounge, talking and sharing news. He heard the latest about the absent members of his family — his mother, brother Jack, sister Jane, plus spouses and children — and thought it would have been great if they had been able to get from London. But he realised he couldn't expect all the family, especially his mother, to travel long distances just for his birthday.

He looked out of the windows and saw the youngsters kicking a ball around the apple trees. It was a happy scene. He glanced across at June and she smiled back at him. She had promised him babies and he couldn't wait to get started. Being patient was going to be difficult. Even as he thought about the future, a stab of pain shot through him — his happiness was at the cost of Arthur's death. A lump knotted in his throat, and he swallowed hard to gain control of his emotions. He saw June's smile change to a look of concern. She was certainly in tune with his thoughts.

Clare caught his attention. 'Well, big brother, what are your plans for the future? You used to talk about setting up in business with that friend of yours… what's his name?'

'Richard. Commander Richard Andrews. His present assignment is working with the design executive in Bath. There was nothing definite about a business, just ideas for the future. Situations change.'

There were shifty glances towards June. She was looking at her hands. Were they all thinking of Arthur's death? Kate spoke up.

'I'll have to visit my old top-floor flat. I hear June's cleared out the workrooms and done up the place. How long are you planning on living up there, Charles?'

'As long as it takes.'

'As long as it takes?'

'Before Arthur died, he asked me to take care of June and the children.'

'So June told us,' Clare put in abruptly. 'Did Arthur expect you to give up plans for your future and move into Bloomfield indefinitely? That's a bit of an imposition.'

'Huh! Daddy wouldn't impose on anyone,' said Rosie angrily. 'We can manage by ourselves. Uncle Charlie doesn't have to be around. He loves Mum, that's why he's living here.'

'I love all of you, Rosie,' Charles put in quickly, looking directly at Rosie and wondering what else she might blurt out. He turned to Clare. 'From today, I'm officially retired from my Navy job at Bath. I'm most grateful to June for putting me up while I map out my future. It's my pleasure to be here and fulfil the role our brother asked of me. Arthur knew of my fondness for June and the children. I can assure you, Clare, being here is no imposition — it's a real joy.'

George laughed. 'Early days, Charlie, early days. Kids — they drive you nuts!'

'Not that you're home much to notice,' Helen snapped, looking at her husband with disdain. She turned to Charles. 'I really admire you, Charlie. Not many men would want to take on four kids.'

Rosie snorted, 'Huh!'

Charles said quickly, 'They were all doing nicely before I turned up yesterday. June will tell you how much help Rosie is. She's a real treasure.'

'Charlie's quite right, Rosie's my right hand. Has been since Arthur became ill. David and Peter are away at school most of the year. Jimmy's no trouble. But, it's good to have a man around the house again. The arrangement suits both of us.'

'Especially a nice guy like Charlie,' said Helen, smiling and looking at June through perceptive eyes.

At that moment Michael ran into the room to tell his mother that Bobby had jumped into the lily pond. The lounge instantly spilled out its occupants, bent on rescuing the miscreant. It was one misdeed that Charles was pleased about.

By mid-afternoon, the visitors said they had to get back to their homes as they had things going on that evening. Charles shook hands or hugged each person and thanked them for making his birthday special.

When everyone had gone, he took June in his arms and asked her if she would go out with him that evening. 'I guess being Saturday, most places will be booked, but we can get some fish and chips and eat them by the river. Just imagine: music from the car radio, dancing by moonlight, swans on the river for company...'

'And midges to nibble my tender bits, while peeping Toms watch from the bushes! Nice thought, Charlie, but George and Helen are taking us out tonight.'

'Really? They didn't say anything.'

'Of course they didn't, they wanted to surprise you. Now I've ruined it for you. Never mind. Would you like to come up and help me choose a dress to wear?'

An evening out with George and Helen was not what he'd hoped for, but an invitation to June's bedroom was a birthday treat in itself. Charles followed June upstairs. The bedroom had been redecorated since he was last there. It was now cream and green, with touches of sunshine yellow and deep blue. The highly-polished walnut furniture was still the same, but the heavy wardrobes had gone. The glass-topped round table and cushioned cane armchairs were still in the large bay window that looked out on trees and flower beds. He knew that June used to sit there with Arthur shortly before his death. Even Arthur's favourite novels, read to him by June, were still resting on the table, next to a vase of sweet-smelling yellow roses.

June was heading for a large walk-in closet next to an en-suite bathroom. The door to the bathroom was partly open and he caught a glimpse of a pink basin, black tiles, mirrors, chrome and glass. That was all new. Her big bed was close to the closet. The prospect of sharing it with her was inviting, but raw memories came rushing back to him — Arthur lying there dreadfully ill. His enthusiasm left him. How could he ever consider taking his beloved brother's place in that very bed?

June's pleasant voice cut into his morose reminiscing. 'I thought I would wear this black silky dress, or maybe this blue one with the full sleeves.'

'Mm, both lovely,' he said, but his eye had caught something else. He walked inside the room with its rows of shelves, drawers and dress rails, and pulled out a white satin gown. 'Would you wear this, June?' He deliberately caught her eye. 'To please me?'

She would know exactly what was on his mind. An evening twenty years ago when she was wearing a white satin dress and he took her dancing. Something happened between them that night: a realisation of a mutual attraction that could never be brought to fruition — she belonged to his brother. Even thinking about that night made his heart beat faster. He watched her looking at the gown with its tight-fitting bodice, slashed neckline and side-split skirt. She was frowning. Considering her widowhood, obviously it would not be right to wear such a revealing dress.

'No, not for tonight,' he said, pre-empting her refusal. 'But how about putting it on for me right now? I'd love to see you in it.'

She smiled. 'I know what you're thinking. It reminds you of another dress many years ago. You're an old softie, Captain Charles Rogers. All right, since it's your birthday. But I know it won't fit. The dress is years old.'

She took it to the bathroom but it was a few minutes before she came out wearing it. The white showed off her becoming tan and dark hair. It was so close-fitting he could tell she wasn't wearing underwear — there wasn't room for any! What's more, she had obviously washed away the heat of the day while she was in the bathroom: she was as fresh as a summer breeze.

He gazed at her and saw a girl of seventeen. He held out his arms.

'Shall we dance?'

'In this dress? And on a carpet? You must be joking.'

He held her tight, her arms around his neck. His hands felt the firmness of her buttocks under the white satin. Enjoying the closeness of her sensuous body, he longed to slip his hand inside that split. He struggled with his emotions. It would not do. After taking a few small steps, he said, 'Let's take another look at the frocks.'

'I'll put the black one on. I'm sure you'll like it,' she said, walking to the bathroom with the dress over her arm.

She came out and did a twirl. Charles looked in wonderment. Although the beaded front only slightly revealed her comely breasts, the back was cut almost to the waist, showing off perfect skin tanned by the summer sun. The full skirt, reaching to her ankles, flared out in a smoky cloud of shot silk.

Charles opened his arms, inviting her to dance. She partnered him willingly, but the bedroom carpet inhibited his style. He stopped dancing and held her at arm's length. 'You look absolutely stunning.'

Her eyes twinkled with pleasure. 'I thought you would like it.'

Determined to be gentle with her, he turned her around and lightly kissed the back of her neck. She pulled back her shoulders and sighed. Encouraged, he ran his mouth down her spine, as far as her dress allowed. She moaned a little. He stood up. Cupping his hands over her breasts, he pulled her hard against him, his cheek resting on her soft hair.

'How I have longed for you all these years,' he whispered.

'I know, Charlie, I know.'

Moved by her sighs, he ran his hands down her body. Soon, he was kneeling on the carpet with his hands under her dress, touching her smooth thighs. Lifting her skirt, he kissed her low on her spine and brushed his cheek against her smooth derrière.

Turn around,' he breathed softly, his heart pounding in his chest.

Trembling, she slowly turned. He had to control his avid appetite and not ruin the moment. Still kneeling, he let go of the back hem and slowly lifted the front of her skirt...

The door burst open. 'Mother can I borrow your—'

June's back was towards the door. Charles alone saw the shocked amazement and anger on Rosie's face. He instantly dropped the skirt of the dress and stood up.

'Charlie was checking the hem of the dress for me,' June said quickly, her tremulous voice betraying her embarrassment. 'I'm wearing it tonight. What was it you wanted to borrow?'

Charles was flushed and sweating. He hoped the hot weather would explain his condition, but he knew Rosie was not stupid — she had seen him on his knees in front of her mother for goodness' sake! He put on a welcoming smile. 'Perhaps you would like to help with the dress?'

Rosie stood with her arms akimbo. 'Don't leave for my benefit,' she snapped. 'I didn't know you were an expert on hemlines, Charlie. Great! You must come and check mine.' She walked out, slamming the door behind her.

Shrugging his shoulders and splaying his hands, Charles looked at June with a sigh of resignation. 'Foiled again!'

He burst out laughing. It was either that or crying!

June grinned mischievously. 'Let's go in the bathroom and lock the door.'

Charles was about to follow her, but he suddenly remembered what June had said about foreplay in the shower. He hesitated: when he made love to her, would she be thinking of Arthur? He decided to risk it. He was burning with desire and she was willing. He began stripping off his clothes.

There was a gentle tap at the door.

'Are you there, Uncle Charlie? Rosie says you are. Please will you to read my pirate story? It's great... there's lots of blood and thunder!'

Charles punched his left palm with his right fist, held his breath and let it out slowly.

'All right, Jimmy, give me a minute and I'll come to your room.'

Chapter Four

At seven o'clock, June and Charles arrived at the Grand. They walked inside to meet up with George and Helen. June thought that George, like Charlie, was looking awfully dapper in his evening suit, especially with his jaunty red-spotted bow tie. Helen was wearing a low-cut red dress, emblazoned with sequins and bugle-beads.

'George, you're looking as smart as ever,' June said appreciatively. She turned to his wife. 'Helen, you look fantastic!'

'You certainly do,' Charles agreed.

To June's amusement, George puffed out his chest in pride of ownership. 'Yes, my wife is quite a stunner.'

Helen gave him a disdainful look. 'Then maybe you'll keep your eyes off the rest of the women here,' she said, loud enough for June to hear.

Knowing Helen, June thought her just as likely to be flashing her eyes at the opposite sex. She was already giving Charlie a welcoming kiss that lingered a few seconds too long. Trying to make George jealous?

When they returned to the foyer after tidying their hair in the cloaks, George led the way to the ballroom. An attendant moved forward and opened the door.

'Happy birthday, Charlie!' rang out a gathered throng.

A band began to play in accompaniment. The room was packed and everyone there was singing.

Emotionally moved, June watched Charlie's face as he looked around the room. He was beyond words, clearly stunned. His brother and sister, with their spouses and offspring, had come all the way from London. In fact, all of his family, including his mother, had responded to her invitation. So had many of his old friends from the area and colleagues from Bath. Charles stood, slowly shaking his head in wonder. 'How did you do it?' His eyes fixed on someone singing his birthday greetings near the bar. 'No wonder Richard didn't answer his phone!'

His expression suddenly changed. For a few moments his face darkened but he quickly regained his composure, smiling and shaking his head once more.

June looked to see what had taken his attention. How the devil had Angela got in? That woman certainly hadn't been invited. When the singing came to an end, she whispered in Charlie's ear. 'Sorry, Charlie, I didn't invite her.'

'Don't worry about it'. He put an arm around her shoulders. 'I guess I have you to thank for this wonderful surprise?'

'This is my present to you. Happy birthday, Charlie.' She kissed his cheek.

The room exploded with clapping and cheers. Overcome with emotion, Charles gave a brief speech and thanked everyone for coming.

The band struck up an excuse-me foxtrot.

'This is our dance to get everyone started,' she told him. 'Will you dance with me, Charlie?'

They set off in perfect time with the music. Others soon joined them. Charlie was a wonderful dancer, and she followed him with ease. As they glided around the floor to the rhythm of the dance, the revolving mirrored ball flashed beams of light around the dimmed room. Happiness welled up within her. It was almost as if Arthur was with her, telling her to relax and enjoy herself. It was what he wanted, just like twenty years ago when he'd left her in Charlie's care while he was abroad. Only now it was the beginning of a new phase in her life. To have two men love her so dearly, she must be the luckiest woman alive. Suddenly she felt a tap on her shoulder.

It was Angela, dressed to kill in a sparkling green gown, its sequinned bodice slashed to the waist both front and back. Her pale blonde hair framed her heavily made-up face like a soft cloud. But that was all that was soft about her. The look she gave June was as hard as nails.

'This is an excuse-me, is it not?' she asked, her pencilled brows raised and bright red lipstick emphasising her slinky smile.

June controlled her emotions and smiled. 'Of course.' When Charles was about to object, she said quickly, 'It's all right, Charlie. I'll see you afterwards.'

She made her way to the reception hall to find out how Angela had got in. The receptionist looked carefully through the list and checked the invitation cards that had been handed in. The numbers and names tallied. Looking embarrassed, she shrugged her shoulders and said that Angela must have come with another guest, or somehow slipped in — unlikely, but not impossible. The woman was most apologetic. 'Would you like me to have a word with the lady?'

'No thanks. As you say, maybe she came with a friend of Captain Rogers.'

June returned to the party, thinking what kind of friend would bring Charlie's ex-wife to his birthday celebration?

Things were livening up. Young people were on the floor, rocking to the latest hit. Charles was talking to his old friends. Angela was close behind him, talking to his mother. Furious with the woman, June crept up behind her, waiting for an opportunity to drag her off. Angela was talking loud enough for a dozen guests to hear.

'Yes, Mother, darling, I'm thinking of going back to Charles. The divorce was a big mistake. We still love each other. Now he's finished with the Royal Navy things will work out fine. Charlie needs me.'

'I'm so pleased, my dear. Your mother was my closest friend. I know she would have been overjoyed to see you together again.'

'Dear Mummy, I do miss her so. Yes, she didn't want the divorce. But things will be different now. I'm looking for a nice house away from here. It's not right for Charles to be living with his brother's wife.'

Putting on a false smile, not easy when her jaw was set with anger, June stepped up behind Angela and gripped her arm. She turned to the old lady. 'Excuse me, Granny Rogers, I have to speak to Angela.' She pulled on Angela's arm. 'Come with me please, Angela.'

'Let go, you bitch,' Angela muttered between her teeth, at the same time trying to smile a farewell at old Mrs Rogers.

'We need to have a little chat,' June said sweetly.

Angela walked a few steps trying to pull her arm free. 'No, thank you.'

June tightened her grip and brought Angela to a halt. 'You had better come quietly, or I'll have the management throw you out. I can assure you, madam, that really would make Charlie happy.'

'All right,' she said sulkily, 'but I'm not going home.'

Still holding on to her, June led the way to a couple of armchairs in a quiet corner of the foyer.

'So, tell me how you got in,' she demanded, pushing Angela into one of the chairs and sitting down beside her.

But she did not get an immediate answer. Angela was straightening her dress — a nipple was half-exposed — and recovering her composure. Her eyes were following a dark, handsome man as he walked across the foyer. Obviously trying to attract him, she lifted a hand to comb through her Hollywood-style blonde hair, arching her back and thrusting her breasts forward. The man smiled in acknowledgement before disappearing into the men's room.

'Angela!' June spat between her teeth. 'Answer my question. Who brought you in?'

'I'm a close friend of an old friend of Charlie's. A *very* close friend, if you know what I mean,' Angela said, smiling at June in triumph. 'You invited Fred and partner. Well, I'm Fred's partner.'

'Since when? The last time I saw him, he had a fiancée called Alice.'

'Well, he has me now. At least, until the end of this evening.' Her blue eyes looked at June mockingly. 'I'm taking Charlie back and you can't stop me.'

'Charlie is free to do as he likes, but he'll never go back to you. That I do know.'

'Really? We'll see. Now I must get back to Fred. Time for dancing.'

June found Angela's quiet confidence most disturbing. She watched her slink her way to the ballroom. The woman was out to make trouble. June took a deep breath, and tried to shrug off the unpleasant feelings Angela had left behind. Not easy to do. Angela's vapour trail of venom was as strong as her perfume.

As June re-entered the ballroom, she saw Peggy leading Charlie onto the dance floor to do a bit of hip and head-shaking. Angela was walking up to them. Charlie saw her and turned his back. Soon he had his head down along with Peggy, acting like a teenager. The younger of the guests quickly joined them, shaking their heads and bodies to the beat of the music played by a lively pop group. June smiled and tapped her feet. It was not her thing, but she loved to see others enjoying themselves.

'Come and dance, Mum.' It was young Jimmy eager to get her on the floor.

'Why not?' she said cheerfully, but inwardly groaning.

They joined up with Charlie and Peggy. Fortunately, the music soon came to an end. The band took over with a waltz.

Peggy took hold of Jimmy. 'Come on, young man, show me what you can do.' She winked at June. 'Take over the birthday boy. He was looking for you when I snapped him up.'

'That's true,' said Charlie, taking June in his arms ready to waltz. 'Where have you been?'

'Tell you later.'

'Sounds mysterious,' he said, leading off to the strains of *Always*. 'So, will you tell me how you found out who my friends are at Bath?'

'Sure. George suggested I contact Richard Andrews. He knows him from that trip they took last year. Of course, you know that already. The rest was easy. What a lovely young man Richard is. It will be great to have him sailing with us. I'm sure he'll get on with Rosie and the boys.'

'I'll take Rosie over to meet him,' said Charlie, 'but right now, I want to concentrate on dancing with you.'

After an excellent buffet meal, dancing began again. Charles saw Angela coming in his direction. He turned to June, grabbed her by the wrist and told her it was time to dance. The band was playing *Jealousy*. Charles took June swiftly over the floor in a rapturous tango.

Other dancers stood back to watch, but Charles was unaware of anything other than June in his arms. To have the woman he loved once again united with him in the rhythm of this exotic dance was something he'd often thought about, but which he never dared to believe possible. They moved and swayed as he took complete mastery over their movements. She was with him every step of the way, her body at one with his. The music stopped as he bent her backwards in an orgasm of rapturous delight.

The whole company erupted with applause, shouts of praise and calls for more. As the tumult settled, a voice rang out:

'Poor grieving widow. How nice to have Charlie warming her bed at night.'

Charles felt June stiffen. She pulled away from him and faced her tormentor.

'Sorry, Angela, my bed doesn't require warming. But then, you wouldn't understand that, would you? From what I've heard, you like yours sizzling hot!'

The women faced each other, eyes blazing. Those who had heard the altercation stood in shocked silence while the rest of the guests, uncertain as to what was happening, whispered to one another. Charles nodded at the band to start playing again. He pulled June away from Angela and started dancing. Holding her close, he could feel her body trembling.

'Well done, June,' he whispered. 'Keep smiling. Don't let her win now.'

Over June's shoulder, he saw Fred drag Angela out of the room. Guests then appeared to relax. But he knew that, as far as June was concerned, the harm had already been done. Although she went on chatting and dancing until the party was over, he could sense the tension in her voice and movements. Clearly, she was putting on a cheerful mask for his sake.

When they arrived home, Rosie went straight to bed. In the taxi, she had been chatting happily about Richard Andrews. Her ebullient mood relieved a highly tense situation. For that, Charles was thankful. But he hoped Rosie was not in for a big disappointment. Certainly, Richard liked and enjoyed women but, so far, not enough to think of a permanent relationship.

'Thank you, June, it's been a wonderful evening,' he told her, as they were about to mount the stairs. 'What a lot of trouble you went to just for me. I don't know how you kept it such a secret.'

She leaned on the newel post and smiled. 'It wasn't easy. I thought the kids would give it away. Richard was exceedingly helpful. I don't know how I would have managed without him.'

He put an arm around her shoulders, wanting to walk her to his rooms but afraid of spoiling the evening with rejection. He must let her lead the conversation. 'He's a good man.'

'Rosie seems to have fallen for his looks and charm. I hope she won't get hurt.'

'Mm. But you can't always shelter her from the pain of growing up. Girls fall in love all the time, don't they?'

She rested her head on his shoulder. 'I guess so,' she said wistfully.

Was she thinking of her own youth? Twenty years dropped away. A desire to consummate his love — a passion that had smouldered and flared over the years — suddenly engulfed him.

'Come upstairs with me,' he whispered urgently. 'Please, my darling… I want us to end this night together.'

She turned her eyes away, anxiously wringing her hands. 'I want to be with you,' she said quietly, 'but I'm afraid.'

Lovingly, he held her face in his hands, gently kissing her eyelids. She looked up. He saw a mixture of love and uncertainty. He pulled her closer to his chest. 'Don't be afraid,' he said tenderly, his desire to comfort struggling with his urge to possess her. 'Just come to my rooms and sleep in my bed. I want to hold you in my arms. We'll take it from there. I won't pressure you for more.' Even as he said the words, he wondered at the truth of them.

June followed him up both flights of stairs. On reaching the hall, she suddenly grasped his arm. 'Whatever you want, Charlie, I want too.'

He felt his heart beat faster. 'Are you sure, June?'

'Yes, I'm sure. Just give me a few moments to freshen up.'

She took a quick shower while he undressed in the bedroom. Hardly able to resist joining her, he walked into the kitchen to get them both a drink. Hearing her leave the bathroom, he turned around to see her naked body enter his bedroom.

He put aside all thoughts of coffee and took a quick shower. After the frustrations of the past two days, he could hardly believe that she was in his bed waiting for him. He must not keep her waiting but neither must he rush things. Wanting his first time with her to be perfect for both of them, he smoothed his face with his razor. Or was he just delaying things? He was confident she would find him an attractive and virile lover, but would her mind be dwelling on those last occasions with Arthur? Especially since Angela had made that nasty crack about her widowhood. Dear brother Arthur, with his emasculated body he'd still done his best to please her. Yes, he must be sensitive to her feelings and take things easy. He took a deep breath to calm himself, turned off the light and entered his bedroom. The bed was empty.

June lay under the sheets of her own bed, cuddled up to a pillow. Torn apart by grief and desire, she was crying bitterly. She had always had Arthur to help and comfort her when she was in distress. He had been her lover, her guide, her comforter, and her father confessor.

But images of her other love kept breaking into her thoughts. Every time she had seen Charlie since her marriage she had been sexually stirred, but she had always refused to acknowledge or respond to her desires. Even so, at such times, unsought arousal had caused her to be more ardently responsive to Arthur's lovemaking. She suspected Arthur knew what was going on, but was confident in her love for him. She knew how much he loved his younger brother and enjoyed having him to stay. June's brain told her it was now all right to respond to Charlie's desire for her; it was what Arthur would have wanted. But…

The door quietly opened. In the dim light she saw Charlie enter the room — this was something she hadn't planned for. Surely he hadn't come expecting her to honour her words? But part of her longed for him to do just that: she felt so alone and bereft.

'Don't be afraid,' he whispered softly, approaching the bed. 'I'm not going to make love to you. But I won't allow you to weep alone. I'll stay with you until the night is over and the sun is shining.' He stood over her. 'Please invite me into your bed, then we can comfort each other.'

It was what she wanted more than anything else: a strong man to comfort and ease her sorrow and with whom she could share the pain of Arthur's death. She threw aside the sheet in a gesture of welcome.

He pulled away the comforting pillow that lay in Arthur's place and slipped in beside her. 'No more pillows,' he said firmly. 'I'm here now.' He opened his arms to receive her. 'Come here, June. We'll shed our grief together.' His voice betrayed emotions too powerful to hide.

'I miss him so, Charlie.' Her mind began to drift. 'Never leave me....'

Charles realised that June now had what she most craved: an Arthur substitute to be her consolation. But would she ever crave for him? Not as another Arthur, nor as a mere sexual partner — but for him, Charles, for better or for worse? No matter, to be near her, he would accept any relationship she was able to offer.

In spite of being late getting to sleep, he woke at his usual time. Early morning sun was streaming through the window. From where he lay, all he could see were the tops of trees that grew in the garden, screening the house from the dwellings on the other side of the distant road. A warm glow came over him as he realised where he was and with whom he was lying.

June still lay cuddled up to him. Her breasts were soft next to the firm muscles of his chest. It was a lovely, and arousing, feeling. Sunlight fell on her dark curly hair and he noticed a few shining silver threads. She was untouched — natural as nature intended. She moved and the sheet fell away to below her waist. Out of curiosity, he peeked under the sheet to look at the rest of her. Clearly her sunbathing had been done in the nude. Had it been for his benefit? That was something he would never ask. He preferred to think of the possibility rather than face a disappointment.

After the emotional storm, she looked peaceful and contented. He felt a sort of contentment himself, just to be by her side — naked together as though it were the most natural thing in the world. But soon he must return to his own room before they were discovered sleeping in the same bed. Neither did he want her to feel under pressure to give way to sexual yearnings.

With the sun warming her body, June threw aside the sheet. Charles watched as she gradually opened her eyes. She slowly smiled. 'Have you been here all night?'

'I couldn't leave you. But don't worry, I'll go now,' he told her, kissing her forehead. 'I'll let you rest a while.'

He began to pull himself away, but she stopped him.

'Don't go, Charlie, please don't go. Make love to me in the sunshine. It's something I've imagined for weeks. I felt bad about thinking such things before, but it seems all right now. I don't know why, but it does.'

His heart started pumping in anticipation. 'Hold on a minute.'

He jumped off the bed, picked up a chair and put it so the back prevented the door opening. 'No intruders allowed in today,' he said, grinning at his thoughts: a trail of youngsters with individual needs, plus Peggy wanting to change the sheets and Mrs Craven asking what was for lunch!

'I must find the key for that lock,' June said, on her way to the bathroom.

He followed her in. 'If you don't mind, I'll take a quick shower and get rid of the night's sweat.'

She ran her fingers down his chest and stomach. 'I'll help you wash, Charlie.'

He pulled her naked body close to his. 'In that case, it might take a little longer.'

Shower over, he snatched her up and carried her to the bed. There they bathed in the sun's warm golden light, paving the way for the ultimate pleasure of their union. After a session of blissful foreplay, Charles rolled onto his back. With his powerful muscles, he lifted June up and, with a grunt of rapturous delight, brought her down to begin their act of copulation.

After timeless moments of ecstatic pleasure, he brought them both to the ultimate climax. Deep satisfaction filled his soul. Twenty years of suppressed desire was over. Their union had been complete and perfect.

Collapsing on the pillows, June sighed, 'I love you, dearest Charlie.'

The flickering embers of an old romance had at last burst into a blazing fire. June had reawakened to love. Charles rubbed his cheek against her hair.

'And I love you,' he murmured softly, 'with all my heart.'

Never had his words, simple as they were, been more sincere.

Chapter Five

Outside June's bedroom door, David looked at Peter and grinned. 'That's it, shows over,' he whispered. 'Watch out, Jimmy's coming. If he catches us listening, he'll tell Mum.'

Rosie's voice was heard calling them to breakfast. 'If you don't come now, you'll go without!'

'Coming!' Peter shouted.

'You silly idiot,' David said crossly. 'Mum and Charlie will have heard you. Come on — disappear quick!'

The boys raced down the stairs and nearly knocked Jimmy over in the hall.

'What have you been doing? Rosie's really cross. She's sent me to get you. I want my breakfast. I've been waiting ages.'

'Oh, nothing much,' said David. 'Just learning about the birds and bees.'

'I'm not daft, our David. You've been up to something.'

'Education is a wonderful thing, Jimmy,' said David, grinning at his thoughts.

'About time,' Rosie said, as they entered the kitchen.

They sat down around the kitchen table. Rosie poured out tea.

'It was good last night. Wish we could have stayed till the end,' Peter said.

Jimmy looked up from eating his boiled egg. 'Rosie, what happened after we'd gone?'

'Not a lot. Charlie danced a lovely tango with Mum. Everybody clapped.'

'Wish I'd seen it,' said Jimmy, egg yolk running down his chin.

'It was ruined by Angela — Charlie's ex-wife,' said Rosie, passing them cups of tea.

David looked up from delving into the box of cornflakes. 'Why, what happened?'

Rosie glared at him. 'Keep your hand out of that packet; it's unhygienic. Anyway, Jimmy found the toy yesterday.' She frowned at Jimmy. 'Clean your chin up!'

'What about last night?' David persisted. He shook flakes into his dish, still hoping for a little plastic spaceman to drop out.

'Angela was being rude and sarcastic. She was horrible. Hinting that Charlie was sleeping with mother. "A grieving widow" is what she called her, and saying something about him warming her bed.'

'It's hot at night,' Jimmy said, wrinkling his nose in puzzlement. 'Why would Uncle warm her bed?'

They all started laughing.

'Ask Charlie,' Rosie said.

Jimmy frowned. 'Anyway, what's wrong with Uncle warming it?'

David and Peter couldn't stop laughing.

Rosie rolled her eyes to the ceiling. 'For goodness' sake, keep your mouth closed at lunchtime,' she told Jimmy, 'Commander Andrews is coming for lunch.' She turned to David. 'As for you, just keep out of the way when he's here. Don't think I don't know what you get up to.'

'I thought we were all going to church,' Peter said.

'We are. Richard is coming here first.'

David grinned. 'Richard, eh? Mm, maybe I'll stick around. Might learn something.'

Rosie aimed him a sisterly clip on his ear.

On the way home from church, Rosie slowed down so that she and Richard were walking behind the others.

'Are you married?' she asked him.

'No. Thought about it a few times, but I guess I haven't met anyone I'd want to spend the rest of my life with.'

'Really? You must be choosy. I can't believe a good-looker like you is short of possible candidates.'

He grinned. 'Thanks for the compliment. I must admit I've had a few affairs, but I'm away a lot and that's not good for establishing close relationships. Apart from which, I enjoy variety.'

'Well, I'd better tell you, Commander Andrews—'

'Richard,' he cut in.

She looked up at his laughing eyes and smiled. 'Okay... Richard. It's no use trying to get my mother for a quickie. She's strictly Charlie's now.'

He laughed. 'What a forward young lady! Now what makes you think I'm after your mother when her lovely daughter is available? I take it you are available, Rosie?'

'I saw you looking at my mum.' She cocked her head and gave him a disdainful look. 'Huh! You're not the only one to fancy her. As for me, I've just lost one rotter and I don't want another, thank you.'

'I'm sorry about that. So you think I'm a rotter? That's sad, I really like you.'

Rosie tried not to show her pleasure. 'Your hard luck.'

She threw him a glance to see the effect of her words. He was grinning.

'We're going to be spending a lot of time together soon,' he told her. 'Do you think you could change your mind about me?'

They had slowed to a halt. Rosie glanced at him. He was a little above medium height, with broad shoulders and a powerful chest. He was carrying his blazer, and his rolled-up sleeves revealed strong, muscular arms. His skin was bronzed by the sun. Constant exposure to sunlight had lightened his blond hair to almost white. His eyes, under their pale brows and lashes, were of a brilliant blue — just like her father's had been. His attractive face, with its dominant features of large nose and strong jawline, bore the rugged contours of a man used to an active outdoor life. His wide mouth easily creased into a smile, revealing unblemished white teeth.

She was thrilled by the way he was looking at her, throwing her emotions off balance. Her heart was racing. She found her cheeks getting hot. Disconcerted, she quickly turned her face away from him.

'Rosie? I think you're blushing. Does that mean there is hope for me?'

She glanced up, daring herself to face his searching gaze. 'Perhaps. I admit I find you attractive. Depends what you're after. I'm not into kinky stuff.'

He raised his eyebrows and smiled. 'Sounds promising. I'm sure there's lots we can do together without getting in the least *outré*.'

She smiled at him shyly, her imagination set alight by a certain innuendo in the tone of his voice. For once she was at a loss for words.

'We had better get back,' he said.

'Yes.'

He took hold of her hand and walked her home in near-silence. It was then that Rosie knew that she was in love again.

'David isn't with us,' June said as they were walking home from church.

'He's gone off with Emma,' said Peter.

'They were holding hands,' said Jimmy. 'Soppy things!'

Charles was puzzled. 'Emma?'

'She's the girl next door,' June told him. 'David sees a lot of her in the school holidays.'

'Would she be the young lady grinning at him in church?'

'Quite likely. I didn't see her.'

The two boys whispered to each other and then ran off.

'See you back home!' Peter called from over his shoulder.

Charles suspected they wanted to spy on David and Emma. His mind went back to earlier events. 'I hope David's habit of listening at bedroom doors hasn't inspired him to action.'

June's cheeks turned pink. 'Don't remind me, Charlie. How embarrassing!'

'I'll have a word with them,' he promised, 'especially David.'

He looked behind them. 'Better have a chat with Richard, too. He's a bit of a charmer, and Rosie's a vulnerable young woman.'

'That's true,' said June, frowning a little. 'But, at least, I don't think we'll hear any more about Paul for a while.'

'I guess so. But he's a lot older than Rosie. He must let her know his intentions from the start. I don't want him breaking her heart.'

'Did you break many hearts, Charlie?'

'Not that I'm aware of. Since I fell in love with you, I've never been able to love another woman — in the sense that you mean. Neither have I encouraged women to love me. But then, who am I to judge the workings of the female heart?'

June stopped walking. 'Oh Charlie, was it terrible for you? Have you never loved another woman? What about Angela? You were married for ten years. You must have loved her at one time.'

'I never loved Angela, and she certainly didn't love me. Our marriage vows were a sham. But I did try, and it was good for a while. If she hadn't trapped me with that phantom pregnancy we never would have married. She received a damn good settlement when we split up. I guess she's run out of lovers and now wants me back. She's just greedy. She takes as much as she can get, wears a man out, and then throws him aside like an old shoe!'

June grinned, 'She didn't wear you out, Charlie — I can vouch for that.'

Memories of that morning rolled over him like a mighty flood. He looked into her smiling eyes. 'I guess you hastened my recovery!'

Oblivious of local gossip, he took her hand in his. In silent communion they walked on to Bloomfield.

There was a lot of animated talk during lunchtime. It gave Richard a chance to assess those he'd be sailing with, and roughly plan a schedule for their coming holiday. It was his job to buy what was needed and attend to essential details. It was something he had done a number of times, for short breaks as well as for longer holidays. Arranging adventure holidays and being skipper of the craft added up to a wonderful life beyond his work at Bath. The sea was in his blood. The prospect of having two beautiful women aboard was an added bonus.

After lunch, it was time for him to return to Bath. It might take him three hours and he had an obliging redhead coming to stay the night. The family came outside to send him off. Rosie was standing back from the others and looking a little forlorn. Now, should he give her a little encouragement? Tempting, but she was little more than a kid and probably a virgin. That would put him in a straightjacket. Apart from the fact that he had scruples about breaking-in virgins when marriage was not on the cards, he did not want to harm his friendship with Charles. Well, as long as she knew the score and she kept her lock-gates closed, maybe they could do a little cruising without getting into deep water.

'Would you object if I had a word in private with Rosie?' he asked June. 'Perhaps we could talk in the garden?'

June smiled knowingly. 'Go where you like, Richard. I'll say goodbye now. Thanks for coming and agreeing to arrange everything. I look forward to seeing you next weekend.'

Richard gave June a kiss on the cheek and thanked her for everything. What a woman! Rosie was a tight bud — even if one with promise — compared with her mother's full-blown beauty and charisma.

'I hope all goes well with you and Charles,' he told her. Jealous he may have been, but he truly wished them well.

'You're a lucky guy,' he said to Charles, lightly punching his shoulder.

Charles shook his hand. 'Thanks for coming.' He glanced at Rosie waiting by the garden gate. 'Treat her gently, Richard. She's rather sensitive at present, what with her father's death and boyfriend problems. Make your intentions clear from the start. We both know you're not the marrying kind. Make sure she's aware of that.'

'Don't worry, Charles. From my conversation with her, I think we both know what we want. How far we go will be up to Rosie. I'm aware of her problems. I'll make allowances. Cheers, see you next week.'

Richard didn't like being told how to treat a woman, but he understood his friend's concern. He had to smile to himself: Charles, the bachelor adored by women of all ages, was already acting the concerned father!

Rosie was looking at them both quizzically. Richard took hold of her hand and led her into the garden. She took over and guided him to the summer house: a wooden structure covered in vines and far from the house. She sat down on a cushioned cane sofa and patted the seat beside her. Knowing what was expected of him, he sat next to her and put an arm loosely around her shoulders. With her leaning against him and manoeuvring her breasts within reach of his hand, he thought it time to get things straight between them.

'Rosie, please hear me out before you say anything. You see, I really like you, and I think you feel the same about me. But I won't beat about the bush. I have to tell you that my affairs don't last long enough for them to get complicated. I hope we get to know each other eventually — if you know what I mean — but only if that's what you really want.'

'I would like that,' she said coyly. 'I find you... sort of exciting.'

'I know, but I don't want to play on it. After the holiday, I'm back at work and it's too far away to carry on a close relationship. We may not see each other very often. You understand that, don't you?'

'Yes, of course.'

'I don't want you to be hurt. Better not start anything rather than have that happen. I nearly asked Charles to find someone else to go. But next year is also being planned. We've already booked the yacht for the Caribbean cruise. We must be clear about this: if you don't want me to come on to you, try not to tease me. I find you too attractive. I can hardly keep my hands off you.'

She looked at him from under her lashes. 'I'm not stopping you from doing what you want to do.'

Richard swept his eyes over her body and smiled. With a lusty man's hunger, he kissed her eager lips. At the touch of his tongue, she opened them up for him to take his fill. A sweet aphrodisiac oyster indeed! Before long, his hand was fondling her firm, young breasts. She moaned encouraging grunts of delight, pressing up to him and thrusting back her head for him to kiss her throat. He felt her fingers touching his groin and was powerfully moved to let a hand stray up that very short skirt, now creased up to the top of her thighs. Her knickers were white and lacy. She was utterly vulnerable for him to pleasure her as he willed.

It must not happen. With an effort of will, he pulled himself away from her. Where Rosie was concerned, keeping himself in check was going to be far harder than he'd realised.

He looked into her glowing eyes and smiled. 'I think we can look forward to a happy voyage.'

She smiled coquettishly. 'A *very* happy voyage.'

But he was wondering if having to keep Rosie's sexual appetite in check might turn the venture into a rather rough passage. At least, for him.

As he drove away, he looked in his mirror and watched her waving. Smiling contentedly, he turned out of the drive and switched on his radio to keep him company. Nat King Cole was singing in dulcet tones, *When I fall in love....*

He switched to another programme.

Charles was in his sitting room, catching up with his correspondence. It was already Thursday morning and there was a lot to get done. June wanted him to go shopping with her sometime and advise on new clothes for the boys. Evidently, she couldn't trust them to choose their own. They were already pressing her to be allowed to buy trendy boots.

'Charlie, are you busy?' It was June calling up his stairs.

'I'm never too busy to see you.'

He was beginning to regret having agreed to sleep apart and keep their lovemaking well-spaced until the children were back at school. She was now part of him and he needed her badly. He met her at the top of the stairs and wrapped her in his arms.

'Stay a while.'

'We have to think of the children.'

'Then come and have a late supper with me tonight. Candlelight, music, and—'

June interrupted him. 'Sounds really wonderful. I'll think about it... promise. But when I tell you why I'm here you might not be so eager.'

He rubbed his cheek against her hair. 'Nothing can dampen the fire of my love for you.'

She burst into giggles. 'Corny, but delightfully poetic! Anyway, what I have to say might prove to be an effective fire-extinguisher.'

He laughed with her. 'Oh, well, in that case, better sit down and we'll have a coffee together.'

'Sounds good to me,' she said, following him to the kitchen.

'I have an appointment to see Robert Watson today,' June told him, as they sat facing each other. 'I promised to see him before going on holiday. He wants to go over my old contract and talk about new designs for the next range of both fabrics and garments.'

Charles sipped his coffee, wondering why she was making a big deal about it. 'Is that a problem? Surely it isn't going to take all night as well as this afternoon?'

June put down her mug and rubbed her finger along the rim, removing the slight stain her lipstick had left. She glanced up at him, lines of anxiety taking away her normal youthful appearance and causing her to look her true age.

'Actually, I'm having lunch with him. Annie Craven is cooking the meals today. So when Robert rang and asked me to lunch with him, I accepted. It seemed like a good opportunity to speak to him about that other matter.'

'Young Jimmy?'

'Yes. Robert needs to know he has a son.'

'June, a man like him could have a dozen sons around the country — daughters too!'

Arthur had told him a great deal about Robert Watson. He looked at June's worried face and instantly regretted his outburst. He took hold of the hand which was still hovering over her coffee mug.

'I think you must have wiped that clean by now,' he said, grinning to relieve the situation.

She laughed with him. 'Yes, I think it is.'

He squeezed her hand. 'Of course he has to know. The sooner the better, before he finds out for himself.'

'I won't be back until late this afternoon. I can't say what sort of mood I'll be in, so don't get your hopes up too high. I'm already nervous at seeing Robert about the business aspect. I just don't know how he'll take it about Jimmy, or what the consequences will be.'

'Can I come with you and give you moral support? You shouldn't be facing this alone.'

'I was alone with him when Jimmy was conceived. I guess I'll start from there.'

What she had told him about that night came flooding back to him. 'That's what I'm afraid of — renewing memories best forgotten.' He cupped both her hands in his and looked into her eyes. 'You've told me what this man does to you. I don't want to lose you. I can't let it happen again. I love you far too much.'

'It's all right, Charlie,' she said, smiling with her eyes. 'Even that wild night spent with Rob was nothing compared with what we shared last weekend.'

'That was just the beginning,' he said, kissing her hands. 'A mere taste of things to come.'

'Not sure if I can handle this love-talk. I have to go now before I weaken my resolve.'

He walked with her to the top of the stairs to kiss her goodbye.

She pushed against his chest. 'I really must go, Charlie.'

He released her. 'Of course.'

Watching her walk down the stairs, he wondered if she would be a changed person when she returned. Sighing deeply, he went back to his correspondence.

Chapter Six

At eleven o'clock, June was ushered into Robert Watson's light and airy private office. As the door opened, her eyes quickly took in the rich green carpet, pale ash furniture and Impressionist prints. As Rob rose from his commodious green leather chair to greet her, all else became insignificant. His presence was overpowering her senses.

He came around his busy, but tidy, desk and held out his hand. 'Good to see you again, June.'

She shook his hand and smiled nervously. 'And you, Robert.'

She used his full Christian name deliberately, hoping it would help distance the past. It didn't work — his touch was electrifying.

He stepped back and held wide his hands. 'Well, here you are, looking as lovely as ever. Yellow suits you.' His eyes dropped to her legs. 'The flared miniskirt looks good with that sleeveless top, and definitely shows off your assets to good advantage.' His eyes swept over her in a final critical appraisal. 'Yes, indeed: high shirt collar with deep plunge neckline, wide belt giving a nippy waistline — could be a winner on the high street.' He sighed audibly. 'Pity I didn't see it months ago.'

'Thank you, Robert, but I only ran it up recently. Anyway, you're looking pretty good yourself,' she said, now feeling more confident. 'With that tan, I take it you had a good holiday somewhere?'

Of course, it wasn't only his tan that made him look so healthy and sexually attractive. His whole manner of dress enhanced his finer features: dark slim-fitting trousers emphasising his flat stomach, and fitted shirt flattering his lean waist and broad chest. Rolled-up sleeves not only revealed his strong muscular arms but gave him a down-to-earth, energetic executive appearance.

'Bahamas, actually. You should have been there with me.'

She gave him a derisive smile. 'That will never happen.'

'Don't be so sure,' he said, his eyes sweeping over her body and weakening the muscles of her legs. He offered her an easy chair by a round coffee table and sat down opposite her. 'You really do look fantastic. I was quite worried about you when I saw you at the funeral.'

She couldn't hide her surprise. 'You were at Arthur's funeral? I didn't see you.'

He cocked his head to one side. 'I doubt if you saw most people there.'

His right thumb began dibbing into the cleft of his chin. It was a gesture that she had always found unnerving — and he knew it.

'That's true,' she admitted. 'There were hundreds in church. Arthur had so many friends and colleagues. Many people held him in high regard, even if they did not share his political views. But you were not on the list given to me by the funeral director.'

'They had a busy time taking names. I had to hurry away.'

'A lot of people only came for the service.'

He nodded. 'So I noticed.'

Realising that from his vantage point he would be able to see well up her thighs, she consciously uncrossed her legs and held her knees close together. 'It was kind of you to pay your respects,' she added.

His full lips curved into a half-smile, as though mocking her modesty. 'I had a lot of respect for Arthur,' he said, his eyes seeking to examine her mind. 'Even if I did think him far too protective of you.'

'That is a matter of opinion.'

'Of course,' he said, 'and my opinion is what makes me a successful businessman.' He sat back in his chair. 'But we digress.' He swept an arm towards a large table arrayed with designs, swatches, samples and trimmings. 'There is much to show you and even more things in need of discussion. I must bring you up to date with our latest enterprises.' He nodded at garments hooked to a rail. 'Then we'll visit the showroom and workrooms.'

Even as he was talking to her, explaining the latest trends in garment manufacture and the need to branch out into new fields of activity, she was rationalising her feelings, putting her excitement down to the ambience of the place. Eventually, she admitted to herself that it was as much Robert Watson as what he represented that stirred up old passions. Being around fabrics and fashions awakened memories of the heady days of working close to Rob. His vibrant energy stimulated her. He had that power to dig into her well of life and keep her spring clear and fast running; to his own advantage as well as hers. She wanted to be part of it all again: to be in the swim of things not just paddling in the shallows; to be in the forefront of fashion; to see the garments through their various stages and be involved with the buyers; to know the joy of success and the power that comes with it. Yes, to be part of Robert Watson's empire. More than that — to be part of Robert himself?

No, no, of course not! What was she thinking of? She tried to concentrate on what Rob was saying.

But he was confusing her emotions. She had been wrong to think that she could handle the situation alone. Without Arthur to negotiate for her, she was completely vulnerable to Robert Watson's magnetic power. She should have allowed Charles to come with her after all. Why had she been so stubborn? Of course, she wanted to be independent, the capable businesswoman, not the poor little widow in need of a man to prop her up and protect her. But Robert Watson was ruthless enough to play on her feelings and heartfelt desires. Just as he was doing now. It was too much, too much. Torn apart by desire and prudence, she began to feel hot and faint.

He stopped talking and cocked his head. 'You look a little warm. Let me get you a drink.'

He poured iced water into a glass and handed it to her. As she drank, she sensed him move behind her chair. She felt her hair being lifted from her neck. Expectations of what he was about to do sent shivers down her spine. *Yes, yes, please yes.* But her mind fought against her desires. 'Rob, I—'

Cool hands descended on the back of her neck. The shock restored her reasoning. She turned her head and saw Robert with his hands on the water jug. He touched her again. It was bliss. She drew herself up and pressed her neck against his hands, sighing deeply.

'Thanks. That's better. I'm fine now.'

But he did not move. His lips replaced his hands, his tongue lightly touching her neck in a most provocative way. An uncontrolled shiver ran down her spine. Damn the man! She resolved not to respond to any of his unprofessional advances.

'It's terribly hot in here. Please may I have another glass of water?' she asked coolly.

He filled her glass and returned to his chair. *'Anything else I can do for you?'*

There was innuendo in his tone of voice as well as in his smile. And oh, that look! That devastating pull of his eyes, sucking her into him. She turned away her face, fighting to control her confused emotions.

'Before we discuss my contract and the new range,' she said, assuming a calm tranquillity she did not feel, 'there is something else of a personal nature... something you need to know. When you hear what I have to say, you might decide to reconsider our business association.'

'Sounds intriguing. Can't imagine what it can be.' He lifted his heavy dark brows and fixed her with that devastating, smouldering gaze. 'Unless, rather than work for me, you would prefer to live with me?'

She turned her eyes away and looked down at her hands. 'I don't intend to do either.'

'Oh?'

'But I am prepared to continue our association,' she said, risking a steely stare. 'As before, working from home. I most certainly will not come back and work for you. Let's be clear about that.'

He shrugged his shoulders and splayed his fingers. 'So, what is it you wish to tell me?'

She took a deep breath. 'You have a nine-year old son.'

The bare statement took Rob completely by surprise. He sat back in his chair, his face deeply puckered into a puzzled frown. 'Would you mind explaining?'

'Do I need to? Think back, Robert. Ten years ago in London?'

'Was something I'll never forget. I've never had such an intoxicating partner. Believe me, that's quite a compliment. Of course, I knew you had it in you.' His gaze intensified. She could feel him searching her soul. 'It's still there, isn't it? I felt it as soon as you walked in.'

The shock of his statement brought heat to her face. She told herself to ignore his provocative remarks: they were putting her under his power.

'We are not talking about me. We are talking about your son.'

Deliberately keeping her eyes unfocussed, she sat staring at him, waiting for her statement to sink in.

For a moment, he rubbed the cleft of his chin. 'Are you telling me that you fell pregnant from that one evening you spent with me? Now come on, June, you weren't exactly leading a celibate life with Arthur. What makes you think that…what's his name, your last child?'

'James. And before you say it must be Arthur's child, I'll tell you that it just isn't possible. Wrong blood group. I did not sleep with another man, so he must be yours. He looks so much like you that before long it will be obvious. I have to tell him before someone hints at it. I don't want my son upset by gossip. People can be so cruel. It will be hard for him to accept as it is.'

'Did Arthur know?'

'Yes. He thought you should be told. He said you had a right to know, but I refused. Arthur accepted James as his own child. You could never be a father to him even if he does have your genes.'

'Really? You are wrong about me. It's the one thing I have regretted — not having a son. I have even considered marriage.' He looked at her rather strangely. 'But the only person I was prepared to have for a wife was not available. However, that's changed now.'

'I hope you'll be very happy with her, whoever she is. But what about James? Do you want to meet him? It's important I know your attitude. I don't want him upsetting. It will be bad enough for him to find out that Arthur wasn't his biological father... he adored him.'

'I doubt my coming into his life at this stage will make much difference to his feelings about Arthur.'

She was taken aback. 'So you want to get to know Jimmy... have a proper relationship with him?'

'Jimmy? I prefer his proper name.' He gave a little shrug of his shoulders. 'Perhaps James will enjoy having a new father. His real one.'

'He will soon have a new father and he already loves him.'

Robert frowned. 'Is that so?'

'Yes.'

'Too bad. Well, suppose I call at your house on business and meet James in his own home — casually? We could get to know each other informally before you tell him the truth.'

'I had thought of that myself,' she said, nodding approval. 'But not until his brothers are back at school. I might have to tell Rosie, though. The similarity is so striking, she might guess the truth when she sees you both together.'

'Rosie? Oh, your eldest child. Looks a lot like you.'

'Yes, and she's exceptionally creative.' June shifted in her seat. Bad enough what had gone before, now he had to know the unpalatable truth about her declining abilities. 'It might be a good time to confess that she's been helping me. In fact, when I was looking after Arthur, and since he died, she's been designing most of your prints.'

He raised his heavy brows. 'You're throwing a lot at me today. First, you tell me I'm a father, next that you're getting married again. I take it that's what you meant. And now you inform me that your daughter has just about replaced you in your design business!'

She didn't want a confrontation. Robert Watson would always come out on top, leaving her emotionally drained and even more in need of him. How she missed Arthur to be their go-between. Why had she turned down Charlie's offer to be there?

'I'm sorry, really sorry,' she said, her throat swollen by unrelieved emotion, 'but I didn't plan to have your child, nor for Arthur to die. If you want me to walk out and never return — fine, I'll go!'

Her eyes welled up with tears. Disgusted at her weakness, she stood up pulling a handkerchief from her bag. Rob came quickly over and put an arm around her shoulders.

Damn! Damn! Damn! she thought, vehemently mouthing the words. She knew he would do just that. Why didn't she get straight out? Why stay now? The answer came, but she pushed it from her mind. Surely it was impossible to love a man who had once raped her! No, she hated Robert Watson. Tears of anger, self-loathing and sorrow continued to flow.

'Don't take it like that,' he said tenderly. 'Don't you see? I want you in my life. You can never be replaced. It was you who helped me get started. We were the perfect team — remember? We can be again.'

She did indeed recollect those heady days of soaring ambitions that were realised time and time again. Of starting from nothing — the ignorant trainee from a lowly background — to rise up a ladder of phenomenal success. Working for and with the young entrepreneur determined to make his mark on life. Yes indeed, the perfect team! A glow of remembered joy lifted her spirits.

His arm closed around her more closely and his face brushed against her hair. 'You know we belong together,' he said, his voice soft and caressing. 'Who do you think was the only girl I would have married? Now you tell me that we have a son. Don't say you didn't enjoy that night ten years ago. We both know you did. You can't marry someone else, you're already mine. Have been since I—'

She snapped out of his bewitching spell. Anger flared within her. 'Raped me on the factory floor twenty years ago?'

He sighed, sat her down again and pulled his own chair closer to hers. He raised his hands as if in open surrender. 'You say I did,' he said resignedly. His brows lowered over his mesmerising eyes. 'But in your heart you wanted it. Deny it if you like, but you know it's true.'

She pulled her eyes away from his gaze. 'No! No! It's not true. It isn't, it isn't!'

He took hold of her quivering hands. 'I set your juices going,' he continued relentlessly, 'and not just your creative ones. Deep down we are the same animal spirits. Like me, you have a zest for life. With Arthur, you suppressed your natural instincts and lived a lie.'

'No! No!'

He took her face in his hands and once more fixed her with his smouldering gaze. 'Start to live again, June. No one forced you to have sex with me that night in London. You came to me. You were more than willing. It was good, *amazingly* good. Admit it. Now we have a son. He's yours and mine, created by mutual desire. You can't change that, nothing can. Work alongside me. Be yourself, not what everyone else wants you to be. We can bring our son up together. It's right for him, and natural for us.'

She pulled her head from his hands and shook it. She must not give way to Robert. Her future was with Charlie. Her dear, dear Charlie. She had always loved Charlie.

Yes, but hadn't she always loved Arthur? Her emotions were tearing her apart. She screwed her fists into tight balls and beat them on her forehead. 'That isn't what I came here for. I'm going. Forget I told you about James. I'll move away and you'll never hear from me again.'

She rose from her chair and was about to rush out when he grasped her arm. 'I'm sorry,' he told her. 'Please stay.'

Out of emotional weariness, she sighed heavily and sat down again.

'Come to the showroom,' he suggested. 'Look at the new fabrics and trimmings, they're really exciting.'

She stood up and walked with him to the room next to his office, glad to be getting down to something tangible and positive. Now she was prepared to listen to his every word.

'We must discuss fashion trends and ideas you have for prints. In fact, just what we planned to do before you dropped that bombshell. We'll go out for lunch and then come back to discuss your contract. What you've told me won't change anything.'

June hesitated about being with him for so long, but the excitement of starting a new range, and the feel of Rob's new premises, had great pulling power. She stepped inside the showroom. Apart from the attractive light ash furniture, there were garment rails slid inside open cabinets, fabrics draped over a stand, trimmings arrayed artistically on a table, print designs pinned to display boards, and a few dresses displayed on trendy mannequins. A huge poster on the wall — a June Rogers gown worn by a top model — finally moved her to stay for the afternoon as originally planned.

She tried not to reveal the excitement bubbling up within her. 'All right, Robert,' she said coolly, 'I'll do as you suggest. But please leave my personal life out of it. When we've finished with business matters we can discuss when you can meet James. He is the one to decide how much of you he wants in his life.'

'Fine by me. Now come and look at these fabrics, they'll bowl you over.'

The next hour-and-a-half went quickly by. Rob's zeal was energising her enthusiasm as of years gone by. Ideas began flowing and she shared them with him. He did nothing to deflate her fervour. She knew that Rob knew she was hooked and would be doing his best to reel her in. But she was determined that whatever ensued would be on her terms.

He took her for lunch at a new Chinese restaurant. Over sweet-and-sour pork, they discussed the latest trends and where they both thought fashion was moving. The need to be in the forefront of style was paramount. Rob disagreed with some of her ideas. She had to admit that she needed to get grounded in what was going on in the world of fashion, and with changes required for growing consumerism. But she was willing to learn, and Robert Watson was eager to teach her.

In the afternoon he took her on a tour of his new building. She was impressed. It was so light, clean, and airy compared with the old factory where she'd worked before her marriage. She realised how much she had missed out on. Since leaving the factory, it had been all right working at home, but she had lost so much, especially with Arthur having done so much of the negotiating to keep her apart from Rob.

She noticed the respect his staff had for his abilities, and it greatly impressed her. He had easygoing ways and yet the ability to troubleshoot difficulties before they became problems. Even as they walked around he was able to give snap decisions to questions asked of him. He was the same person she had worked with so many years ago, but now he radiated the power of a self-made millionaire.

Robert took June to meet his only salaried designer. All the others submitted designs on a freelance basis. Rob explained that he was tired of building up talent only to have the best of his designers headhunted by his competitors. He now preferred to employ first-class pattern-cutters and buy designs from young, talented designers eager to get started. But this young designer, Steven Blake, was more of a personal assistant to him. When June met him, she could see why — he was another Robert Watson, bursting with ideas and energy.

When they returned to Rob's office, he had a tea tray brought in. They sat back in the comfy chairs and relaxed. Soon his secretary arrived with the contract.

'Look it over carefully before you sign anything,' Rob told her. 'You may want to make changes.'

'I take it you don't mind Rosie working with me, accepting her designs under my name?'

'Not at all. In fact, I'd like to meet her.' He rubbed his thumb into the hollow of his chin, looking at her as though to gauge her reaction. 'Perhaps she would prefer to work directly with me. I'll arrange a visit for her to look around.'

Her eyes flared in alarm. 'No, Robert. Rosie is not coming here under your influence. Anyway, she's only seventeen and has to finish her education.'

'I seem to remember you were only seventeen when we first worked together. You surely don't regret it? It would do

Page 88

her good to visit here, at least, especially since she's already designing for us.'

His comments were undeniable. She visibly sighed, relaxing her tensed nerves. 'I'll talk to her about it. She'll soon be eighteen and has a mind of her own anyway. But, until she completes her A-Levels, I prefer to have her included in my contract.'

'No problem, and I look forward to meeting this talented young lady.'

Still feeling uneasy about her daughter becoming involved with Robert Watson, June looked briefly at the contract in front of her. 'Apart from the addition of Rosie, there are other things I want to think about. I will take this home with me and discuss it with Charles.'

'Charles? Would this be the new man in your life?'

'Charles is Arthur's brother.'

'Ah yes. I remember him. The handsome sailor.' His lips twisted into a mocking smile. 'Another prop to take Arthur's place? So he's to be the new father for my son?'

'Don't do this to me, Robert. You have no idea how much I loved Arthur.'

'Yes I do. But your need of him as a support was far greater. Perhaps it was the difference in age. Admit it, June… your husband was more of a father to you than a lover. Now you need another Arthur to take his place. Of course, his brother is the obvious choice. I assume he is quite a bit older than you?'

'You can be so cruel. Charles has always loved me, and in a way, I've always loved him. Arthur knew about it. It was Arthur's dying wish that we would get together and that Charles would be a father to our children.'

'Our child too, don't you forget. So, Arthur still props you up from the grave?' His eyes narrowed. 'Why don't you live your own life, woman? I can tell how being here with me thrills you. It's in your blood.'

She knew she couldn't argue with him any longer. The pull of working beside him once more was too great, apart from which, he was far too perceptive. Her emotions were tying her in knots.

'I must go, Robert,' she blurted out, reaching for her handbag. 'I'm expected home.'

'That's another thing. Calling me Robert instead of Rob. Your way of distancing me? It won't work.'

'I have to go.'

She was shocked to find her voice unusually high and strained. She swallowed hard to control it. 'It's been an interesting day, I'll admit that.' She rose quickly from her chair — a bad move, as it made her dizzy. She halted a moment to recover. 'I'll be in touch later,' she muttered.

He put a hand on her shoulder. 'Think about what I've said.' His voice was gentle and conciliatory. 'You have the chance for a new beginning. Don't live the rest of your life wondering what might have been.'

June refused to look at him. The hand on her shoulder was now burning into her soul and setting her body alight, but she was powerless to tear herself away. His other hand was moving under her chin, gently lifting her head.

She looked up and saw his lips — moist and swollen with sexual desire — coming to meet hers. With an effort of will, she forced her head aside. 'No!'

His hands gripped her shoulders. 'I love you, June. Is that what you want to hear? I have never said that to another woman. I want you. *All* of you. Yes, I admit it. But you want me too, no matter how much you deny it. We're soul mates: made for each other.'

Her heart was thumping in her chest. 'No, you're wrong! I'm in love with Charles.'

'Maybe that's so. But what we have is much more than mere love. We are twin souls burning with a lust for life.'

His arms closed around her. She shut her eyes against the world. Oblivious to touch and sound, she began floating... lost in a blanket of utter silence.

'Mrs Rogers. Wake up, Mrs Rogers.'

She opened her eyes. Rob's secretary was dabbing her with cold water.

'Feeling better?' asked Robert.

June looked around her, trying to think what had happened.

'It's the heat. You fainted,' Rob explained. 'Don't worry, I'll drive you home in the Daimler.'

'No!' June objected, suddenly brought to alertness. 'I'll be fine in a moment or two. Anyway, I came in my car. I can't leave it here.'

Robert helped her to her feet. 'Nonsense, Judy will drive it back.'

'No, I....' Feeling unsteady again, June sat down and delved into her bag. She brought out her keys and handed them to Judy. 'It's the green Rover. Parked just down the road, not on your parking area.'

June watched the secretary leave. She turned to Robert. 'Please tell me you didn't... didn't—'

'Rape you while you were out cold?' he cut in. 'What point would there be? I can have a woman any time. I want your soul as well as your body.'

She stiffened. 'Never!'

He grinned. 'If you say so. Now we must get you home.'

The smirk infuriated her. 'It will not happen,' she told him with exaggerated confidence. 'I love Charles. Accept it.'

So I have a son, Rob thought to himself as he pulled his golden Daimler up at the traffic lights.

June looked across from the passenger seat. 'What was that?'

He smiled. Soul mates, indeed — she could even hear him thinking! 'You know, June, I'm really warming to the idea of fatherhood.'

'I don't want Jimmy to see you yet. Or anyone else. When we get to Bloomfield, please drop me off in the lane.'

No need to argue with the woman. She was hooked. He would give her a few months before pulling her in. 'You know best,' he said pleasantly.

A few minutes later, he turned the corner of the lane leading to Bloomfield. A red Mini came straight at them. He screeched his Daimler to a stop, but the damage was already done. The Mini had caught the side of his front bumper.

The female driver jumped out of the wretched little car and stood in front of his Daimler with her arms outstretched. 'It's your fault!' she yelled. 'You took up all the road with that golden monster. Look what you've done to my precious Mini!'

Robert Watson preferred to look at the lovely young woman, rather than examine her tin-pot car. She looked incredibly sexy in her state of fury: flashing hazel eyes, flushed face, rich brown hair tumbling in curls about her bare shoulders. Moreover, her breasts were almost falling out of their boob tube, and her rumpled miniskirt hardly covered her crotch! For a few seconds he amused himself by imagining taking her by her hair, throwing her in the back of his Daimler and teaching her some manners.

It was Rosie Rogers. No mistake about it. On recognising her, his mind went back over twenty years to when he first met her mother. Of course, her mother had been much less exposed. In those days, miniscule skirts and revealing tops had been reserved for the beaches! But the daughter was highly spirited, as well as talented. She was going to be quite a challenge to his masculinity. Yes, he must have Rosie Rogers for his clothing empire and, of course, for himself.

He was about to leave his car to face Rosie, when he turned to June to make sure she was all right. She was sitting, horrified, her pale face staring at the Mini. He followed her gaze. Then things started happening all at once.

Rosie had seen her mother in the Daimler. 'Oh, no!' she exclaimed, raising a hand to her mouth.

A boy sitting in the front passenger seat jumped out and ran to the Daimler. 'Mum, are you all right?'

Two other lads were scrambling out of the back of the Mini.

'What have you done, Rosie?' yelled one of them — a fair-haired boy.

'Mum!' yelled an older dark-haired boy. 'Are you hurt?'

They all arrived at the Daimler together. June opened the door. 'Stop fussing, all of you. I'm fine.'

Robert stepped out of the car and took a card from his wallet, offering it to Rosie. 'Get your car repaired and send me the bill. I'll sort it out myself. Don't worry your mother about the damage.'

'How do you know she's my mother?' she said, sounding highly suspicious. 'Oh yes! You must be Robert Watson. Mum said she was visiting you today. Why is she with you? Where's her car?'

He truly admired this presumptuous young woman. 'It's all right, Rosie — you don't mind me calling you Rosie, do you? Your mother isn't feeling well. My secretary is bringing her car back.'

The boys were still fussing around their mother, and Rob took the opportunity to observe his son. 'Strange,' he muttered to himself, 'it's as if I've known him for ages.' Then he realised he was looking at his own likeness, as he had been so many years ago. His heart warmed towards the lad — a child of his own loins and born of the woman he loved. He blessed the day that June found Arthur alone with his half-dressed secretary.

In the midst of his thoughts, he heard Rosie thanking him. 'I suppose it was just as much my fault. Thank you, Mr Watson. And I don't mind if you call me Rosie.'

'You're a talented young lady, Rosie,' he told her, running his fingers through his hair and pushing back the heavy forelock. 'You must come and visit my place sometime and meet my staff. Talk it over with your mother. But don't worry about this little mishap — worse things happen at sea.'

'I hope not, Mr Watson, at least not to us, we're off in a yacht on Saturday.'

The rest of them had been listening. They all laughed except June, who was now getting out of his Daimler to look at the damage.

June shook her head. 'Oh dear,' she groaned, her face strained with worry. 'Rosie has made a mess of your bumper.' She took her things out of the Daimler. 'I can walk from here, Robert, so I'll say cheerio. I'll get in touch when we're back from holiday.'

The older boys were looking at Rob's Daimler with admiration. But James was not interested in the car; he was eyeing Rob rather quizzically. Robert was about to speak to him when June intervened.

'The boys will have to go back home.' She grabbed Jimmy by his arm. 'Mr Watson is a busy man. We must let him get on.'

Rob smiled as they walked away. No doubt about it, James was his son!

Chapter Seven

June glanced back and saw Rosie talking to Robert. It worried her.

Jimmy was rattling on about the accident: 'And it was Rosie's fault really. She took the corner too sharp. I told her she was too far over. The Daimler was on the right side of the road. That man's nice. Is he the one you design for?'

'Yes, Jimmy. We may be seeing a lot more of him when we get back from holiday.'

The older boys came up from behind and ran ahead. Just as June and Jimmy arrived home, Judy was turning into the drive. She gave June the keys to the Rover P6.

'I do hope you're feeling better, Mrs Rogers,' she said anxiously. 'Mr Watson is concerned about you. What happened? Was it just the heat?'

'Probably, but it's been a busy day. Thanks for driving my car home. How are you getting back?'

'Mr Watson is waiting for me with the Daimler. He's just down the lane. I'll be getting a lift straight home to my flat.'

June wondered what would happen when they arrived there. Then she chided herself — why should she care? Robert Watson's affairs meant nothing to her. But for whatever reason, her mind continued to buzz with possibilities that refused to go away.

Charles was coming down the stairs as June entered the house. The boys were telling him what had happened.

Jimmy was talking excitedly: 'And, Uncle Charlie, Mum looked terribly ill. Rosie nearly killed her!'

Charles walked over to June and put a steadying arm around her. 'You look washed out, June. Why were you in Watson's car? Are you ill?'

'It was hot in Rob's office and it's been a rather busy day,' she told him, trying to steady her taught nerves. 'I just passed out, that's all. Nothing to worry about. Rob was just making a fuss. I could have driven myself home.'

His worried frown deepened. 'I'm glad you didn't. Go and lie down, you really do look tired.'

Made worse by feelings of guilt and remorse, June's nerves were on a razor edge. 'Don't tell me what to do, I can look after myself!'

'Sorry, I'm just concerned for you.'

'Don't be. I'm fine.'

'Okay, but let me—'

'Don't fuss, Charlie. I don't want anyone fussing. I want to be left alone!' She broke free of him and ran, sobbing, up the stairs.

She heard Jimmy calling after her and Charles saying calmly, 'Don't worry lads, it's just the shock of the accident.'

But she knew that he knew it was much more than that.

Although he tried not to show it, Charles was feeling agitated. June had cut him off, and it really hurt. But more than that, he was concerned as to what had happened that afternoon. June was a tough cookie. Passing out because of the heat? No, there was more to it than that. Then David broke into his thoughts.

'Rosie was taking us to the swimming baths. It's club-night. Can you drive us there, Uncle? Please? It's too late to go on our bikes.'

'No, but you can still go.' Charles put his hand in his pocket and brought out his loose cash. 'Here's some money for bus fares and anything else you need. You can be in charge. Get back for seven. I'm cooking for you tonight.'

'Gosh, thanks, Uncle Charlie,' David said, taking the money and picking up his gear. 'Come on you two,' he called to Peter and Jimmy. 'There's a bus in five minutes.'

'Just a minute, boys, where's Rosie?' Charles shouted after them.

'Taking her Mini to a garage,' David called back. 'Mr Watson said he'd pay for the damage. He's crazy! It was Rosie's fault, not his.'

Having arranged to be alone in the house with June, Charles went upstairs to talk to her. He knocked gently on her bedroom door. There was no answer, so he slowly opened it. June was lying on the bed, weeping.

'Don't cut me out, June,' he said, standing by the door. 'You don't have to say anything, just let me be with you.'

She didn't answer. Charles went over to her, sat on the bed and took hold of her hand. She gripped it hard, held it to her face, and cried all the more. Charles sat with her, waiting for her to calm down.

After a minute or two she sat up and dried her eyes. 'I'm so mixed up, Charlie. I want to go back to work, but I'm afraid of Rob. And yet he's the reason why I want to go back. It sounds crazy, I know. I want to be home with you too... for us to have a life together. But most of all, there's my poor little boy. Rob's thrilled he's got a son. I'm afraid he will spoil things for Jimmy. And for all of us.'

She gave her nose a good blow on a wet handkerchief. Charles produced a clean one from his trouser pocket.

'Thanks,' she said, making an effort to smile. She looked at him through sorrowing eyes. 'What will Jimmy do when he knows? What will Rosie and the boys think of their mother? Everyone will know I'm an adulteress. They may think I've been carrying on with Rob for years. And now they'll see my husband's brother living with me while Arthur's hardly cold in the grave. They may even think Peter's your child. He looks so much like you.' She burst into tears.

Charles lifted June to her feet and held her close. 'Weep as much as you want, but don't send me away. I want to stay beside you.'

He kissed her wet cheeks and continued to hold her close until her tears ceased. She stood exhausted in his arms. He put her down on the bed with her head on a pillow, and lay beside her until she fell asleep.

He thought through all that June had said. He'd expected Rob to be pleased to find he had a son. He certainly would be, especially a lad like young James. Everything was bound to come out into the open some time, June had known that. What disturbed him most of all was Robert Watson's power over her. What had happened that afternoon?

After an hour, he pulled himself away from her and was about to leave the room when she woke up. 'Please don't go, Charlie. Stay with me, I need you.'

He returned to her side. 'I'll stay a little while, but I must go soon. Rosie will be home any time now and I'm getting a meal ready for them all. Later on, I'll get us something to eat. We can have a quiet time together.'

'That will be nice. Hold me tight, Charlie, I want to feel your strength.'

Nothing could have pleased him more. But she pushed him away again. 'Take off your shirt,' she said softly. 'I want you really close to me.'

He unfastened the buttons but she took over, hastily dragging the shirt from his back. Gripping his arms, she pulled him by her side. He felt her hands moving across the hardness of his back and shoulders, as though seeking his protective power to guard her against the problems that threatened to engulf her.

She begged him, 'Hold me tighter... much tighter.'

The intensity of her need was arousing. The closeness of their bodies quickly became a blissful agony. He knew he couldn't hold on much longer.

'I want to feel your strength inside me,' she yelled breathlessly. 'Now, Charlie, now! Please, oh, please!'

It was all too intense, sudden and lacking in tenderness. But he wanted to please her. He stripped off the rest of his clothes. She lifted her skirt and ripped off her pantyhose. As he came over her, she gripped his back so hard her nails ripped into his flesh.

He flinched with the pain. 'Take it easy, June.'

'No, Charlie. Harder, harder, harder! I want you to hurt me, really hurt me. Please, please, please!'

Charles could not go on. He pulled himself away from her. Something she had said about that night in Rob's hotel bedroom flashed through his mind — guilt! Once again she wanted to be hurt. Yes, punished. For what? Well, he wasn't going to oblige her. Not his style.

'I'm sorry, I can't do it,' he told her, pulling on his underpants. 'I don't know what happened this afternoon but you haven't told me all of it. I can't hurt you, I love you too much.'

June began weeping. Charles nursed her in his arms. 'What is it, June? Tell me what's wrong.'

She shook her head.

'Then let me help you, just by being here. Please don't ask me to cause you pain. I just can't do it.'

She lay in his arms like a hurt child in need of comfort. After a while she whispered, 'You wouldn't love me, wouldn't want to know me, if I told you what really happened.'

'Nothing could stop me loving you. Whatever happened today could not possibly be worse than my imaginings. So you might as well talk about it. Remember you're not talking to some innocent kid.'

'Rob tried to kiss me. I turned my head away, but he knew I wouldn't be able to resist him for long.' She gave a little shudder as she tried to control her voice. 'I was terribly confused. I'm not sure what happened next. I passed out.'

'I take it you — that is, part of you — wanted more than just his kisses. Is that what you're trying to tell me?' He waited a brief moment for an answer, but she didn't respond. 'Then you couldn't cope with your feelings and you simply lost consciousness?'

'Yes, something like that.' Her body visibly relaxed.

Handing the problem over was clearly a relief. But what a responsibility for him! In a way he would rather not have heard her confession. Having to deal with the jealousy and anger her disclosure had engendered was no easy matter. But, as in battle, it was better to face the enemy rather than give way to faintheartedness. Robert Watson was no simple contender for June's affections: the man had a deeper relationship with June than he could possibly understand. Arthur had known about it. He had dealt with the problem by dividing June's need of Rob in her career from the fascination that drew her to him sexually. Did she love the man? He didn't think even June herself knew the answer to that question.

'June, nothing actually happened, thank God. But we have to face this problem or it will forever come between us,' he told her kindly, but forcefully. 'You don't have to work for Watson again, but I know how much your association with him means to you. Of course, I could negotiate with him on your behalf, just as Arthur did, but frankly I don't think that is the answer. Working from home cuts you off from the stimulation needed to produce your best work, as you know only too well. And Arthur told me that you would have to work in London to get a job equivalent to what Watson can offer you — if indeed anyone would take you on.'

She shook her head. 'No one would even consider me on my present showing. And, like before, I wouldn't want to move away.'

'As I thought. In any case, even if you don't work again with Watson, you may still be seeing more of him now that Jimmy is involved.'

'I haven't told you everything. Wedded or not, Robert wants me and my son. He says we can bring up our son together.'

'Well, at least he's made his intentions clear. He might possibly have a moral right to see his son, but he has no rights over you. But that isn't the problem, is it?'

She lowered her head. 'No.'

'I think you're just going to have to see how things go. But don't try and punish yourself for having natural feelings. God knows, I would have been whipped around the fleet if I'd received my desserts for yielding to temptation!'

The corners of June's lips flickered into a smile. 'You make yourself sound like a lecherous rake.'

He pulled her to him. 'All I'm saying is... ask yourself what you really want from life. You could up sticks and move many miles away. But, no doubt your past would catch up with you some time or other: Watson is not a man to let go of what he wants.'

June nodded, but said nothing.

'Clearly, you want to be back working with the man. He really does something for you beyond my comprehension. If it means you'll occasionally give way to him, I guess I'll have to accept that. But I don't want you torn apart by love for me, and whatever it is that Rob can give you. Just accept what happened today, remembering you are emotionally vulnerable for a number of reasons. And yes, learn to live with your feelings. As long as you're afraid of them, they'll just torment you. As our relationship deepens, maybe his hold over you will eventually diminish. Let's hope so.'

She rubbed her face against his chest. 'Thank you, Charlie. I'll think about what you say.'

'Don't think too long, June, it will only make you unhappy.' He heard Rosie's car in the drive. 'I must clean up now and get the evening meal ready for the kids; they'll be back any time now. You stay and rest, it's been an exhausting day for you.'

He slipped on his trousers, put his shirt over his arm, and headed for the door.

June jumped off the bed. 'Charlie, stop! Your back is bleeding.' She hurried to him. 'I'm so sorry. Let me bathe it for you.'

He turned his back to the long dressing mirror and looked over his shoulder. Deep scratches, red and raw, were scored into his flesh.

He smiled. 'You can kiss me better tonight.'

On opening the bedroom door, he found Rosie at the top of the stairs heading his way in rather a hurry. He walked towards her to head her off.

'Is Mother in her room, Charlie?' she asked, without slowing down.

He caught hold of her arm. 'Yes, but she needs a rest.'

She looked up at his tussled hair and flushed face. 'Huh! I can see that.'

He ignored the suggestive remark and headed for his rooms. 'I'll be down shortly. I'm cooking tonight.'

'Hey, Uncle,' she shouted after him. 'What have you done to your back? Cut yourself shaving?'

He turned to see her grinning at him. He shook his head to hide his embarrassment. 'Very funny, Rosie. I caught my back on the rosebush by the summer house. I must get it pruned back.'

'Oh yes?'

'Yes. Now I must get on.' He started to walk off.

'Well, you don't have to cook for me, I've got a date tonight.'

He stopped and looked her in the eye. 'I hope your date isn't with Paul. That would be a good reason to disturb your mother.'

'Don't either of you worry, I'm not seeing that rotter again.'

Having stripped off her clothes and put on a dressing gown, June was in her bathroom scrubbing at her nails when Rosie came up behind her. She gave a startled cry and dropped the nailbrush into the soapy water.

'I didn't hear you come in. You made me jump, Rosie.'

She left the brush hidden under the lather as though it were evidence of a heinous crime, and started to wash her face.

'Charlie says you're resting,' said Rosie. 'Do you mind if I come in for a little chat?'

'Of course not. Your uncle is an old fusspot.'

June patted her face nervously on a soft pink towel and walked over to her dressing table. Picking up a pot of face cream, she turned and saw Rosie in the bathroom, pulling the plug from the washbasin. Her heart missed a beat. 'Leave it, Rosie, I'll wipe it round later.'

Rosie was grinning. 'You left your nailbrush in the basin.'

'Oh, did I? I'm going to do my nails. Some of them must have been broken on the Daimler dashboard.'

June knew exactly where, and when, the nails were damaged. The thought of what she had done to Charlie's back stirred up deep feelings of shame and remorse. Heat rose to her cheeks. She picked up her small tray of nail cosmetics and carried it to the table in the bay window. 'Come and sit with me,' she said, sitting down in one of the cane armchairs.

In the garden beyond the shadows, trees and flowers glowed in late afternoon sunlight. The scent of roses, pinks and lavender drifted in through the open windows. She began to relax and feel more at peace with herself.

'I'm sorry about the accident, Mum. I didn't expect Mr Watson's tank to come sweeping round that corner. Did it shake you up a bit?'

June glanced at her daughter. Rosie might be apologising, but there was still a curl to her lips and laughter about her eyes that did not sit well with what she was saying.

'I'm fine,' she told her, hoping she sounded better than she looked. 'It's been rather hot today. I'm just a little tired, that's all.'

'Looks like poor old Uncle's been in the wars too. Gosh, his back is covered in horrid scratches.'

'Really? Oh, come to think of it, he did say something about scratching his back on something or other.' Had Rosie guessed and was trying to divert the conversation away from herself and the costly accident? Well, she was not going to play her little game. 'What about you, Rosie? Are you all right?'

'Of course. It was only a bit of a bang.'

'Even so, you caused expensive damage to both cars by your carelessness,' June told Rosie sharply. 'Was Robert Watson angry with you after I left? He should have been.'

'Not at all,' said Rosie, smiling triumphantly. 'He's invited me for dinner tonight. Isn't that great? His designer, Steven Blake, will be there too.'

June's fears were being realised and she felt sick at heart. 'Don't let Robert Watson carry you away with his grand schemes. It's something he's good at. And, whatever happens, don't let him persuade you to give up your education and work for him. He may appreciate your talent, but there will be plenty of opportunities for good designers once you are qualified. Don't promise Robert anything — anything at all.'

'I'm not stupid, Mother,' Rosie snapped. 'I have a mind of my own. But if he wants to talk business, I'll listen. I'd be a fool not to.'

June sighed: her daughter certainly did have a mind of her own. But a short while in Robert's presence and she could lose it to him! It wasn't only Rosie's mind she was concerned about.

She put down her nail file and looked out of the window, wondering what advice Arthur would have given. She turned resolutely to Rosie.

'Don't let him bring you home in his car; take your own.'

'Mother really! Do you think he's going to rape me?'

June thought it more likely he'd use seduction, but no use telling Rosie that. 'He drinks a lot, that is good enough reason.'

'If he gets drunk, I'll drive,' Rosie retorted.

'After what you've already done to his Daimler? Robert's not that forgiving!'

Her daughter pulled a face. 'Anyway, it's all arranged. Robert Watson is picking me up. He'll be here at half past seven. He's collecting Steven Blake as well, so I won't be alone in the car with Mr Watson. I don't know why you're worrying, you know I can look after myself.' She stood up and headed for the door. 'I must get ready.'

'Try not to be out late, it's a busy day tomorrow,' June advised, trying to hide her dark fears behind a screen of motherly concern.

June continued with her nails, thinking through Rosie's situation. After many 'ifs' and 'buts' about her daughter seeing Robert that night, she decided it might prove a good thing in the long run. Rosie had to talk with him sometime, and she was going to be seeing quite a bit of him soon when Robert did his father thing. What a problem that was going to be! How will Jimmy take it? How will all of them take it? As she finished her nails she sighed deeply, full of regret for her past indiscretion. And yet, she was thankful for all of her children, including James. Yes, indeed. And now, with Charlie beside her, she could be full of hope for the future. Having shrugged off her demons, she walked to the bathroom and ran the water for a good relaxing soak.

At seven-thirty, June, dressed casually in a sleeveless, yellow-and-white-flowered dress, was in the hall sorting through the glove drawer of the dresser. It was the only excuse she could think of to be present when Robert Watson called to pick up Rosie.

'What are you doing, Mother?' Rosie was walking regally down the broad ornate staircase, wearing a stunning red dress with shoes to match. 'Lost something?'

June muttered something about mislaying her yellow gloves. Just then, a car's engine sounded in the drive. Peeping from behind the lace curtain of the hall window, June was surprised to see a maroon Alvis drawing up in front of the door with Steven Blake at the wheel. So, where was Robert Watson?

'Really, Mother, you're acting like a spy!' said Rosie crossly. 'How embarrassing! Do come away from the window, Mr Watson will see you.'

'Robert Watson is not here. Steven Blake has come for you, thank goodness.'

When June opened the door, the young man was standing in the porch with finger poised to ring the bell. He was just as June remembered him: tall, dark, square-jawed, large mouth with full lips, and deep blue eyes framed by heavy-rimmed glasses. He was smartly dressed in a light grey suit with white shirt and maroon silk tie. He gave her a broad smile, revealing his immaculate teeth.

'Good evening, Mrs Rogers. The Daimler has gone in for repair. Mr Watson asked me to pick up your daughter. I hope you have no objection.'

'Not at all.' June hoped her relief was not too obvious. She introduced him to Rosie.

Steven eyed her daughter appreciatively. 'I must say you look absolutely gorgeous, Miss Rogers.'

'Rosie, please, Steven. You look pretty good yourself.'

He grinned. 'I'm a lucky man to be escorting you. If you're ready, shall we go?'

June watched as Steven opened the passenger door for Rosie.

'This frock is rather lovely,' Rosie was saying. 'It's one of mother's designs.'

'I wasn't talking about the dress; you would look fantastic in anything.'

As Rosie slipped into the low seat, her skirt was pulled high up her thighs, showing off her long, slim legs.

'You're a beautiful young lady. I hope I'll see more of you." Steven said, with a dazzling smile.

June wondered exactly what he meant by that. Was Steven even more like Robert than she already suspected? A storybook quote came to mind: 'Oh Granny, what big teeth you have!'

'Take good care of her, Steven,' she called, as he stepped into his Alvis. 'No under-age drinking, please.'

'Don't you worry, Mrs Rogers, my boss will be around to make sure of it.'

June sighed. Robert Watson was going to make sure of a number of things — that was the problem!

The driver's door slammed shut. The Alvis backed, turned, and then was driven off — gravel flying.

June caught Rosie's angry face staring at her through the car's window.

As June walked up Charlie's stairs, a lovely savoury smell met her nose. She went into the dining end of the kitchen and found the candles on the table already lit. Soft romantic music was playing and the whole ambience was soothing to her strained nerves. Charles left his cooking to give her a welcoming kiss.

'What are the lads doing?' he asked, rubbing his cheek against her hair. 'I hope they have their instructions to keep away.'

'Don't worry, Peggy is here for a while. They're watching a film and then going to bed. They're quite excited about the holiday. It's such a good opportunity for you to get really close to them. I know you've been with us before, but Arthur was with us then — now it's just you.'

'Don't forget there's Richard too. I hope all goes well with him and Rosie.'

'Yes. But I think Rosie may now have another young man in tow, as well as Richard. What it is to be young and carefree!'

'Come on, June, don't look so wistful. Have you forgotten Rosie's boyfriend problems?'

June laughed, 'You are so right!' Thoughts of her own youth came to mind. She looked at Charles with love and admiration. 'I'm so lucky to have you, Charlie. How come you waited so long?'

'I haven't exactly waited, have I? I'm too fond of women to live a celibate life.' He kissed her cheek. 'Few people get what they really want in life. I'm really blessed to be here with you after so many years.'

'Oh Charlie, I….'

'Now please don't go all maudlin on me. Let's live for today and enjoy what we have.'

A smell of burning meat suddenly sent Charles off to the grill. He finished preparing the meal while June just relaxed. Watching him deftly preparing a tossed salad, she wondered how many women he'd cooked for. That thought made her realise how little she knew about Charlie, his work or his love life.

When he brought the food to the table, she asked him, 'What are you going to do, Charlie? Now that you've retired, I mean. If you continue to live with us, you won't want to just hang about. I can't see you at home being a house husband while I'm working.'

'I've thought a lot about it. Quite honestly it really depends on you. That's why I haven't talked to you about my ideas. I don't want you to feel in any way pressured.... Just leave it for now.'

June did not want to let the matter drop. 'Do you mean whether I go back to work with Rob or not? Or whether we get married?'

'Just leave it, June,' he said, piling salad onto her plate. 'Enough?'

'Yes, thanks,' she said, putting up a hand. 'But what you want to do is important to me. You are an essential part of my life now.'

'Very well, if you insist.' He helped himself to salad and pushed aside the bowl. 'If we agree to live together—married or not — and if you go back to work...' He was looking at her searchingly. 'I intend to set up a business — health and leisure — somewhere local. If you don't want a committed relationship, I might try a boating or yachting business on the coast. Maybe something in the Lake District. But, if you reject me for someone else, I will do what I'd planned before I knew Arthur was dying. That is, start a holiday business in the Caribbean with Richard Andrews, hiring out fully-equipped and manned sailing boats and launches.'

June was taken aback. 'Gosh, I had no idea you had such ambitious plans. I guess I've ruined them for you. To think, you are prepared to sacrifice so much for me... I feel so ashamed.' She put her head in her hands, thinking how selfish she had been worrying about her own future.

'I knew that's how you'd react,' he said, pulling her hands away from her face and looking deeply into her eyes. 'Sacrifice? Of course not. I love you and want us to be together — can't you understand that? But I don't want you to worry about my future. Certainly, it may depend on what you want to do, but I'm happy to be flexible until something evolves.'

She grasped the hands that were holding hers. 'Charlie, please do what you really want to do... even if you decide on the Caribbean thing. Wherever you are, I want us all to be.'

Charles lifted her hands to his lips and tenderly kissed them, but his eyes were shadowed by concern. 'June, you already have enough decisions to make without this intruding into your life at present. We'll talk about it again, but for now let's just enjoy each other's company and see how things go.'

She knew he was right, and it gave her a warm feeling to have a strong man once more supporting her. 'Yes, let's do that.'

'Now eat up, woman,' he said with a twinkle in his eye. 'I've been sweating over a hot stove all evening to get you in the mood for love.'

'Yes, Charlie,' she said with false meekness. She ate a few mouthfuls of tender steak. 'You know you're a wonderful cook, this is quite delicious. I wonder what you have prepared for afters?'

He grinned. 'You have quite a wicked gleam in your eye. Perhaps we should leave the dessert until much later. Exercise on a full stomach is bad for you.'

'Are you planning on a few press-ups, Charlie?'

'A few? You will be surprised what I have in mind.'

Sitting in Charlie's sitting room ten minutes later, they relaxed, listening to classical music on the radio. She snuggled close to Charlie, enjoying the scent of his masculinity and the feel of his firm muscles. He was a strong tower to keep her and her family from harm, and yet a voracious lover ready and willing to satisfy her more earthy needs. She looked up into his soft brown eyes; they were fuelled by longing, and it thrilled her.

He whispered, 'Shall we?'

She silently nodded her head and allowed him to lead her towards the bedroom. By the bed, he held her close and carefully pulled down the zip at the back of her dress. She wanted him desperately; her body was already tensing with desire. But she must restrain herself and allow him to make his unhurried love-play. Yes, allow him to lead her into realms of rapturous delight, until that final release when stressed flesh and muscles suddenly find release in a glorious indefinable erotic climax!

He framed her face with his large hands. Locked in the rapture of his kiss, she felt his fingers move from her face to under the narrow shoulders of her dress. Moving a little from him, she allowed the dress to fall to the floor. She was wearing her pretty white silk and lace camiknickers just for him and she wanted him to see them.

'Very pretty,' he observed. 'Convenient too.'

His kisses were stimulating her stiffened nipples, turning them into hard peaks, and the gusset of her camiknickers became damp against her hot flesh. His hands were caressing her body most delightfully. Such a soft touch. She threw back her head for him to kiss her throat.

'Take your clothes off,' she said breathlessly, unbuttoning his shirt. 'Hurry, hurry.'

She stood captivated by his firm masculinity. He slipped off her camiknickers and consumed her with his eyes. Warm oil seemed to be flowing over her body as desire swelled her flesh. He put his arms around her and pulled her against him. She stretched on her toes and tilted up her pelvis — his hardness connecting with her softness.

She lifted her eyes to his. They were soft and deep and full of lustful love. Now, it had to be now....

His arms were lifting her up....

'Mum! Uncle Charlie!' It was Peter's voice bellowing from the stairs.

Even as Charles hastily dropped her on the bed, Peter was bursting into the bedroom yelling that Peggy had cut her finger off!

'What? Okay, Peter, just wait outside a moment,' Charles said with remarkable calmness, reaching for his dressing gown.

While Charlie went off with Peter, June hurriedly slipped into her clothes. The situation was so absurd she didn't know whether to laugh or to cry. But her sister's welfare soon had her mind focussed on the emergency. She ran down the stairs ready to give comfort.

Peggy was sitting on a kitchen chair looking rather pale. Her blouse and flowered pinny were stained with splashes of blood. Blood was dripping off the table onto the floor. David was giving Peggy first-aid. She may not have severed her finger but, judging by the quantity of blood, she had cut it rather badly. Charlie was attending to James who, according to Peter, had passed out at the sight of so much blood.

'Peggy, we must get you to hospital,' June said, putting an arm around her sister's shoulders.

'No thanks, I'll be okay. David's done a good job of binding the edges together. He should be a doctor.'

David beamed at the praise. 'I'll make you a nice cup of tea, Aunt Peggy. That will soon get you better.'

'You're right there, kiddo,' Peggy said. 'Maybe your mum will let you put a spot of brandy in it.'

'Peggy, you know you don't need my permission for anything you want in this house,' June told her, feeling rather peeved. 'I'll get it for you myself.' She was back in less than a minute. 'Like it or not, I'm taking you to the hospital. That wound needs stitching.' She poured a good helping of brandy into a glass.

While Peggy was protesting that she didn't need stitches, James stirred on the floor. June rushed over to him. 'Poor

Jimmy, I guess you had a bit of a fright.' She hugged him to her bosom.

Charles stood up and patted David on the back. 'Well done, lad,' he said. 'I must say, I'm impressed with your coolness. Tea is a jolly good idea for all of us. While you're doing that, I'll clean up this mess.'

'Kind of you, but I can do that myself,' Peggy insisted. 'It's my fault and my blood.'

'Don't be ridiculous, Peggy, I'll clean up after I get Jimmy to bed,' said June. Why did her sister have to be such a martyr?

David poured them all tea. Jimmy said he wanted lemonade.

'Will you read my pirate story, Uncle — please?' pleaded Jimmy, looking pale and pathetic.

'Okay, young whippersnapper. Drink that up and off you go. I'll be up in a minute.' He pulled his dressing gown around him a bit tighter. 'Perhaps I'd better get dressed first.'

Much to June's annoyance, Peggy looked at Charles and grinned. 'I'm sorry, Charlie, looks as if you were disturbed in the middle of something.'

'Yes,' piped up Peter. 'Uncle and Mum had nothing on. Just like Adam and Eve!'

'That's enough, Peter, no need for details,' said June, wondering what was going through her son's mind. 'I'm sure Peggy has the picture. You and David can clear off now. It's bedtime soon.'

David was grinning knowingly. As he and Peter left the kitchen to finish watching a programme on television, they were heard chuckling. June just caught the words, 'It was this big!' She looked swiftly at Charles. He was clearly mortified. His deflation was surely now complete!

Since it was useless pushing for a hospital visit, as soon as the mess was cleared away June insisted on taking her grinning sister home. At least Peggy kept her thoughts about Peter's remarks to herself.

It was getting on for eleven before arriving back in Charlie's flat. He was dressed casually and making them a drink in his kitchen.

She flopped into a chair and sighed. 'The joys of family life! Are you sure that's what you want, Charlie?'

'It won't always be like this. Anyway, I'm impressed by David's behaviour. A good show of initiative.'

'Impressed?' June smiled at her thoughts. 'Well, I suppose you *impressed* Peter tonight. He'll have something to tell his classmates when he gets back to school!'

'Well, I am proud of my achievements,' he said, laughing. 'Though I must admit, there's little to boast of at present. But we could soon change all that.' He looked at her uncertainly: 'How do you feel about it?'

Having previously reached a peak only to be left high and dry with muscles aching to the point of pain, June was both physically and emotionally tired. It had been an incredibly long day and her nerves were shattered, but she wanted to please him. 'Suppose we have that dessert now and see how we progress?'

'Where would you like it served, madam?'

'Do you mind crumbs in your bed?'

'No crumbs, I only have trifle. We could have a sticky mess,' he said, nodding seriously with his eyes laughing.

'The sheets can be changed tomorrow. Come on, Charlie — let's eat!'

She walked to the bedroom, stripped off her clothes and slipped into bed. Her eyes were closing when Charlie came in with a dish of trifle piled high with whipped cream.

'Mm,' she murmured, slowly licking her lips in an effort to be seductive. Her eyelids became heavier....

June woke up with a start. She opened her eyes. The room was in semi-darkness. As her mind cleared, she recognised the engine of the Alvis disturbing the warm summer air in the drive below. After a moment or two, muffled voices could be heard approaching the front door. She put her hand out to touch Charlie, but he wasn't beside her. Slipping out of bed and going over to the open window, she could just see Rosie and Steven Blake.

'I'm not a bit sorry Rob went early,' she heard Steven's unmistakable voice say. 'He gave us time to be alone. I was thinking, perhaps we could see more of each other when you return from holiday?'

'I would really like that, but I'm a busy girl... what with homework and helping mother with her designing. And, of course, I do have various student commitments and close friends to see.'

'Are you playing hard to get, or just trying to make me jealous?' There was amusement in Steven's voice. 'Come here, Rosie,' he said, his voice deep and compelling.

Silence followed. Realising they were kissing, and maybe more, June felt suddenly ashamed of her eavesdropping. She was just about to leave the window when she heard a snippet of a sentence, 'If you accept Rob's offer.'

June returned to listening with intent. Too late, they had moved closer to the door and their speech had become a soft mumble. Her constant worries about Rosie came to the fore: the revealing clothes she wore and the impression they gave of availability; her sexual teasing and bolshie attitudes that lacked the seriousness of approaching adulthood. But right now, mingling with those concerns was 'Rob's offer' to Rosie. Had he actually approached her daughter to join his company? Why did Rob leave early? Had he arranged with Steven Blake to have Rosie seduced?

Determined to rescue her daughter, she began pulling on her clothes when the door opened and Charlie, drying himself on a large towel, walked into the bedroom.

He threw the towel on a chair and came over to her. 'You seem rather anxious. What's the matter?'

'I don't know, but I'm going to find out. Rosie's outside with Steven Blake.'

He caught hold of her. 'Leave them, June. She won't thank you for interfering in her life. You have a stubborn daughter. Don't turn her against you. You must trust her to be careful. If she starts screaming, I'll go and deal with the rascal.'

'I suppose you're right.'

'I know I am. Look, instead of going off to worry yourself sick, come back to bed and spend the rest of the night with me.'

She pulled off her clothes and climbed back into bed. Snuggled in Charlie's comforting arms, she told him what she'd heard.

'That could mean anything: a promise of a future career, part-time training to fit in with schoolwork, or simply doing a few designs. Would you deny your daughter the start you had? As for Rob seducing Rosie by proxy, aren't you letting your wonderful creative imagination get the better of you?'

'You're quite right, but—'

'Rob's in his mid-forties, he's hardly likely to—'

'Be attracted to a young kid?' June cut in. 'Charlie, you're fifty and Rosie has the power to turn you on.'

'Well, a hard-nosed businessman is not likely to be sexually attractive to young Rosie.'

'I'm not so sure about that. Anyway, Steven Blake is working for him. He's young, and quite handsome.'

Charlie drew her closer to him and ran his hand through her hair. 'If you're saying Rob is deliberately using Steven as bait, it's a bit far-fetched isn't it? He already has both of you designing for him. And since you're thinking of going back full-time, he wouldn't want to spoil his chances there.'

'You're right, as usual. I can go to sleep now.'

'Do you really want to sleep?' he murmured, ducking his head under the sheet and exploring her body.

Later, although exhausted by Charlie's lovemaking, June did not fall sleep at once. Something was getting at her. Suddenly, she realised what it was — jealousy! Was she actually jealous of her own daughter? It could come to that if she found herself taking second place to Rosie in the fashion business. If Rob had intended to use Rosie as a spur to get her working back with him, then he had succeeded. She would arrange to see him soon after they returned from holiday.

Yes, with Charlie giving her full emotional support, to be back in the swim of things was an exciting prospect. The business with Jimmy would fall into place. It was surely in Robert's interests to be discreet. She had simply got herself into an emotional tangle and been unable to think clearly. Anyway, what the hell did it matter what other people thought? Most of Arthur's colleagues had engaged in the occasional affair; some of the wives had regular lovers. This was the late sixties, and women were now liberated. She snuggled up to Charlie's sleeping body and sighed with contentment. He made her feel secure in an uncertain world. There was nothing to be afraid of.

Chapter Eight

It was clear to Charles that coming back to reality after three weeks of adventure was a drag for the children. None of them was looking forward to school. David told him that seeing Emma again was the only bright spot to look forward to. Rosie said she was going to miss Richard. She had volunteered to assist the skipper by working in the galley. Richard had been frequently disappearing below deck, ostensibly to give her instructions, but they all knew what was really going on. It wasn't instructions on how to cook fish that Rosie would be missing!

The boys had done quite a bit of training to equip them for all types of weather and conditions and were just itching to be aboard the larger craft they would be crewing the following year. David, in particular, was an excellent crewman, and he reminded Charles of himself at his age. Peter was pretty sharp and eager to learn, and young Jimmy was no slacker when it came to jobs in need of doing.

Altogether, it had been a wonderful holiday. The beauty of the coastline and the charm of the places they visited had again inspired June's creativity. Charles had watched her sketching and painting. She had an ability to draw out from her surroundings a sort of essence that she applied to good effect in her design work.

June seemed so fresh and alive, so youthful and full of energy. Charles had no desire to hinder her happiness. He enjoyed bathing in her sunshine, happy to share her with her children. He knew for certain that she had to be part of his future, whatever path she decided to choose. Being a highly emotional subject, it was something that could only be properly discussed once they were back home and the children settled in their schools.

Just before they set off home, June suggested they go ashore to buy a few mementoes and some food for the journey. The boys were keen; anything to delay going home. They hurried to their cabin to get their things. But Rosie said she would stay behind.

'I've got a dreadful headache. You're better off without me,' she told them, wrinkling her nose and wiping a hand across her forehead.

Charles smiled at the theatrical gesture. 'She wants to say goodbye to Richard,' he whispered in June's ear. 'They may not see each other again for a long time.'

June looked worried. 'I'd better have a quiet word with her about being careful.'

It was said quietly, but Rosie overheard. 'Huh! You're the last one to preach about precautions,' she said crossly. 'I know about Jimmy, Mother. Seeing him next to Robert Watson made me suspicious. Robert himself confirmed it when I asked him that night. So perhaps you had better teach *yourself* a few things unless you intend starting another family with Charlie.' She put her hands on her hips. 'Oh yes, and have you talked to David? The way he was behaving with Emma in the summer house before we came away made me wonder what sort of practical lessons he's been having lately.'

Charles looked at June with a mixture of sympathy and quiet resignation. Rosie was her daughter and he felt he should not interfere.

'Rosie, we'll talk about these things when we get home,' June told her, keeping her voice lowered and glancing around her. 'Now is not the right time. You must not say anything to the others. The matter will be sorted out in the proper way when I'm ready to do so. Jimmy must not be hurt. Now please watch your tongue, young lady, and treat others with respect.'

Rosie glanced at Charles and muttered an apology. She turned to her mother as she went below. 'I'm sorry, but it's time someone told the truth.'

June was about to go after her when Charles grasped her shoulder. 'Leave it, June. Talk when you get back home. Now is not the time for a row, the boys will hear.'

She sighed. 'Another problem: David and Emma. He's too young for that sort of thing.'

'I'm not so sure about that. Would you like me to have a word with him?'

'Please, Charlie. He'll talk to you. I would just embarrass him.'

Charles took June's hand. 'Cheer up, the holiday isn't over yet. We'll leave Rosie to sort herself out. Let's see if the lads are ready to go ashore.'

When the rest of the family had gone, Rosie went along to Richard's tiny cabin. He was lying on his bunk in just his shorts, his normal wear in hot weather. He put down the book he was reading and pulled her beside him.

'Now what do you want, Rosie? An aspirin for your headache? Or would you like some exercise to take your mind off the pain?'

'I can help myself to aspirin,' she said softly, rubbing up to him. 'I'm going to miss you — really, really, miss you.' She lightly kissed his sun-tanned cheek.

He turned and placed his soft lips over her mouth. She drank in the pleasure of his exploring tongue and pressed her naked breast against the hand that had pushed aside her bikini top. 'Mmm,' she mewed, 'More, more.'

While nuzzling her neck, he adroitly removed her top completely. She vaguely wondered how much practice he'd had with tricky fastenings. She allowed him to push her backwards onto his bunk, anticipating further demonstrations of expertise.

'Miss me? Or what we do together?' he whispered softly. 'I hope the latter, Rosie kitten. You won't be seeing much of me when we get back. But, with your looks, you can't be short of this sort of thing.' His mouth moved downwards.

'Won't you miss me just a little?' she asked. He certainly knew how to please a woman. 'Just a teeny bit?'

'Just take it for what it is,' he murmured. 'Two people using each other in a most enjoyable way.' He pulled the bikini top out of the way and threw it across the cabin. She felt his eyes burning into her breasts. 'I hope to see more of you before next year's holiday. I'll be visiting your uncle on business. But don't waste your time hankering after me, life's too sweet to waste it. Now, enough of this chatting. Relax, Rosebud. Enjoy your assets. I certainly am.'

Pleasurable feelings overtook all thoughts of the future. She ran her fingers through his pale blond waves, suddenly gripping his head as a shock of rapturous anticipation swept over her — his hand was slipping up her shorts....

Charles knew that returning from holiday was going to be hectic, especially for June: so much to sort out, put away or wash, jobs to do before school began, and just getting back to a normal life. He could see she was desperate to get her design ideas sketched out too. So he did what he could to help out by being available as and when needed. Taking the lads shopping for school items brought back many memories of his boyhood. But more than that, he enjoyed the company of the youngsters and having it assumed that he was their father. More than ever, he realised how important family life was to him and what he had missed through marrying Angela.

Since the gardener was on holiday, Charles volunteered to keep things in trim. Turning over soil made friable by a handsome crop of potatoes was a particularly relaxing occupation, and gave him time to muse on the pleasures of his new life. He looked up to see James hovering around.

'Hi, shipmate, want to work or just chat?'

Jimmy bent over, picked up a wriggling worm and threw it to a blackbird hopping around the turned soil. The boy's face was wrinkled in deep thought. 'If Mum hadn't married my dad, would you have been my father, Uncle Charlie?'

Charles stopped digging and carefully considered his response. 'There was never any question of my marrying your mother, Jimmy. She was in love with your father, and I didn't stand a chance.'

'If you marry Mum, will I become your son and you be my dad?'

'Do you want to have a new dad?'

Jimmy frowned. 'I think so. I miss my old one. It's nice having you here.'

Charles looked into the lad's eager face and a warm glow filled his chest. Pleasure was quickly replaced by anxious concern: Jimmy's life was going to be turned upside down yet again. Holding onto the spade, he squatted on his haunches to be more at Jimmy's level.

'Supposing someone else, not me, became your new dad... that would be good too, wouldn't it?'

'Don't know,' Jimmy answered, looking at his feet and kicking away a stone. 'A boy in my class had a new dad and they don't get on. John says he's going to run away.'

'That's sad. But it's not always like that.'

'Guess not,' Jimmy said, shrugging his shoulders. 'But I want you to be my new dad, Uncle Charlie. Can't you marry my mum... please?'

Charles only wished things were that simple. 'We'll see. But you know, Jim, I'll always be your uncle and I'll never stop caring about you.'

'You won't go away and leave us, will you?'

'You ask some hard questions. But I can tell you for sure, I'll try to be there if you need me. Who knows, you may find yourself with a dad that's much better than me.'

'I don't want anyone else, you're like my real dad.'

Charles put a hand on Jimmy's shoulder. 'You know, young Jim, we get a lot of surprises in life.'

'I like you calling me Jim, like in Treasure Island.'

'Then you will always be my godson Jim. No more little Jimmy.'

'It's my birthday in December. I'll be ten. No one can call me little then.'

'Frankly, Jim, no one can call you little now!'

Jimmy looked pleased. 'I'm good at digging. Can I give you a hand, Uncle?'

'Tell you what. Suppose you do a bit of raking? Then we can get this job done in no time at all.'

David arrived. He looked apprehensive. 'Mum said you wanted to talk to me.'

Charles footed his spade deep into the earth and left it there. He touched David's shoulder. 'Quite right. Let's go over to the summer house.'

'Can't I come too?' James pleaded.

Charles turned and gave him a sympathetic smile. 'Sorry, Jim. This is man-to-man stuff. But we can have the same talk when you're a little older.'

They reached the summer house. David grunted peevishly, 'I do know the facts of life.'

Charles sat down in a cane armchair and nodded for David to sit close by. 'It's what you're doing with your knowledge that concerns your mother,' he said casually, not wanting to sound heavy-handed and turn the matter into a big issue.

David frowned. 'What's Rosie told her? It is Rosie who sneaked on me, isn't it?'

'It doesn't matter how your mother found out. She doesn't want either of you getting into trouble.'

'Huh! We haven't done anything yet that would get us into trouble. You can't call petting trouble-making activity!'

Recalling his own youthful sexual activity, Charles shrugged and raised his hands apologetically. 'Emma's parents may not see it that way.'

'Well Emma is sixteen now. That's the age of consent, isn't it? So she can do more than pet if she wants to. And believe me, Uncle Charlie, she wants to!'

'Maybe, but her parents would not approve. You must be responsible, even if Emma wants to go all the way.' Again remembering his youth, Charles felt a bit of a hypocrite.

David pulled a packet of French letters out of his pocket. 'I do intend to be responsible, that's why I bought these.' He looked Charles in the eye. 'You're not telling me that you never did it when you were young.'

'Actually, not when I was as young as you are. Though I admit I was not much older. Look, David, you don't want accidents, so keep those with you, but do your best to resist. Your father would not have approved, he always believed marriage to be the proper path to full sexual experience.'

'I know, he told me. But you have never believed that, have you?'

Charles met the boy's questioning gaze. 'I am not your father.' Since David looked so much like Arthur, it was a strange experience telling him the things that Arthur had told him when he was a lad — like a reversal of roles. Wanting to get emotionally closer to the boy, he sat forward in his chair and opened his hands in a pleading gesture. 'This is rather difficult for me, David. I'm a poor role model for you to have around. I just beg of you, wait at least until you're a little older. Your mother would be much happier about it if you did.'

'I know, and you want to make mother happy. Can't promise, Uncle.' His brow wrinkled into immature furrows. 'You know jolly well how women can lead us men astray.'

Charles shook his head. 'That, my boy, is just a lame excuse. Show yourself to be a man by taking the lead in this relationship.'

David grimaced. 'I don't think Emma will be happy about that.'

Charles thumped the arms of his chair. 'Be the man of your family,' he said with verve. 'Take the moral lead as Arthur did for us when our father was away. He was worth ten of me. What you do in life will influence your younger brothers. Be strong — you'll never regret it. I lost your mother to your father, but she had the better man.'

Silence descended for a few moments. Had his words made any impression on his nephew? He watched David rubbing at his small growth of facial hair, deep in thought. So like Arthur. Sweet memories of his dead brother threatened to engulf him. As if David could read his thoughts, he looked up and smiled sadly.

'I'm going to miss you when I go back to school. Will you come to our sports days and, you know, that sort of thing?'

'I'll be everything you want me to be, David. When you're away, ring me when you need to talk. Same goes for Peter. If you're ever in trouble, I'll be alongside your mother giving you support. Can't say more than that, can I?'

David's lips tightened into a determined thin straight line. 'Thanks, Uncle Charlie. I'll do as you say. I mean about Emma. At least, I'll try.'

Charles stood up and shook the hand David had thrust towards him. 'That's all I can ask of you. I'll tell your mother, it will ease her mind.'

Charles went back to James, who was still busy raking. 'That's a good job you've done there, Jim. Not a weed in sight.'

Peter turned up. 'Can I join in?'

'You boys are wanted indoors.' It was Rosie, dressed in skimpy red shorts and blouse, calling from the garden path. She came over to the vegetable patch.

Jimmy offered her the rake. 'Come and join us.'

'No thanks, I get enough gardening — raking up your grubby clothes! You'd better get going. Mother's sorting out the washing for Annie Craven. She wants a word with you lads about missing socks and pants.'

Rosie looked keenly at James as he ran towards the house. 'He will have to be told, Charlie. Gosh, when I saw them together it was so obvious they were related. It doesn't make any difference to me, or any of us, but it will to him. Anyway, Rob is keen to get to know him. He does have a right. He told me he's always wanted a son.'

'Really? Then he should have married and done something about it.' He knew he was being testy, but what right had Robert Watson discussing personal family business with young Rosie? 'Claiming Jim now might be convenient for Watson, but the child has to be considered. Your mother will decide what happens next.'

'You're too hard on Robert Watson. I like him. I like him a lot. It will be nice to have him around when he visits Jimmy.' She took hold of the spade and casually dug it into the rich soil. 'Mother must like him or she wouldn't have slept with him, nor would she be going to work with him again. That day mother spent with Robert — the day I bumped his car — I reckon it wasn't just the heat that made her faint.' Glancing up, she gave him a knowing look. 'You'll have to watch it, Charlie.' She lifted a scoop of soft earth and turned it over.

He watched her stirring the soil with the edge of the spade. A squirming worm was trying to get away but she would not let it go. Soil was falling over the path. He took the spade away from her and turned her to face him.

'You have no idea what you're saying, Rosie. I know all about Robert Watson. It isn't as you seem to think.'

She looked up. Her face was a mask of sweet innocence. 'Oh really? Well, I find Rob sort of… impressive. He's more of a man than his sidekick Steven. But I'm not complaining. Steve is fun, I like him a lot.'

'You seem to have a few admirers at present. You made quite a hit with Richard.'

'Now, he's a *real* man.' Smiling, she looked at him from under her lashes. 'Are you jealous, Charlie?'

He placed his hands on his hips and laughed. 'Age is always jealous of youth, but I assure you, dear niece, it's no more than that.'

'Well, from what Peter told me, you have nothing to be jealous about. Angela told me a few things about you too. But I've seen most of your body for myself, and I've sort of felt what I haven't seen.'

Behind her coy expression, she was laughing at his embarrassment. Refusing to play her little game, he folded his arms and slowly shook his head.

'Don't tease men, Rosie. It's dangerous. As for Robert Watson, keep your relationship strictly business. He's much too old for you to be thinking of him as a possible lover. He's quite ruthless and will take advantage of you, and any other young woman he can lay his hands on.'

She moved to lean provocatively on a nearby apple tree. 'You're not telling me he took advantage of my mother ten years ago, are you? Not according to Rob. He said it was mutual attraction. I don't blame mother for having her little fling. He certainly has something about him, and it's not just looks. It's a sort of power… energy… vitality.'

She picked up a fallen apple and polished it on her blouse in a seductive manner. 'No wonder mother fainted resisting him. If she did indeed resist him.'

'Don't speak of your mother like that,' Charles said, exasperated by her persistent aggravation. 'Why are you doing this? You have a choice of men, but you're still not happy. What's wrong with you? Are you jealous of your mother?'

She took a bite out of the apple. Juice ran out. She stuck out a pink tongue and ran it over her plump lips. 'I'm very happy. What have I to be jealous about?'

Angry with himself for letting her rile him, he picked up the spade and thrust it into a patch of weedy ground. 'You're an enigma, Rosie. Only you can answer the question you pose. I have work to do.'

She threw the apple over her shoulder and sidled up to him. He took no notice. She picked up the rake and combed through clods of earth.

'I saw Steven last night,' she confided. 'All he could talk about was mother going back to work for Rob. He said Robert was always singing her praises. When Richard came over for your party he couldn't keep his eyes off mother. On the yacht he made do with me, but I knew who he really wanted.'

Exasperated, he thumped the spade into the ground, and turned towards her. 'You're wrong, Rosie,' he said firmly, 'especially about Richard. Stop harbouring these silly ideas. June is an attractive mature woman. Men look at you and then at her, thinking that's how you will look at her age. It's no more than that.' Even so, he suspected there could be a small element of truth in her suspicions — men admire women without intending a sexual encounter — but why go down that track?

'Do you really think so?'

'Of course I do. As for young Steven, you must separate Steven's appreciation of your mother's talent from what you may think is physical attraction.'

'Guess so.' She was fiddling with her thumb nails. 'I'm sorry for being a pest.'

She looked so forlorn: a troubled, insecure young woman. Set free by Women's Lib and the Free Love movements, she was like a boat drifting aimlessly on a tide of her own emotions. Arthur — moralistic but kindly, firm but fair, and always loving — had been both her anchor and guiding light.

'What is it, Rosie? What do you really want from me?'

She wiped her eyes with the back of her hand, and shook her head.

'Missing your dad?'

She nodded.

Putting an arm around her shoulders, he walked her along the garden path.

'We missed him on the yacht, didn't we? It was always great to be together. But you know you can't substitute sexual love for a father's love. Yes, it may distract you for a time, but the pain will still be there. Arthur will always be part of us. A good and better part. Hold on to the things he taught you.'

'I'll try.'

'Come and talk to me any time. But please don't try to get my attention by teasing, it will only destroy our relationship. Just tell me when you're hurting and we'll talk. Okay?'

She hung down her head. 'Yes.'

'There is one thing you might like to tell me, but only if you want to. Did Robert Watson make any proposals to you?'

'He was really nice. He said he liked my work and that I could have my own contract when I'm eighteen. But he was happy for me to go on working with mother while I'm still at school.'

'Is that all? Did he say anything about your mother working alongside him again?'

'Yes. He said he hoped she would. But if she declined his offer, would I like to work with him. He wants to have at least one of us on the premises. Actually, he said that if I would like to join the company when I leave school he would take charge of my training… either under mother or alongside Steven Blake. I guess he was offering me a job. Quite exciting really.'

'I thought you were going on to higher education?'

'Well, mother didn't and she's done okay. I'd love to be trained by Robert Watson – he's got real magnetism. But Steven is a good designer and a brilliant pattern-cutter. Rob's training him to do a lot of his work too.' She suddenly stopped walking. 'I'd better get back, I'm supposed to be helping mother.'

She made her way back to the house. Charles watched her, thinking how much richer his life had become in spite of the complications. Of course, to some extent, he had already been part of Arthur's family, but now he was forming deep relationships. He would find it hard to tear himself away from them all. But, within a couple of days the kids would be back at school. What about June? Life at Bloomfield was going to be somewhat quiet during the daytime.

He insisted on driving June and the boys to Plowden Manor College. David was resigned to being back and chatted about the clubs and the rugby team he would be joining. But Peter seemed unsettled and distant. Charles tried to draw him out, but the boy was keeping tight-lipped. Charles recalled his own youth and understood the need to keep control of one's feelings in front of other boys, but Peter's silence worried him. He took him aside and told him to phone or write if he had any problems or wanted to talk. Without looking up, Peter just nodded. 'Mum told me. Thanks, Uncle.'

On the way home, June said, 'Robert rang me before we set off this morning. He's coming to see me tonight.'

'At least you'll be meeting on home ground.'

'Yes, but after that fainting fiasco, the thought of seeing him again just makes me tremble. Anyway, it will be good to get everything sorted out.'

Charles turned the Mercedes onto the main road, glad to have a straight run so he could concentrate on what June was telling him.

'You'll get used to being with Watson again,' he told her sympathetically, even though the thought of it sickened him. 'You really enjoy your work. I know you already have quite a few designs ready.'

'How do you know that?'

'You've been tucked away in your studio since we got back. What else would you be doing there?'

He didn't tell her that he had sneaked in late one evening to see her work and had been staggered by what she had produced. Clearly, love for her work was all-consuming. He glanced at her sitting in the passenger seat, looking so far away.

'It's been quite a while since we made love,' he told her. 'We only managed a cuddle on the yacht, what with your monthly and kids everywhere. I really need you. You have no idea how my body aches for you.'

'You managed twenty years without me in your bed. You'll be okay – we'll get together soon.'

Her dismissive attitude both annoyed and worried him. He stopped the car in a lay-by and took hold of her hand. 'It's been years since I've been this long without a woman. When Rosie came on to me the other day, she stirred up my loins.' He felt June stiffen. 'No need to worry, your daughter is quite safe. But I find it hard, really hard.'

She gave him an apologetic smile. 'I'm sorry, Charlie. Yes, it's true what you say. I've been working day and night since we got back. But once this business with James is resolved, and when a working arrangement with Robert is finally concluded, and I get settled into full-time employment—'

'And you have a minute to spare?' Charles cut in sharply. 'No, June. We have to get our relationship worked into your programme or there will be no relationship. I'm prepared to risk you working with Robert, but don't let him, or your work, take over your life. It's not just me, your children need you, too. Rosie will go right off the rails unless you give her some of your time. If you don't, she's going to be creeping into my bed one night just to get attention. I'm not sure I'll be able to handle that.'

'She wouldn't do such a thing. Surely not!'

'You have no idea, do you? You get so absorbed in your own grief, your own problems, and your own work, that you don't see what's happening around you. You don't want to lose Jimmy to Robert, do you? All your children have needs. I love them all and I'm prepared to share responsibility for them, but I need some encouragement from you. The children need to see us working together. That way we function as a unit. But a family is also cemented by love. We *all* need to know we are loved.'

'But I do love you, Charlie, you know that. Arthur understood about my designing and we worked things out okay.'

'Really? Not quite what I've heard. What with Arthur busy with his directorships... Parliamentary work in the later years... you running a business from home. A hired help is a poor substitute for keeping a family together. And, of course, all that business with Watson didn't help — still doesn't. I know things are different for you now, but I want to be more than a prop in your life, enabling you to do your own thing. As for your children, they deserve more than just a mother figurehead.'

June's face wrinkled with unhappiness. 'I know you're right, but I just get carried away. Arthur knew that, but he still wanted to marry me, and for us to have children.'

'By all means get carried away: I want you to be happy, and I'll soon have my own work to think about too. But let's work things out together — don't exclude me. The children had Arthur to turn to with their problems, at least when he was home. I'll do my best, but I'm not used to kids. We need time too. Just you and me, to talk, and to love.'

'I know, Charlie. I feel really bad about it.'

'Good!'

She bit her lip. 'I didn't realise how unhappy you are. Maybe you—'

'I'm not unhappy! Far from it.' He cupped her face in his hand, looking into her worried eyes. 'I'm just glad that you now realise the situation. I want you near me. Please don't keep us apart.'

He lifted her chin and gently kissed her lips. 'Come to my room and stay the night. We can talk. Make love, or just be together. Surely that's what kept you and Arthur together and in love?'

'Yes, you are right.'

'Are we in agreement then?'

'I guess so. And I'll try and involve you in what I do. Tell you what. Why don't you join us while I discuss things with Robert?'

'I'll do just that.'

At eight o'clock the doorbell rang. June, dressed casually in a bright flowered dress, jumped up nervously and hurried to the door. In spite of the hot weather, Robert Watson was dressed formally in an immaculate grey suit, blue striped shirt, and a knotted, blue silk tie. He had a briefcase in his hand and a parcel under his arm. Steven Blake was with him, similarly dressed, but in brown.

'Good evening, June. I've brought Steven along. It will save having to give him the details tomorrow. He may want to make some input too.'

'I don't mind,' June told him. 'Nice to see you again, Steven.' She closed the door behind him and turned to Robert. 'Charles Rogers is joining us too.'

'Your brother-in-law? Perhaps we should have Rosie too. Make it a family party?'

His sarcasm was profoundly irritating. 'Perhaps that might be a good idea since you've already discussed intimate details of my private life with her.'

Robert shrugged his broad shoulders. 'The truth will come out. She had already guessed the relationship.' He raised his heavy eyebrows. 'Did you want me to lie about my part in his birth?'

June was caught in his mesmerising gaze. Erotic memories of Jimmy's conception welled up and disturbed her composure. Steven Blake broke the pregnant silence.

'Perhaps it would be good for Rosie to join us. After all, she will be designing for us one way or another.'

'Good thinking, Steven.' Robert turned again to June. 'Is Rosie here?'

'Yes.'

'Perhaps you would ask her to come to the meeting?'

'I'll ask. It's up to her if she wants to come.'

June showed them into her studio before looking for her daughter. Charles was coming down the stairs with James. June sent her son in search of Rosie.

Just as June was introducing Charles, Rosie arrived. She seemed pleasantly surprised to see Steven. 'I didn't know you were coming,' she said, giving him a welcoming smile.

Steven rose from his chair and held out his hand. 'Nice to see you again, Rosie. Sit here by Robert. I'll go the other side of the table and sit by Charles.'

After polite preliminaries, June discussed her contract with Robert Watson. Rob said he was pleased that she had decided to come and work with him. 'You won't regret it,' he said. 'Now that you're coming on board, you have a great future ahead of you. But you know that already.'

Charles asked pertinent questions about the hours June would be working. His intrusion into the conversation clearly riled Watson.

'June knows the rag trade better than any sailor, no matter what his rank,' Watson retorted. 'She is fully aware of the pressures we can be under.'

'Of course. I am merely concerned for June's health and her family life,' Charles said placidly. 'We single men can so easily forget there is a life beyond work.'

Watson was looking at him through narrowed eyes. Suddenly he smiled. 'Of course, is there anything else that concerns you?'

June sat back in her cushioned armchair and relaxed. It was like having Arthur back with her. She could leave Charles to sort out contractual details. She looked across at Steven. He was in eye contact with Rosie and they were smiling as though sending coded messages to each other. But Robert soon broke into their sweet communion.

'Rosie, we can discuss the possibility of you working in-house at a later date,' he told her. 'But, if you would like to submit designs while you're still at school, we would be pleased to consider them.'

'Thank you, I would like to do that.'

'I expect you to come in occasionally. Perhaps you would like to work closely with Steven? Better for you to develop away from your mother's influence. I don't want another June, I want to see what you can do. The young approach, fresh as a daisy.'

June watched as he swept his eyes over her daughter's long tanned legs, slim waist, and youthful breasts.

'Or should I say, fresh as a Rosie?' Rob added, lifting an appreciative eyebrow.

June was completely abashed; not only had Rob bypassed her as regards Rosie's future, but he'd also repeated words and sentiments spoken to herself over twenty years before. She looked at Rob as he gazed at her daughter, practically undressing her with his eyes. She felt utterly humiliated, and yet what Robert had said was surely the truth: Rosie needed to develop her own youthful style. She glanced at her designs on the low coffee table. Fear of them being rejected suddenly gripped her as Rob bent over to pick them up.

'As always, your holiday has inspired you.' He gave her a penetrating glance from under his dark brows. 'Perhaps it was also your visit to my office before your holiday?'

All eyes were on her and she felt herself blushing.

Charles suddenly put in, 'No doubt about it, our holiday was an inspiration to all of us, but especially to June. In that fantastic environment she couldn't help herself. Could you, darling?' he added, smiling in her direction. 'Of course, her visit to your new premises had greatly impressed her. I heard all about it. I wouldn't mind a guided tour of the place myself.'

June smiled at Charles, grateful to him that eyes were no longer focussed on her. Robert muttered something about being pleased to show Charles his factory and continued looking at the designs, passing them over to Steven so he could also give an appraisal.

A feeble knock sounded at the door and Charles jumped up. 'I'll go.'

June's heart started racing. She knew it would be Jimmy seeking Charles. She heard Charlie speaking to him the other side of the door.

'Go along and get ready for bed, Jim. I'll be up in a few minutes.'

Rob stood up quickly and hurried to the door. 'I thought I might see you, James. I have a present for you. I'm sure your mother won't mind me giving you a little something. Come in.'

June knew Robert Watson never expected anyone to object to anything he did. She sat back as he took Jimmy over to the studio work table where the parcel had been left.

'I believe you like cars, James. These are not just toys, they are a set of genuine scale models,' Robert said in a friendly voice. 'Perhaps I could come over some time and we could talk about them?'

Jimmy looked both puzzled and pleased. 'Is that all right, Mum?'

'I'm sure Mother won't mind a bit,' said Rosie. 'Especially since we're all going to be working together, Robert will be like one of the family. Isn't that right, Mother?'

June ignored Rosie and went over to Jimmy. 'Unpack it now and then you can thank Mr Watson before you go to bed.' She did not want an excuse for another contact, although she knew it was going to happen anyway.

James quickly undid the parcel. His face lit up at the sight of eight model sports cars. 'They're great! Golly, they have headlights that light up. Thank you, Mr...?'

'Watson,' said June.

'Thank you, Mr Watson.' Jimmy's face wrinkled with thought. 'You're the gentleman my mum designs for. You brought her home that day Rosie bumped your Daimler.'

Robert grinned. 'There's an honest witness.'

Rosie blushed. 'I'm sorry, Mr Watson, I know it was my fault. It was so kind of you to pay for the repairs, but I should really have contacted my insurers.'

'Don't worry, I can afford it. It was worth it just to meet you, Rosie.' He turned to Jimmy. 'And my young friend here.'

Jimmy beamed up at him. Charles moved forward and put a hand on his shoulder. 'Time for bed, Jim.'

Jimmy looked at June. 'Must I?'

June nodded a decisive, 'Yes! Go with your uncle. Now, please.'

Jimmy picked up the large box of cars. 'Thanks again, Mr Watson. It's been very nice to meet you.'

Rob sat down. 'Come over here, young man, and let me see if you've got any muscles.'

Grinning, Jimmy put down his box and gave Robert an arm to feel.

'Oh yes, splendid! And what a big lad you are. I like your thick curly hair.'

Rob put his fingers through Jimmy's thick mop and ruffled it. He then gripped his shoulders. 'I bet you're a good rugby player.'

'I am actually. I'm in the first team. When I'm older, I might play in the City Junior League.'

'Really?' Rob rubbed at the cleft in his chin with his thumb, as though in deep thought. 'I played rugby at school.'

Jimmy's dark eyes widened. 'Gosh, Mr Watson, we are alike. I've got a deep dimple, just like yours.' He placed a forefinger in the hollow and gave a broad grin.

June was feeling tense. Damn Robert Watson! He was deliberately drawing attention to the features he shared with his son. Breaking the news of the relationship was something that should have been discussed first. It was typical of the man. 'I'm sorry, Robert, it's Jimmy's bedtime,' she said firmly.

Charles, standing near the door with hands loosely on hips, cleared his throat. Jimmy turned his head and nodded. 'I'm coming, Uncle Charlie.'

Jimmy gave Robert a downcast smile. 'I must be going now, Mr Watson. I have to go to school tomorrow.' He walked towards the door with June willing him to get to bed. Suddenly, he turned and looked at Robert quizzically. 'Are you a relative, Mr Watson?'

'Come on, Jim,' Charles broke in quickly. 'Mr Watson has business with your mother. I'll come up with you and make sure you get to bed.'

Robert grinned. 'You the *au pair*, Charles? I am impressed.'

Charlie left the room with Jimmy in front of him. He closed the door without looking up. But June could see the anger registered on his face.

'I don't know what I'd do without Charles,' she said, the heat of indignation burning her cheeks, 'he's great with the boys.'

'Apparently, my boy especially. When are you going to tell him, June?'

June glanced briefly at Steven and Rosie. 'I think that is something we should discuss in private.'

'Don't mind Steven, he knows James is my child. Rosie does too, so where's the problem? The sooner James knows the better. He's a great kid who needs a father. I can see us getting on rather well. What do you think, Rosie?'

June was furious. 'Leave my daughter out of this, Robert. Anyway, I think it's time Rosie went upstairs to sort her school things out. She has to be up early in the morning.'

'Oh Mother, don't treat me like a kid! I'm eighteen soon. What's more, next year we get the vote — about time too! We're old enough to fight in a war!'

'I like a woman with spirit,' said Robert. 'Don't worry, my dear, your mother forgets she started work at fourteen, and was working with me when she was only seventeen. And, I might add, she looked exactly like you — fresh, and sweetly innocent.'

June did not like the way Robert was flirting with her daughter — flirting he most certainly was doing, with his eyes devouring her body. If she had worn such revealing skirts in the late forties, Rob would never have believed her to be sweetly innocent — quite the contrary! What was Rob really up to?

Steven sat forward in his chair. 'How about you showing me the garden, Rosie? I expect it looks lovely in the moonlight.'

Having seen Robert giving Steven a nod, with a glance that took in her daughter and the glazed door to the garden, June was not surprised by the request. 'Yes, do that, Rosie,' she said, glad to get them both out of the way.

As Rosie led Steven through the door, Robert drew his chair closer to June. 'I'm really looking forward to having you working beside me again after all these years.'

'It's been a long time, Rob,' she said, determined to remain calm. 'I look forward to being in the swim of things again.'

'You know, you really came alive in my place.'

She knew he was waiting for her to respond, but she remained silent, afraid of the emotions he so easily engendered.

'You haven't lost your touch, either. The majority of these designs are great.'

This was something she had been waiting to hear. Her confidence soared and cast aside the tension of being alone with him. 'I'm pleased you like them.'

He drew a little closer. 'They have a youthful look that will appeal to a wide market.'

It was exactly what she had been trying to achieve. 'Looking young without aping teenagers is what women want.'

'Appealingly youthful, but seductively mature,' he said softly.

His voice and eyes were mesmerising her. Her whole body was becoming sensuously alive. An exciting but dangerous feeling!

She looked down at the sketches and fought to break the spell he was weaving around her. 'I'm looking forward to being back, but please keep our relationship strictly business,' she said, her voice a little strained.

'Ah, not so easy with my son involved.' There was a hint of amusement in his voice.

'As for Jimmy,' she continued, annoyed that he had gained the upper hand, 'all right, you can see him. But don't push it. And I rely on you to be discrete about the relationship. Enough that you have already told Steven Blake. Jimmy will be told in due course. He already sees Charles as a substitute for Arthur. Charlie gets on well with all my children.'

'That's good, he can keep house while you give me your full attention.' He sat back in his chair and rubbed at the cleft in his chin. 'Now tell me about James. Do you have pictures of him, school reports — that sort of thing? I want to know all about my son.'

Glad to get away from the charged atmosphere, June left the room to gather photographs and information.

Charles sat listening to Jimmy's thoughts about Robert Watson.

'It's funny that Mr Watson is a lot like me, isn't it?'

'It certainly is. Now where did we get to in this story? Oh yes, Blackbeard was about to—'

'Do you think he's related?'

'Blackbeard?'

Jimmy laughed. 'Don't be silly, Uncle. I mean Mr Watson.'

'Perhaps. You should ask your mother about that.'

'But you're my uncle, so you should know.'

'Not necessarily. I do know Robert Watson is not a blood relative of mine.'

'I look a little bit like you, but I don't look like my dad. I don't really look like Mum either. I don't look like any of my family. Not my sister, not my brothers, not my uncles, not my aunts, not my cousins, not my—'

'I get the message,' Charles cut in, before Jim explored the entire family tree. 'You are definitely your mother's child. I felt you in her tummy not long before you were born, and I saw her nursing you when you were tiny.' He turned a page of the weighty book. 'Now I think this is where we got to in the story.'

'Do you think that Mr Watson could be a long-lost uncle?'

'Would you like him to be?'

'Think so… I like uncles. It's nice you're here. I miss my dad, and my brothers when they're away. Dad used to help me with my homework, if he wasn't too busy, which he usually was.' His face wrinkled into a frown. 'He used to drive me to school on the first day back. When he could, that is. Will you take me tomorrow in your Merc? You don't have to fetch me, I come home on the bus.'

'I'd like that. Now let's see what Blackbeard is up to in this story.'

'Uncle, my friend at school has two dads. He gets lots of presents. Of course, only one can his real dad. I do know how babies are made.'

'Two dads and lots of presents? I guess he's made a fuss of.'

'Uncle Charlie, do you think I've got two dads? I mean, had two dads before dad died.'

'Suppose you did, Jim, how would you feel about it?'

'Don't know. Do you think Mr Watson could be my real dad?'

'My brother was the best father a boy could ever have, Jim. He loved you. That made him a real dad. But I know what you mean.' He snapped the book closed and threw it on the bed. 'Put your dressing gown on and come downstairs with me.'

Robert Watson and June had their heads bent over photographs when Charles walked into the studio with Jimmy in front of him.

'Jim has been asking me questions. Only you two can answer them. It's important to him to know the truth.'

June looked stunned, but Robert pleasantly surprised. Charles turned to Jimmy: 'Just ask your mum what you want to know. She won't lie to you.'

Jimmy stood with Charlie's protective hand touching his shoulder. He looked at his mother and then at Rob who was smiling at him.

'Come here, James,' said Robert, holding out his hand. 'What do you want to know? If I'm your father?'

'I guess so,' said Jimmy, his frown emphasising his inherited features. He ignored Rob's invitation and looked at his mother. 'Is he, Mum? Is Mr Watson my father?'

'Arthur has been your dad ever since you were born,' said June gently, only her eyes betraying the strength of her maternal feelings. 'You were always his son. But yes, Robert is your biological father. That is, your real father.'

Robert held out his hand again and Jimmy took hold of it.

'I've only just found out about you,' said Rob, 'but I hope we can make up for lost time. I'm jolly pleased to have a son. Perhaps we can go places together. Rugby matches, swimming, skating — you name it.'

'Will you come too, Mum?'

'Mr Watson is an exceedingly busy man,' she told him, dodging his question. 'Don't expect too much of him.'

'Can't he live with us like dad did?'

'I don't think—'

'That would be a delightful prospect,' Watson interrupted, 'but your mother has other plans at present. Maybe we—'

Charles butted in: 'I think Jim has had enough for one night. Come on back to bed, shipmate. We'll finish that story and you can get some sleep.'

Rob glanced at Charles with thunder in his eyes. But his expression quickly changed as he turned to Jimmy. 'Goodnight, James,' he said, smiling broadly, 'I'll see you again soon. We must let Captain Rogers carry out his duties.'

Charles held in his anger. 'Say goodnight, Jim,' he said firmly, 'it's getting late.'

With James as his son, Rob had one over on him as far as June was concerned, and he knew for certain Watson had every intention of pursuing the fact to his own advantage. Well, he was not going to play into the man's hands by taking the part of a jealous lover. Everything must always be in the open and June given every opportunity to pursue her goals. Surely love could, and would, triumph over all of Robert Watson's dark plans.

When he went back downstairs some time later, June was still talking to Robert. They were discussing the latest fashion trends. With the important issue of her son's future, Charles wondered how she could just switch off from Jim and talk so animatedly about fashion. Bile rising in his throat, he left the house by the back door and strolled out into the garden to clear his mind.

Robert Watson was doing his best to cut him out. But, on occasions, June was pretty good at doing that herself. He was beginning to realise the extent of his brother's patience. Perhaps he should go to bed and call it a day. As he approached the summer house, he heard the familiar sounds of a couple involved in love-play. He decided not to disturb Rosie. She would not thank him for being reminded that it was school tomorrow! But what he heard in the sweet night air brought on his urge to get June alone and in bed.

He returned to the house. As he approached June's studio, he could hear her discussing James with Robert. He turned back and went up the stairs. Looking into Jim's room, he saw that the boy was fast asleep. Whatever the outcome of his relationship with June, he was determined to keep faith with his brother and watch over his children. But then he remembered — James was not his brother's child. Well, he was his godson, and as such would always be there for him.

As he reached the hall of his flat, the phone started ringing. He took the call in his bedroom. He was surprised to hear Angela's voice.

'I'm lonely, Charlie darling. Will you come over? I need you. Really need you.' It was the familiar pleading he'd heard many times. 'Please, Charlie, come now. Please come. Let me show you just how much I love you. I'll—'

'Angela, you've been drinking!' Charles snapped. 'Where are you?'

'I'm at the new motel down the road. Please come, darling, I need you so much. Remember our good times together? I could really turn you on. I still can. Come and let me prove it.'

Charlie stood by the bed with the phone in his hand. A fiery flashback of the exciting sex they once shared fired his loins, and he was sorely tempted.

'Sorry, Angela, we finished years ago. Try one of your lusty gigolos, I'm not available. Goodbye, Angie. And don't ring again.'

Charles slammed down the phone and punched his bed with both fists. In spite of himself, he found that Angela was still capable of arousing him. He took a shower and prepared for bed. At nearly midnight he heard the visitors leaving, and a few minutes later he picked up June and Rosie's voices. They seemed to be having an argument as they came up the stairs. A door banged shut and then silence fell over the house. He could just make out the clock in the hall striking twelve o'clock.

Sounds of the night drifted in through the open window. He saw the moon glowing brightly in the sky and wondered if June could see it from her window. Should he go to her? No, she needed her sleep. He thumped his pillow in frustration. Then he turned on his back and tried meditation techniques that he'd practised years ago when he was engaged in dangerous missions. The controlled breathing helped to calm him. He could, and would, be patient. There was much to be thankful for. He started counting his blessings....

Chapter Nine

Thoroughly rested, Charles woke at his usual time and did his exercises. Returning from a short run, he found Jimmy on his way to the kitchen.

'Hi, Jim. I'll just get a shower and something to eat. See you soon. Half past eight when you go?'

'Yes, Uncle. Rosie's not up yet, neither is Mum.'

'Rosie is old enough to get herself up and off. I expect your mum is tired. Don't disturb her. You'll be happy with me taking you to school, won't you?'

'Yes, but Mum gets my breakfast and packs my lunch.'

'I'll do it.'

'I can get myself some corn flakes and pack up bread and jam.'

'You need more than that to start school on.'

After cooking bacon and eggs for them both, Charles packed Jimmy some sandwiches and gave him money for general needs. Looking his nephew over, he gave Jim full marks for smartness and clean ears. 'Now, hang on five minutes while I change out of my running gear.'

Rosie, dressed in school uniform — tight white blouse pulling at the buttons, navy skirt just below her thighs and blazer slung over her arm — was coming down the stairs as he went up them. He stepped out of her way. 'Good morning, Rosie,' he called to her hurrying figure.

Grunting an inaudible greeting, she went rushing through the hall with her school bag in one hand and her car keys in the other.

'See you when you get home,' he shouted, but the front door was already slamming shut.

He smiled to himself, thinking that he was going to have a whole day with June. His thoughts were interrupted when he saw her rushing out of her bedroom. She was buttoning the cuffs of a white silk blouse whilst trying to keep the straps of a handbag over one arm and the jacket of her blue suit over the other. He took the jacket from her arm.

'It's all right, no need to rush. Rosie has gone and Jim is ready for school. I'll be down shortly and we can take him together.'

'Sorry, Charlie, I promised Robert I'd be in for a meeting before nine. I'll only just make it. Would you take Jimmy yourself?' Having fastened her cuffs, she grabbed her jacket back and made for the stairs. 'I must have a word with Jimmy. Is he in the kitchen?'

He followed her down. 'Yes, I'm sure he'll be pleased to see his mother. I'm pleased to see you — I waited long enough last night!'

'Please don't be difficult, Charlie,' she said, stopping to look at herself in the hall mirror. 'We'll talk when I get back — promise. Now I must see Jimmy. Robert wants to take him out.' She hurried to the kitchen, calling behind her, 'See you tonight, Charlie.'

When Charles arrived in his bedroom, he punched his right fist into his left palm. 'Damn the man!' he muttered to himself. He took a deep breath and slowly let out the air. 'Right, so be it.'

While he dressed, he worked out his day. After taking Jimmy to school he would start working on plans for his own future. Plans he hoped would include June, but that would be up to her.

On the way to school, Jimmy talked continually about his father and what his mother had told him. 'He's going to take me to all sorts of places, and he says he'll come to see me play rugby at school.'

'That will be nice.'

'Uncle, you won't leave me now will you? You will still live with us — you will, won't you?'

'Can't promise, Jim, that's up to your mother. But I'll always be your friend.'

'I like Mr Watson, but I love you, Uncle Charlie.'

Such simple words to gladden his aching heart. 'I love you too, Jim.'

As he was driving home, he suddenly thought about the boys away at boarding school. He must make sure they knew about Jim before they found out elsewhere. Then he realised he was doing June's thinking for her. Would she resent it? Or did she now rely on him to think about the family for her? Either way was not good.

When he arrived home, Annie Craven met him at the door and told him that his sister-in-law had called to see June. 'I told her that June had left me a note saying she would be at work all day. She said she would like to have a word with you. I was going to ring to see if you were in, but Mrs Rogers was already on her way up. She said she wanted to surprise you.' Anxiety dragged her pleasant face into a worried frown. 'I'm sorry, Captain Rogers, I didn't know you were out.'

'I took Jim to school.' He had a sudden thought. 'Should Angela — my ex-wife — turn up sometime to see me, don't even let her inside the house until you speak to me first. In fact, if anyone calls to see me, best to give me a buzz and I'll come down. Mm… perhaps I should have a bell by the front door.' He gave Mrs Craven an encouraging smile. 'Don't worry about Helen, Annie, I'll be pleased to see her.'

'I don't know if she's still here, Captain Rogers. I haven't heard her go out though.'

Charles ran up both flights of stairs. Helen, looking radiant in a pale blue dress and jacket, met him in the hallway.

'Helen, it's great to see you.' He put a hand on her shoulder and led her towards his sitting room.

'Nice to see you too, Charlie. I was just about to leave when I heard your car.' She looked up and her violet-blue eyes smiled at him from under their blonde lashes. 'Can I stay a few minutes?'

'Do you have to get back, or could we have lunch together?'

'That would be lovely.' She sat on the sofa. 'Michael and Bobby are back at school, and George is at work. In fact, he's working away for a couple of days. I called to see June. I felt like a bit of a chat.'

'You can chat to me. Want a coffee?'

'Yes, please.' She was fidgeting with her wedding ring. 'I didn't expect to see you,' she said, slipping the ring to the tip of her finger.

'Surely you wouldn't have called without saying hello to me?'

She gave him a coy smile. 'I did want to see you, Charlie. Actually, I hoped June would be out. I wanted to talk to you about George.'

'Hang on, I'll get that coffee.' He hurried to the kitchen and put on the electric kettle. He came back. 'Instant all right for you?'

'Fine thanks. As it comes, milk but no sugar.'

He sat down at the other end of the sofa and turned to face her. 'What's my younger brother been up to? Not another woman, I hope?'

She sat back and crossed her shapely legs, slowly rolling a slender ankle. 'Your Angela's been after him. I think they had something going at one time. She's been ringing him up.'

'She's been in touch with me too. I would rather not see her, I don't want to set her off again.'

She slipped off her little jacket. The silky material of her dress caressed her breasts in a most seductive fashion. 'As far as I know, George hasn't responded to her either,' she said, slipping off her ring and pushing it back on again.

'Then what's the problem?'

'George doesn't seem to want me any more,' She dropped her eyes and wrung her hands nervously. 'Can I be frank with you, Charlie?'

'Of course you can. Anything you say will go no further.' He was puzzled. How could George, or any man, want to stray from such a gorgeous creature?

She continued playing with her ring. 'We haven't had sex for weeks,' she whispered. 'He says there isn't anyone else and gets angry when I ask him.'

A tear was rolling down her soft honey skin. He leaned over, gently wiped away the tear with a thumb, and then took hold of her hand — the symbolic ring action was driving him crazy. 'Perhaps there's a medical problem that he doesn't want you to know about.'

She kept her eyes lowered. 'I thought of that and asked our doctor. He hadn't seen George for ages. Do you think George has someone else?'

He took out his fresh white handkerchief and dabbed another tear from her cheek. He put the hanky in her hand and sat back a little. 'Quite honestly, I just don't know. Perhaps he has a lot on his mind at present and just isn't up to it. Give it time.'

Helen looked at him wistfully. 'I married the wrong man, Charlie. It's you I really wanted. Why didn't you divorce Angela sooner? Your marriage was already on the rocks when we first met.'

He tried to let her down gently. 'We were never serious, Helen. Nothing happened for us to regret later. Anyway, I was much too old for you, and I was trying to save my marriage at the time. I admit I found you attractive — still do — but you became my brother's wife.'

She looked at him with pleading eyes. 'Why is it all right for the husband to have affairs but never the wife?' she said with considerable passion. 'Why should I go without love? Women need it as much men — you must know that.'

'Angela is a constant reminder of that fact, Helen. As for George, he would have to be out of his mind to put his marriage at risk. Let's face it. You don't know that he *is* having an affair.'

'I guess not.' She pulled her ring off and twiddled it. 'Are you and June intimate? Is there no hope of us getting together occasionally? Just being near you….'

She hesitated, clearly sensing his growing embarrassment. 'I'm sorry, I'd better go.' She stood up and reached for her jacket, dropping her ring on the floor.

Charles picked it up. 'Better not lose this.'

'Thanks, Charlie.' She held out her finger for him to slip it on.

He ignored the finger and pressed the ring into her palm. 'Lunch is still on, Helen. Believe me, I have my own problems at present and I would value your friendship. Maybe it would be best if we skip coffee now and I pick you up at your house. Twelve o'clock okay?' He helped her on with her jacket. 'At least, we can give each other a bit of company.'

Her lips curled into a bewitching smile 'You're so understanding. I certainly would enjoy some company.'

'I'll get you home for two-thirty. That all right?'

'Fine,' she said, looking at him intently. Her violet-blue eyes seemed to be illuminated from within and for a moment he was utterly captivated. Her plump rosy lips slowly parted and he was sorely tempted to kiss them. She suddenly laughed — white even teeth making her even more attractive. 'What a silly girl I've been. Sorry I've embarrassed you, Charlie. But at least I know where I stand, and it's not a bad position to be in.'

Charles walked with her to her car, sighing as he waved her off. It had been difficult to say no to such a desirable woman. There was no doubt about it; she had done wonders for his ego.

At the appointed time, Charles picked up Helen in his Mercedes. He drove her for lunch at The Black Boy. They chatted about old times and he enjoyed sharing old memories of people they both knew. Arthur came up a few times and he was surprised to hear that his brother had once helped George out of a gambling debt. 'He found him a better paid job too,' she told him, a tear glinting in the corner of her eye.

That touch of sorrow for the loss of his brother was most endearing and drew her closer to him. 'That was Arthur, all right,' he said, slowly nodding his head as fond memories welled up into consciousness. 'He was firm in discipline but he never let any of us down.'

Throughout their time together, Helen made no demands, and was not in any way sexually provocative. She was a perfect companion: laughing at his jokes, listening intently to his salty tales of both sea and land, and discussing various topics in an intelligent and lively manner. Afterwards, he took her straight home. Thankfully, she did not ask him in. She had clearly accepted the situation. It was with a contented spirit that he opened the car door for her, said goodbye, and then drove on to Bloomfield

Chapter Ten

On Friday of the second week of June's return to work, Charles sat mulling things over. A routine had settled into place. Seeing to Jim in the morning, home each afternoon to receive him back from school, talk to him, help him with homework and generally be a friend. According to June's instructions he supervised both Mrs Craven, whose main tasks centred on the kitchen, and Peggy, who cleaned, helped with the laundry and did most of the shopping.

Most afternoons, Rosie drifted in, did some homework or sketches and was off out again as soon as she had eaten. Or, if she was eating out, just disappeared into her room until it was time to go. At least, no longer subject to her sexual teasing, he could now relax in her presence. What a relief!

June came home at six the first day back at work, but her times gradually became erratic. The first weekend she was busy in her studio day and night — she said a special customer wanted to get an early viewing of her designs. Eating his meals with the family so as to get regular time with her had made little difference: her mind was elsewhere. But at least he was able to give Jim some companionship and keep an eye on Rosie's comings and goings.

At June's request, he had been to see the boys at boarding school. Strolling around the school grounds, he told them about Jimmy's parentage. They did not appear surprised that their younger brother had a different father to themselves. David said that he'd suspected it for a year or so. 'We're all different, but Jimmy more so. What does it matter who his father is? After all, Jimmy is still our brother.'

'He's not going to live somewhere else, is he?' Peter asked, looking worried. 'I don't want him to leave Bloomfield.'

'I very much doubt it. But he'll get a few more toys, and a lot of confusion.' The bitterness he felt was not entirely suppressed. He put a hand on Peter's shoulder. 'You are a family, brought up by a dad you've known and loved. Nothing can ever change that.'

But something else was worrying his nephew. When David had to run off to join his rugby team, he was able to draw it out of Peter. The lad was being teased to the point of bullying. Charles guessed that it was because he was clever and exceptionally good-looking, but being a gentle soul and still torn with the grief of losing his father, he was not able to deal emotionally with the jealousy he aroused in his classmates. Tears, however hard he may have tried to hide them, brought out the beast in his tormentors.

Being able to talk about it had helped. Charles had left him with tips on toughening himself up, and seeing his problem more as a challenge. Peter had decided to do a bit of body-building and to join the Judo club. Charles knew only too well from experience that only time would heal his grief.

A visit to the headmaster had not helped a great deal. Dr Robinson appeared dismayed at having a complaint, but said he would ask Peter's housemaster to keep an eye on the situation. 'We rarely get complaints of actual bullying at this establishment, Captain Rogers. But boys will be boys. The cut and thrust of schooldays toughen them up for later life. Being a naval officer, you must know that for yourself.'

'I'll make sure it stops, Uncle Charlie,' David said, when told about Peter's problem after his rugby match. 'I have an idea who's behind it. I'm having a boxing session with him tomorrow.' He nodded his head and grimaced. 'I'll be having a little chat with him first, don't you worry!'

Putting thoughts of the boys aside, Charles now began looking at his own situation. He had to admit he missed his friends and colleagues, and it had been going through his mind whether he'd done the right thing in leaving Bath and the things he'd enjoyed doing. But, considering the distance involved, it would be difficult to have a foot in both camps. He would soon get used to family life.

Family life? 'Be realistic, Charles,' he muttered to himself, 'the older boys are at boarding school, Rosie is rarely around, Jim has a father interfering in his life, and June?' He sighed deeply: 'My intended bride is totally distracted by her work.' Well, he knew the score when he encouraged her to take it up again. At least she didn't appear to be getting into any more emotional tangles with Watson. Things would settle, early days yet.

Apart from fellow officers, he missed his women friends. He harboured thoughts about ringing an old flame; perhaps go down to Bath and visit her at the weekend? In his present circumstances with June, it was a possibility hard to resist.

His mind drifted to the previous day. He had not intended to see Helen again for a while, but she boosted his masculine ego. This time, he'd taken her for a short drive before returning her home, just for her stimulating company. But his body craved for something much more intimate than a friendly chat.

Angela had rung twice and said that she would come round to the house if he refused to meet her. He told her the doors were kept locked. But he had to admit, if only to himself, that it was getting harder for him to resist those women who desired his body, when the woman he wanted in his bed was otherwise engaged. Engaged, that is, with Robert Watson and his clothing business.

But, of course, the situation was not that simple. Watson loomed like a spectre over all he held dear. The man had collected James on the Saturday of the previous week to take him to a rugby match. Jimmy had come back excited. 'Dad's going to take me out every Saturday, Uncle Charlie. Rugby again next week!'

But would Watson keep his promise? Apart from which, such things should be negotiated with the boy's mother. The ringing of the telephone broke into his thoughts. It was June on the line and she sounded rather anxious.

'Let Jimmy know that Robert can't manage it tomorrow. He's going to his London office tonight and will be staying over for a week.'

Charles was not pleased. 'Damn Watson! He's made promises to Jim he can't possibly keep. What's more, he has no right to disrupt your family life. It's time you put—'

'Mind your own bloody business!' Watson cut in. 'Some of us have work to do. Get yourself a life and stop interfering in mine!'

June came back on again. Her voice was strained and apologetic. 'Sorry, Charlie, I will be late home tonight. Don't prepare anything; I'll be eating with Robert and Steven to discuss business. Robert is catching a late train. Let Rosie know that Steven can't make it for their date. Must go.'

With Robert's grinning face in mind, Charles thumped his left palm. He then took a deep breath to calm himself. He did not look forward to making excuses for Robert Watson, nor did he wish to tell Rosie about Steven. And, once again, a promise of an evening together had been broken. Would they ever get together again? His arrangement with Helen for Jimmy to spend the evening playing with his cousins would just mean him being alone in the house to comfort Rosie. He was beginning to feel like a geriatric go-between.

A cheerful sound lightened his mood. Friday was the day for Peggy to clean his rooms and he could hear her singing in the bedroom. Here was another woman hungry for love. He wondered how long he was going to hold out. Only that morning she had joked about the sheets being spotlessly clean: 'Shame to change them, Charlie. How about we mucky them first?' She had stripped the bed, laughing in that carefree way of hers.

'Charlie, you look tense,' Peggy said, walking into his kitchen with a bundle of bed linen. 'How about I massage your shoulders for you? It's something I'm good at — no kidding.'

Peggy didn't wait for an answer; she was already working her hands over his taught muscles.

'Mm, yes. That feels really good, Peggy. When did you learn to massage?'

'Years ago. You see, I trained to work in a massage parlour, but my husband objected. It was no use telling him it was quite genuine and that most of my clients were women — he wouldn't believe it. My career ended before it began.'

'That's a real pity,' he said, pressing his neck against the fingers that were now working on his spine. 'I've often had a massage and believe me, Peggy, you are as good as any that's had a go at my body.'

'Praise indeed! A go at your body, eh? Good idea,' she said with a wink. 'I'll get a rug and some cushions. You can lie on the table while I do your back and legs.'

Before he had chance to consider Peggy's proposal, she was off to get the things, telling him to get changed into his shorts. 'Unless you prefer to be free and easy?'

Her saucy manner and jolly laughter were infectious and he found himself grinning at his thoughts. He stripped down to his pants and sat on the table edge waiting for Peggy to return. He looked down at himself and raised an eyebrow. Peggy was no beauty, but she did have a certain sexual attraction and it was beginning to show! She returned with the rug and cushions and arranged them on the table. She began rubbing a little oil over her palms.

'Baby oil,' she said in answer to his unspoken question. 'I used it on Arthur.' As if to dispel the sadness of why Arthur needed her ministrations, she glanced at his crotch and grinned. 'I see Peter was telling the truth.'

He quickly rolled on to his stomach. 'How many people has that lad been talking to?'

'You should be proud of your assets,' she said laughing. 'I expect you were the envy of every sailor in the fleet! Now, let's concentrate on your muscles.' She let out an exaggerated sigh. 'Poor me. Some areas of tension I have to leave to others.'

In Bath, he'd been getting a massage every week. It had been a social occasion as well as being both relaxing and invigorating. What Peggy was giving him was just as enjoyable. When his shoulders and limbs were finished, she asked him to move to the centre of the table so she could get to his back easier. Kneeling astride him, she worked on his muscles and his spine. After a while, she said she would be pleased to give his belly a gentle massage. 'But I don't want to cause you problems,' she added, with a twinkle in her eye.

Massage his stomach with her sitting astride him? Phew! 'Nice thought,' he told her, 'but not today, thanks.'

'You know, Charlie, when I first saw you all those years ago, I thought you were fantastic and longed to get my hands on you. Now here you are, fantastic as ever, and my hands have not left your body for half an hour. Wow! There's a dream come true.'

She was laughing merrily, and he had to smile. It made him feel good to be appreciated. Peggy had given of herself without complaint, asking nothing in return. He slipped off the table and flexed his muscles. 'Thank you, Peggy, it's been great. I feel much better now.'

'How about I make you a coffee and a sandwich? I'm supposed to finish at twelve but I don't mind staying on, you deserve some tender, loving care.'

'How about I take you out for lunch?' he said, putting an arm around her shoulders. 'Just a little thank-you for making me feel more civilised?'

'Tempting, I must admit. But, as you see, I'm in my working clothes and I could do with a shower. I'm only fit for a transport café fry-up.'

'Ridiculous. You can use my shower, and your clothes look fine.'

'Tell you what, I'll borrow one of June's old dresses; she won't mind. I'll just nip downstairs while you're dressing.'

Charles was surprised at the change in Peggy, when she walked out of his bathroom ten minutes later. Not only was she dressed well, with make-up skilfully applied, but she also looked quite attractive.

'You look fantastic, Peggy. Which would you prefer, the Grand or a country inn?'

'I'll leave that to you, Charlie. Surprise me.'

Within half an hour, they were sitting in the Grand's dining room, looking at menus. A loud voice was heard close by:

'Sit here, my dear, and you can cast your magic on our guests and bewitch them!' Sounds of laughter followed.

'It's June!' Peggy exclaimed.

Charles looked up in surprise. 'So it is.'

'Who are the mobsters with her?'

He laughed out loud. 'Peggy, you have made my day!'

He saw June look up with a puzzled stare, and then whisper something to the group of men with her. Robert and Steven turned to acknowledge their presence. June was looking uncertain as to what to do, but when Rob spoke to her, she gave him and the others her full attention, discussing the wine list

Charles found Peggy to be good company. She was friendly and chatty and could be quite witty in a raunchy sort of way. She reminded him of his early years in the Navy and the women he knew then. Her conversation helped him to ignore what was going on at June's table, although he did not care for Watson looking in their direction with a supercilious grin and raised eyebrow each time Peggy laughed out loud.

At the end of the meal he paid the bill and they made their way out, passing June and her companions on the way. Peggy bent over her sister, gave a thumbs-up sign, and quickly whispered something in her ear. Charles saw June colour up and wondered what had been said. Once outside, Peggy told him without waiting to be asked. 'I said that six men should keep any working girl busy. With that sexy devil next to her she should keep her finger on her halfpenny. Don't think she appreciated my bit of advice.'

Charles headed for the car, chuckling not only at Peggy's cheeky remark, but at the expression on Robert Watson's face when Peggy had winked at him.

Peggy slipped into the passenger seat. 'I take it you're not too happy with our Junie at present?' she asked, when Charles was sitting beside her.

'I'm not being fair to June, really. I encouraged her to go back to work, so it's my fault if I don't get to see much of her. It'll work out, she just needs time to settle into the job.'

'I take it a shortage of copulation is getting you down.'

'Something like that.' He put the car into neutral and started the engine.

'We could do something about that, Charlie,' Peggy said softly, lightly smoothing his hand holding the gear lever. 'I have the afternoon free.'

Charles felt a stirring in his groin. He was sorely tempted, if only for a bit of slap and tickle, but he shook his head. 'You're a sexy lady, Peggy, and I appreciate the offer, but I don't think so. Apart from my attachment to June, you being her sister would make it even more an act of disloyalty. If June were to find out, it would cause trouble between the two of you, even if she was generous enough to forgive me — which I doubt.' He put the car into gear with a determined grip and drove out of the car park.

'Is that what you really think, or are you making an excuse? It doesn't have to be all the way. How about we complete that massage I gave you?'

Charles slowed the car to take a corner. 'Believe me, I'm tempted,' he said, feeling her eyes on his crotch, 'but I don't want to make June unhappy. As you know, she's still bearing the loss of Arthur. Apart from grief, it could be that guilt over me is part of the reason for her overworking. But I shouldn't be talking about June. Forget what I said. Thanks for the offer, though.'

'Good psychology, but I think you've a lot to learn about my workaholic sister. My offer will remain open as long as you're around.' She stretched her limbs like a contented kitten before a fire. 'I've really enjoyed myself today. It's been great, absolutely great! Thanks ever so.'

'It has been quite an experience for me too — just what I needed. What with the massage and your company, what a day! We must do it again sometime.'

Since it was a pleasant, sunny afternoon, Charles decided to take the longer route home. He turned the Mercedes into a country road.

'Hello, 'ello! What's this then?' she said, touching his hand on the gear lever.

He put both hands firmly on the wheel. 'If you're not in a rush, let's enjoy the weather. Could be raining tomorrow. Okay by you?'

'Fine,' she said, 'I'm game for anything. Which reminds me, have you heard the story of the woodcock and the weather vane?'

'Not yet. Am I old enough to hear it, or is it X-rated?'

For the rest of the journey, she was telling him jokes that kept him laughing and her giggling. Finally, he stopped the car in front of her terraced house and thanked her again for the massage. 'I appreciate the other offer, Peggy. I hope you understand why I have to refuse. In other circumstances, who knows? See you next week, if not before. Oh, I've just remembered, I haven't given you your wages.'

He pulled out his wallet and put a few notes in Peggy's hand. 'You're worth every penny.'

She laughed. 'I hope my neighbours didn't see the money — or hear what you said!'

She suddenly bent over to his side and kissed him on the cheek. 'You're a lovely man, Charles Rogers. I hope my sister realises just how lucky she is.'

Only half-an-hour after Charles had arrived home, James came in and headed straight for the kitchen. He helped himself to a big bowl of cornflakes, topped it up with milk and ate greedily. It was his usual routine when he had games last thing in the afternoon. Anticipating Jim's homecoming, Charles had made him a strawberry milkshake.

'Thanks, Uncle Charlie, my favourite.' He sucked hard through the straws, consuming half the liquid within a few seconds.

Charles sat at the table next to him, ready to break the bad news. He picked up the cup of tea he'd poured out seconds before a whirlwind had told him of Jim's arrival. 'How did it go today, shipmate? Score any goals?'

'I got a try in the first half and two more in the second and converted both of them.' His eyes were wide and shining with excitement. 'I've been picked for the school match tomorrow, even though I'm only a junior. My father is picking me up. He'll be able to see me play in the team. Isn't that great?'

Charles put down his cup and placed a hand on Jimmy's shoulder. 'Sorry, Jim, Robert Watson has to go to London on business for a week, but he should be back next week.'

Jimmy's face screwed up into a heavy frown. 'But our school won't be playing then. He said he wanted to see me play.'

'And your father meant it.'

'Huh!'

Charles could not help but notice how much more Jim resembled his father when he became angry. The dark brows over his narrowed eyes and the determined chin with its deep dimple became even more prominent.

He leaned forward and patted Jim's shoulder. 'Suppose I take you? I'm going to see you play anyway.'

Jimmy's face creased into a huge smile. 'Thanks, Uncle Charlie. Can we go for a burger afterwards? Mr Watson took me last week. We had fried onions as well.'

'Fried onions? Fantastic! Now you'd better get your homework done. Do you need any help?'

'No thanks, I'm good at maths, and French. My dad taught me. That is, my real dad — no, I mean my....'

'The one you called daddy when you were little, and will always be your daddy. Robert Watson is your biological father. I'm sure he'll be pleased if you want to call him dad.'

'That's what he told me to do, but it seems funny when I don't know him very well.' His face creased in thought. 'Is he going to marry Mum?'

'That's up to your mother, Jim. Now finish your snack and do your homework. Don't forget, you're visiting your cousins this evening.'

Jim noisily sucked up the rest of his milkshake, grabbed his school bag off the kitchen floor where he'd dropped it, and ran out of the kitchen and up to his room. Charles was about to go up to his rooms when Rosie came in. Standing in the hall, he gave her the message about Steven being unable to see her that evening and why.

Rosie's face first went pale and then suddenly flushed with anger. 'But it was going to be a special evening. He said he had a hotel room booked. We were going to spend the night together.' Her eyes flashed. 'How could he do this to me? Is mother spending the night with him instead?'

Charles put an arm around her. 'Now, Rosie, you know your mother is not staying the night with him. This is purely business. Robert Watson will be there too.'

'Huh! What do you think of that? Are you just mother's housekeeper now?'

'You're understandably upset.' He guided her to the kitchen. 'Come and get a cup of tea and have a slice of Annie's cake. We haven't had a chat for ages.' He sat her down at the table and poured out the tea. 'What's all this about spending the night with Steven? Perhaps it's as well he can't make it tonight.'

'Don't be so old-fashioned, Charlie,' she said, helping herself to a large slice of sponge cake. 'Steven wants to do it and I want him to. I don't want to be a virgin for the rest of my life. When Richard found out I was a maiden — his words, not mine — he wouldn't do it. He probably thought you would be after him with a shotgun! Steven doesn't have silly inhibitions. It was going to be a special evening for us tonight, but obviously Steve has better things to do.'

She broke down in tears. Charles handed her a large handkerchief from a neat pile of laundered clothes Annie had left for him on the end of the table.

'You don't know what pressures of work he may be under,' he said gently. 'Like your mother, he wants to get on and get somewhere in the fashion world. Don't they work in seasons? I expect he will give you more time when the rush is over. His job is obviously important to him, but I'm sure he would rather be with you. '

'Oh yes? I doubt it. I don't want to hang around waiting for him like you do with mother.' She looked at him from under her tear-soaked lashes. 'Don't you get sick of it, Charlie? She's always like this when she gets going, only it's worse now she's not at home working. You only saw us at holiday times and occasional weekends – you have no idea what dad put up with. Mind you, he could be just as bad after he was elected to Parliament, but at least he could switch off from work when we really needed him.'

'I had no idea, Rosie. Do you feel your parents let you down?'

'Not really,' she said disconsolately, pushing her finger into the slice of cake on her plate and watching the filling ooze out. She absent-mindedly licked at the cream smudged on her fingertip. 'I felt sorry for the boys being sent off to school but no doubt it did them good. Mother gets lost in her own world and then she gets a bad conscience about it. She tries to make up for it when the rush is over.'

'I suppose it's all part of being creative. You should know something about that, after all, you do take after your mother.'

'I also have my father's brains. I don't want to end up like my mother. These past two weeks have made me think. I don't want to be a slave to anything or anybody. And now Steven has let me down. Oh, Charlie, why are men so horrible?'

'Some of us try not to be. How about we have a snack now and I take you to the pictures? We can leave Annie's casserole for another day and get fish and chips on the way home.'

'That would be nice, there's a film on at the Palace I want to see. We can sit on the back row and have a cuddle.'

'Rosie, you're at it again. But it's nice to see you cheering up. I'll get you a snack while you start your homework. Jim's going to your Aunt Helen's tonight. We can pick him up on the way home.'

'What a slave you are to Mother,' she said, stuffing the rest of her cake into her mouth. 'See you later.'

Charles was not happy with that remark; it was too near the truth. He sighed deeply and cleared away the cake and crockery, wiping the table as he did so. He made his way upstairs to write a few business letters.

Oliver! was a good film and Rosie seemed to enjoy it as much as he did. Charles missed Jim being with them, but he'd already seen the film with his cousins. Helen had taken them.

On the way home, they bought the fish and chips and picked up Jim. Helen would have liked him to stay there to eat his supper — George was away for the night — but when she realised Rosie was in the car, she smiled sweetly and said goodnight.

James soon went to bed. Charlie and Rosie finished off the fish and chips.

'The best ever,' said Rosie, 'but I've eaten too much.'

Before she went upstairs, she kissed Charles on the cheek and thanked him for a lovely evening. 'By the way, Paul met me from school this afternoon. He must be desperate, leaving work early. He says to forget about what he wanted — you know, what I told you — he just wants me back. He said he's calling for me tomorrow night. I was just going to leave him standing, but now I'll take up his offer. Goodnight, Charlie.'

Charles cleared away, thinking about what Rosie had just said. He must get June to talk to her. His thoughts were interrupted by the arrival of June's car outside. The front door slammed and seconds later she entered the kitchen.

'How could you, Charlie? You were having lunch with my sister. You know what she's like. She tried to make a fool of me in front of our new clients! And she was making eyes at Rob. What's more, she was wearing my dress!'

'Sit down and I'll get you a coffee.'

'I don't want a coffee.'

'Well, I'm having one.'

'All right, but not too strong.' She sat at the table, her face a picture of weariness.

He refused to give way to pity. 'Guilty as charged,' he said, pouring a little milk into a pan to warm it up. 'I escorted Peggy to the Grand and bought her lunch — a jolly good one, too. This morning she gave me a wonderful massage. So, a fair exchange don't you think? As for the dress, Peggy said you wouldn't mind if she borrowed an old frock.'

'Old? I only bought it last week!'

'So? Surely you don't mind your sister sharing in life's little pleasures?'

'I do if it includes you.' She frowned. 'What was this massage she gave you?'

'Just that,' he said calmly, 'a simple massage.' He put a cup of coffee in front of her. 'I assure you, nothing more.'

She did not look convinced. 'Really?' She slowly turned a finger around the rim of her cup. 'Knowing my sister, I find that hard to believe.'

He sat down opposite her. 'I'm surprised it bothers you what kind of massage Peggy gave me. After all, you have no use for my body these days. You know, June, you are beginning to treat me like the red dress Peggy borrowed — hanging around until wanted, but not for others to touch.'

She looked up. He saw disbelief, pain and then anger flashing in her eyes. 'How can you say that? You know I love you, Charlie. Of course I want you — and not just for sex! Are you trying to make me jealous? Well, don't do it with my sister. And while we're at it, keep out of Helen's knickers — she's your brother's wife, for goodness' sake! Oh yes, I know she's been here, and that you've been seeing her.'

'Hold on, June—'

'And I know you've been seeing Angela,' she snapped. 'She made sure I knew about your little affairs. She actually came to see me at work to warn me!'

'You know that Angela is trying to split us up. She seems to be doing a good job of it.' He looked at her intensely. 'Now listen to me carefully. I have not been with another woman. I haven't even been with you! Have you any idea what that's doing to me? You spend all your waking hours working. Do you care at all about me? More to the point, do you care about your children?'

'Of course I care about my children, but I know they're in safe hands with you.' She turned her eyes away and started stirring her finger around the cup's rim again. 'I'm sorry about us. I didn't plan the last occasion to be disastrous, nor did I intend to be out tonight, it's just that Rob—'

'That's the problem,' he cut in, 'you let Robert Watson rule your life. He obviously rules Steven's life too. Well, you'll be pleased to know that you and Robert between you have made your daughter very unhappy. At least she has come to a decision about her future. Wisely, it seems to me, she does not intend to follow in your footsteps.'

June put her head in her hands, 'I can't cope with this, I'm too tired. Go back to Bath if that's what you want to do, I can't stop you. When Angela told me—'

'Forget what Angela told you. She's nothing but a troublemaker!'

'Angela said you'd say that. With your reputation, why should I believe you?'

Charlie pulled June to her feet and gripped her by the shoulders. 'Now listen to me. Arthur gave me a job to do, and I'm damn well going to do it! Apart from that, I love you. Did you hear that, June? I love you — you! Not Angela — Peggy — Helen — or any other woman. I have no intention of sleeping with any of them. Do you hear me? Do you want me to repeat it? I love you, only you. I have always loved you, ever since you were a kid. The problem is, do you really love me? Or am I just a convenient prop to support your true love?'

'I do love you, Charlie, you know I do.' She was now sobbing and shaking with emotion.

He held her to his chest. 'Look, I can't tell you what to do, but I suggest that whatever you've planned for tomorrow, drop it! Be with me tonight. In the morning, I'll get your breakfast and you can rest while I go for a run. When you get up, talk to your daughter. Did you know she intended staying at a hotel with Steven? It was going to be a special occasion for her. She was devastated when I told her that Steven couldn't make it. Now she intends to go back to Paul

Bicksworth. Her first experience should be with someone better than that slimy toad!'

She pulled away from him. 'First experience? How do you know she's a virgin?'

'Don't worry, I haven't touched her, in case that's what you're thinking. She told me herself, but I already knew. Richard told me that he was concerned for her. He has scruples concerning teenage virgins, and would not go as far as Rosie obviously wanted.' He shrugged his shoulders. 'It could be a moral thing. But more likely Richard is afraid of expectations of commitment. He enjoys a bachelor life and doesn't want to be tied down.'

June sat down and sighed heavily. 'I will talk to her and I'll explain about Steven too. I can assure you, he wasn't happy about breaking the date, but Robert demanded it. After Rob left us, we had a chat about the situation. Steven is actually considering leaving Rob, but it's a big step to take. Anyway, he intends ringing Rosie for a date tomorrow night.'

Charles sat down and took June's hands in his. 'I'm sure Rosie will appreciate knowing that. Now this weekend is special. Jim's match is tomorrow and David's birthday is on Sunday. How about we all go out in the morning to get David a present? Afterwards we can go for lunch and then watch Jim's rugby match. Helen has already agreed to have Jim again tomorrow night — I asked her just in case. So, with Rosie having other plans, the evening will be ours alone.'

She smiled. 'That's wonderful. What would I do without you?' A determined expression tightened the muscles of her face. 'I hear what you say, Charlie. I must try and work fewer hours. After all, Rob was managing fine before I went back to him. It's just that he's taking an opportunity to expand and—'

'Frankly, June, I don't want to hear about Rob's problems.'

She dropped her eyes and he was immediately sorry for the harshness of his tone. He took her hands in his. 'How about you go up to my place and we can take it from there? Meanwhile, I'll check everything's okay for the night.'

'Yes, Charlie, and thank you.' She gave him an apologetic smile. 'I'm sorry I thought the worst about you. I guess Angela caught me at a time when I was feeling insecure.'

'I think you've been feeling a little vulnerable since Arthur died.'

She nodded, but said nothing.

'You have me now,' he said softly. 'I want you to make your own judgements, but don't let Robert, Angela or anyone — including me — determine your life for you. You are an intelligent woman, creative and single-minded about your work, but everyone needs space to live a full life. Without love we shrivel up inside.'

She gave him a weary smile. 'You're quite right,' she said, getting up from her chair. 'I'll see you upstairs. I won't keep you waiting.' She made her way to the door and then turned. 'And neither will I be asleep... promise.'

Charles threw away the coffee left in the cups and put the dirty supper dishes in the sink. He then walked around the ground floor of Bloomfield to check that windows were closed and the doors locked. Picking up his clean washing from the kitchen table, he made his way upstairs. June was already slipping into his bed. Uncertain as to what she would want from him, he quickly pulled off his clothes and hurried to the bathroom. He was soon naked beside her and ready to respond to her slightest whim.

'I really do love you, Charlie,' she murmured. Her eyelids closed. Within seconds, she was fast asleep.

Chapter Eleven

June was still by his side when Charles woke up. He slipped out of bed and made himself a cup of tea in his kitchen. He took it to the bedroom and sat looking at June, who was sleeping like a child. He left her to rest and went into his sitting room to do his exercises. He'd just about finished when he saw her standing watching him, her open dressing gown revealing her readiness for bathing.

'Do you always exercise in the nude, Charlie? You certainly get a sweat on. I'm most impressed by your exertions.'

He jumped to his feet. 'Did I disturb you?'

'Not until I walked in here and saw the view.'

He grinned. 'Get in the bath and relax — sounds as if you need it. I'll come and join you with tea and toast.'

'Relax? With you looking like that on my mind?' She laughed like a young child. 'See you soon.'

Charles first went to his stairs door to hang up his new noticeboard telling any would-be visitor not to disturb him unless it was very urgent. He then locked the door, pleased that he'd managed to get the much-needed lock fitted that week.

By the time breakfast was ready, June had run the water and was relaxing under a frothy heap of bubbles. He stood the tray on the stool by the bath. She looked so young and lovely that Charles could not help but stand and gaze at her. 'Beautiful, beautiful, truly beautiful.'

'Get in, Charlie. Eat your toast, you're going to need the calories.'

When June and Charles arrived downstairs an hour later, James was in the kitchen getting his rugby gear ready and toasting bread at the same time.

He talked incessantly about the coming game and what they could get for David's birthday. He rescued beans that were bubbling in a pan and heaped them on top of toast thick with melting butter. 'Can I get you some breakfast? I can cook you know.'

'So I see. Looks good and smells good,' said June, 'but we've already had our fill.' She glanced at Charles and gave him a knowing smile. 'Thanks for offering, Jimmy,' she said, picking up the messy pan and putting it in the sink to be washed. 'Another time, maybe.'

'I came upstairs to ask but there was a message on the door.' He looked at them both and grinned. 'I guess you were busy, Uncle Charlie.'

'I saw that notice too,' Rosie said, entering the kitchen and yawning. 'Been working, Charlie?'

'You know Uncle does his exercises every morning, Rosie,' said Jimmy.

'Apparently, he was doing them with mother this morning.' Rosie gave June a sweet smile. 'Seems to have done you good, Mum.'

'I expect so,' June said, trying to keep her voice normal. 'But never mind me and my health. We need to talk. A walk in the garden after you've had your breakfast?'

'Why wait? I'm intrigued — let's go now.'

June sat with Rosie in the summer house. Morning sun, paled by a light mist, caught the top of the copper beech, rich in its autumnal glory. The nearby orchard glowed with ripe baubles of fruit. Many varieties of chrysanthemums, secured by canes, stood sentinel in a great display of colour, and late roses added sweetness to the stillness of the morning. Where the sun broke through the mist, dew sparkled like a scattering of diamonds. It was great to be alive. It was great to love and be loved. It was great to be home.

June took Rosie's hand. The happiness she was feeling flowed out to her daughter. 'I'm sorry, Rosie. I guess I've been a bit distant lately.'

'That's all right. I'm a big girl now. I don't need a mummy to run to. I can look after myself.' She pulled her hand away and sat back in the cane chair. 'So, what's this all about then?'

June explained Steven's problem of not being able to see her the night before, and that he was going to phone her. 'I can tell he's fond of you. Give him a chance, Rosie.'

Rosie frowned. 'I don't want a man that prefers to spend an evening talking shop with my mother to honouring his commitment to me. It isn't as if we were just going to the pictures and having a cuddle on the back row — like your lot did in days of yore! Last night was going to be an important event in my life. So Steven Blake can forget it.' She leaned back in her chair, put her hands behind her head and stared at the rustic ceiling, a half-smile on her face. 'I phoned Paul and he's taking me out tonight.'

'But, Rosie, you know what Paul's like and what he's after.'

'He just wants to take me out like we used to.'

June found it hard to believe that Paul had given up his sexual preferences. But, knowing her daughter, argument would only make Paul out to be a redeemed character of saintly status. So she changed the subject.

'How are your studies coming on? Do you need extra help with anything?'

'I'm coping nicely with most things. Tops in art and history. Not bad in English and geography. I'll get a good grade in French. Biology's fine but I'm only just coping with maths and physics. Jack Cummings — he's in my maths class — is helping me with some stuff I'm not good at. Jack's really brilliant and better than our teacher at explaining things.'

'Jack Cummings? You haven't mentioned him before.'

'Don't get ideas, Mum, Jack's all right as a friend but he will never be anything else. He doesn't go out with girls.' She grinned. 'Even if he did, he's not my type. From what I know of him, I'm certainly not his!'

By half-past ten they were all setting off to buy presents for David. All thoughts of work had completely left June's mind. Charles and the family were all that really mattered in life. By five o'clock they arrived home, laughing and chatting. Jimmy's team may have lost but he'd done all the scoring and was quite elated. He was sent upstairs to shower and change ready to go to George's house. Rosie went straight up to her bedroom to spend an hour getting ready for Paul.

Now alone in the kitchen, Charles put his arms around June and brushed his face against her silky hair. 'You know, I now feel part of your family. To me, your children are my children. Tomorrow we visit David and Peter. I promise I'll be everything to them that you, and they, want me to be.'

June knew that what Charlie really wanted was to be their acknowledged stepfather. Her heart swelled with love for him. She wanted to give him more than that. She wanted to bear him children of his own seed. Aroused by overwhelming desires, her whole being became vibrantly alive. In her imagination, she believed the time must be right, for she was seized with a powerful longing for them to grasp the moment of ripeness and make love — the joining of body and soul in the creation of a new life. In her imagination, she could already see the fruit of their union. 'Charlie, it has to be now,' she whispered, 'and we will call him Adam.'

Puzzled, he gazed into her upturned eyes. His face suddenly glowed with youth and love. And she knew that he understood.

Robert Watson did not get back from London until the following Saturday. He phoned to say he was too busy to take Jimmy out. 'And, June, I want you in this morning. Get yourself here at once!' The line went dead before she could answer.

She put down the receiver and walked to the kitchen where Charles was cooking breakfast for them both. They had been out for a short jog together and had returned to find they were alone in the house. Rosie had taken Jimmy for an early morning swim. June's happiness, generated by a week of hard work at the office, contented motherhood and loving togetherness with Charles, was now completely shattered. She knew something had happened and Rob needed her creative input. As adrenaline pumped through her body, excitement kindled her desire to be inspired, to perform and to achieve. But it was more than that.

Damn, damn, damn the man! She did not want to be under his spell. She tried to ignore the feral feelings his call had produced, for, in spite of her love for Charlie, she knew herself to be sexually aroused. She took deep breaths. She could, and would, keep control of such maverick impulses. After all, since starting her new job, nothing had happened to suggest otherwise.

'I'm sorry, Charlie, I have to go in this morning,' she said, sitting down at the kitchen table. 'What's more, the rotter is letting Jimmy down again.' She sighed heavily. 'Perhaps it's for the best, it will give you chance to be a real father to him — the kind he needs. Robert is incapable of being a dad.'

Charles, still wearing his jogging shorts and top, was standing by the range, frying bacon. He ladled the bacon onto a plate and picked up an egg to crack. 'So you are going in today?' There was sadness rather than anger in his voice. Could he read her thoughts and sense her torrid emotions?

'I have to, Charlie, if only to have it out with Robert about the hours I work, and his ridiculous expectations of loyalty. He can't have it all his own way with Jimmy, either. I have to be strong and face him.' She heard the fear in her voice and found it most unnerving.

Charles took the pan from the heat and went over to where she sat at the table, rubbing a finger around the rim of her coffee cup. He laid his hands gently on her shoulders. 'Do you want me to drive you there? I can wait for you. Give you time for a brief conference and then come knocking on the door.'

'No, Charlie,' she said, pressing her cheek against his comforting hand. 'I have to do this myself. If Robert knows you are waiting outside, he will be even more difficult.'

When June walked into her office, Rob was waiting for her with hands on hips. The sleeves of his finely striped shirt were rolled up and his dark eyes were blazing angrily. 'What's the matter with you?' he barked. 'You haven't completed that order we promised to get out. Are you sick? Or has Arthur's replacement been keeping you busy in bed?'

There was a touch of jealousy in his tone of voice and that made her fearful as well as angry. 'I don't like your attitude,' she snapped back. Without stopping, she told him everything that she'd promised Charlie she would say. Robert listened as if she were a petulant child that couldn't get her own way.

'If you just want a nine-to-five job then you're no use to me,' he snarled. 'Clearly, you're only interested in your pay!'

'That's not fair. I worked really hard while you were away. You ask the impossible. I have a home life too, you know.'

He stepped forward and gripped her shoulders. His narrowed eyes burned into her soul. 'Oh June, where is your spark? Where is your lust for creative power? Do you know what I've been doing while your mind has been on Charlie's body? I have been getting contacts for extending our business into the sports and leisure arena. Think of it, June. Once we get established we will have our own labels. Not tucked away somewhere, but our own logo blazing where it can be seen and proudly displayed — on the chest, a sleeve, or anywhere else where it will be noticed. Designer gear for discerning fashion-conscious customers. It's the biggest thing since pantyhose and we're going to lead the market. It may take a year or two to build up but I already have the promise of contracts to get us started.'

Her creative inner self sprung to life. 'That sounds fantastic! Can we really do it?'

His voice rose excitedly: 'You know we can. But it's up to you whether you come with me. Think of all those ideas you got from your sailing holiday. Imagine channelling some of them into natty clothes. Think of the swimwear, beachwear and sports clothes you could design. The colours, textures, prints and everything that puts a bit of glamour into holiday clothing. Think of all the different sports and team events — all needing outfits. Before long, we'll even be marketing hats, shoes and any other accessory with the same logo. This is a huge market to cater for, and I intend to make us market leaders.'

Her mind was already working — ideas flashing through her brain in psychedelic colours. 'Do we have the capacity for such a project?'

'Before long we won't have to rely on our own workers and local contractors. Bulk manufacture will be extended abroad where labour is cheap. If it proves successful, only the designing and management will be based here.' His eyes flashed under their heavy brows. 'The market is wide open and we're going straight in!'

June's heart was racing with excitement. 'Gosh, Rob, what a prospect. The whole thing takes my breath away.' She sat on the edge of her desk. 'Where do you want me to start?'

'Go look in the shops and come back with better ideas and better designs than are already on offer. Come with me soon to London, and later to Europe. We're thinking international and you have the opportunity to be in at the start. Before long, we'll have our own chain of sportswear shops too — big stuff!' He gripped her shoulders so tight she winced. But she cared nothing for the pain — in fact, she welcomed it. He gave her a little shake as if to force words out of her. 'What do you say? Are you with me? Or are you going to be the little housewife while Charlie plays chess down at the pensioners' club?'

The remark stung her conscience, but she refused to be sidetracked from such an ambitious project. 'Yes, Rob, I do want to come with you. I only ask that you don't push too hard. My family – and that includes your son, remember – needs me. So does Charles. Quite frankly, I need him more than he needs me. We both need him, Robert. You know he supported me coming back to work with you. Please don't ruin things now that I'll be needing him more than ever.'

'I'll get you a personal assistant,' Rob told her, with a careless flip of his hand. 'No need for you to do the run-of-the-mill stuff. I'll look into it.'

'That will be marvellous. Thank you, Rob. Charles will be pleased too.'

'Well, we have to keep the boyfriend happy. Now, how about you making me happy?'

She looked at him, wondering what he was about to demand. But he said nothing. His lips were curled into a mocking smile and his eyes seemed to be laughing at her. Damn him, what was so amusing? Then he began stubbing his thumb into the cleft of his chin and a change came over his face. There was no mistaking now what he wanted. His eyes were penetrating her body and making her sexually alive. She could not control the flushing of her face, the stiffening of her nipples, the heavy breathing, or the flow of juices. She became aware that her body was trembling. Was it fear or desire? She dare not even consider the answer. Suddenly, he took her in his arms, pulling her against his hard body. Nervous excitement paralysed her brain from even thinking of resisting. His mouth became one with hers. A kind of psychic energy was streaming into her.

Magnificent sensations were setting her body on fire. She knew what must follow.

No, no! It must not happen. 'Please don't, Rob,' she moaned, pushing him away from her, 'you will ruin everything.'

He grasped her arms causing her to wince. 'We are soul mates, and you know it. One day you'll be completely one with me — mind, body and soul. You can't resist me. Admit it, June — I bring you to life. You're panting for me at this very moment. Can't you feel your whole body yearning to be one with mine? I certainly can!'

He was far too perceptive. 'Let me go, please let me go.'

He made a gesture of opening up his arms. 'I keep telling you, you're free to go any time you want to.'

She did not move. She felt as though she were riveted to the spot, looking at him through eyes half-closed and lips slightly parted. Lust for his body was tearing her apart. She heard herself whimpering, 'Don't do this to me.'

He wrapped his arms around her again and kissed her passionately, his tongue seeking hers in sensual communication. She felt his hand inside her blouse. Her mind was telling her to resist, but still she could not find the strength, or the will, to stop him. She felt the desk hard against her back and his hand moving up her thigh. Her flesh was quivering at his electric touch. Memories of the night of Jimmy's conception, so long ago and yet vividly near, brought to life deep primitive instincts of carnal lust. Then Arthur's kindly face drifted into her mind. She had been faithless once; she would not be so again. She would be true to Charlie. She turned her face from his mouth and pushed at the hands eager to pleasure her. 'No, don't do this to me. Please, Rob, please — let me go!'

He stepped back, pulled her to her feet and held her shoulders in a firm grip. His eyes were cold and piercing. 'I promise you, next time you will be begging me to take you.'

She straightened her clothing, shaken but triumphant. She had not yielded!

He turned aside and picked up papers fallen from the desk, as though nothing had happened. 'Right, now it's time you brought me up to date with what you've done while I've been away. I'll only keep you an hour and then you can go home to our son.'

Exactly one hour later Robert Watson stood at his office window, watching June drive away. Smiling with satisfaction, he held his fingers to his nose and allowed his tongue to run over his full lips. He could still smell and taste her scent. The chase was so gratifying. Soon she would be his mistress; she couldn't help herself.

Yes indeed, she wanted him all right — always had, but could never admit it. It had been twenty years since she'd accused him of rape. Rape of an innocent young virgin? Never! She wanted him to make a woman of her. Putting up a fight was just part of an act for Arthur's benefit. She knew Arthur would be no match for a real man when it came to sexual gratification. All women wanted a lusty male to break them in. He should know, he'd done it often enough. Apart from which, it had been right and just to seal their business partnership, and on the factory floor too! She may have refused to acknowledge the pleasure he'd given her on that occasion, but she showed her true colours the night young James was conceived. She was like a bitch on heat — ready and willing for anything. What a night that was.

Of course, there was far more to their relationship than sexual attraction. She had creative flair — a rare gift. He had the means to control and direct it. In spite of the separation, he was the one who had kept her freelance business afloat for all those years — her other clients were small beer. But she could have done better — much better. Now he had the woman in the palm of his hand, she would reach her full potential — good for her, lucrative for him.

He smiled at his thoughts: no need to keep her in the office, as soon as she was home she would be producing ideas for their new line as fast as a golden goose with ovulation diarrhoea. She was right, Charlie Boy had to be kept happy — at least, for now. The poor mutt! He knew he could never hold her down. Try to control her and he would surely lose her. Well, lose her he most certainly would. Once James was under his control, June would become his wife — Mrs Robert Watson. But for now, someone else must supply his urgent need. He picked up his phone and rang his secretary. 'Judy? Be ready in ten minutes.' He slammed down the receiver and hurried from the building.

Chapter Twelve

When June arrived back at Bloomfield, she told Charles about the firm branching out into a new line. 'What's more, Charlie, Robert is getting me a personal assistant so I can keep reasonable hours. Isn't that wonderful?'

Charles was wondering what the catch was, but when June started talking excitedly about the details of Rob's new project, he thought it no wonder the bastard was giving her an assistant. When she told him she would be going with Robert on business trips for at least a month, he began inwardly groaning.

But June was alive with an energy he'd rarely seen in her. Her eyes glowed and her whole presence radiated life. Ideas she had gleaned from her recent holiday were being redirected in a creative way. June seemed to believe that some kind of enlightening power was taking over her life. She could even talk of next year's Caribbean holiday as if it had been planned especially for the coming design task. Charles could put another name to the influence June was under, but he listened to her animated talk and kept silent.

He thought he'd already seen her at the peak of inspirational excitement, but this was something else. Now he could see for himself what Arthur had so often told him about June and her creative genius. She had only been with Robert Watson a little over an hour and yet he'd completely energised her. A pang of jealousy stabbed at his heart. He tried to brush the feeling aside and accept what June had said about her work and Rob's powers — that it was nothing to do with love. But Charles knew sexual attraction came in many guises and could override the deepest affection. It was for certain that June was on another planet far beyond all the previous ones he'd seen her flying off to. What happened when she was up there with Robert Watson? He inwardly groaned. He must not let such thoughts enter his mind and poison their relationship.

The following Friday, June arrived home from work looking tired but happy. Over a cup of tea in the kitchen she told him that Robert was collecting Jimmy the following morning and keeping him until late evening.

He sat down with her at the table and stirred his tea. He avoided eye contact lest she see the deep longing of his heart. 'What about you?' he asked casually, 'anything planned?'

June put down her cup and smiled impishly. 'Actually, I have a few ideas,' she said, her sparkling eyes betraying her thoughts. 'That pudding Annie's made for tomorrow looks delicious, but I have a craving for something much more satisfying. How about—'

The door burst open and a distraught Rosie entered. She threw her bags on the floor, pulled off her jacket and slumped into an armchair by the range. 'The rotter, the absolute rotter! I hate men! They're disgusting liars!'

'Sounds a bit harsh,' Charles said, trying to hide his own annoyance for being interrupted at a crucial moment. 'Any male in particular?'

'Paul, that's who! No need to tell you what he's been after again. I've finished with him. He's had it, had it, had it!'

'Apparently not,' said Charles, trying to lighten the situation. 'And a good thing too! A rotter indeed.' He rose from his chair. 'How about a nice cup of tea?'

The phone rang. Charles answered it. 'For you, Rosie. It's Steven Blake — for the umpteenth time this week. Will you talk to him?'

Delight lifted the frown on her face. 'I'll take it in the sitting room,' she said, excitedly jumping from her chair. She hurried from the room, her creased-up skirt revealing the top of her pantyhose.

'Eyes front, Captain Rogers!' June said, laughing at his reaction. She rose from her chair and put her arms around his neck. She took the lobe of his ear into her mouth, and tickled it with her tongue in a most seductive manner. 'Jimmy's out for the day tomorrow,' she whispered. 'From what Steven asked me, looks like Rosie is going to be occupied too. That leaves just the two of us. Are you up to a romantic weekend?'

'Up to? What do you think? Use your eyes, woman. With you in this mood, I think my condition could become permanent.'

Giggling like a teenager, June took him by the hand and led him to the door. She was making him feel young and virile, and he fell for her all over again.

Monday morning, Annie Craven and Peggy arrived as usual to do the domestic chores. Charles retreated to his rooms and made himself a coffee. He wanted a quiet time to mull over the past two days and nights. Sex had never been so good. Instead of feeling jaded, as often happened after a weekend of intense sexual activity, memories of their love-play were kindling within him a terrific sense of well-being. June had been fantastic! She was leading him to experiment in ways he'd not attempted before. No wonder Arthur had wanted June to keep her connection with Robert Watson. Whatever his methods for inspiring June, the fall-out from her creativity was certainly worth the bearing of her problems. What a woman!

The following weeks were some of the happiest Charles had ever experienced. Everything was running so smoothly. Both Rosie and James were happy and contented. They required no urging to get homework done, were punctual at mealtimes, and did their best to be helpful in the running of the household. June kept regular hours and slept with him most nights. He'd found it necessary to cut down on his exercises. June's appetite for sexual activity took up time and absorbed much of his energy first thing in the morning. But he was not complaining.

But it wasn't only June keeping him happy. Through James playing at his cousins' house twice a week, he'd been invited by Helen to play badminton at her health club. He was now a fully paid-up member. Apart from badminton, occasional use of the swimming bath and various items of equipment helped to keep his weight down and his muscles in trim. But he had to admit, having lunch with Helen and the other people he met regularly was also part of the attraction of the health club. He had been missing the social interaction of his work at Bath and it was good to meet up with others for intelligent conversation during the daytime when June was at work.

Helen was not the only female whose company Charles enjoyed while June was working. It had become a regular routine for Peggy to give him a weekly massage. Taking her for a good lunch afterwards was part of the pleasure. Although she was nothing like her sister, he thoroughly enjoyed her company. Peggy was firmly attached to her working-class roots while June had done her best to escape them. Peggy's sense of humour made him laugh and her conversation, easy and uncomplicated, was light-hearted and straight to the point. He admired both women for their hard work and endeavour. He was fond of Peggy, but June was the only woman he could possibly give his heart to.

Rosie was none too pleased when the time came for her mother to go off with Watson for an unspecified time. 'This means Steven will be working all hours to make up for Rob being absent. Huh! After saying he was leaving Robert Watson, he's now climbing up the managerial ladder. Men! They're all the same lying creeps.'

'Please don't shoot the messenger,' said Charles, busy polishing his car by the garages. 'If you were downstairs earlier this morning, your mother could have explained

Steven's situation.' He stood back to admire his handiwork. 'Don't you think you are being a little hard on the man? He can't just give up a job without careful consideration. Give him time, Rosie.'

'Trust one man to stick up for another. You'll see, Charlie — we'll both lose out to Robert Watson.' She pouted her lips and strode off to her car.

Was she really concerned about Steven's workload, or was she just a little jealous of her mother? Probably both. But he refused to think about Rosie's comments. Hard enough to have June leave him for a while without being reminded with whom she was going. He put more effort into his polishing. He didn't need to do it himself, but it gave him great satisfaction and dissipated stress. He stood back and gazed at his sleek Mercedes. 'Beautiful!' he said, admiring the glossy paintwork.

'Talking to yourself, Charlie? That's a bad sign,' said Rosie from her car window. She suddenly accelerated her engine and squealed down the drive, throwing up a cloud of dry crumbling leaves and dust.

'Thank you, Rosie!'

All too soon the morning arrived for June to set off on the long trip abroad. Charles admitted to himself that he was pleased it was not easy for her. He knew she wanted the excitement of it all and he wanted her to enjoy herself, but he also wanted her to suffer a little for leaving him. Losing her to Robert Watson was a constant fear.

He lay in bed with June beside him. They had made love well into the night as though to drown all thoughts of separation, but now the time had come and June was having second thoughts.

'I shouldn't be going, Charlie. My poor Jimmy is unhappy, Rosie is cross with me, and we're going to be parted. I'll miss you terribly.'

'Don't worry about the family, I'll hold the fort,' he said, giving her a squeeze. 'Better get up or you'll have to rush.'

June slipped out of bed. 'You're so kind to me, Charlie. I don't deserve you.'

Charles led the way to the bathroom. 'I'll be the judge of that. Now, you enjoy this opportunity. I'm with you all the way — as far as you want to go. I made it to the top of my career, you do the same.'

He turned on the shower. 'Go with the flow!' He smiled as he said the words, but his heart felt tight within his chest.

Watson arrived early. Charles put June's cases into the Daimler boot while Rosie and James hugged their mother. He then opened the passenger door. June looked at him with a hint of tears in her eyes. With a nervous smile, she stepped into the car beside Robert.

Unexpectedly, Watson suddenly jumped from his car, walked up to Jimmy and took hold of his shoulders. 'Now you be a man, James. No fretting after your mother, she's only with me. When we get back, we'll all go out together.' Behind Jim's back, he smirked at Charles. 'Just the three of us.'

As Rob walked back to the car, he slapped Charles on the shoulder. 'Thanks for taking care of things, Charlie boy. I appreciate all you do for my son. And keep an eye on young Rosie there, she's one of my treasured assets too.'

Charles refused to let Watson have the satisfaction of seeing his anger. He contained his rising bile and forced himself to nod an acknowledgement. With June calling and waving goodbye, the Daimler swept out of the drive, leaving a misty trail of exhaust and dust. As the sound of the engine trailed away, silence settled. Not even a bird twittered in the trees. Charles, feeling bereft, was left standing with the youngsters, one arm around James and the other around Rosie.

'Why do you let her go with him?' Rosie said angrily. 'He intends to marry mother, you must know that. He's just sucking up to young Jimmy so he'll put pressure on her.'

'No he isn't. You shut up, Rosie!' Jimmy snapped. 'He's just my dad. Uncle's going to marry Mum.'

Charles tightened his grip on Jim's shoulder. 'I hope to, young whippersnapper.' He looked down into Rosie's angry upturned face. God help him, she looked so beautiful with her cheeks flushed and her eyes flashing. He let go of both of them and turned towards the house. 'I'm not your mother's keeper,' he said softly. 'She has to make her own decisions. Robert Watson has a lot going for him but he's already married to ambition. I think your mother can see that for herself.'

Rosie looked across him at Jimmy. 'But Rob has one up on you.'

'You'll never leave us, will you, Uncle?' Jimmy said, suddenly digging his fingers into Charlie's arm.

Charles could not help but empathise with Jim's deep concern. He gave him a reassuring smile and put an arm around his shoulders. 'Whatever happens, we'll always be shipmates. Cheer up, big Jim, your mother is not away for long, and she'll be popping home soon.' But would she want to leave her exciting business abroad for a day or so at home? Would Watson beguile her into having a break with him? Her tale of Rob's allure came vividly to mind — no, shut it out! There were far sweeter memories for him to dwell on.

Charles walked Jim back indoors. Out of the autumn frost it was warm inside the house, but there was a cold sensation deep within him. He shook off the unwelcome feeling and concentrated on getting Jim ready for school. Rosie was soon off in her car and he was left in the kitchen drinking coffee while Jim ate his breakfast.

Jimmy picked up the cereal box and shook it. Looking inside, he found a toy spaceman. Absentmindedly, he twiddled it in his fingers. 'If Mum did marry my dad, would all of us go and live with him? You too, Uncle Charlie?'

'You worry too much. Can't see Robert Watson wanting a whole crowd living with him. Come on, we must be off. I've a game of badminton this morning.' Helen, with her pale blonde hair and full-lipped smile, her shapely breasts and long, slim legs came into his mind — in full Technicolor glory.

'But, Uncle, I don't want us to be split up. Perhaps Dad could live with us instead. We've got a very big house.'

No house would be big enough for him to share with Robert Watson. He suppressed his desire to laugh hysterically. 'Somehow, I don't think it would work out, Jim. But you'll be seeing plenty of me in the future, don't you fret.'

Jimmy studied his plastic toy, wrinkling his nose in disgust. 'I've already got this one,' he said, pushing the spaceman into his pocket. 'I'll do a swap at school.'

Thankful that Watson had been dropped in favour of a free toy collection, Charles gave an inward sigh of relief. What a pity his undesirable antagonist couldn't be replaced so easily.

Chapter Thirteen

June had been away a couple of weeks when Richard Andrews came up from Bath to see Charles. There was a need to confer on a mutual investment concerning a property in Bath, and to discuss other financial matters. Papers needed signing with witnesses being present. As far as Charles was concerned, Richard did not need an excuse to visit Bloomfield. They enjoyed each other's company and that was reason enough. Charles asked him to stay the night.

'I really appreciate having you here,' he said, walking into the kitchen to make them tea and cut Richard a slice of Annie's farmhouse cake. 'I must admit I do miss my friends and colleagues. But living in this place does have certain compensations.'

Richard sat in an armchair by the range and grinned. 'I can imagine.'

'You may well smile. An old bachelor like me, used to freedom and choice, especially where women are concerned, happily tied down to a beautiful widow and her children. With June now sleeping with me most nights and her kids being quite fond of their old uncle, commitment feels pretty good.'

'But what about when June's away — like now — or when she's busy, don't you ever feel like coming back to Bath and growing old in the company of fellow officers? And, of course, with the comfort of your women friends, and with one or two new ones to keep your spirits up?'

Charles sliced into the rich fruit cake. He placed a generous helping onto a gold-rimmed china plate and handed it to Richard. 'Not so long ago, I was considering exactly that. I hardly saw anything of June. I just seemed to be the housekeeper and childminder. But now, you wouldn't believe the change in June. You know, Richard, to be loved, not just by a woman but by her kids too, is something you have to experience to really appreciate.'

Richard bit into the cake. 'Delicious! You bake it?'

Charles laughed. 'I'm not that domesticated!' The kettle whistled. He warmed the pot and poured boiling water over the tea leaves.

'You could have fooled me,' Richard said. 'I don't remember you ever making tea, never mind bothering to warm the pot!'

Charles grinned. 'Milk, but no sugar?' He poured out the tea and handed a cup to Richard. 'I don't need training to make tea or prepare a few meals. Anyway, June's sister and a domestic look after most things.'

'Ah, yes. I remember Peggy. Likes a bit of fun.'

'She does a lovely massage.'

'Mm. That all? Sorry, I don't believe it. No wonder life is sweet!'

'The body massage is pleasure enough. You have a dirty mind, Commander.' It felt good to be having this light-hearted conversation with an old friend. He sat in the chair opposite Richard and sipped his tea thoughtfully. 'I must admit, when extras are offered, it's hard to turn them down. Old habits die hard!'

Richard laughed. 'There's an honest sailor. Let me know when your next massage is due — I can take over where you leave off!' His cheerful face suddenly became more serious. 'How's Rosie? Now she's a girl I could think of settling down with. Pity there's such a difference in our ages. But there's no chance of a serious relationship between us. Hasn't she got a serious boyfriend? When I spoke to June on the phone a couple of weeks ago — you know, when I rang about next year's trip — she said Rosie was going out with Watson's assistant.'

'I think he's too much like Robert Watson for her liking. He thinks more of his work than his relationships. He really let her down a few weeks ago. They were going to have a sort of honeymoon weekend, but he went into work instead.'

'What an idiot! So it was to be Rosie's first time? I feel quite angry about her let-down. But, I must admit, not a little jealous.'

'They got going again, but she's seen little of him these past two weeks.' He put down his cup, sat back in his chair and regarded his friend. Maybe he did look his age — outdoor activities had weathered his face and bleached his hair almost white — but there was no doubting his good looks and manly appearance. It had little to do with his well-tailored clothes: Richard had the physique to look sexually attractive in anything — including a frog-suit! His handsome strong-jawed face and broad shoulders, muscular chest and narrow waist were not his only assets; his vibrant personality drew women like butterflies to a flower-rich meadow. When it came to affairs of the heart, did age really matter?

'You know, Richard, you're wrong if you think Rosie is too young for you. She's a lot like her mother. June married a man twenty years her senior and now she's considering marrying me. On holiday, you and Rosie seemed to be getting on fine.'

'I don't deny it, I found her hard to resist on the boat. She was fun to be with. If she had been eighteen... well, you know me. It's hard to resist a girl who's keen to experience what I so much enjoy myself.'

'Rosie is eighteen next month. Better watch out, she might pick up the scent of your renewed interest. With her cunning wiles, she'll capture your heart and—'

Rosie suddenly burst into the kitchen. 'He's done it again! That's it! He'll never get another chance to get me into bed.'

Richard stood up. 'Hello, Rosie. Sounds as though you have a boyfriend who doesn't appreciate you.'

'Richard! I didn't know you were here. I'm so sorry, please forget what I said.' She was looking down at her feet, cosseted in trendy pink boots. 'I feel so embarrassed.'

Richard walked quickly over and gave her a friendly hug. 'Lovely to see you again.'

'I should have told you Richard was coming today,' Charles said, getting out of his chair. 'But I haven't seen much of you since yesterday morning.' He nodded towards his seat. 'Both of you sit by the range. I'll get another chair. Want a cup of tea, Rosie?'

'Yes please,' she said, glancing at Richard from under her lashes.

'I didn't know you planned to be out all night,' Charles said, taking on the role of a concerned parent. 'I would have been worried sick listening for you coming in.'

'I would have told you,' she said, pulling off her jaunty multicoloured coat and throwing it over the back of the chair. 'I was going to ring from the hotel.'

'So it would be too late for me to talk you out of it?'

'Well you don't have to now. That should make you happy. You know, Charlie, I'm almost eighteen. I bet you and Richard didn't wait that long to get on with it.'

Richard grinned.

Rosie's cheeks flushed bright pink. 'Oh, I didn't mean you two were... well, you know, jumping in bed together.'

Richard laughed. 'It's okay, Rosie. When Charles was your age, I was just a toddler! And you're quite right about me. In fact, I'd been with more than one girl before I was eighteen. Not actually in bed with them, as I remember, but that's being pedantic. Your uncle must speak for himself.'

Charles handed Rosie a cup of tea and pulled up another chair. 'Rosie already knows my reputation. You have to understand that I matured early. Girls wouldn't leave me alone.'

Richard slapped his knees and laughed loudly. 'That's your uncle's excuse.'

'And I'm sticking to it!'

Richard looked across at Rosie. 'You must tell me how you're getting on. Are you still designing for your mother? How do you find time to do your school work in spite of your torrid love affairs?'

Sipping his tea, Charles sat back and let the others do the talking. He was pleased that Jimmy was staying with his cousins overnight, it was giving Rosie a chance to speak with Richard without her brother butting in. Clearly the girl needed a diversion after Steven's let-down.

After a few minutes, Charles rose from his chair. 'I'll leave you two to catch up on things. I'm going for a short jog. Later on, I'll fetch some fish and chips for supper.'

'My favourite food,' said Richard. He smiled at Rosie. 'But don't you have to watch your waistline, young Rosie?'

She looked at him coyly. 'Not really, but you can if you like.'

Charles laughed along with Richard. But, as he left the two on them chatting and eyeing each other in a sexy manner, he realised that his friend's resolve regarding Rosie's virginity was being seriously eroded.

The evening was spent playing Monopoly on the large coffee table in Bloomfield's congenial lounge. The room, with its imposing cornice and ceiling mouldings, was where Arthur had entertained his Conservative friends and workers. It was also the room where family, friends, colleagues and neighbours had gathered to pay their last respects after Arthur's funeral. June seldom used it, but Charles thought it was good that it was now witnessing a happier event.

It was obvious that Richard couldn't take his eyes off Rosie. No wonder! Apart from the provocative figure-hugging pink outfit that showed off her breasts and legs to good advantage, she was looking incredibly bright-eyed and flushed with excitement. The fact that she was giving Richard little coquettish glances heightened the intensity of the atmosphere. He was pleased Rosie was being distracted from her disappointment, but was he doing right to encourage her relationship with Richard? He sighed inwardly: it was surely jealousy forcing him to question his motives. Watching the two of them eyeing each other and giving off little signals of lustful intent made him only too aware of his own sexual needs. He was saved from further introspection by the ringing of the telephone.

'I'll take it in the study,' said Charles. 'It's probably June.'

It was half-an-hour later when he returned to Rosie and Richard in the lounge. Sitting together on the sofa, they had obviously done a quick shuffle apart as he opened the door — hair was ruffled, faces were flushed, and Rosie's top was badly creased and twisted. The Monopoly game had not progressed since he'd left the room, but, apparently, Richard had made a few advances passing 'go'!

'How's Mum?' Rosie asked quickly, getting up to turn on the electric fire as if to divert his attention from her disarray.

'Things couldn't be better, or so it would appear from what she told me. The people she's met love her ideas and, so it would seem, business is booming. You know your mother, Rosie. When things are going well, she's riding high. She asked after you and Jimmy.' Charles looked meaningfully at the dishevelled Rosie sitting once more on the sofa close to the equally untidy Richard. He grinned. 'I brought her up to date.'

Rosie blushed. 'We were only kissing, Charlie,' she said, somewhat unconvincingly.

'I'm sure,' said Charles, his grin even broader. 'Your mum wanted to know if David and Peter had been in touch. I told her about them ringing me: David needing a new rugby shirt and Peter wanting money for a school trip. June said she loved and missed you all.'

'We miss her too. Did you tell her that?'

'Of course. She was going to speak to you herself, but Watson turned up and she had to go.'

'You were on the phone for half-an-hour, you must have talked about lots of things before her boss barged in.'

'Well, yes. I asked her if she was coming home for a short break. It took some time for her to tell me why she couldn't. She's too tied up at present.'

Charles had no intention of telling her the main content of his conversation with her mother: of how deeply he longed for her presence, and what thoughts of her did to him when he was alone in his bed. Even as he recalled her speaking to him — in intimate detail — of her body burning with desire at the sound of his voice, sweat was beading his brow. Her whispered recollections of their passionate lovemaking were still echoing in his ears. Her heavy breathing as, lying on her hotel bed, she had played out their familiar acts of love. He had listened to her whispers, her sighs and her gentle moans, with his masculinity responding accordingly. He was there with her every step of the way. God help him, he was still!

Such deep sexual intimacy over a telephone line was an experience new to him. He would never have thought it possible to gain such pleasure. Had it not been for Watson disturbing their little interlude by knocking on June's door, he most certainly would have ended up changing his clothes before going back to the others! Thoughts of Robert Watson brought him back to earth.

He was pleased that Richard was there to take the edge off his heartache, but he knew the ache would grow as soon as he went to bed. He worried how soon it would it be before Rob came on to her, catching her off-guard when she was high with achievement.

'Penny for them,' said Rosie, looking at him quizzically.

'Time for those fish and chips,' he announced, glad of the diversion. 'I'll put some plates to warm.'

After supper, Rosie made them coffee while Charles rang Helen to check on Jimmy. Helen asked him if he would like to go to her place for lunch on Monday: 'It will give you a bit of a break after a lonely weekend, Charlie.'

'That's kind of you, Helen. Actually, I'm far from lonely. An old friend is staying over. Tell you what, I'll let you know when I pick Jimmy up tomorrow. Can't talk now. Okay?'

He put down the phone. Richard, sitting nearby, raised an eyebrow. 'Overtures from the fair Helen? Watch it, Charles. I don't like to mention it, but I had problems with that young woman on the yacht I skippered for them last year. Marital difficulties, or so I was led to believe.'

'Things are fine now. George and Helen are perfectly happy with their marriage.' Charles knew that he was lying, but he felt a kind of loyalty to the woman who was such a good friend to both him and Jim.

On Rosie's return to the lounge, coffee was served and the Monopoly game resumed. Helen was not mentioned again, but Richard's warning still rang in his ears.

It was after half-past eleven when Charles asked Rosie if she should be in bed.

Rosie grinned. 'Who with, Uncle Charlie?' she asked, her eyes wide and innocent.

Charles shook his head and told her to clear off. 'Take your teddy bear with you if you feel that lonely.'

'And what will you take?'

'Sweet memories. Now off you go, I'm going to bed myself soon.'

Richard lay naked in bed, his hands behind his head. The clock in the hall struck twelve, its deep melodic gong breaking into his thoughts about Rosie. He was remembering their time together on the yacht. A reverie he often enjoyed in spite of its frustrations.

The door quietly opened. Burglars? Hardly — a girl was briefly silhouetted in the doorway. He switched on the bedside lamp. Rosie was already slipping off her flimsy dressing gown. What a gorgeous sight!

'Stop gawking and move over,' she said. 'I'm getting cold.'

'Do you really want this?' he asked, pulling back the bedclothes. 'Shouldn't we discuss the implications first?'

Rosie slipped into his bed and cuddled up to him. 'Quite honestly, do you really want to talk? A certain something tells me otherwise. You know what I would have done with Steven tonight. Too bad for him. I'd rather be doing it with you anyway. It's what we both wanted on the boat, isn't it? That is, until you chickened out when you knew I was a virgin and still seventeen.'

She felt delicious sprawled across his chest. Her hair was soft against his cheek; her breath was sweet, and her body yielding to his own.

'But that hasn't changed, has it?'

'I'm almost eighteen. Anyway, are you allergic to virgins or something?'

'Of course not.' What a question! 'I just take your virginity rather seriously. I don't want to spoil things for you and Steven.'

'Never mind Steven. He's mated with his job. Does virginity matter these days anyway? Surely you're not telling me that you've never slept with a virgin?'

He wished she wouldn't entice him with that word; it had the potential to inflame his hormones. 'I was just sixteen at the time. Both of us new at it.'

'Are you afraid I will get all serious?'

'Actually, I'm just as much afraid that I'll get serious about you.' That certainly was the truth of the matter. 'Trouble is, I'm so much older than you. I lead a free and easy bachelor life. Getting serious about someone would mean a hell of a change to my lifestyle.'

'I'm not expecting a lifetime commitment. But I really do like you. Can't you feel me trembling?' She said, pulling herself up to him. 'Oh, why don't you stop arguing? We both know what we want.'

With such a desirable young female willing and waiting for him to deflower her, Richard's doubts were completely overtaken by instinctual urges. His cravings could no longer be denied, even if the affair ended in a lifetime commitment. At such a moment as this, that prospect seemed more like a prison sentence in paradise.

Rosie was now rubbing herself up next to him in a seductive manner — a hand urging him on. Sweat was beading more than just his brow. He was about to respond when his conscience pricked him with a point of honour. He pulled himself away. 'It's no use, Rosebud, I'm your uncle's guest in your mother's house. I'm taking advantage of their trust.'

Rosie jumped out of bed. 'Right,' she said, eyes blazing, 'then I'll get Charlie's permission. Will that make you happier?'

She ran out of the room, slipping on the see-through dressing gown. By the time he had slipped on his trousers, Rosie was well ahead of him. He was just in time to see her burst into her uncle's bedroom.

Charles put on his bedside light. 'Rosie!' he yelled. 'What the hell are you doing here with practically nothing on?' He pointed to his plaid dressing gown, draped over a chair. 'Put that on at once, and don't argue!'

Rosie was already in full flood: 'We both want to have sex. Richard wants it as badly as me. He won't do it because he's your guest.' She stood hands on hips, ignoring the dressing gown. 'Tell him, Charlie. You tell him not to be stupid. You don't give a damn! Mother doesn't either! Nobody gives a damn! Everybody does it in other people's bedrooms. Tell him, Charlie. You tell him—'

'I'm really sorry, Charles,' Richard cut in, holding the dressing gown and trying to get Rosie to put her arms into the sleeves. 'You shouldn't be bothered like this. I, well... you know.'

'Don't try to explain, Richard, I know what my niece is like. You won't get permission from me because you don't need it. You must take responsibility for yourselves.' He waved his hand in the direction of the door. 'Now clear off both of you, and let me recover from the shock.'

Richard took Rosie by the hand and led her back to his room. She was most submissive. He sat on his bed and put her across his knee. Trying to stop himself from laughing, he made a mock display of spanking her bottom.

'That was a very naughty Rosebud. I can see you're a little madam used to getting your own way.'

She pulled herself away and stood up, pink chiffon misting her nakedness in a most alluring manner. 'I only want what you want. It will be a while before we get another opportunity.' She slipped off the dressing gown and offered him her bare cheeks. 'You can spank me again if you want to.'

He spanked her a little harder. She squealed gleefully. With considerable pleasure, he kissed her flushed, peachy bottom. Aware of her desire to be subjugated, he pulled her into bed with him. Being masterful was a game he enjoyed playing with willing women.

'This will be a night to remember. Trust me, Rosie.'

An hour later, Rosie lay in his arms, relaxed and smiling, almost asleep. Breaking the veil had been as much an awesome experience as it had been ecstatic. The latter he had expected; the former had surprised him.

'From now on, Rosebud,' he whispered, 'you will always be someone very special in my life.'

Chapter Fourteen

After performing his usual morning exercises, Charles trotted downstairs to cook bacon and eggs in the main kitchen. Sunday was the only day he ate a large cooked breakfast. But he didn't get it that morning: Rosie was up early with Richard and did what she never did — tucked into a huge fry-up. Watching the two of them clearing their plates and munching into toast and marmalade, their eyes sending each other coded messages, there was no doubt in Charlie's mind that Rosie had spent the night benefiting from Richard's considerable experience.

The phone rang. It was June. She told him that as a result of last night's meeting she would not be home for another three weeks. Things were going well and they had extra appointments to fit into their already busy schedule. They would be in Italy next week, Scandinavia and the Netherlands the following week, and Robert was hoping for snow so they could go skiing before returning to Paris.

'Where we go depends on the weather. Rob is in contact with a number of resorts, but prospects seem uncertain. Robert wants me to experience the sport before I start designing suitable outfits. Of course, he's right. I could easily bring back outfits and copy the fitting, but that would restrict my designing. I need to experience the movement — you know, the twists and turns. When I know what is needed, I can create garments accordingly.'

He took a deep breath, trying to keep disappointment at bay. 'I'm sure they'll be great,' he said pleasantly.

'It is so exciting, Charlie. With increased travel abroad, the market is wide-open for attractive sports and leisure clothing. I've already been given samples of terrific new fabrics that move and stretch like a second skin. I have absolutely no idea what skiing is like. No use just having a couple of days at the resort, I have to learn what to do.'

'You'll enjoy every moment of it.'

'Thanks. I knew you would understand.'

He understood all right. She would have more time with Watson while he kept the home together and spent each night alone. So be it. 'Well, since you will soon be an accomplished skier, and I've done a bit myself, we'll be able to take the kids on a winter holiday.'

'Maybe, in a year or two. Anyway, I'm getting time off when I get home and extra for Christmas. I'll be home for the school holidays. Won't that be great?'

Time off? From work, or merely going into the office? After such an exciting trip, how could she possibly resist jotting down ideas and working in her studio? Clever Watson! He knew exactly what he was doing. But June was so elated and happy that he didn't want to upset her.

'Absolutely wonderful. A time for togetherness and family parties. Make sure you don't wear yourself out while you're away, we'll have a lot of catching up to do.'

June asked him to explain things to Jimmy and Rosie and tell them she loved them. She was beginning to get rather emotional. 'Make sure you tell them, Charlie. I do miss them, I really do.'

Was she afraid of being a bad mother? Probably. Guilt followed her around like a constant shadow. 'Of course you miss them.'

'I miss you too. You know that, don't you? Perhaps I should have said no to Robert, but... well... you know how it is with me. I get carried away. I feel on top of a wave and it's all happening. Ideas are flowing and I can't stop them. Rob is so encouraging. He really is, Charlie. I feel so young again. But I do miss you all.'

He could have done without the reference to damn Watson! 'Now stop worrying. Everything is fine. Jimmy's okay. He's been having a great time with his cousins, and with me. I keep in touch with David and Peter. They are keeping fit and studying hard. As for Rosie, I've never seen her look so happy. She ate a huge breakfast this morning after a night with Richard.'

'Rosie spent the night with Richard? I thought that was going to be with Steven.'

'That didn't happen. But with Richard it did. Yes, here! Would you believe she came up to my bedroom to ask my permission? Keeping up with this lot is quite exhausting for an old bachelor like me!'

'Oh, my poor darling, is it all getting too much for you?'

'Don't worry, I love it — thrive on it. Enjoy your time away. You've been through a lot these last eighteen months. It's good that you're flying high again. Once you're home, we'll deal with any domestic problems together, not that I'm expecting any.'

He hoped he was right. Events of the past year had already caused her enough stress without added worries associated with Watson and Jim, Rosie and her boyfriends, and any problems David and Peter might throw up. Her work took a lot out of her, but she gave herself little rest. At least, there had been no suggestion of Watson seducing her. For that he was most grateful.

The morning was spent mulling over business plans with Richard. Ideas were kept rather fluid. Although Richard was free to plan his future, Charles needed to prepare for a number of eventualities. So much depended on June. He had no intention of pushing her into yet more decision-making. No, he and Richard would have to be flexible and patient, get together ideas and work on possibilities. At least they were able to agree on some kind of partnership that would make the most of their individual talents and combined experiences. They knew each other well. They were bonded in a kind of brotherly love, founded on mutual trust when in extreme circumstances of valour, the secrecy of which could never be shared with others — at least, for many years. When the time was right, he would discuss their ideas with June.

Rosie worked hard at her studies and then prepared lunch for the three of them. Did she want to make a good impression on Richard? All through lunch, they only had eyes for each other. Was Rosie going to be added to an already complicated equation? It certainly seemed that way. All remaining doubt was dissipated when, just before Richard left for Bath, he asked Charles if he could come to stay the following weekend and whenever he could get away. 'And, since I've been invited to stay for Christmas and for Rosie's eighteenth, would it be possible to stay on until New Year?'

'No problem. I know June will be delighted to have you here. I'm always pleased to see you.' He looked at Rosie hovering in the drive by Richard's sleek Triumph Spitfire and grinned. 'With Rosie around, I don't suppose either of us will be seeing much of you anyway.'

Charles left Richard and Rosie to say their farewells while he went off to collect Jimmy. There was no doubt about it; Richard had got it bad. Charles had never known him so infatuated — at least, not as far as travelling many miles just to be with a woman. He wondered if his new love would be able to hold on to him when the wind and the waves beckoned Richard to adventure. But, as he knew only too well, love for a woman had the power to overrule all other claims on one's affections.

As Charlie stopped outside Helen's house, he remembered her invitation to lunch with her the following day. He was in two minds about it. He enjoyed her company, but he didn't want her to get the wrong idea. Jimmy shouting and running out to meet him broke into his thoughts.

'Will you take us swimming? Please, Uncle Charlie. Please, please, please.'

Helen, wearing a nifty blue miniskirt with a matching soft jumper, appeared behind Jimmy.

'George was going to take them,' she said, 'but he had to go off on business down south. Something urgent came up.' She gave him a winning smile. 'It would be lovely if you could manage it. The children were so looking forward to going and I can't swim.'

'Actually, I was going to take Jim to the club pool. I have his things in the car. Why not all of you come?'

Within twenty minutes the boys were jumping into the water. Charles sat on the edge of the pool, waiting for Helen to change. He was pleasantly surprised when he saw her walking towards him. She was wearing a black one-piece costume with a deep, plunging neckline and high legs. She had quite a figure, definitely worth showing off: long curvaceous legs, full breasts, firm round bottom, slender waist and flat tummy — Lastex and breath control? She obviously noticed his admiring glance and responded by smiling coquettishly and breathing in even harder, swelling up her bosom to even better advantage. And why not? As far as he was concerned, she had a body to be proud of.

He suddenly realised what was happening within his groin. It was normal, so why did it bother him? It was what was going on between the two of them that needed subduing. He waved in greeting, jumped into the water and then swam quickly to the diving boards at the other end of the pool. Pulling himself out of the water, he looked back to see Helen walking by the pool. By the time he reached the top board, she was standing, almost beneath him, a curious smile on her lips. Damn it! She was doing it to him again. He prepared to dive.

'Mummy, Mummy, Mummy! Mickey's drowning!'

Bobby was running towards Helen, screaming and yelling.

'Charlie, Charlie!' she yelled up at him.

'It's okay, Helen!'

With a run he dived off the board and did a fast crawl towards the other end of the pool.

Jimmy had already reached Michael and was keeping his head above water. Within seconds, Charles took over. He soon had Mickey to the side. Helen pulled him out.

Charles checked Michael over.

'Don't worry, Helen, he'll be fine.'

Helen wrapped a towel around Michael and held him in her arms. 'What a fright you gave us.'

'It wasn't my fault,' Michael spluttered. 'Someone jumped in and knocked me under. I don't know what happened after.'

'Thank you, Charlie,' Helen said, 'You saved my Mickey's life.'

'It's Jim you should thank, Helen.' He turned to Jimmy and ruffled his wet hair. 'Well done, lad. You deserve a medal.'

'So do you, Charlie,' Helen told him. But the smile on her lips made him suspect she had something more personal in mind.

When Charles took Helen and her sons back home, she invited him inside. 'I refuse to take no for an answer. Anyway, I would feel happier if you were here for a little while, just in case Michael has a relapse or something.'

He could understand her concern. Thinking it would be the decent thing to do, and since the children were present to prevent any hanky-panky taking place, he accepted. She led him to the sitting room and sent the children to another room to watch television. She sat him on the sofa and poured him a large glass of brandy. He protested, but she insisted he needed it. Her gratitude for saving her son was becoming far too embarrassing. Now he was beginning to feel trapped.

A guarded coal fire had been left slowly smouldering in the grate. She quickly poked it into a cheerful blaze and put on more coal. The room was cosy with heavy curtains shutting out the gathering dusk. A single lamp placed on a table in a corner added to the mellow light. The sofa of the chestnut-brown velour suite had been pulled close to the fire and piled with soft feather cushions.

There was no mistaking her desire for him to make love to her. It was as if she had planned it. The heat forced him to remove his jumper. Unfortunately, this seemed to be a signal she had been waiting for.

She threw herself at him, took his face in her hands and kissed him ardently. 'Thank you, Charlie.'

'I appreciate the gift,' he said, swallowing hard. 'But you have thanked me enough already. I really must go now.'

'No, don't go, please don't go,' she said, clinging to him. 'Stay with me. You won't regret it.'

'Sorry, Helen, I can't accept what you want to give.' He extricated himself from her arms and stood up. 'You're my brother's wife. It wouldn't be right.'

Her eyes glittered angrily in the firelight. 'What is right? Is it right that my husband is always working? Is it right that he's often away? Is it right that he ignores me in bed? Is it right that he ogles young girls in their miniskirts?' Her fury trailed away into sobs. She put her head in her hands. 'Is it right that my husband — your precious brother — comes home smelling of perfume that's not mine?'

He thought she was overdoing the drama somewhat. But, moved by her brokenness, he sat down again — at the other end of the sofa. 'I'm so sorry, I had no idea. How long has it been going on?'

'A long time. Not so bad to start with.' She pulled a hanky from her pocket and carefully dabbed at her damp cheeks. 'Now George finds me repulsive. I know he does. He's forty but he still acts like a randy student when girls are around. The way he treats me you'd think I was a geriatric.' She crept closer to him and ran her fingers down her smooth pink cheeks. 'Do you think I'm old and ugly? Is that why you don't want to make love to me?'

Of course he'd like to make love to her. What man wouldn't? She was a most desirable woman — and she knew it! The situation was getting overheated. He took out a handkerchief from his pocket as an excuse to move away a little, but the sofa arm brought him to a halt. 'I'm sorry if George doesn't appreciate you, but—'

'I'm just fat and disgusting?'

He mopped the sweat from his brow — the fire and her close proximity were getting him to boiling point. 'You are nothing of the sort. And I'm absolutely certain George doesn't think so either, even if he does like to ogle the girls. There's nothing unusual in that. You are a beautiful young woman. George is lucky to have you for a wife.'

She looked at him with her big violet-blue eyes. 'Then why don't you want me, Charlie?'

'Don't want you?' He sighed deeply. 'You know better than that. But men can't make love to every woman they desire. We are both committed, Helen.'

Her head came down on his shoulder. Her hair, gleaming like strands of gold in the fire's flickering light, was soft on his cheek. Her light perfume was strangely intoxicating, drawing him closer to seek its source. Her soft pouting lips were parting even as he looked at them. He felt her hand moving over his knee.

Her lips moved in soft whispers. 'Come with me upstairs, Charlie. You don't have to be unfaithful to June. We can just kiss and cuddle.'

The invitation was hard to resist: the hand had reached his groin sending wild messages of what was to come. But he had no intention of giving in. He put his hand on hers to push it away. 'Helen, I don't think—'

She didn't give him chance to reject her. She flipped his hand away and half-lay across him, pulling down his head to reach his mouth. Between soft wet kisses that were sending him crazy, she whispered, 'Touch me, Charlie.' She lifted her skirt and feverishly grasped his hand, pushing it high on her inner thighs.

Suddenly, the phone started ringing. He quickly straightened up and tried to look composed. He felt like a schoolboy caught in the act. Just as he had been when he was just fourteen and the head's daughter had lured him into biological research of a somewhat intimate nature!

'Whoever is ringing can't see us,' Helen said, laughing at his confusion.

The phone went on ringing, but Helen ignored it. She started kissing him again, her fingers on his zip. Charles grasped her hand just as the ringing stopped.

'Relax, Charlie. You worry too—'

'Mummy, Daddy's on the phone,' shouted one of her sons from the hall.

Helen went out of the room. In a minute she was back.

'George forgot to tell me he would be going straight to work when he gets back on Wednesday. And that he will be late home!' She frowned angrily. 'So, what's new?'

Charles stood up, thankful for the intervention. But he was feeling dreadfully guilty. Had he really wanted to be saved by the bell?'

'Please don't go, Charlie.' She said, as he began slipping on his jumper. 'We were getting on so nicely.'

'I must get Jim home,' he said, putting up his hands as if to fend her off. 'I really appreciate your company — please believe that, Helen — but Jim has homework to do for morning.'

She nodded her head, as if accepting defeat. 'I'm free for the next three days. Have you decided about lunch tomorrow?'

'Quite honestly, I think it would be unwise for us to see too much of each other,' he told her, walking towards the door. 'We do meet for badminton and we can lunch occasionally, but not too often to cause problems.' He turned, and saw she was looking rather sullen. He kissed her on her forehead. 'Thank you for today.'

She brightened up. 'No, I must thank you, Charlie. For everything.'

Charles dragged Jimmy away from the television. Helen went with them to the car. 'Goodbye, Jimmy. It's nice to have you here, any time. Thanks for what you did for Michael. Your uncle is right: you do deserve a medal. Please come again soon. Just ask Charlie to bring you.'

Jimmy clambered into the Mercedes and settled himself into his comfortable leather seat. 'I will. Goodbye, Auntie, and thank you.'

Helen turned to Charles. 'Goodnight, Charlie. Thanks for everything.' She gave him a coded smile. 'And I mean... everything.'

Charles felt distinctly uncomfortable. 'Cheers, Helen. Keep smiling.'

He slipped quickly into the driver's seat. Switching on the engine and putting the car into gear, he let in the clutch and, releasing the handbrake and pressing down the accelerator, the Mercedes sped off. Except for checking the traffic, he didn't look back. Even so, he felt Helen's eyes following him to the end of the road.

James turned to him. 'Have you been kissing Auntie?'

Guilt sent a rush of adrenaline through his body. He tried to stay cool. 'Why do you ask, whippersnapper?'

'You've got lipstick on your face and you smell like her.'

He made a mental note to go straight to his bathroom as soon as they arrived at Bloomfield. 'You'd make a good detective, Jim. Don't mention it to anyone though, they might think we did a bit of snogging.'

'Snogging? Is that the same as copulating?'

'Where have you heard that?'

'I know what it means. I've seen frogs and dogs copulating, and it's in a book at school. David talks to Peter about copulating because he thinks I don't know what he's talking about, but I do.'

'Sounds like it. But no, we haven't been copulating. Anyway, snogging doesn't mean quite that. Your aunt just kissed me to thank me.'

'She didn't kiss me when she thanked me.'

'Some boys don't like their aunts kissing them.'

'Yes, I know. But I'd like Aunt Helen to kiss me. She's different.'

Charles changed the subject and they chatted about school activities until they arrived home. He was about to hurry upstairs when Rosie caught him.

'You're late back. I've prepared a meal for the three of us. I'll get it out of the oven.' She looked at him more closely. 'What have you been up to? You smell like a woman. A bit too musky for my taste. But I like the colour of your lipstick.'

'It's all quite innocent. Something happened at the baths. Ask Jim, he'll tell you about it.' He ran up the stairs. 'I must change.'

'Oh yes? Better not mention it to Mother,' she called after him. 'She rang you. Said she will ring again about eleven.'

Hoping for a distant love session, Charles was in bed in time for the call. In spite of trying to block them out, the events of earlier that evening were emblazoned on his mind. The phone rang and he hurriedly picked up the receiver. All thoughts of Helen, guilty or otherwise, were quickly dispelled.

Charles found it hard to grasp how quickly time was passing. The three extra weeks of waiting for June to return had not been spent in idleness. Moreover, with Richard now coming over each weekend there had been greater opportunities to discuss future plans. They had been examining details of businesses and properties sent to him from agencies near and far. He could see many possibilities, but so much depended on where June was heading, and with whom. Richard also had many creative ideas, but he too wanted to keep things open and fluid. With Rosie now high on his agenda, he was quite willing to tread water until they both had a clearer view of future responsibilities. Even so, it was good to examine the range of possibilities, especially those that could include June and maybe Rosie.

Charles had to admit to himself that he had not been short of female contact since June's departure. Apart from occasional telephone sessions with his beloved, he had been seeing Helen for badminton and taking her, her sons and Jim swimming each weekend. Then, of course, there was Peggy and the massage sessions. It had been only right to reward her by taking her to lunch occasionally, and including her in visits to the cinema with Jim.

It was Friday evening. Rather foolishly, he had invited Helen out to dine before June's return on the morrow. But it couldn't be helped. She had received some disturbing news about George and wanted to see him to discuss what to do. But now he was wondering if Helen had other things on her agenda while George was absent for a few days: a last ditch effort to get him to make love to her before June's return? At least he was seeing her outside of her home, so what could she get up to?

He harangued himself for such unworthy thoughts about a friend. The poor woman had sounded quite desperate about George's philandering. But, did part of him want to make love to Helen? In truth, that was a question he had to keep asking himself. Mental pictures gave him the answer even if he refused to acknowledge them.

He picked Helen up outside her home. She came tripping out to the Mercedes wearing a shimmering blue outfit and a white fur coat over her arm. She looked absolutely fantastic, with white glossy high-heeled shoes showing off her slim ankles and long shapely legs. Sitting next to him, her expensive perfume filled his nostrils in waves of erotic allure. He took a grip on himself. 'I hope your appetite is good, Helen, I'm told the Black Boy has a new chef.'

She looked at him, her bewitching eyes peeping from under their mascara-coated lashes. 'I'm prepared to try anything new, Charlie.'

Once they were sitting in the restaurant, it didn't take her long to come out with her problem.

'I've seen a letter from the mother of a sixteen-year-old girl called Janet. The woman says her daughter has been sleeping with my husband.' Her eyes widened. 'The girl's only sixteen, Charlie — a mere child! Having it off in a flat paid for by George. Can you imagine it? Your forty-year-old brother — my husband — keeping a young girl for sex!'

He could indeed imagine it, but he preferred not to. Over the years, girls younger than sixteen had offered him their bodies, and not always for financial rewards. He may have turned them down, but that did not mean he had never been tempted. Young Rosie was not yet eighteen and she had considerable power to turn him on — and well she knew it! Even so, although it may not have been difficult to understand age irrelevance regarding mutual attraction, what did puzzle him was that George already had a fantastic woman to come home to. So why risk losing everything — a beautiful wife, home and family — to satisfy a sexual fantasy? The eventual cost was far greater than the rent of a flat. Could it be genuine love? Or did George have an unruly predilection for young flesh, and young Janet was merely the latest, and probably not the last, in a string of teenage lovers?

'For years we've been short of money,' Helen was saying to him. 'It was his excuse for working away so often.' She sipped at her glass of wine. 'I feel so humiliated.'

The waiter came with their starters.

When they were alone again, Charles asked her, 'How long has it been going on?'

'No idea,' she said, stabbing at a large prawn. 'Surely not that long — the kid's only sixteen!' She pouted her pretty lips and shrugged her shoulders. 'Would he risk illegal sex? Maybe he would. I doubt he has moral objections. He's probably been seducing kids for years.'

'Does he know about the letter?'

'He hasn't been home for me to tell him.'

'What do you want to do about it?'

Tears gathered in Helen's eyes. 'I don't know. I would divorce him, but I have to think of the boys. They don't see much of their father, but they love him just the same. Anyway, how would I manage on my own?'

Charles put down his fork and gave Helen's hand a comforting squeeze. 'I guess you'll have to see what he says. Perhaps when he's presented with the truth it will bring him to his senses. Why on earth would he want to mess with kids and ruin his marriage? No, when he's faced with the choice, I'm sure he'll do the right thing. That is, if you'll still have him.'

'I can't go on as we've been doing. I need loving just as much as he does.'

Of course she needed loving, and the way Helen was looking at him it was quite clear whom she would like to satisfy that need. Was that why they were dining together? Little was said for the rest of the meal, but occasionally they looked at each other — her eyes burning into his with lustful desire. As soon as the meal was finished, he made an excuse to take her straight home. There would be no hanging around either; Helen was a dangerous lady.

He helped her out of the car and went as far as the front door. They were sheltered by a partially-glazed portico.

'Would you mind dropping my childminder off on your way home?' she asked him. Her voice dropped to almost a whisper: 'And, Charlie, please come back later to talk some more. It really does help.'

Charles knew it wasn't talking Helen wanted, and his whole body was urging him to satisfy his own need as well as hers. No, it must not happen. 'I'll gladly drop off your sitter,' he said, genuinely pleased to have a reason for a speedy departure. He shrugged his shoulders apologetically. 'Sorry, Helen, but I can't promise to return. Don't wait up for me. By the time I've done all the jobs ready for June's homecoming, it will be very late.'

'If you say so. Anyway, come inside while Julia gets ready.'

'I'd better wait in the fresh air. It will keep me alert after the wine.'

The door was left open as Helen called to Julia. At the other end of the hall money was exchanged and the girl, a teenager wearing woollies and glasses — unlikely to attract the likes of George — soon arrived at the door. 'Goody,' she said, 'a lift in a Merc.'

Charles opened the passenger door and Julia clambered inside. Helen had followed her down the few steps from the house and was standing behind him. She stood on her toes and kissed his cheek, her perfume luring him to return.

'Well, come back if you can, Charlie. I'll put the kettle on, just in case.'

Put the kettle on? He was already getting steamed up! 'Don't expect me back, Helen,' he said gently, 'I think it most unlikely.'

'We'll see,' she said, and returned to the front door. Light, warmth and her perfume were beckoning him inside. She stood smiling. 'Goodnight, Charlie, sleep well.'

As the door closed he was suddenly swamped by memories of his last time inside that house. He pulled himself together and joined the awkward teenager, hoping she was more interested in books than fooling around with men. It turned out she had been into Beatlemania since she was about eleven, and now her loyalty was drifting towards the Osmonds. She didn't stop talking until they arrived at her home. He had to almost drag her out of his car.

When he arrived at Bloomfield, only the hall light was on. He hoped Rosie hadn't gone out and left Jimmy alone. He went straight away to check. The boy was tucked in and fast asleep. He went quietly by the guest room, wondering if Richard had arrived that evening — he wasn't expected until the morning. Bumping and grunting met his ears; both sounds indicating the guest room was indeed occupied. Not wanting to eavesdrop, nor desiring to be stimulated, he hurried to his stairs.

A message had been pinned on the little noticeboard by his stairs door. He took it over to the light. Evidently, June had phoned to say she would be staying in London and it would be Monday before she arrived home. After five weeks on the continent with Watson, she was giving the man a weekend in London! Didn't she care for him at all? He decided he could do with a bit of company, and he knew where to find it.

Helen was ready for him. She had brought the fire back to life and the room felt warm and cosy. She offered him a drink. He refused alcohol and just had soda water. She poured herself a large gin and lime and swallowed it straight down. Slipping off a silky shawl that covered her bare shoulders, she lay down on the thick rug in front of the fire and propped herself up on feather cushions from the sofa. Then, stretching herself like a kitten, she motioned to Charles to join her. 'Come right here, Charlie. Join me in the firelight glow.'

He took off his jacket, threw a cushion the other side of the fireplace and sat down, leaning on an armchair behind him. He couldn't take his eyes off her.

Her soft pouting lips, big baby-blue eyes, and blonde hair framing her face like an angelic halo, belied the rest of her appearance. From the neck down, she was incredibly alluring. Her heavy breathing was exposing her breasts in a most provocative manner. The slightest movement and her shimmering skirt creased further up, revealing bare shapely thighs beyond her stocking-tops. If the blend of contrived childlike innocence and *femme fatale* was meant to seduce him, it was certainly having its effect.

'You look fantastic, Helen. Quite irresistible.'

Sensuously, she ran a moist tongue along her parted lips. 'Then why resist?' she whispered. 'We both know why you came back.'

'Helen, I....'

'Don't say anything, Charlie,' she said, creeping towards him like a cat. 'Let your lips do the talking.'

He kissed her open mouth, savouring what he had been missing since June had left the country with Watson. It felt good. Soon, Helen rolled back her head, encouraging him to caress her neck. He lapped up her sighs of pleasure and responded to her every move. She began stretching backwards, deliberately allowing her breasts to pop up from the boned confines of the dress. His mouth followed the dictates of her desires and his own unruly urges.

'Unzip my dress,' she whispered, turning on her side and lifting an arm. 'That's better,' she said, standing up and letting the dress fall to the carpet in a glistening pool. Rolling her hips in a provocative manner, she stepped out of her skimpy knickers. Wearing just her black stockings, pretty blue garters and high heeled shoes, she posed in front of him. 'Now it's your turn, Charlie.'

But he was too fascinated to move. All evidence that she was a true blonde had been removed. She was soft and smooth as a juicy peach.

'Come on, Charlie,' she said, starting to unbutton his shirt. 'I'm waiting.'

The shirt was thrown aside. He hesitated to go further. A bit of petting was one thing, but once he was undressed there would be no holding back.

'Helen, I don't think—'

'Better not to,' she cut in. 'Are you being coy, Charlie?' Dropping to her knees, she quickly unbuckled his belt. 'Let's see what you're trying to hide.'

'Helen, please….'

The zip ran smoothly down.

Chapter Fifteen

Someone had a thumb on the doorbell whilst hammering the door knocker. The noise echoed through the hall. Charles, who was eating his breakfast with Jimmy, Rosie and Richard, jumped up.

'Seems someone is anxious to see one of us.'

The racket, made worse by angry bellowing, continued as Charles hurried to the front door. As soon as he pulled aside the bolts and unlocked the door, a furious George, dressed in a creased business suit with the neck of his shirt wide open, burst into the hall.

'You swine, Charles! You'd better have a good explanation or I'll bloody-well kill you!'

Charles gripped his brother's elbow and guided him across the hall. 'Lower your tone, George. Come into the study where we can talk quietly.'

Even in their father's day the study, with its book-lined walls, huge leather-topped desk and heavy drapes at the long windows, had a sobering effect on the most excited of spirits. An oil painting of their father, Colonel Arthur Percy Rogers, looked down on them as in the days of their youth – his posture stern and unyielding, but a certain glint in his eye betraying his innate kindness and good humour.

George was dragging his feet. 'Talk quietly? I'll bloody shout it from the rooftops!'

Charles was wondering when his brother had arrived home. He looked dishevelled, his speech was a little slurred, his eyes were puffy and his cheeks flushed. He was obviously lacking in sleep, and full of alcohol. 'You've been drinking, George. Calm yourself if you want me to listen.'

He led him to an armchair by the fireplace and switched on a bar of the electric fire. 'Do you want a coffee?'

'I haven't come here for bloody chit-chat! What have you been saying to my wife?'

Charles sat himself in a chair opposite his brother. 'Saying to Helen?'

'Don't come the bloody innocent! She says that you — yes, you dammit! — have advised her to get a divorce. What the devil do you think you're playing at? Are you having an affair with her? Do you want my wife as well as Arthur's?'

Tears flooded his eyes. He wiped them away with the back of his hand. 'You're a greedy bastard, Charles. One woman has never been enough for you to—'

'Stop!' Charles snapped. 'That's the drink talking, not you. What has Helen told you?'

'You know damn well!' A huge sob exploded from his throat. 'The bitch! My Helen, my beautiful….'

Charles watched helplessly as his brother fought to control himself. What had Helen told him? As sympathetic as he felt, he could hardly allow George to get away with his own philandering. 'Helen did mention the possibility of a divorce,' he said calmly, 'but only after she discovered your adulterous affair with a teenager. Don't you—'

'What the hell are you talking about? *Me* — adultery? Don't start telling lies to excuse your fornicating habits.'

Charles leaned forward. 'Have you forgotten Janet?' He raised his hands in exasperation. 'Really, George, sleeping with a kid and paying the rent on her flat. Hardly surprising if Helen's decided to go it alone with the kids.'

George looked at him wild-eyed. 'What's she been saying?'

Charles sat back and told him about the alleged letter.

'I don't know anything about that,' George said, looking genuinely mystified. 'But, yes, I did get a letter from Janet's mother.'

'You admit to the affair then?'

'There is no affair! Just listen instead of jumping to conclusions.' He rubbed spittle away from the corner of his mouth. 'It was a letter from the lady who cleans the flat. Yes, there is a flat. Some of us reps rent one, it's cheaper than hotels.' He slapped at his forehead as though trying to rid himself of a severe headache. 'The cleaner wrote to me. Her daughter helps her out and they both want the same rates of pay. Janet is very accommodating, but not in the way Helen's told you. She comes in to cook breakfast and clear away.'

Charles frowned. 'If I recall, Helen said the girl was sleeping with you.'

'Helen got it wrong. The girl sometimes sleeps at the flat when we're having an early breakfast. She enjoys getting away from home.' He shook his head as if to clear his brain. 'Come to think of it, I wouldn't be surprised if Janet has a boyfriend sleeping with her in the flat when we're not there. But, I can assure you, she does not sleep — or otherwise perform — with *me!*' He bent forward towards the fire and rubbed his hands together. 'It's bloody cold in here.'

Since the background heating was on it wasn't chilly in the room but Charles, wanting to placate his brother, switched on an extra bar of the portable fire and turned it in George's direction. He sat down again, trying to make sense of what Helen had told him in the light of George's explanation.

'Well, that's not what I heard. Perhaps there has been a misunderstanding. I would have to see the letter myself and draw my own conclusions. But if Helen wants a divorce, no doubt there are other reasons.' Charles paused, waiting for a reply. He received none. 'Perhaps she gets lonely,' he finally suggested.

But George shook his head. 'Then she'll be even more bloody lonely if I go altogether.' He gave a deep heartfelt sigh. 'Helen wants too much. She wants to send the boys to private schools, live in a big house, have expensive holidays and wear nice clothes. Where does she think I get the bloody money? I manage to save a bit on my expense allowance, and now she's accusing me of double-dealing! No wonder I'm worn out when I get home. Even then she's not satisfied, while I'm away she'll jump into bed with any man who'll have her.' He put his head in his hands.

Charles was feeling uneasy at the message he was receiving. Had Helen deceived him? It seemed incredible that having once been with Special Services he could be deceived by such a homely woman. Homely? Surely not that innocuous! She was hardly the virtuous little woman not many hours ago. He tried to analyse the situation. Had he been duped?

'You aren't saying anything, brother Charlie. Are you one of those men stupid enough to fall for her lies?' He gave a brief hysterical laugh. 'You're hardly likely to admit it.'

'I don't know what to make of it. Helen has been great at looking after Jimmy occasionally. And yes, we have been swimming with the children. I don't deny lunching with her — and others — after a game of badminton. And I did take her out for dinner last night.' He could hardly tell George the details of what happened afterwards. 'So I can't deny having been seen with your wife. If you object, I won't see her again.'

George stood up. 'I won't put you in a position of having to lie about your sordid affair. We both know your reputation. You had sex with her all right. You probably thought you were doing her a favour. The sort of favour you enjoy doing! I just hope you feel bloody stupid at being made a fool of.'

George walked out. Hurried footsteps sounded in the hall and then the front door slammed. Feeling somewhat bewildered, Charles returned to the kitchen and sat down at the table to finish his coffee.

Richard stood up. 'I'll make a fresh pot, Charles. You look as if you need it.'

'Is Uncle George cross?' Jimmy asked, looking a bit sheepish. 'I could hear him shouting when he came in. Have I made him angry?'

Charles was jerked out of his unpleasant, guilty thoughts. 'Of course not. What makes you think that?'

'Because I had a fight with Bobby. I hit his nose and made it bleed.'

Rosie was appalled. 'Why on earth did you do that? I thought you were friends?'

'He called me a bastard.'

'You can't hit someone just because they call you names. What had you done to upset him?' Charles thought Rosie sounded just like her mother; even her voice had changed in tone.

'Nothing!' He dropped his eyes and frowned.

'You must have said or done something. Bobby's a good little lad.'

Jim kept his eyes lowered. 'He was jealous because my dad gave me those cars and his dad won't get him any. He said I only got them because I was a bastard. I didn't know what he meant. I thought he was swearing.' He paused a moment, his cheeks turning pink. 'But he said I was a proper bastard because Mum isn't married to my real dad.'

Jim's lips were gripped tight as he fought to control his feelings. Charles put a comforting hand on his arm. 'When parents aren't married to each other, their children are sometimes called bastards. Unfortunately, people use the name to insult you and make you feel inferior. If you allow the word to hurt you, they've won. It's not worth fighting over.' He ruffled Jim's hair in a friendly gesture. 'Do you understand, whippersnapper?'

Jim looked at him, his eyebrows drawn together in thought. 'If my mum married Mr Watson, I wouldn't be a bastard then, would I?'

Charles winced at the idea of June marrying Robert. It was something he didn't want Jimmy to even think about. He told him gently, 'You have a birth certificate saying who your parents are. Arthur and June Rogers. My brother was always a dad to you. Isn't that true?'

'Yes.'

'You are James Rogers. That is your identity. Rogers has always been your name and there is no reason to change it. I have every intention of marrying your mother. She will still be Mrs Rogers and you will still be James Rogers.'

Jimmy beamed. 'Are you really going to marry Mum?'

'I hope so. Now go get your swimming things. Your mum phoned to say she wouldn't be home until Monday. So we've lots of time for fun and games. Get going and make sure you get a clean towel.' He was relieved to find Jim accepting the delay in June's homecoming, in spite of his growing excitement during the last few days.

'So why did George come?' Rosie said, as Jimmy disappeared from the kitchen. 'He didn't even say hello to me.'

'Perhaps that's none of our business,' said Richard, as he poured freshly-brewed coffee into Charlie's cup. 'Tell you what, Rosebud, how about we go swimming with Charles and James?'

Rosie's sullen frown disappeared. 'Great!'

'Go get your things. Mine are already in the car.'

Rosie swallowed down the rest of her coffee and left the kitchen. She could be heard yelling at her brother: 'Make sure your feet are clean, you scruffy tyke!'

Richard turned to Charles. 'It's Helen, isn't it?'

'Too right!'

In between sips of hot, reviving coffee, Charles told Richard the gist of Helen's story. But before he could finish telling him George's version of events, Jimmy arrived with Rosie close behind.

As they were leaving the house, Peggy, retrieving a large key from her bag, was walking up Bloomfield's drive. 'Hello, Charlie,' she said cheerfully, 'Make the most of your freedom!'

She may have been laughing, but Charles could see the sadness in her eyes. They had become rather close during June's absence, but now he was going to have to be much more circumspect about their time together.

'No rush, Peggy. June isn't back until Monday.'

Peggy frowned and shook her head. 'Typical!' She gave an exaggerated shrug of her shoulders, and continued up the drive.

When they arrived at the swimming baths, Richard had a chance to ask what the problem had been with George. Charles told him the gist of everything that had been said.

'I won't ask you if George was right about your involvement,' Richard said. 'But I must admit, I found it hard to resist Helen on that sailing trip.'

'That's the best of it, when it came to the crunch, I didn't do it. Oh yes, a bit of petting and before long all her clothes were off. And most of mine. She looked fantastic lying there in the firelight glow, willing and ready for anything. She pulled down my zip and helped me remove my last bastion of defence. Then she said, "Who could believe you're so much older than George, you're terrific"... or something like that.'

'So you suddenly felt your age?'

'No, it wasn't that. I suddenly felt guilty of trespass on my brother's property.'

'Property? Ouch! Wives are hardly property these days, Charles.'

'I don't mean property in that sense... or maybe I do. She belongs to George. I'm not a wife-stealer and don't want to be one. I also became aware of a responsibility to my much younger brother. Not only that, but I began feeling disloyal to June too. It was thinking of June that finally tipped the balance.'

'How did Helen take it?'

Charles put down his cup and sighed. 'She probably felt I was rejecting her, as she claims my brother is doing.'

'Do you think she deliberately told George that you had advised her to get a divorce? You know, either to punish you, or cause some sort of showdown?'

'Frankly, I just don't know. I must admit, I do enjoy her company. She's a good badminton player. She's youthful, vibrant, and quite knowledgeable about a lot of things. If George is going after youngsters then he's a fool.'

Charles led the way to the pool. Jimmy gave them a wave and then jumped in. Charles watched him and a warm glow of love filled his heart. He turned to Richard, 'You know, I love that kid as if he were my own.'

Richard may have been listening, but he had his eyes on Rosie, who was walking sinuously towards them. She was dressed in a skimpy, tiger-patterned one-piece swimming costume. He said with feeling, 'And I love his sister. I never thought it would happen, but I intend to marry her.'

Rosie walked up to Richard. As their eyes met, she smiled with her whole body. Laughing merrily, she pointed to the other side of the pool. 'Race you there and back?'

They both dived into the water and set off at speed.

Charles watched as Richard caught hold of her in the water, kissing her with the passion of a man in love. Seeing them so happy together, he wondered if the mutual attraction would last. Certainly, Richard had never before spoken of marriage to any of his previous lovers, but Rosie was still young and relatively inexperienced. She was likely to be pursued by many attractive men who could offer her considerably more than Richard. But why concern himself? The couple were happy and enjoying life.

His thoughts turned to June. Watson had so much going for him: considerable wealth, career opportunities, creative energy, entrepreneurial skills, power in the right places, and that certain something — a kind of ruthless, rugged sexuality — that drew her like a magnet. Was it possible that she had been faithful all that time alone with the man? But then, who was he to judge others? Being drawn to Helen had not been difficult. Would he have succumbed to her exquisite charms had she not been married to his brother? That was something he felt too ashamed to answer, not even to himself.

His longing for June's presence caught him off guard. Soon they would be together and making up for lost time. He could almost smell the scent of her body. It would not do! He deliberately turned his attention to Jim. That lad was not short of courage, but he needed stability in his life. Time to do a little more cementing of their relationship. He jumped in the pool and swam over to him.

'How about I give you a diving lesson?'

'Super!'

Chapter Sixteen

It had been an excellent meal: good food, good wine and stimulating company. Although tired, June was sorry it had come to an end. She felt somehow restless, almost cheated of a climax to the evening. The men had retired to the bar for a last drink together. She had been excluded because she was a woman, and that made her feel inferior. Rob said it was to save her from the smoke of cigarettes, which he knew she hated, but she knew the real reason — they wanted to be free to tell their bawdy jokes and eye up the women who were drinking alone.

It was their last night in Paris, the final stop-off before London and whatever Robert Watson had planned for them. Of course, she knew the essential details, but Robert always kept much to himself. Nearly everywhere they went, part of the time he would keep her occupied while he negotiated financial affairs of which she knew nothing, and with men she never met. Sometimes she wondered if this whole trip was a front for something other than his clothing business. Of course, she was being ridiculous. Robert had negotiated for a vast expansion of his present trade and opened doors for his sports and leisure clothing and accessories. She knew he was looking at possibilities for cheaper manufacture as well as outlets for their goods. They had travelled throughout Europe, attended trade fairs, met agents, visited stores, manufacturers, boutiques, and design agencies. They had been shown around workrooms and factories, looked at garments, fabrics, trimmings and accessories. She had seen some of the latest materials produced especially for their qualities of stretch and breathability and others for warmth and lightness. There had been much to see and handle, causing ideas to buzz in her brain until they found expression in presentable drawings for garments likely to be fashionable in the near future.

Her week in the Alps had been fantastic. Robert had been absent most of the time, but she had met lots of interesting people. It was good that she could speak French. Memories of learning the language brought Charles to mind. He was the one who had started teaching her so many years ago. Dear Charlie, if only he had been with her. But that was stupid; he belonged to a different world. He could never be part of what she did with Robert.

Did with Robert? An unsought thrill ran through her body. So far, he may have kept their trip strictly business, but he had left her in no doubt — by glances and innuendoes — that he intended bedding her before they arrived home.

She knew he had been with women in every hotel they had stayed in. She could smell them. He knew she could. It was part of his teasing. He would be a little late for dinner and arrive at the table looking smugly satisfied, or he would disappear from the lounge for a while and return with a hint of perfume about his person. He would look at her as if to say, 'What do you think I've been doing? Eat you heart out, woman!' Yes, she was jealous. She was missing Charlie and was in need of love. But soon she would be with him — what joy! She must not succumb to Robert's advances — not ever. But deep in her soul, she knew resistance would not be easy.

She looked around the bedroom. It could have been the bridal suite. Soft lighting and luxurious furnishings. A four-poster bed with down bedding. In her mind's eye, a little hazy from too much wine, she could see herself having her wrists tied with soft cords — no, no, no! It must not happen. But she knew Rob would get his way. A shiver of erotic expectation set her nerves on fire. She walked around the room. 'Resist, resist, resist,' she kept telling herself.

She looked at herself in the long, gold-framed mirror. She ran her hands down the sheen of her black silk dress and quivered at the sensuous feeling. She touched the sparkling necklace around her neck, felt for the clasp and let the jewels run into her hand. She stroked her neck, now devoid of clutter. She felt good, alive and desperate to be loved. She looked into her eyes, hazel with gold flecks and bright with lust. She ran her tongue over her lips, swollen and moist with desire, and touched her cheeks flushed with growing expectation of what must surely come.

She pulled out the pins holding up her bouffant hairstyle and let the curls spill over her shoulders. 'No, it must not happen,' she moaned, running a comb through her glossy hair. 'Get a shower, go to bed and get some sleep. Too much wine, far too much wine. Don't even think of Robert. Soon you will be with Charlie. Dear, dear, Charlie. Keep thinking of Charlie.'

A sharp knock on the door broke into her thoughts. Her heart began racing. All thoughts of refusing Robert entry into her room — into her body — quickly dissipated. She opened the door of her bedroom and of her soul.

'May I come in? There is something I would like to discuss with you.' His voice was brisk and businesslike.

She looked at the folder under his arm. 'Of course,' she said, trying to keep her voice steady. She closed the door behind him. 'What is it you want to go over?'

He looked straight into her eyes. 'You,' he whispered.

She felt that familiar thrill, knowing he would beguile her into submission. She turned from his gaze. 'Don't do this to me.'

'Do what? I only want to go over your contract. Certain details need adding. What did you think I meant?'

She looked at him quizzically. Was he playing games with her? Suddenly, she felt stupid. All that dreaming about his intentions — ridiculous! It was all in her mind, triggered by her own desires. Surely the wine had gone to her head. 'I'm sorry, it's just that I....'

He was smiling at her embarrassment. 'Have I disappointed you? We must do something about it.' He casually dropped the folder he was carrying onto a small writing desk set in the bow window. 'Your contract can wait until morning.' He pulled his tie loose and threw it over the cushioned ornate chair.

He slipped off his jacket — his eyes never leaving hers. It was a simple but sensuous movement, full of meaning. 'Been waiting for me?'

'No! Of course not, I....'

'You don't need to say anything. I understand.'

Almost brutally, he grabbed her arms and turned her around. His hands were on her shoulders. Moist lips were kissing her neck. Her body was beyond control, softly quivering like a leaf caught by a gentle breeze. She moaned in agony of spirit, telling herself to resist.

Impossible! She was held in the grip of his ruthless magnetic sexuality. Movement touched her spine. Her dress fell to the floor. She vaguely wondered how it had got there. Of course, she wanted it off; she wanted everything off. She wanted him to take her and do with her as he willed. But no, no, no. She loved Charlie.

'No, Rob, don't, please don't. You know I can't—'

'Resist me? So don't. Let go and enjoy it.' His words came softly from his wandering lips.

Fingers were caressing her shoulders. She rubbed her cheek against them, softly sobbing. The straps of her camiknickers left her shoulders. Without any urging, the pretty lacy garment touched her legs as it slithered to her feet. Now his fingers were deftly undoing her bra. A hot tear ran down her cheek. She found herself whining like a child. 'Don't, Rob, please don't.'

Robert stood back, looking at her; hands on hips, head to one side. 'I like the black stockings. I think we'll leave those on.' He paused, moving his eyes from her legs to just above, his thumb rubbing suggestively into the deep dimple of his chin.

She followed his movements, picking up the signals, her nerves tensing for what must follow. 'No more, no more.' Her lips were saying the words but no sound was leaving her mouth. Earthy desire was overruling love.

'Ah, a tear. Poor darling, I'm keeping you waiting.'

Her eyes followed his movements as he stripped off his clothes — silk shirt, fine leather shoes, black silk socks, drainpipe trousers, briefs that barely covered his manhood — excitement welling up within her. He looked so ruthlessly masculine — his muscles and facial features hard, his loins girded and ready for action. She closed her eyes. She must resist. She must, she must....

He was behind her again. She gasped as he pulled her to him — he was so hard, so aroused. His hands were moving down her body.

'You're exactly the same as I remember you. Firm in all the right places, and deliciously soft where a real woman should be.'

She felt lulled by his gently spoken words. Suddenly, he grabbed her shoulders and turned her around, kissing her with lusty passion. Her mind was saying no but her primitive instincts were refusing to be denied. His lips were wet, his tongue rough and forceful. Her whole body reacted, alive to every nuance of his love-play.

Suddenly his grip loosened. She knew what he was going to do to her. 'No, Rob, please don't.'

'Don't push you away? Or do you mean... don't do this?'

His hand began moving down. She was held in its grip, moaning with both pain and ecstasy. He was working his erotic magic too powerful to resist. His voice was soft and husky in her ear. 'Tell me now to leave you alone.'

His mouth moved passionately over her lips, her throat, her breasts. Flashing pictures of what was about to be were appearing before her closed eyes. Groans were exploding from her throat. Her spine was arching. Anticipation was forcing little gasps of intoxicating delight. She wanted to yell, 'Now, please, oh please, now!' But she held it back. She loved Charlie.

He suddenly stopped and held her face in his hands.

'Well, what is your answer?' he demanded. 'Am I to leave you? Tell me, please… I'm waiting to hear.'

She tried to avoid his penetrating gaze. It was impossible: his eyes were hooked into her soul.

'I can't… I can't… you know I can't.'

He moved over to the bed and threw aside the covers. Curling his finger, he beckoned her to join him. An invisible cord was pulling her and there was no breaking free. She lay before him — a willing offering on the altar of desire. He slipped off her shoes and threw them across the room. Now he was standing over her in his naked manliness — his eyes sweeping over her body and burning into her inner depths. Her heart was thundering in her breast. The caged animal within her had to be set free.

He grasped her wrist, pulled her off the bed and down onto her knees before him. His lips twisted into a smile. 'Now, my dear, let me hear you beg!'

Chapter Seventeen

June arrived with Rob at London Heathrow. His Daimler was waiting for them. Rob drove straight to the hotel.

He'd said little to her throughout the homeward journey. On the plane he had been making notes and now he would be mentally preparing his speeches. She knew she had a part to play in the coming discussions, and the enormity of the task was making her both nervous and exhilarated. Robert had a large number of colleagues that he wanted her to meet and there were many proposals that needed her input.

She was going to meet some hard-nosed businessmen and employees of the Watson empire. Robert expected his minions to be able to get on with mundane activities of the company; that was why they were executives receiving good salaries. But he was planning something new, and he wanted the top boys with him every step of the way. She knew how ruthless Robert could be: those who dragged their feet would be out and someone with enthusiasm would take their place. He rarely found opposition. He chose his staff relying on his instincts, not their qualifications. She knew how hard Steven Blake worked, but he was a beginner compared with the men she was about to meet.

Robert had been on the phone to Steven almost every day, to be kept informed and to give instructions. It was necessary for his personal grooming towards top management. But these guys had full control over whole sections of the company. Soon, a new branch of business would be launched, requiring flexibility on everyone's part with extra responsibility for some. Upward movement within the company was a real possibility for those with drive.

Occasionally she was assailed by memories of the previous evening, but she blocked them from her mind. Now was not the time to dwell either on the incredible ecstasy experienced or the guilt it had brought her. It happened, and could not be undone. Confess to Charlie?

'Don't even think about it.'

Robert glanced her way. 'What was that?'

'Sorry, just thinking aloud.'

Robert merely grunted and concentrated on the junction rapidly approaching in front of them. A foot on the brake cutting down the car's speed, a glance at the mirror, indication of a right turn, and the Daimler smoothly took up its position on the road and sped off into the heavy flow of traffic on the main highway. At their six-thirty breakfast, he had said nothing about the previous evening. His mind appeared to be totally centred on the task ahead. What else had she expected? Words of love, or appreciation? Ridiculous! Robert Watson was a focussed businessman.

On arrival at their hotel June was tired, and more ready for bed than a heavy meal of words. The room where they were meeting was part of the hotel's expensive conference suite: well-lit from recessed ceiling fittings, attractive Impressionist reproductions to gladden the eye, light oak table and panelled walls, comfortable cushioned chairs, a long dresser bearing an endless supply of hot coffee, tea and biscuits. But it was hot and stuffy after her refreshing week of crisp mountain air.

Clearly, Robert had no intention of allowing her to waste any opportunity of furthering business by mentally dozing off. 'Pull yourself together, woman,' he whispered during a coffee break. His top staff had made themselves available for the whole weekend; she must make a greater effort and come up to scratch.

At the end of the session, she hurried to her room and took a cold shower. Now wide awake, she combed up her hair, put on a grey suit and crisp white blouse — just returned from the hotel laundry — and rejoined the men who were walking around, stretching their legs. They gave her admiring glances. Her self-esteem was restored.

After a light meal of sandwiches, taken by all in the conference room, she was given the opportunity to discuss ideas for future sportswear, based on what she had seen and experienced. She spoke of materials readily available and went on to discuss merchandise that was possible to produce but, so far, was not generally for sale — mainly due to the expense of manufacture. This she thought could change. With the right machinery, she believed skilled staff could overcome problems and develop techniques to bring down costs to acceptable levels. Moreover, as it became possible to set up manufacturing abroad — and this was something they had been investigating — they could develop wider markets in countries beyond their present sphere of operations.

The designs would have to be spot-on. Here June came to life, with ideas flowing into her mind even as she spoke. She glanced across at Rob. He was nodding in agreement and giving her a smile of satisfaction. She felt utterly elated by his approbation. Creative energy flooded her being, with sparks of inspiration firing her imagination. She was on an all-time high. Words flowed clearly and without hesitation. Her notes were seldom glanced at.

Eventually she handed over to Robert. He spoke about the negotiations he'd had with manufacturers of known brands who were interested in buying rights to original ideas, and how others had expressed interest in manufacturing garments under license for home consumption, or acting as outworkers for the British-based works. He also mentioned the media interest in June herself, and how this had resulted in many enquiries and requests for meetings.

June watched and listened to Robert with complete admiration. She glanced around the long table and was not surprised to find the rapt attention he was receiving. When he spoke of facts and figures, little greedy smiles appeared on most faces. He was as good at beguiling them into working his will, as he was at drawing her under his spell. What a man! When he finished speaking — precisely at six o'clock — enthusiastic clapping broke out. Waiters appeared on cue with glasses of champagne and the liquid was swallowed down with gusto. There may have been much in need of discussion, but June knew that Rob had every one of them eating out of his hand.

Robert seemed to sense her eyes were on him. He turned to face her. Those eyes, those penetrating eyes under their heavy brows, were inescapable. He folded his arms and smiled knowingly, his head cocked to one side. Memories of the previous evening overwhelmed her. Leaning back in his chair, he skewered a thumb into his chin. 'You did well,' he said. 'A beautiful performance.' She found herself blushing.

That evening they had an early dinner. Conversation revolved entirely around how the meeting had gone. Robert walked with her to her room. After the day's intoxicating activity, topped by good wine, she was on an all-time high and expecting him to come inside to end the day in a more intimate manner. Maybe part of her did want him to make love to her, but she was determined it would not happen — no, never again. Last night he had won, but tonight she was stronger. She would show him he was not the master of her soul. Her conscience would then rest easy. She unlocked the door and stepped inside. He didn't follow her.

'I'll say goodnight. Another busy day tomorrow,' Robert said, lolling on the doorframe.

'Goodnight, Rob. It's been a wonderful day. Thank you.'

'It has rather. But no need to thank me, you give as much as you take.' His eyes were looking at her quizzically, as though plumbing the depths of her mind. 'A good business relationship is founded on close co-operation, and, of course, knowing who's ultimately in charge. We work well together. You made a good impression today, but don't let your enthusiasm flag, we must keep them on their toes.'

June suddenly felt the weight of the responsibility being thrust upon her. A lot was at stake. An incredible amount of money was being put into Rob's new venture. At this initial stage, her role was vital. So far, so good; her enthusiasm had carried her along. But when it came to the nitty-gritty of long term commitment, was she really up to it? Inspiration was not something quantifiable, neither could it be simply switched on — a collapsed business had told her that. Her self-confidence began to crumble.

'Won't you come in? We could go over what you've planned for tomorrow.'

'We've already been over tomorrow.' His eyes fixed on hers as though exploring her inner depths. 'What is it you really want tonight? You have only to ask. I would hate you to go to bed disappointed.'

Damn it! He was playing games with her. It was all part of his humiliating technique to gain power over her. Well, he would not succeed.

Lift doors suddenly opened at the end of the hallway. A chatting couple came out and stopped by the first bedroom door. A few moments later and they were alone again.

Afraid to look him in the eye, she gazed at her feet. 'Nothing! You've got it wrong. I just thought… never mind.' She held the door ready to close it. 'It's late. Goodnight, Robert.'

He didn't move. 'Nothing? Nothing at all?'

She lifted her chin defiantly. 'Nothing!'

'Really? We both know different.' His penetrating eyes took in her breasts and then travelled downwards. 'Why are you trembling?'

'You swine, how can you be so brutal?'

He pushed her inside, kicked the door closed with his heel, and grasped her shoulders. 'Oh, easily, my love,' he hissed between his teeth. 'I just want you to be honest about your feelings.'

'I am being honest, I only wanted to—'

'No you didn't. The mother of my son must always be honest. All those years you denied him to me, Not only James, but yourself too.' He gripped her wrists. 'Now you must beg for what you want.'

'You're hurting me,' she whimpered.

He dragged her down onto her knees. 'We both know what turns you on.'

'No! No! Let me go!'

He ripped open the top of her dress and dragged it off her shoulders. A potent blend of fear and sexual excitement welled up within her, flushing her cheeks and drying her throat. Tremors of expectation racked her body. She knew it was the thrill of the chase and that she must resist. 'No, no, I don't want this,' she cried, but her voice held no conviction.

Soon, all her clothes were on the floor. She crouched, panting, her body charged with earthy lust, hating herself for wanting what he would do to her. She watched him take off his jacket and throw it onto the bed. He stood over her, dibbing his thumb into the hollow of his chin. His eyes were regarding her closely. His lips gradually curled into an enigmatic smile.

Suddenly, he pulled her to her feet and held her by her hair, kissing her with his whole mouth. Erotic sensations were setting her body on fire. She felt his lips, tongue, teeth and hands, moving sensuously down her body. She heard herself moaning, 'Oh, yes, yes, yes.'

He put her from him. 'I think that's enough for tonight,' he said, picking up his jacket from the bed. 'You must be tired. Far too tired for this sort of thing.' He walked to the door. 'I'll see you tomorrow at breakfast — prompt at seven. It's going to be a heavy day. Get some sleep.'

He walked out of the room without looking back. She guessed a woman would be waiting for him. Overcome with frustration and humiliation, she beat the bed with her fists. 'I hate you! Hate you! Hate you! Damn you, Robert Watson! Go to hell and take that whore with you. You'll never touch me again. Never! Never!'

She lay back on the luxurious quilt and closed her eyes, trying to rid herself of the images tormenting her body. No, no, he must not win. She suddenly leapt from the bed. 'Keep your women, Robert Watson. I don't need you, you swine.' She threw her shoe at the door. 'I have Charlie. He loves me. We love each other. No one will ever love you.'

She walked to the bathroom. Under the shower, she flushed Robert out of her mind and down the drain. Cleansed of his touch, she went to bed and mentally slept in Charlie's arms. But Robert still haunted her dreams.

June was happy that the following day passed just as busily as Saturday had done. It was good to have her mind focussed on the job in hand. Robert had arranged a grand party in the evening to celebrate both a successful year and the promise of the year to come.

June soon realised that his staff worked as hard at their play as they did at their work. Apparently it was just as much a requirement, and every one of them was keen to prove their worth to the company. In an expanding business, promotion prospects were excellent and Robert had every one of them well motivated. Hate him she might, but admiration for him could not be denied.

She dressed herself in a simple long blue dress and matching jacket embossed with touches of velvet appliqué. She mixed with the wives and tried to avoid Robert, and the attentions of bachelors on the lookout for a woman to bed. She also made one glass of wine last the whole evening.

She left the party at eleven-thirty and went to her room. She undressed, washed and changed into her nightdress.

Sitting at the dressing table, she brushed her hair, wondering if Robert would come to her room. Surely not. It was late and they had an early start in the morning. She tried to put him from her mind, but her spirit was restless within her. She walked over to the bed, pulled back the covers and slipped inside.

Soon she would be home and there was a lot to think about: her job, her children, her home and her darling Charlie. Suddenly she realised how divided she was. She longed to be home with her family and yet she was still hyped up with her job, restless to get on and see it reach a conclusion. And Charlie, dear Charlie, so patiently waiting for her — or was he? In a way, for the sake of her own conscience she hoped he hadn't been that patient. Even so, thinking of him in bed with another woman was quite unbearable. She would make it up to him; spend every night with him and take an interest in his plans, his hopes and desires. Yes, she owed him that much.

The sound of men laughing reached her ears. Farewells were being said, and doors noisily closed. Footsteps sounded and stopped outside her door. It was surely Robert. Her heart raced in anticipation of his knock.

June woke up as the Daimler approached the East Midlands. It was so embarrassing to have dozed off for most of the journey. But she had no intention of apologising; Robert had given her little time for breakfast before dashing off. He'd even had reception call her at six o'clock to make sure there would be no delay. The man could be so irritating. Why was he in such a hurry?

With thoughts of her homecoming, a warm glow came over her. Soon she would see Rosie and Jimmy, and be held in Charlie's arms. But Robert slowed at a junction and took a turn that led to Castle Donnington — some miles from Bloomfield and in a different direction.

What on earth was he thinking of? Her imagination ran riot.

'Where are we going?' she demanded. 'I'm expected home this afternoon.'

'Relax, woman. You are going home. You'll see. Sit back and enjoy the ride.' He glanced in her direction and grinned. 'By the way, it's nice to know you don't snore.'

He slowed the Daimler and steered up a country lane lined by hedges and trees. No other cars were in sight.

Surely he wasn't planning something devious. 'Rob, where are we going? Please take me home. I don't want a trip in the country.'

'Nearly there.'

She looked at the fields and woods stretching out each side of the narrow lane. Apart from a couple of barns, there were no buildings in sight. She crossed her arms in agitation. After half a mile, he turned a corner and a group of cottages and a village church came into view. A short distance on and the car ran alongside a high stone wall. They slowed almost to a halt. A sign told her that they had arrived at the Old Rectory. Wrought-iron gates were already open and Rob swung the Daimler into a yew-lined drive leading to a splendid old residence complete with a number of outbuildings. He stopped the car close to the house.

June was baffled. 'What are we doing here? I hope you don't think—'

'I want you to see my new home,' he cut in quickly.

She gasped. 'This is your place? It's huge!'

'Yes, it even impresses me. It was built for the son of a wealthy landowner. He held the patronage of the living here. Very useful if your youngest son fancies donning the cloth. It was the hired curates who lived in near-poverty, ran the parishes and cured the souls of the local peasants. The original parsonage, in the village close to the church, was quite modest compared with this pile. You know, some of those country rectors led opulent lives. Hunting, shooting and fishing during the day and socialising most evenings. I expect to do a bit of entertaining myself. Quite impressive, don't you think? My overseas clients will be bowled over.'

The handsome three-storey brick building was partly covered in a tracery of Virginia creeper, a vestige of ruby-red leaves hinting at its former autumnal glory. Tall multi-paned sash windows twinkled in the sun's rays. Picturesque chimneys stood proudly against a backdrop of bare oaks and chestnuts, rich green pines, and a majestic cedar with dark, sweeping branches. June guessed the house to be eighteenth-century, with later additions.

Robert stepped out of the Daimler and stretched his legs. 'Now stop worrying about getting home. We left earlier than planned, and we both know you are not due back for a while yet.'

Of course, he was right. And she had to admit to curiosity. Rob's new acquisition was rather intriguing. He already had a splendid property in the most exclusive area of Nottingham. Why a huge house in the country? She joined him on the newly-surfaced tarmac drive, admiring the tranquillity of her surroundings.

'Before we go inside, I'll show you the outbuildings, garages and stables. A nice bit of land came with the property too. Fields, woods, orchards, paddock and laid-out gardens with a hard tennis court. A swimming pool is in the conservatory at the side of the house. Cost a bomb to get the pool built and the garden restored to its former beauty, but worth it.'

In spite of the season, the garden looked impeccable: neatly trimmed box borders, fine gravel paths, and weedless flower beds raked over and planted ready for spring flowering. A young man was working in a sunken garden that had a full size statue of a well-endowed female at its centre. He nodded his head at Robert in recognition and then went on with his planting of rose bushes. Near to the house were a fish pond and a couple of fountains, water spraying upwards from urns carried by groups of naked nymphs. After a quick walk around the gardens, June had a brief look inside the stables. 'Are you going to keep horses? I didn't know you could ride.'

'There are a lot of things you don't know about me. Not only do I ride but I also plan to teach my son to ride with me. You too, if necessary.'

June laughed. 'I can't see myself in a saddle, but I expect Jimmy will enjoy it.'

But Rob was right about how little she knew about him. Much of his life was a closed book to her. It was twenty or more years since she had first met him. He was the son of John Watson, the managing director of Watson and Sons, an old established knitted-cloth and garment-manufacturing business, housed in a huge nineteenth-century factory within the City of Nottingham. Although only in his mid-twenties, he was the successful sales manager of the clothing section. It was his entrepreneurial skills that had kept his father's firm afloat, and also launched him into a highly successful organisation of his own making.

She had been his protégé in those early years. Yes, she had helped him with the beginnings of his empire, but he had brought out her talent and turned her into a highly successful designer. These last weeks had proved how well they worked together. But what of that other side of their relationship? A chilling thrill ran down her spine as recent memories of his torrid lovemaking flashed through her mind. Certainly, not what she was used to. Charlie was a magnificent lover, as Arthur had been — powerful but considerate. Robert was powerful all right, but aggressive and hedonistic with it. The shadow side of her personality longed to be taken and made part of him. He not only energised her creativity but also released her demons of dark desire. How could she possibly have understood all this when she was but a young virgin? No, he had been wrong to do what he did. He had stolen what was hers and Arthur's. If only....

'This way. Better get on before you start complaining.'

With keys in hand, Robert shook her from her musing and led her up a few steps to the large solid door at the front of the house. Within a splendid escutcheon were two keyholes of mortise locks. With obvious pride of ownership, he opened the door and bade her enter. 'Not completely furnished yet, but all the alterations have been done.'

A vestibule opened into an impressive vaulted hall. A wide staircase wound its way upwards to a gallery supported on marble columns, off which were rooms, corridors and a further stairway. All the woodwork was solid with elegant carving. Marble fireplaces graced the walls to her left and right. Radiators were discretely built into fitted fretwork cabinets. Most of the downstairs doors were open with glimpses of the rooms beyond. The place was warm and light. June spread out her arms, taking in the scene before her. 'Gosh, it's absolutely beautiful! I am impressed.'

'In its heyday, the place must have needed a hell of a staff to run it. Just keeping the fires stoked must have taken a small army. Thank God for central heating. Although fires in the few open grates will be most welcoming. You have to admit, those old country rectors certainly knew how to live the life of a country gentleman.' He beckoned her to follow him. 'Come upstairs and see the elegant bedrooms.'

All the main rooms were light and airy, with tall windows and high, exquisitely moulded ceilings. The whole house had been tastefully redecorated, and had bathrooms fitted in all the main bedrooms. The ground floor rooms were even more splendid: original floors, fireplaces, woodwork and ceilings all of the highest order — as befitting the son of a man of considerable property. However, the kitchen block had been completely stripped out and modernised according to the latest in kitchen design, and furnished with the latest equipment.

'Fantastic, absolutely fantastic,' she said, agog at the marble surfaces and the superb accoutrements. 'What else can I say? This place is a cook's paradise!'

'Not bad,' he said, shrugging his shoulders with false modesty. 'But then, I need somewhere suitable, not only for entertaining but also for a large family. Of course, I expect Rosie and the others to live here with James and us.'

'Robert, what are you talking about? I have a home.'

'You don't need two homes. You will marry me and we'll bring up our son together. James will eventually take over the business.' He waved a hand airily. 'This too, and more besides. Would you deny our son the best?'

'I've no desire to deny Jimmy anything, but you assume too much. Surely you haven't bought this place with marriage to me in mind?'

'Of course not. Along with another property, I acquired it more than a year ago. Clearly, it was meant to be. Don't you think your family will love it here? There's everything they could possibly want. As for you, my dear June, you need me. Always have. Be honest with yourself, woman. I've brought you back to life. Anyone can see that.'

He moved behind her and placed his hands on her shoulders. She could feel his breath on her face, and smell the maleness of his body.

'Every night could be like Friday night,' he whispered. 'No more leaving you unfulfilled. I know you were waiting for me last night. That's why you were so tired this morning. Disappointment was written on your face. Admit it, your whole body is greedy for my touch.'

Mixed emotions were tearing her apart. 'It's not true,' she said, but her physical reactions were telling her otherwise. With an effort of will, she twisted her shoulders and pushed at his hands to move away from him. 'Let me go!'

He was too strong for her. He merely moved his hands to grip her breasts. 'Mm, that's better.'

She heard herself whining like a child: 'Don't, please don't. I want to go home. Take me home.'

'In due time. Now just relax.'

His sensuous touch was enveloping her like a soft mist. She began to quiver. It must not go on. She had to be strong. 'I can't marry you. I don't love you,' she blurted out.

He moved his hands inside her jacket. 'What is love?' he murmured in her ear. 'We both know you want me. You always have. From the moment we met all those years ago.'

'You may satisfy my animal instincts....' Her back stiffened with the pleasure of his love-play. 'But that's not enough for marriage.'

'What you call love will come, my dear. When we live together things will be different.' He slipped a hand inside her blouse.

'No, never! I'm in love with Charlie.'

'I don't think so,' Rob said dismissively. 'He's just another prop like his brother was. You need a real man, not one that bends with your will.'

'No, I love Charlie. You don't know him.' Rob's romancing had to stop. Prepared to use her nails, she gripped his hands to drag them from her breasts. But he quickly moved them lower on her body. She squirmed. 'Don't do this to me, Robert.'

'You can keep Charles around,' he muttered, moving a hand downwards to pull up her skirt. 'He'll come in handy to help with the kids. We'll be otherwise engaged.'

'You can't make me marry you.'

'You want to keep your job, don't you?'

'You know I do. I will think about marriage. Truly I will. Just give me time.'

'That's better,' he said, running down his zip. 'Of course I'll give you time. I can be very generous.'

He lifted her onto the table and snapped open her camiknickers, breaking off the tiny buttons. She didn't care. She wanted him to be rough. She wanted him to punish her for giving way to him and for being unfaithful to Charlie. His harsh foreplay arched her spine with masochistic pleasure, forcing little gasps of air from her lungs.

He dragged her to the edge of the table. 'Now it's time to give you a little on account. Something you will never forget.

Chapter Eighteen

Charles was up early Monday morning to cook Richard a good breakfast before he drove home to Bath. After seeing his friend off, he performed his exercises and showered, his mind fixed on June's homecoming. He prepared breakfast for Jimmy and made sure Rosie ate something before going off in her car. After taking Jimmy to school, he went back home and Peggy gave him a massage — complete with a few raunchy jokes to cheer him up. Not that he needed much cheering; June would soon be in bed with him again! Ah, yes, but would she be changed?

He was due to go to the badminton club and lunch there after the game, but he hesitated in doing so. Over coffee with Peggy, he debated with himself as to the best course of action as regards Helen. Would it be best to let the dust settle before seeing her again? He had to face her sometime. Perhaps it was better to carry on as normal, have the match, skip the lunch and agree to sort things later.

'Penny for them,' said Peggy.

'Keep your money, dear lady. My thoughts are pretty worthless.' Decision made, he put down his cup. 'Must be off. I'm playing badminton this morning.'

He arrived at the club just in time for the match. Helen was looking as lovely as ever and waiting for him with a beaming smile. Perhaps the letter business had been sorted out.

'Charlie! Good to see you again.'

'Helen, we have to talk,' Charles tried to keep his voice calm. 'I don't want June upset with wild gossip.'

'Wild gossip? What are you talking about, Charlie?'

'Come on, you two.' Their badminton partners were waiting to start the game

'I'll have to see you later this week,' he said to Helen. 'June's home this afternoon, so I can't stay for lunch. For goodness' sake, keep quiet about our relationship. Nothing happened. Well, nothing worth upsetting June about. But we can't talk now. I'll give you a ring sometime.'

Agitated voices sounded from the doorway: 'Come on, Charlie and Helen, we'll miss our slot!'

Robert Watson was driving June home. She was hardly hearing what he was saying to her. He was talking enthusiastically about future business, but she could only think about his plans for her and her family. The business side of life was straightforward — exciting, compelling, creative, incredibly rewarding — compared with her personal life. That was getting far too complicated for comfort. Out of the blue, Rob brought Charles into his one-sided colloquy.

'A retired Naval officer with zest and initiative would be an asset to the company. Yes indeed. We could find a prominent place for Captain Charles Rogers in our organisation.'

June was staggered by the suggestion. 'Charlie would never work for you. He doesn't even like you!'

'He doesn't have to. I have acquired a new leisure complex in its last stages of completion. Since it's on the site of an old gravel-pit, water sports and activities will be prominent features. It has accommodation and facilities for conferences. I need a partner to run it. Someone prepared to invest his own capital as proof of commitment. I intend being a sleeping partner. So as long as I make a profit, I keep out of it.'

'You really are amazing. I thought you would try to get rid of him.'

He glanced her way and grinned. 'Now that would be foolhardy. I don't mind you having your pets around as long they don't interfere with my plans.'

June ignored the sarcasm, it was only done to rile her. 'I'll discuss it with him. I don't want to lose him. He's done so much for me. I really do love him, Robert.'

'So you keep telling me. I've told you, I've no objection to him staying your faithful skivvy. I don't even mind you favouring him occasionally with your body, but marriage is out.'

Skivvy? June began feeling dreadfully guilty. Is that really how she treated the man she claimed to love? Well, Rob would not get his own way. Once their new venture got off the ground — which wouldn't happen overnight — she would break free of Robert and set up a completely new business. With her new contacts and knowledge, and with Charlie's help, surely she would succeed. But could she break free of Robert? He was now so much part of her, how could she ever be independent of him? She was deluding herself. But surely things could change? She looked across at him just as he glanced at her. His eyes narrowed and his heavy brows drew together.

'You're quiet,' he remarked, slowing the car at a sharp bend in the road. 'I hope you're not planning to deceive me. I would hate to see you grovelling on your knees in front of me. Come to think of it, it could be a rather pleasant experience for both of us.' He saw her blushing. 'Just joking, my dear. Don't take life so seriously.'

Could Robert read her mind? She knew he was not joking. He most certainly would get her on her knees — one way or another! Resolutions were all very well; keeping them was something different.

Before long, Rob was turning the Daimler into Bloomfield's drive. 'I'll see James before I go,' he said, as the car slowed to a halt. 'My son is now an important part of my life.' He turned to face her. 'That is, our lives. Don't ever try to change that.'

Jimmy came running out of the house. June guessed he must have arrived home from school much earlier than usual. Keen to have her back home? Or was it Robert he'd been waiting to see? A stab of jealousy touched her heart. Sharing him with Charlie was one thing, but losing her youngest child to Robert was unthinkable.

'Mum! Dad!'

June sprang out of the car and opened up her arms. 'How are you, Jimmy? I've really missed you.'

Robert came up behind and ruffled Jimmy's hair. 'You're coming with me, James. I have something important to show you.'

Frowning, June looked at Jimmy. 'I suppose you do want to go with your father?' She wondered if this was the right time to be putting ideas into her son's head.

'Of course he does,' interjected Rob. 'He has to see where his new pony will be kept.'

'A pony? Am I getting a pony?'

'I have to get my son something for Christmas. Get in the car and we'll go.'

June decided to let Robert have his way. At least it would give her time to be alone with Charlie. 'All right, but don't keep him out late.'

As Jimmy clambered into the Daimler, she saw Rob give Charlie, who had been getting her cases out of the boot, a smug grin. 'Thanks for looking after my son while we've been away.' He started up the engine and then waved his hand. 'Cheers!'

The expression on Charlie's face as he watched Robert drive off with Jimmy was one of resigned indifference. But she knew how much Rob's insensitivity would rankle with him. Bad enough that Jimmy had greeted them as his parents, missing from his life for the past five weeks. How was Charles going to react to the house that came with the pony?

It was now bitterly cold outdoors. Shivering in her travelling clothes, June picked up the smaller of the cases and followed Charles inside. In the warmth of the hall, she put her arms around him and savoured the gentleness of his responding embrace. 'Don't mind Robert,' she said softly. 'He's a bit of a swine, but he really does love Jimmy. Thank you for everything, Charlie. I couldn't have gone if you hadn't been here. I owe you a great deal.'

'Nonsense, caring for your family has been nothing but joy for me.' He kissed her with utmost tenderness.

Scenes of her unfaithfulness were flashing through her mind. She fought against the feelings of remorse they inevitably engendered. Although tired, she managed an enthusiastic smile. 'Let's not wait. Let's go straight upstairs before Rosie gets home.'

As they lay on the bed, she nestled up to Charlie's broad chest; glad to be back home and revelling in the warmth of his uncomplicated love for her.

'It's lovely to be home. I've been in another world these past five weeks, just a beehive of exciting activity. It's funny — no, not funny, *odd* — I don't feel the same person when I'm away. I do things I—'

'It's all right, I do understand,' Charles cut in quickly. 'My service years on land and sea taught me many things about life and passions.'

'You know don't you? I'm sorry, Charlie. I don't love him, but—'

'June, I said I understood. Please don't go on about it.' There was pain in his voice.

'It only happened—'

'This weekend?'

'How do you know?'

'Do you really need to ask?' His chest heaved in a deep sigh. 'But don't punish yourself, it only hurts me more.'

'I didn't plan it. You see, Robert—'

'Spare me the details!'

'I'm sorry, Charlie, I couldn't—'

'Please, June, drop it! We've been over the whole business already. Just accept it happened, like I have to. You're home now. You have me to lean on. Hopefully, I'll supply your needs in that area.'

If only things were that simple! 'There's something I need to tell you,' she said, hoping that he would listen without jumping to conclusions. 'Robert wants me to live with him, so we can bring Jimmy up together. He's bought a fantastic house with swimming pool, stables, gymnasium — you name it, Rob's got it all. He wants all of us living there with him, including you, Charlie. Of—'

'That's big of him! As chief cook and bottle-washer, no doubt. Do I get the best servants' quarters?'

'Of course it's impossible. But Rob has more than hinted that my future with his company is linked to marriage. He knows I can't resist the excitement my job gives me. Somehow I have to string him along until he gives up the idea.' Weariness and remorse overwhelmed her. 'Oh Charlie, Charlie, why do you put up with me?'

'Why do you ask when you know the answer?'

'I guess I want to hear you say it.'

He rubbed his cheek against her hair. 'Because I love you.' He turned his face away. 'That doesn't mean I'm not angry,' he told her, thumping the bed. 'I'm bloody furious!' He released a deep sigh. 'But not with you, June, not really. We'll sort something out.'

She pressed herself up to him, comforted by his forgiving love. Her heart stopped pounding and she could think more clearly. She kissed his hairy chest. 'I'll hold out, Charlie. I promise. Now I'm home things will be different. You're here to keep me on the straight and narrow. What happened this weekend was an aberration. It won't happen again. Once my present work is finished, I'll break free and start my own business. I know so much more now I'm back in the swim of things. I have contacts in many areas of industry and commerce. We'll get married and have children and—'

Charles sat up. 'Hold on, June, we've been here before. If we're going to chat, I'll make some tea.'

She leapt up and grasped his arm. 'But, Charlie, I have something important to tell you. Rob has a plan that may interest you.'

'Whatever Watson is planning, believe me, it won't be for my benefit.' He left the bed and slipped on his dressing gown. 'Let's take a break in my kitchen. You can tell me about it there. I'll not have Robert Watson joining us in my bed.'

She knew he was right. She slipped on Charlie's shirt — it was like having him wrapped around her — and walked to the bathroom to freshen up and get her thoughts together.

Sitting at the kitchen table, she told Charlie about the leisure complex and what Robert had said about the partnership. 'Isn't that the sort of thing you want to do, Charlie? When everything's going to plan, maybe you could buy Robert out. I'll support you, Charlie. I really will.'

But Charles just sat there, slowly stirring his tea and listening with his head down. When he finally looked up, his face was twisted with fury.

'Dammit, June! Don't you understand what he's doing? He could be in a position to completely break us. Worse than that. I don't know how he found out, but just recently I was in negotiations for that property myself, along with Richard. We could put up most of the money between us. Now that devil has outwitted us. I wondered who the opposition was, waiting to gazump us at every turn.'

'Surely Robert couldn't have been spying on your activities, that's ridiculous. Aren't you being just a little paranoid?'

'Am I? You know my plans, at least in embryo. Rosie does too. Steven Blake went out with Rosie and is still in contact with her. Need I say more? I saw that place as being right for all of us. I even planned a boutique for you. That is, should you wish to be part of the scheme. I told Rosie all about my idea so as to seek her views and see if she would be interested in being part of it. Are you telling me Rob didn't know that from Steven? Steven's probably angry because Rosie now has Richard. Oh yes, he would have me as the active partner all right — with him pulling the strings! And waiting to pull out when we were at a vital stage of needing market confidence.'

June felt personally responsible for Charlie's plans being ruined. She touched his hand. 'Do you want me to give up my job? Just say it and I'll do it.' She knew it was a mere gesture. Hadn't Charlie encouraged her to pursue the work she loved?

He took hold of the hand reaching out to him. 'I can't tell you what to do, and I wouldn't if I could. Before long I'm bound to confront him because of the way he treats you. But taking a swipe at him, and believe me, that's what I'd like to do, would be useless. After all, he's not exactly forcing you to have sex with him, and marriage is not in your contract. You want to be part of his new enterprise. That's what he's gambling on. He may pressure you by withholding promotion, but let's face it, you would willingly work with him whatever he did.'

How could she deny it? 'Yes, you're right.'

'If you marry me, no doubt, he will make life difficult for you. He may be prepared to end your contract in some devious manner, but I doubt it. As for the rest? Only you can make the effort to resist him when you're alone with him. But I can't stand back and let him ruin both of our lives. I have no intention of toadying to him — let's be clear about that. The ball is in your court, and only you can play it.'

'If I don't give up my job, will you leave us?'

'June, I don't want you to use me to make such a momentous decision. It has to come from your own heart. I can cope if you just stick to your job. Maybe I can even accept the odd indiscretion — not that I do so willingly. But if you live with Robert Watson — sharing his bed or not — there is no way I can be a hanger-on. You must see that.'

She held his hand and touched it with her face. 'I can be strong when I'm here with you. But when I'm living in that exciting world, and when Rob looks at me the way he does, somehow I just....' She let out a deep sigh. What could she say that he could possibly understand?

'I know that already. How many times have we talked about it? Your work — and yes, Rob too — do a lot for you. You come alive when you are deeply involved in new and creative activities. Certainly, you can be an exciting woman to be with.' He took her face in his hands and looked into her eyes. 'Perhaps the best thing is for me to go ahead and develop my plans, keeping in close contact with you and your children. It's not long since Arthur died. You shouldn't be under pressure about marriage, or about anything else for that matter. Of one thing you can be sure: I'll always love you.' He pulled her from her chair and gently kissed her.

'I'm afraid, Charlie. Will you be leaving us soon? Will you find somewhere else to live?'

'Not until you kick me out,' he said, nestling his cheek against her hair. 'But I will have to go away sometimes while I'm looking around. While you want me near you, how could I leave for good?'

'You're so good to me and my children, yet I treat you so badly.'

He held her more closely. She found his strength comforting. He smoothed her hair and kissed the top of her head as though she were a child. She sighed within herself.

Indeed she was a child: she wanted everything and was afraid of losing what she already had. But she knew within her that one day, soon, circumstances would force her to make choices.

The winter afternoon had turned dark. Both Rosie and Jimmy would be returning home. 'I'm sorry, Charlie, I've ruined my homecoming. I wanted so much to please you.'

He caressed her half-naked body beneath the shirt and grinned. 'Kinky! Wear it more often.' He let go of her. 'I think we should get dressed now. Plenty of time for romance later on.'

'Yes, you're right,' she sighed, wishing the pleasant interlude could go on.

'Look, you have some days off now, and you have that long Christmas break to look forward to. The children will be home and you will be able to get things into proportion. Christmas is a great time for family life. Hang on, it will all work out, you'll see.'

Charles slipped on his clothes and went quickly down both flights of stairs. He thought he'd heard Rosie's car in the drive, and he was right. She was home earlier than expected. Jack Cummings, looking somewhat bedraggled in a shaggy oversized jumper, tatty flared jeans and an old school scarf hanging from his neck, was with her.

'Hi, Charlie, I've brought Jack home for something to eat. I can't have him working on an empty stomach.' She noticed the cases in the hall. 'Is Mother home already?'

'Yes. Don't you remember? I told you this morning she would be home mid-afternoon.'

'I know, but we all know what mum's like. I'll go up and say hello.'

Charlie put up a warning hand. 'Wait until she comes down. She's probably asleep now. It's been a rather tiring day for her.'

She looked him in the eye. 'Mm, I can imagine, especially if she's been home a little while.' She looked around the hall. 'Where's Jimmy? Jack was going to give him a hand with his maths homework.'

Jack looked at Charlie through his thick glasses and grinned. He could not be any older than Rosie, but he certainly looked it. His face was thin and serious, his mousy hair unkempt, and his body too lean to give any kind of shape to the jumper that hung from his slack shoulders. But Charles liked the youth. He had seen him on one or two occasions and the young man had given him the impression of being seriously dedicated to his teaching ambitions.

'That's kind of you, Jack. Jimmy will be home soon. Why don't you dine with us tonight? We have a great casserole in the oven; one of Annie's specials. Can't you smell it? That should whet your appetite.'

Jack accepted Charlie's offer with thanks. Before going off to the study, Rosie led him to the kitchen for a chunk of cake. Charles smiled at memories of his own youth, and of the cakes and pastries consumed on night raids of the pantry. Annie Craven was a live-in domestic for a few years, bringing up a young daughter on her own while her husband was away in the army. Recalling how Annie's Jenny was a forward young miss, forever trying to tempt him with her buns, he had to laugh to himself — the young madam! Just as well he was often away from home, and she was back at her own house before he returned from sea. But there was no doubt about it; Jenny produced some lovely buns — complete with icing and a cherry on top!

Still smiling at his colourful musings, Charles took June's cases upstairs to her bedroom. He then set the table in the main dining room and prepared the wine. His thoughts were taken over by concern over young Jimmy, and the ideas being put into the boy's head by Robert Watson. Everything a boy could desire would be given to him unreservedly. But the reckoning would surely come. Rob wanted his son to grow into his own image. To achieve that, whether June married him or not, Watson would make sure Jimmy lived under his roof and picked up his father's habits.

The voices of Jimmy, Robert and Rosie, coming from the far side of the hall, interrupted Charlie's thoughts. He hadn't heard the bell ring. Rosie must have heard the Daimler and reached the door before they did. He moved quietly to the hall. Jim was already disappearing towards the kitchen. To his horror, Rosie was listening with rapt attention to Watson's boasting. Casually dressed in black jeans and a blue jumper embossed with some kind of badge, Robert was posing like a rugby star: hands on hips, stomach in and chest puffed out. Even his rugged looks boosted the image — the aggressive game player. The only thing missing was a ball resting under a foot. But then, the games Watson played used people, not balls!

'Well, Rosie, you must come and see the Old Rectory,' he was telling her. 'The house will suit you. It has a certain grace about it.' He was bewitching her with his hypnotic eyes. 'Yes, indeed. Like you, my dear, a charm of its very own.'

She smiled demurely. 'From what Jimmy said, it sounds like a palace.'

'You must pick your own room,' he said, airily lifting a hand. 'There's plenty to choose from.'

Charles was furious. 'Rosie already has a home,' he snapped, 'and it's ridiculous to assume she will be living under your roof. She also has serious work to do: school to attend and exams to pass.' He walked to the door and held it open. 'Thank you for bringing my nephew home,' he said with forced politeness. 'And goodnight!'

Rosie stared at him in amazement. 'Uncle Charlie!'

Robert was smiling sardonically. 'Your nephew? I think you mean *my son*. Somehow I don't think we are related. Do you?'

Resisting a desire to kick Watson out with the toe of his shoe, Charles remained unmoved by the open door. 'I sincerely hope not,' he said with deliberation. 'That certainly would be a misfortune difficult to tolerate.' He nodded towards the exterior. 'Do you mind? It's getting draughty in here.'

Robert turned to Rosie. 'Forgive me, my dear. I have an important engagement and I'm late already. Remember that you're welcome any time. The permanent staff will be moving in tomorrow, so you'll be able to get inside to look around. I'll tell them to expect you.' He picked up her hand and gently kissed it.

Charles looked on, longing to get hold of Rob's wrist, twist it round his back and eject him from the house forthwith. Yes, and a severe kick in the right spot might just prevent him from pestering June for quite a while! But he held his peace and, standing back, gave Watson a polite nod as he walked past him and out to his Daimler. 'You'll get your comeuppance,' he murmured under his breath.

After the door had closed, Rosie was still standing in the hall looking utterly confused. 'Is mother going to marry Robert Watson?' she asked him. 'I suppose it will be nice for Jimmy. He'll love having a pony. Gosh, a large swimming pool too! But what about you? I hope you're not leaving us.'

'Rosie, that man is a devil. He may flatter you and make you feel good, but he's dangerous. If you want to design, go somewhere else. I'm sorry, I can't discuss anything to do with your mother.' He turned his back to hide his feelings. 'I must go now and finish off in the kitchen.'

Rosie was annoyed. 'What's happening, Charlie? I've never seen you so angry,' she called after him. He ignored her, but she followed him to the kitchen. 'I can understand your jealousy, but what right have you to speak on my behalf? That does annoy me. I'll decide what work I do, not you!'

'Fine by me, Rosie. But either get back to your studies with Jack, or help me in the kitchen.'

She walked out, muttering to herself.

Aware of their guest, June tried hard to keep the dinner conversation light and cheerful. Her tales of her early attempts at skiing put smiles on faces, and made Jimmy giggle.

'Can I go skiing? If Mum's too busy, will you take me, Uncle Charlie? We could go to Scotland. Robbie Drummond goes skiing every winter with his real dad. He's going to Nice in his summer holidays. They've got a huge villa there. His new dad bought a super motorboat — it goes ever so fast. He's going to show Robbie how to ski on water.'

June caught Charlie's look of disgust at the rivalry going on in the youngster's life. She cut in before he could answer Jimmy's question. 'I've already discussed a skiing holiday with your uncle. We thought the whole family might go next year.' She smiled at her daughter, whose look suggested she had better things to do. 'Rosie might have other plans, of course. But I'm sure David and Peter will be keen.'

'I'm sure they will,' said Rosie, picking at her food with her fork. 'Richard will probably be working. Maybe I'll take a break in Bath.'

'Well, lots of things can change before next year. Best not to make plans for any of us just yet,' said Charles.

'Things *are* going to change, aren't they, Mum?' Jimmy piped up excitedly. 'Dad showed me my bedroom in our new house — it's huge — and the stable where my pony will be kept. The swimming pool is fantastic. Dad's going to swim with me every day. Did you know my dad does weightlifting? Well, he does, and he's got a gymnasium next to the swimming pool. Dad says Uncle Charlie can live in the flat above the stables. Won't that be great?'

'Eat your dinner, Jimmy. I'll talk to you afterwards,' June said, feeling annoyed with Robert for having put her in such an impossible position. But she knew Rob never did anything without some purpose behind it, and that worried her. Come what may, she would not allow her son to be the pawn for Robert to gain the queen.

She glanced at Jack Cummings. Had Rosie told him about Jimmy's parentage? If the young man was confused and embarrassed, he was doing a good job of hiding his feelings. Not only was he ignoring the tension surrounding him, he was keeping his head down and eating with gusto.

The telephone rang. Charles gave June a questioning look.

'Yes please, Charlie,' she answered to his unspoken question. 'I have no desire to speak to anyone tonight, other than family.'

When Charles returned, he was looking most concerned. 'Bad news, I'm afraid.' He went over to Rosie and put a hand on her shoulder. 'Now don't get anxious, Rosie, but there's something you need to know. Richard won't be ringing you tonight. There's been an accident.'

Rosie jumped up from her chair. 'I want to speak to him.'

Charles held her back. 'It was just a message. Richard is in hospital.'

'What happened? How bad is he? Is he going to die? I must go and see him. Tell me where he is, Charlie. I must go now. I must see him. I must be with him.'

As she was about to leave the room, Charles caught hold of her arm. 'You can't go now. Don't worry. He's broken a few bones, but they should mend okay. Evidently he's been slipping into unconsciousness, but he's getting more stable. You'll be able to go down and see him soon.'

'I must drive down and see him *now*. Tell me where the hospital is, Charlie. I'll go tonight and—'

'No, Rosie!' snapped June and Charles together. June was totally with Charlie. It would be madness for her daughter to drive off to Bath at night, especially in frosty weather. 'Rosie,' she said softly, 'just try and think clearly. You are quite naturally upset, but Richard would be horrified if you set off to see him tonight. Don't add to his worries. Send flowers and best wishes by all means, but go down later when you know more. Or if he asks for you. Try to be sensible as well as loyal.'

'But I love him,' she sobbed. 'I want to be with him.'

Charles held on to her shoulders. 'I have known Richard a long time. I know how he thinks. He would be most upset if you left your work to go down there. Heavens, Rosie, think about what you are planning to do. Richard has an advanced driver's qualification. He's been driving for years in all conditions, but he came a cropper on icy roads. He'd be worried sick if you go off in your Mini. Just wait a while. If he asks to see you, or if his condition gets worse, I'll take you there myself... promise.'

Jack jumped up from his chair. 'Tell you what, Rosie, if you still want to go we could use my car. It's bigger than yours.'

June had forgotten their guest. Apart from the weather and time of night, knowing that the young man had an old banger that barely made it to Bloomfield made her quickly intervene. 'That's a kind thought, Jack, but I would hate your studies to suffer on Rosie's behalf. You have no idea what the weather is going to be like for the next few days. You could be stuck down there for ages.' She stood up. 'Since Rosie is upset, perhaps you should abandon any further study for this evening. Would you like to take the rest of that cake you had earlier with you? I noticed Annie has been busy and we have more than enough. Come with me to the kitchen.'

Within minutes, Jack had said goodnight to anyone who was listening, snatched up his books and scarf from the study, visited the kitchen, and was leaving the house with a bag of cakes and pastries. June escorted him to the door.

'Goodnight, Mrs Rogers,' he said, tying his scarf around his neck. Not an easy task whilst balancing his goody bag and books with one hand. 'I hope things work out okay for Mr Andrews. Let me know if I can help in any way.' He jumped into his car and started it up. There was a minor explosion and a cloud of exhaust filled the air.

June watched him drive away, praying that he would arrive home safely, and giving thanks that he wasn't off to Bath with her daughter. Poor Rosie, and poor Richard. Just how bad was the accident?

'Where's Rosie?' she asked Charles when she returned to the dining room.

'Probably in her bedroom, crying her eyes out.'

'Is Richard going to die?' Jimmy asked, getting up from the table.

'We all have to die sometime, whippersnapper,' Charles told him. 'But I think Richard has a bit more mileage in him yet.'

'More than can be said for Jack's car,' Jimmy grinned. 'The last time he was here, I thought Rosie would have to tow it away with her Mini — or me with my bike!' His expression quickly changed. 'I liked Richard's Spitfire though,' he said, wrinkling his forehead. 'I guess any car can be dangerous on icy road. I hope Richard is okay. I really like him. I don't want him to die like my dad.'

Later that night, June discussed Richard's condition with Charlie.

'Is it worse than you were making out? I had the feeling you were trying to spare Rosie.'

'It could be very serious indeed. I'm going down to see him tomorrow.'

'But, Charlie, the roads are dreadful down south. I don't want you to have an accident too.'

Don't worry, I'll take the early morning train. No need to tell Rosie before I go, she'll want to come too. When I've seen him, I'll let her know how he is. If he asks for her, put her on a train. Whatever happens, don't let her drive down. If all goes well, I'll be back to take her down myself at the weekend.'

Chapter Nineteen

As soon as the train arrived at Bath Spa station, Charles took a taxi to the Royal United Hospital. Visiting hours did not apply to seriously ill patients in the private ward and Charles was taken directly to Richard's room.

The nurse paused outside the door. 'Commander Andrews is conscious at the moment, but that could quickly change. Your friend is very poorly, don't expect too much of him, Captain Rogers. The surgeon will be here shortly, but Doctor Witherspoon is making his rounds. He may be able to tell you something about the commander's general condition.'

Charles entered the room, put down his bag in a corner out of the way, threw his coat over a chair and quietly approached the pale figure lying under crisp white sheets. A tunnel-like frame over the lower half of Richard's body supported the bed linen.

Richard opened his eyes. 'Kind of you to come, Charles. But as you see, I'm fine, except for a few broken bones. They'll soon have me running around chasing the pretty nurses.' His grin quickly turned to a wince. He closed his eyes and recovered his composure. 'Sorry, I'm not good company this morning.'

Charles moved a chair close to the bed. 'Your company is always beyond reproach, Richard. No need to make conversation. Being here with you is enough for me.'

'With the treatment I'm getting, I'll soon be dancing a....'

A flicker of pain cut him short. He closed his eyes and gave a restrained moan. 'Sorry, I'm rather....' He slipped into unconsciousness.

Charles went off to catch the doctor making his morning rounds. He was told that Richard was suffering from concussion, but was now conscious for most of the time. His condition was being constantly monitored. He had broken ribs, severe bruising and internal injuries were also suspected. The foot and ankle of the right leg were badly damaged. Charles was advised to have a word with the consultant surgeon, Mr Franks.

When Charles returned to his friend's bedside, Richard was awake again, 'I can see they've told you the glad tidings. I'm a lucky cripple. By all accounts I should be dead.' He made an attempt to laugh, but the noises he made were merely croaks.

Charles sat by him waiting for his friend to gain control.

'Richard, we've been friends a long time,' he said softly. 'However things turn out, nothing can change that. We'll still be business partners, supporting one another. Hold on, we'll see this setback through together. Just as we did years ago when we rode out severe storms.'

The lines on Richard's face deepened. 'I'm worried about my Rosebud, Charles. She must not see me like this. Keep her away. She's too young to be saddled with a cripple. She must let go of me and live her own life.'

Charles gently placed his hand on Richard's shoulder. 'I think Rosie may have something to say about that. You must let her decide for herself.'

Richard moved his head from side to side. 'No, no. She's just a kid.'

'You talk as though you'll be helpless. It's your leg they're worried about, not your brains.' He waited for a response, but nothing came. 'If I know my niece, she'll want to hold on to you whatever the outcome.'

Richard fixed him with his pained eyes. 'Keep her away. I can't bear the thought of her seeing me like this. If, *a big if*, I don't lose my leg, then all right, I will see her when I'm well again.' He closed his eyes. 'Promise me, Charles. You must promise me. Keep her away.'

'I'll do what I can. But you know Rosie, she has a mind of her own.'

'Do your best. I don't want her weeping over me.' His voice was thin and tired.

'Weeping? What do you think she'll do if she can't see you?' Charles said gently. 'Rosie will imagine the worst and be inconsolable.' He sighed deeply. In Richard's situation, would he not make the same request? Of course he would. 'I'm sorry, Richard; you know what's best. Yes, I will try to keep her away.'

'Thank you, Charles.' The muscles of his face seemed to relax.

Charles sat watching over him, wondering what he was going to say to Rosie. The truth was going to be painful. Would she understand? His eyes roamed around the pleasant private room with its pastel drapes and carpet, its comfortable armchair, and en-suite bathroom. The usual accoutrements of the sick room were in evidence on the bedside cabinet, including a monitor registering — with pulsating lights — the condition of the patient. A drip on a stand rhythmically fed fluids into Richard's arm. Drip... drip... drip....

A loud groan suddenly escaped Richard's lips. The monitor's signals peeped and flashed rapidly. Charles pressed the alarm bell, but he could already hear feet hurrying in their direction.

Richard's face was twisted with agony. 'Sorry... crying like a big baby.' He gritted his teeth while a huge groan escaped his lips. His face was turning a greenish-grey, and he was sweating profusely. 'Dear God... such pain!' he almost screamed.

Nurses arrived, quickly followed by Doctor Witherspoon. The following few minutes were hectic as Richard was hastily examined and taken off for immediate surgery.

Charles stayed with him until he went through the doors of the operating theatre.

Then came the waiting.

Charles sat on a chair close to the theatre with his head in his hands, praying for his friend and willing him to live. He brushed away the tears gathering in his eyes, and made an effort to be positive and manly. Richard had been in danger before, but his courage and strength of will had pulled him through. He had a strong, healthy body; surely it would not let him down now?

A pleasant female voice broke into his thoughts.

'Captain Rogers, your friend is going to be in theatre for quite some time, may I suggest you take a break and have something to eat and drink? There's a nice little pub in the village. A little fresh air would be beneficial.'

He wiped his face with his hands as if to remove the misery he was feeling, and looked up. He thought he knew that voice. 'Hello, Sarah. In other circumstances, I would say it was lovely to see you again. I see you have made it to staff nurse — well done!'

'Nice you have remembered me.' Tears filled her eyes. 'I was here when Richard was brought in. I'm so sorry, Charlie. I know how close you both are.'

'You went out with him not so long ago. Must be hard for you, too.'

'More than you think. I have always loved him. But you know Richard — not the marrying kind. I was quite happy to be just part of his life, but I think he must have met someone he's really serious about. I haven't seen him for ages. He hasn't even been in the club at weekends. And now....'

A tear rolled down her cheek. She wiped it away with the back of her hand, and quickly dived into her pocket to fish out a couple of tissues. She gave her nose a good blow and recovered her serene composure. 'Well, I must get along,' she said with a brilliant smile, 'I'm on afternoon shift until eight tonight. I'll see you again. Richard is on my ward.'

Charles watched her go. Such a lovely woman: medium height, a curvaceous ten stone, lovely round face with perky nose and full lips that curled at the corners. Her crown and glory — bouffant red hair — was partly hidden under a stiff white cap. Obviously, she knew nothing about Rosie. Poor Sarah, to love in vain. Well, at least she would have the privilege of caring for Richard while he made his recovery. That was, if....

He pushed negative thoughts from his brain, picked up his coat and bag and made his way to the hospital entrance. He needed to deposit his things at his flat — thankfully not rented out since he was considering selling it. He could phone June and Rosie from there. His tummy rumbled. Yes, he must also pick up something to eat at a sandwich bar.

Twenty minutes later, he phoned June.

'Charlie, thank God it's you,' she said, deeply agitated. 'Rosie is about to set off in her car to go to Richard. I'll rush and tell her you're on the line.'

June came back on, and Charles just had time to tell her Richard's condition when Rosie's voice bellowed in his ear, demanding to know where to find the hospital Richard was in.

'Rosie, now listen to me. I understand how you feel, but it's no use rushing down here. Right now, Richard is in the operating theatre. I doubt they will let you see him for a while. You certainly must not drive here. The roads are still bad. Wait until Richard asks for you. When he does, I'll let you know straight away and you can take the train.'

'But, Charlie—'

'No, Rosie. Richard hasn't been able to say much, but I know he wants you to get on with your work. He does not want you to come racing down here. I know it's hard, but that's how it is with him. He needs to lick his wounds. Please accept his decision. Wait until he feels a little stronger.'

'But you are there.'

'You have to understand, Rosie, we have known each other a long time. Before I was working from a desk in Bath, we served together in Special Services and formed a bond through mutual tribulations. Blood brothers, you might say. But it's hard for a man like Richard to show weakness in front of a woman. Just give him time.'

He heard her weeping. 'Doesn't he want me, Charlie? Doesn't he love me any more?'

'He most certainly does love you... perhaps too much. But there's nothing you can do at the moment. Just wait a day or two. I'll keep in touch.'

'No, I will *not* wait. I'll catch the afternoon train. I want to be near him, even if he won't see me. How can I work knowing how ill Richard is? I must be near him, Charlie. I must. I must!'

Charles sat in the waiting room, thinking of long ago when Richard had saved his life. They were doing underwater surveillance of a new type of submersible craft docked ready for sea trials. It was suspected that certain foreign agents were in the area, if not to destroy the vessel, then to examine its secrets. There had been a struggle involving knives. His oxygen airway had been cut, and he was being held down when Richard came to his rescue. The intruders were not so lucky; they were eventually swept out to sea. Finding diving equipment in fishing nets nearly caused a diplomatic incident.

And now his friend was fighting for his life and there was nothing he could do to help him. A patch of ice, a heavy lorry out of control and Richard's Triumph Spitfire had become a heap of squashed metal. That much had been printed in the local paper on the table in front of him. He thought of Richard's last moments in the driving seat. He sighed deeply; his fight for life was still in the balance.

The door opened. 'Captain Rogers?'

Charles nodded and stood up.

'I'm Sean Goodwin, one of the surgeons looking after Commander Andrews. We seem to have you down as the commander's next of kin. He has no close relatives?'

'That is correct. I'm his closest friend. Is the situation serious? Will he lose his leg?'

'Well, I'm not the bone man. You will have to see Mr Franks, the consultant orthopaedic surgeon. But I can tell you what I know. The ankle and foot of the right leg are in a poor state. Commander Andrews has instructed us not to amputate except as a final resort. He's had extensive surgery but eventually there may be no other choice. He knows the risks… delay much longer and he could lose his life.'

Charles grimaced. 'Richard enjoys an active life. Disablement would be hard to bear. What happened this morning?'

'The emergency just now was a different matter. We've been monitoring Commander Andrews for possible internal injuries. We were already considering taking a look inside on this afternoon's list, but his sudden deterioration made immediate surgery imperative. A kidney has been removed — there was no choice — but he can manage well enough with one. We were able to repair the rest of the internal damage and the wound should heal without further complications. But, as I have already emphasised, our good work will be as nought if this leg business is not dealt with.'

'Thank you, Mr Goodwin. I'm sure Richard is in excellent hands.'

'I must go. Don't expect too much of Commander Andrews for a day or so. He's been through a hell of a lot these last twenty-four hours, and it's not over yet.'

It was some time before Richard was taken back to his own room. When he opened his eyes and saw Charles by his side, he smiled weakly. 'I have died then. Archangel Gabriel, I presume?' His voice was only just audible.

Charles smiled. 'Sorry, Commander, you'll have to make do with a fallen angel. Welcome back to the land of the living. I thought I'd lost you. You gave me a hell of a scare.'

'I gave myself one. Coming close to death makes you think... what is....' His eyes closed and he drifted into a drugged sleep.

Early evening, Charles arrived at the station to meet Rosie's train. He refused to answer her many questions until they were in a taxi heading for his flat. He gave it to her straight. It was the only way for her to be able to grasp Richard's motives for not wanting her by his bedside. She was devastated that Richard had been through so much suffering and still could lose a limb, but happy to hear his life was out of immediate danger.

'Maybe I can see him now. I promise not to upset him.'

'He's still a very sick man. He may not want you to see him in his present condition. Don't make an issue out of it, Rosie.'

'Please let me go to him, Charlie. Just to tell him how much I love him.'

'I'll take you to the hospital so you can be near him,' he said, understanding her grief. 'But please don't try to enter his room. Don't push to see him against his wishes, or you may lose him for good.'

'Lose him for good?'

'Try to understand, Rosie. He's worried about you. He's much older than you are, so naturally he's concerned for you. Give him time to get stronger. Prove your love by respecting his wishes. He still doesn't know how things will go with his leg, so don't add to his concerns. He needs time to think about his future before he can offer to share it with you.'

She looked at him quizzically.

'Yes, Rosie. This has been no casual affair for Richard. Believe that he loves you. Believe also that he loves you enough to deny himself of your love for him.'

The taxi stopped outside his flat in the Crescent. 'Now, we must get you inside. Freshen up, get a snack, and we'll be off to the Royal.'

It was almost eight o'clock when they were approaching Richard's private room. Sister Landers met them at the door.

'Good evening, Captain Rogers. Can you hang on a minute? I'll let Commander Andrews know you're here.' She smiled at Rosie. 'And the young lady's name is?'

'I'm his girlfriend, Rosie Rogers.'

A shadow passed over Sarah's face, but the smile quickly returned. 'Right, I'll make sure the commander is comfortable and ready to receive visitors.'

'Does she know you?' Rosie asked him, when Sarah closed the door after her.

'Yes, she's an old friend. She knows Richard too. Her name is Sarah Landers. She's the ward sister.'

He saw Rosie frown. What she jealous that Sarah was looking after Richard while she had to plead to even see him? Sarah emerged from the room.

'He's awake at present. Would you like to go in first, Charles? He's asked to see you. He's rather tired, I'm not sure he's up to seeing another visitor just yet. I'll let you tell him about Miss Rogers.'

Richard looked up as he walked into the room. 'Nice to have you back. Sorry I dropped asleep.'

'Glad you did. I have someone outside longing to see you. Her mother had to stop her driving down. Am I to let her in? It's up to you, Richard.'

'I'll see her. Just for a little while.'

Charles opened the door and invited Rosie to sit by Richard. He then went along to the waiting room so as to give them a little privacy.

Rosie walked over to the bedside, sat down, and took Richard's hand. She held it gently, afraid it might be bruised.

She avoided looking towards the ominous sheet-covered tunnel and kept her gaze fixed on Richard's face, trying not to let him see how much it hurt her to see him brought so low.

'Hello,' she whispered.

'Hi, Rosebud. Nice of you to come all this way to visit an old sailor.'

She felt hysterical, wanting to cry out in protest. Anything but sit there passively making small talk while Richard's whole future hung in the balance. Just two days ago they were making magical love with limbs entwined, energetically moving in unison to a passionate rhythm that could not be halted until finally spent. Now her lover was lying broken and weak. That dance of love may never be repeated. She made an effort to smile.

'Hello, my handsome buccaneer. I had to see my lover, you might run off with — I'm so sorry, I didn't mean....'

'Don't be upset, Rosebud. We all have to get used to the idea. Come closer.'

He held her hand to his face and then kissed her palm. He folded her fingers. 'Keep that kiss inside you,' he said tenderly. 'Remember the good times, but don't feel committed to me. You're too young to be tied to an old sailor. You have your whole life ahead of you.'

'My life is nothing without you.'

'You think that now, but you may feel differently later on.' He winced. 'Sorry, can't talk any more. Must close my eyes....'

Rosie said no more. She sat by the bed, holding his hand as he slipped into sleep again. After a little while, he suddenly jerked and groaned loudly. Alarmed, Rosie clasped his hand. 'I'm still here,' she whispered, a tear rolling down her cheek.

Richard opened his eyes and tried to smile, but his whole face told her that he was in considerable pain.

'Shall I get the nurse?' She tried to stop her voice from quavering, but her emotions were too strong to be controlled.

Just then the door opened and a nurse came in with a covered tray.

'Would you like to wait outside a few minutes, Miss?' she said, giving Rosie a sympathetic smile. 'I have to give Commander Andrews an injection and make a few checks.'

Rosie was outside the room a few minutes when Charles arrived.

'How is he?' he asked anxiously.

'Oh Charlie, he's so poorly. The nurse is giving him an injection. He's hurting and I can't help him.'

'I know. It's hard to watch a loved-one suffer, but you know that already. It was hard for you when your father was in so much pain. Don't worry, Richard is expected to recover. He's being well cared for, but he'll need time to heal. Hopefully, we should see a change for the better by the end of the week.'

But Charlie's worried face told her not to be too hopeful.

Chapter Twenty

With Jimmy at school most of the day, and the others away, it was a relatively quiet, if exceedingly busy week for June. But her thoughts were constantly with Richard, Rosie and Charlie. After a call from Charles each night, it was impossible not to hope and pray for Richard's full recovery. Although at home, supposedly resting, she threw herself into a heavy work schedule: assembling and filing sketches from her trip away; drawing working sketches of those designs chosen by Rob to start off the new range; and, at Rob's request, making visits to Nottingham's top stores to view the latest in furnishings.

On Saturday, Rob rang her at seven in the morning to say he was picking up both her and Jimmy. 'Be ready for nine,' he told her bluntly. 'We're going shopping.'

Arriving at the store of Rob's choice, they went straight to the bedroom furniture department. First Jimmy was given the choice of what he wanted — no messing about or changing his mind allowed. The furniture for the master bedroom came next. June wondered why he was involving her: Rob had impeccable taste and was capable of making snap decisions. Was it to get her mentally attuned to being the mistress of his home? She refused to dwell on such possibilities.

An assistant approached while they were looking at the beds. June, having suggested the suite, had tried to steer clear of selecting a mattress. As far as she was concerned, if Robert wanted that bed, he could lie on it. But the girl insisted they both give it a try.

'You see, madam, some of our customers find these particular mattresses rather soft. You may prefer one that is much firmer. It really is best to try it.'

Rob grinned. 'Madam definitely prefers a firm one,' he said in a rather suggestive manner. He turned to face her, his thumb pressing into his chin. 'Why don't you try it, darling?'

June felt her cheeks growing hot, as much with anger as embarrassment. 'Mr Watson must decide what he wants to lie on,' she said curtly. 'He's doing the buying.'

'If you recall,' Rob said slowly, his penetrating eyes regarding her from under their heavy brows, 'that is a decision already made.'

She was totally flustered. It was the wrong place and the wrong time for him to be pressurising her with his innuendoes. Jimmy, who had been busy bouncing on the mattress in question, broke the tension.

'Are you're going to sleep with dad?'

Finding herself at the centre of an embarrassing and bizarre comedy, June didn't know whether to laugh or to cry. Ignoring Jimmy's question, she glanced at the assistant, who was finding it hard to keep a straight face. 'Mr Watson will take this one — the whole suite, not just the bed.'

Without waiting for a reply, she moved off to another department, leaving Robert to finalise the purchase.

Allowing but a short break for lunch, the buying spree was completed by four o'clock; the task having been made easier by June having already studied the patterns and colours of furnishings available, and choosing curtains and carpets for Robert to consider. The store was left to organise measuring and fitting, Rob insisting the job be done according to his schedule or they lose the whole order.

While they were enjoying afternoon tea — entertained by a pianist playing pleasant music in the store restaurant — June told Rob that she was unhappy with the way he'd spoken to Rosie and Jimmy. She kept her eyes down and her voice low. 'For goodness' sake, Robert, you made it seem as though marriage is already arranged. And that the kids will be moving into the Old Rectory any time now.'

'You have it all wrong,' he told her, casually spreading a scone with butter. 'James wants to come over and stay occasionally, so he must have his own room. Obviously, he wants his sister and brothers to come too.' He reached across for the jam, touching her hand. Instinctively, she glanced up. He caught and held her gaze. 'Of course, it would be preferable for us to be married.'

She pulled her eyes away. 'I can't marry you,' she murmured for his ears only.

'Can't?' He lifted an eyebrow. 'We'll see about that.' He turned his eyes towards Jimmy, who was busy scoffing sandwiches whilst keeping an eye on the tiered cake stand. 'We have to do what is best for the boy, don't you think?' Jimmy looked up. Rob gave him a fatherly smile. 'I'm sure James would prefer his parents to be married rather than be called a bastard.'

'Robert, how can you be so cruel?' she muttered angrily. 'Leave Jimmy out of this.'

'I want what is best for James,' he said, loud enough to cause glances in their direction. 'You just want to be selfish.'

'It's all right, Mum,' Jimmy said, worry creasing his face into a likeness of his father's, 'I don't mind being a bastard.'

'Don't you worry, son,' said Robert, with a satisfied grin. 'I think your mother and I will be married soon. It will be much more convenient. We'll see much more of her, especially you.'

Embarrassed at the attention they were receiving, June kept her voice low. 'Married soon? How do you make that out?'

'We can discuss that later. As soon as James has finished his tea, we'll go to the house and try out the swimming pool.'

'I don't carry a costume around with me,' she told him, annoyed that she was being taken for granted. 'You can take me home, and let Jimmy do the swimming.'

'Wait here a moment,' he told her, somewhat brusquely. He disappeared for ten minutes. She was furious at being kept waiting. Jimmy was happy to eat more cake, and talk about Robert's new house — that made her even more annoyed.

Rob returned with a satisfied look on his face. What had he been doing? When they reached the ground floor, an assistant handed him a large parcel.

'You now have several outfits, plus a robe and towels,' he told her, as they left the building. 'So no excuse for not swimming. And James has a few things to match my swimming gear.'

He was taking over her life. Well, he might win the odd battle, but she was determined he would not win the war. 'All right, I'll try out the pool. But please get me home by eight. Charles will be ringing.' She gave him a determined look. 'I must be home for then, Robert. Jimmy too. If necessary, I'll ring for a taxi.'

By six o'clock they were swimming in Rob's splendid heated pool. The room had been completed since she was last there. The tropical plants, stage lighting and Romanesque tiling, decorating and furniture conjured up a world completely apart from the rest of the house. The ambience of the place induced relaxation. Coming out of the pool in the stunning red costume bought at the store — one-piece and shaped to hold in the tummy, and firm the buttocks — she lounged on a sun-bed watching Jimmy and Rob swimming and playing in the water. With Jimmy there, she felt safe and immune from Robert's charms.

She had to smile at Rob: the tough businessman was playing like a big kid. If he was always like that with his son, it was no wonder Jimmy enjoyed being with him. Sipping a gin and lime, June pondered what it would be like if her family did spend some time at the house. She had to admit she might enjoy certain aspects of it. But would Robert always be like this?

Her mind turned to Charles. What if Charlie grew tired of her preoccupation with her job? Who could blame him? He was planning on being with Richard in some sort of partnership. If she kept her job, how could she possibly fit in? Was Richard more important to him than she was? Poor, dear Richard; if he lost a limb he would need Charlie more than ever. The two were closer than most brothers were. Suppose Charlie decided to clear off with Richard and follow his own star? Logically, it was the best thing he could do — she was just a drag on his ambitions. Would he still keep faithful to his promises? Or would he get tired of travelling and tired of her? 'Don't leave me, Charlie,' she whispered. 'Please don't leave me.'

Her attention was caught by loud laughter and splashing. She found herself laughing too, not just at Jimmy, but also at Robert. This was a side of him she hadn't seen before. Was living with the man such a terrible prospect? She and Rob were in tune with the business side of the relationship, and he constantly inspired her and stretched her to the limit of her creativity. Life with him would always be exciting. Yes, God help her, especially the sexual side of it. If Charles had not split from Angela, she might well have ended up marrying Rob, even though she did not love him like she loved Charlie.

No, no, no! She must put such thoughts from her mind. Charlie would never leave her and she would not leave him for Robert Watson. They belonged together.

She diverted her thinking away from the happy scene in front of her. Would Rosie and Charlie get home tomorrow? Poor Rosie, it was too soon after her father's death to be worrying if Richard might die. Hard for Charlie, too. Clearly, the crushed foot and ankle had become a huge issue. Rosie did not seem aware of the situation, but Charlie most certainly was. Poor Richard, what a choice! If he managed to keep the limb, he would never walk straight again and he could be in constant pain. But, if he agreed to amputation, would that really make him less of a man? Evidently, Richard seemed to think so.

Of course Charlie had to support his friend, but she missed him so. It had been six weeks since they had made love; mostly her fault, of course. Had he been with another woman? If he had, she could hardly blame him. And most certainly it would only be a casual affair. Oh, yes, there had been hints from various sources about him and Helen, but she couldn't believe that Charlie would break up a marriage. He was much too honourable. No, she was the unfaithful one.

June realised she was looking across at Rob again, and the sight of his near-naked body was arousing her. She must think only of Charlie. Mentally, she sent a plea to heaven for Richard to get well, and for Charlie to come home.

Jimmy cut into her thoughts. 'Come on, Mum.'

Although feeling tired, she joined them in the water. The weariness soon left her.

'Well, that was fun,' said Robert, holding out her robe as she climbed out of the pool ten minutes later.

June had to admit, it had been quite refreshing to leave her heavy thoughts behind and play in water like a kid. 'Yes, it was rather,' she said, looking at Rob's face and thinking how its appearance had changed. The lines were softer and the eyes warmer.

'He's a grand lad,' Robert said with deep feeling.

She tied the belt of her robe and sat down. 'Yes, he's never given us any trouble.'

'Well brought up,' he remarked, sitting down next to her. 'I guess it's time for me to be a family man. Ease up on work and give space for play.'

June was overcome by Rob's attitude. Was this really the hard-nosed businessman — the self-centred entrepreneur? The man who whipped her with his eyes and stung her with his tongue? Could he possibly be a changed man, or was it make-believe for her benefit? Rob stretched an arm across her shoulders. She felt herself warming to this softer side of his personality.

'Are we going to be a family then?' Jimmy said excitedly, running over to join them. 'Will we all live here?'

Robert smiled and glanced from Jimmy to her. 'What does your mother have to say about that?'

'We'll have to wait and see.' She knew she was stringing them both along, but Jimmy would be spending time there anyway, so she didn't feel guilty about it. Once she was firmly entrenched in her job and Charlie was settled — Richard too? — maybe she would get married. But not living at the Old Rectory, and living together as Jimmy imagined. Certainly, Robert would be part of her and Jimmy's family — a distant part, if Charlie had anything to do with it!

Dressed and hair dried, Rob insisted on taking them out to a family restaurant. He was being so fatherly with Jimmy and considerate towards her that they seemed no different from the happy, chatting families around them.

When Rob took them home, he ran his fingers through Jimmy's thick curly hair. 'Goodnight, son.'

Jimmy beamed and hugged his father. 'I love you, Dad,' he said shyly. Watched by Robert, he ran up to his room.

June was greatly touched to see the adoration softening Rob's facial features. Was that a tear in his eye? Surely not! More likely the effects of the pool water.

But why shouldn't he be emotionally moved? Had Robert ever known true love? She remembered his father, always distant and brusque. Had John Watson ever shown his son fatherly affection? The relationship had always seemed to her to be strictly business. She knew his mother had died when he was young and that he'd been the only child.

Living in his own flat, rather than in his father's spacious but emotionally cold home, had been common knowledge. The girls at the factory had boasted of their visits there. Genuine affection being in short supply, maybe sexual love was the only kind he understood. And yet, he had expressed his love for her, knowing she did not return that affection. Used to getting what he wanted through sheer hard work and bullying tactics, he had no conception of sacrificial love. Even so, her heart warmed to this man who clearly suffered from inner loneliness.

She watched Robert giving Jimmy a wave as he disappeared from view. A shot of fear ran through her — now he had her alone, would Rob come on to her? Oh, please, not now, not tonight when things had gone so well.

'Goodnight, June,' he said, turning to kiss her on the cheek. 'Thanks for what you've done today. I appreciate it. I'll see you Monday morning.' He was about to pick up his coat from the hall chair. 'Would you like to bring Jimmy to the house for Sunday lunch tomorrow?'

She warmed even more to this new Robert. 'Unless I hear from Charles to say that he's coming home, that would be lovely. Can I give you a ring later?'

'We're both alone tonight, how about I stay a short while with you?' It was said without any sort of pressure. His eyes were gently smiling as well as his lips.

'I must go up and see Jimmy,' she told him, as much afraid of her own feelings as what Robert might really want from her. 'I want to read a few pages to him. Charlie usually does it. I think Jimmy's missing him.'

'Show me his bedroom. I'll read to him. Will you allow it?'

That Robert should ask, rather than demand, was something she wasn't used to. How long would it last? She took Rob up to Jimmy's room.

The phone rang. June left Robert with Jimmy and went downstairs to answer it. She did not intend to give him an excuse to enter her bedroom.

'Charlie? How's Richard? Is he getting better? How's Rosie coping?'

Charles brought her up-to-date with the situation. 'So that's how things are. Not good, but Richard is keeping the worst of it from Rosie. He wants time alone for a while. If the leg has to come off — quite honestly, it's looking that way — he doesn't want Rosie near.'

'Oh Charlie, how awful. Is it certain?'

'No, but the surgeon says it's a mess and that no amount of pins and rods will restore it to a fully working limb. But it's more than that, June.' She heard him sigh. 'The infection hasn't cleared. I can smell it. I think Rosie chooses not to. She hasn't mentioned it. She talks all the time of Richard getting better and of the things they will do together.'

'Poor Rosie. She was just the same when Arthur was dying. She could not face the facts. But Richard will get better, won't he? Even if he loses the leg he will still be the same person.'

'I'm not sure that is how Richard would see himself. Anyway, I'm bringing Rosie home tomorrow. We'll be visiting Richard first, so it will be evening before we get to Bloomfield. I'll tell you more tomorrow. What have you and Jim been up to today?'

She told him the bare bones of the day's activities. But she did not mention Robert was still in the house. Why make him suspicious? He had enough to cope with.

Just as she was putting down the receiver, footsteps sounded on the stairs.

'Everything all right?'

'They'll be home about six tomorrow evening. So you can expect us for lunch. Thanks for asking us.'

'My pleasure.'

A smile lit up his face. 'I now realise what's been missing from my life. I'll go now.' He picked up his coat left on the hall chair, and kissed her tenderly on the cheek. 'I love you, June. Perhaps, one day, you will learn to love me.'

He turned and quickly crossed the hall to the front entrance porch. June watched him, full of wonder at his changed personality. The door opened. He hesitated for just a moment, and then walked out of the warm house into the bitterly cold night.

Chapter Twenty-One

Sister Sarah Landers came out of Richard's room carrying a tray covered with a cloth. 'You can go in now,' she said to Charles and Rosie, who were waiting by the door. She smiled sympathetically at Rosie. 'Don't stay too long, my dear. I've just given Commander Andrews his injection. He will be very sleepy.'

As Rosie eagerly entered the sick room, Sarah glanced at Charles. 'One at a time please, Captain Rogers.' Her look suggested she wished to speak to him alone.

'Charles,' she said quietly, as soon as the door closed. 'Mr Franks would like to see you.'

Charles detected a putrid smell coming from the bowl on the tray, covered with a white cloth. 'I think I know what he will tell me,' he said, resigned to know the worst.

After his conversation with the surgeon, Charles returned to Richard's room. He popped his head around the door. 'Do you mind if I see Richard for a moment, Rosie?'

She frowned but, smiling at Richard, said she would be back in a few minutes.

'You've seen the bone man,' said Richard, after Rosie had closed the door behind her. 'You know what must happen. Please listen to me, Charles. Rosie must go home and not visit me again. There can be no future for us....' A shadow of pain crossed over his face and he groaned wearily. 'Make her understand. Please, Charles, make her see sense. She's too young to be hanging around waiting for an old crock to get his life b....' His face suddenly creased with pain. He closed his eyes as if to hide his feelings. 'Go back with her. Keep her away. I love her too much to ruin her life.'

Charles nodded. 'Whatever you say.'

'I'll speak to Rosie tomorrow... tell her... go home. Can't do it now... sleep....'

Saturday afternoon, Richard spoke to Rosie with Charles present.

'I've made good progress. I'm not in danger.' He squeezed Rosie's hand. 'You must get back to school and finish the term. Not long to Christmas. Soon after it's your eighteenth.' He closed his eyes a moment. When he opened them, he forced a smile. 'Promise me, Rosie. Go back with Charles.'

'If that is what you really want, Richard,' she told him tearfully. 'But let me stay until tomorrow. I'll go back to school on Monday.'

Richard nodded his consent. Rosie might have been pleased but Charles knew the sacrifice his friend was making, and his heart bled for him.

June was waiting for them at the railway station, looking concerned. As soon as they left the train, carrying four pieces of luggage — three of them Rosie's bags — she came hurrying towards them. She took one of the bags from under Charlie's arm. 'Let me help you. How's Richard?'

Rosie didn't give him chance to answer. 'Oh, Mummy, he's so poorly,' she burst out. 'I want to stay with him but Charlie won't let me.'

Charles looked at June and shook his head. 'We have to respect Richard's wishes.'

'Of course,' June agreed. 'Rosie, you have to give Richard a bit of space. He wants what is best for both of you. Surely you can see that?'

'I know but—'

'You still have your whole lives ahead of you. Right now, you have to catch up with your studies. Richard is old enough to understand these things.'

Charles thought June was putting on a good act. Her eyes told him how much her heart ached for her daughter, for him and for Richard.

They arrived at the station car park. He put down the bags by the Rover P6. 'June, you had better sit with Rosie. Give me your keys, I'll drive.'

On the way to Bloomfield, he glanced in the mirror. June was almost weeping with Rosie. He felt like weeping with them. It was on a night such as this, a year earlier, that June had picked him up from the same Bath train. It was also the same car and the same people in it, but on that occasion he had arrived alone to visit his sick brother. Arthur had undergone surgery, but the prognosis was not good: he had a few months to live, maybe only weeks.

When they walked inside the house, the phone was ringing. June answered it and then handed him the receiver. 'It's a friend of yours wanting a word with you.' She turned to Rosie. 'Suppose you take your bags upstairs, I'll go make us some tea.'

A few minutes later, Charles joined her in the kitchen. He took off his coat and sat in a chair by the range. June handed him a cup of tea. 'It was the hospital, wasn't it?'

'Yes,' he sighed wearily. 'Sister Landers said she'd keep me informed. Richard has agreed to amputation. Mr Franks told him a week ago that the limb is worthless. Nothing but a source of pain and disablement. By hanging on this long, he's put his life at risk. They intended operating in the morning, but it's become an emergency. He's being prepared right now.' His throat tightened as he fought to control his emotions. 'You know, June,' he almost croaked, 'I think he deliberately waited until Rosie was out of the way. How that man must have suffered for love.'

Rosie appeared in the kitchen. 'What is it? What's happened? It's Richard, isn't it?'

Charles stood up. As gently as he could, he sat her down beside him and told her the news.

'Oh, no, no!' Rosie wailed. 'My poor Richard. No! No! No!'

June put her arms around her daughter, but she would not be comforted.

Thinking it best to leave June to comfort Rosie, Charles left his seat. 'Sit here, June, I must go upstairs and sort out my clothes.'

He walked to the hall to collect his case. Rosie came running after him. 'You're going back, aren't you? Take me too. I want to see him. Please, Charlie, take me with you. I'll drive myself if I can't go with you.'

Charles put down his case and gripped her shoulders. 'You must understand, Rosie, Richard does not want you there at the moment. He wants you to get on with your own life. It isn't because he doesn't love you — he does, more than you'll ever know. Don't make things harder for him. Be brave. Give him time. Push him now and you may push him away for good.'

Rosie was shaking her head. 'Sarah Landers is there. She looks after him. I want to be there too. I can help Richard. I can help nurse him.'

'Sarah is a nurse, trained to be objective as part of her caring role. Look, Rosie, Richard is much older than you. He has a sense of responsibility towards you.'

'I can be responsible for myself,' she yelled. 'Richard needs me. I don't want him to push me away.'

How could he possibly explain Richard's fear of disablement and what it could do to their relationship? Surely she would be even keener to prove her love, without giving thought to the future. What's more, how could he explain Richard's need to be strong and fearless in order to accept himself? Women adored him because he was so manly: a bold-hearted sailor who loved life and acts of derring-do. Richard did not want the girl he loved saddled with a cripple. On his own he might well face the challenge of disablement, but with Rosie anxiously watching for progress he might feel maimed in spirit as well as body.

'If you cannot accept his wishes,' he said gently, 'what use would you be to him? Don't you see? He has to be in charge of himself. Rightly or wrongly, he wants you to stay away. In his position, I think I would do the same.'

Rosie clung to him and wept bitterly. He held her close, face on her head and tenderly patting her shoulder. She suddenly pushed him aside and ran up the stairs. He heaved a sigh of heartache: there was nothing he could say to her that would ease her pain. After all, having free access to Richard made him part of Rosie's problem. Had he handled it badly? Now the poor girl was feeling a deep sense of rejection as well as grief.

He looked up as a door slammed above him. Rejection indeed, but only Richard could change that. He had been in no position to reverse his friend's heartfelt decision, nor, with Richard so weak and debilitated by pain, had he wished to try.

He took his case upstairs, unpacked his clothes and replaced them with clean ones. Footsteps sounded on his stairs. Rosie? Well, he would not give way and take her with him. Richard must be his priority. But, to his relief, it was June's voice reaching his ears.

'Charlie? It's me.' She came into his bedroom. 'Are you going back to Bath tonight?'

'I'm driving there first thing in the morning. Having the car there will make things easier. Sorry, June — just back and I'm off again.' He looked at her worried face. 'Come here,' he said, opening up his arms.

She snuggled up to him. It was wonderful to feel her in his arms once more. The warmth of her love kindled the smouldering fire within him. Kissing was not enough. He moved her towards the bed.

'No, Charlie,' she said. 'Jimmy isn't home. He's with Robert. I'd better fetch him or Rob will bring him home. It's not a good time for him to come here.'

'It's never a good time for Watson to be here as far as I'm concerned, but I know what you mean. You stay here, Rosie might need you. I'll collect Jimmy. Time I faced my adversary on his home ground.'

When Charles arrived at the Old Rectory, Robert himself admitted him. He was obviously surprised to see him.

'Come to collect James?' he said, eyebrows raised and his lips twisted in a mocking smile. 'No doubt you want to see what's on offer for the future Mrs Watson. Well, step inside and I'll show you around.'

Charles, hands on hips and forcing a casual smile, shook his head. 'Nice of you to offer, but no thanks. If you would just call the boy, I'll wait in my car.'

Before Watson could answer, Jimmy's voice rang out from the other end of the hall.

'Uncle Charlie, come and see my room — it's huge!'

'Coming in, Captain Rogers? Or do you want to disappoint my son?'

What Charles would have really liked to do was go a few rounds with Watson — no holds barred! He raised his hands in open surrender. 'I suppose I have a few minutes to spare. Can't say there is much here that will interest me.'

'Maybe you will change your mind when Mrs Watson is installed?'

'I'm absolutely certain I have not met your wife — present or future — so I reserve my judgement.' He stepped inside and drank in the ambience of the splendid hall. 'Quite impressive. Like being in my club at Bath.'

'Uncle, come on,' Jimmy called from the stairs. 'I want to show you my room.'

'I'll let James show you around,' Watson said, smiling with parental pride. 'I'm sure he will do a good job of convincing you where his future happiness lies.' He turned towards a door at the far side of the hall. 'I have a phone call to make. I'll see you again before you leave.'

It didn't take long for Charles to realise why Jimmy enjoyed going to the place. Apart from furniture, his room had a television and the latest hi-fi equipment. An adjoining room had a train set in the process of being set up on a large table. Electric guitars, a full set of drums and recording equipment were in a playroom, waiting to be used by Jim and his brothers plus any invited friends. Next to the swimming pool conservatory was a fully-kitted gymnasium.

'You should see my dad lift those weights, Uncle Charlie. And do you know you can run for miles on that treadmill? You can listen to music at the same time. Of course, that's only for when it's raining, we've got plenty of land to run and ride on. Did you know we've got our own stream and pond to fish in? Well, we have.'

Outside, the stables were bathed in security lights. Even though the woodwork was still receiving touches of paint, the brick buildings with their quaint dormer windows, and tubs and hanging baskets filled with winter pansies, made a pleasant scene. Soon, horses and Jim's pony would complete the picture.

'Isn't it exciting, Uncle Charlie? Look up there,' he said, pointing to the row of dormers. 'There's a big flat above the stables. It's got a huge bathroom and a kitchen. My dad says you can have it. You can even use one of the garages for your Merc. Isn't that great?'

'Great? Certainly interesting.' Watson had everything worked out. 'Damn the man,' he muttered softly. Of course, Watson knew he could never live anywhere near him.

'What was that, Uncle Charlie?'

'Quite a plan,' he said, as pleasantly as he could muster. 'I think we had better go now. The car's parked at the front of the house.'

'Don't you want to look at the flat?'

'Another day, Jim.' He started walking. 'Since you're wearing your coat, I assume you have nothing to go back inside for?'

Jimmy looked disappointed. 'I can't go without seeing Dad first. Are you sure you don't want to look at your flat? Dad will give us the key.'

'Look, Jim: say cheerio to your dad if you must. I'll wait in the car. Don't be too long, I have things to do.'

'Dad will take me home.'

'No, Jim. Your mother wants you home *now*.' They reached the house door they had come out of. 'Now hurry inside. I'll expect you at the front in two minutes.'

Feeling agitated, Charles sat in his Mercedes waiting for Jimmy. With Watson's plans being put into action so fast, it was not a good time to leave Bloomfield. By the time he returned from Bath, would Jim be living with Watson? Of course, it would begin with weekends, and then holidays, and then what?

Driving back home, Charles soon grew weary of Jimmy's chatter. It consisted entirely of praise for his dad. It seemed there was nothing Watson could not do, and nothing he would not buy him. Hardly surprising if his mind began to drift. Richard became uppermost in his thoughts.

'What's the matter, Uncle Charlie? Are you cross with me?'

'What was that, whippersnapper?'

'You're not listening to me.'

'Sorry, things on my mind.'

'You look sad. Is it because I wanted to stay a bit longer with my dad? I do love you, Uncle. I've missed you ever so much.'

Charles smiled. 'Well, that's nice to know. I guess I am sad, but not because of you.' He paused to concentrate on his driving. A sharp bend was just ahead and headlights told him a vehicle was approaching the corner too wide. 'Hold on!' He quickly braked, changed gear and drove close to the hedge. The car passed him by with a few inches to spare.

'Phew! That was close, Uncle Charlie.'

'Yes, some people think they own the road.'

'You mean like my dad? Sometimes he drives like that. He does own a lot of things, but I don't think they would sell him the road!'

Jimmy giggled. Charles laughed with him. It was good to know that, as far as Watson was concerned, Jim was in touch with reality after all.

'About what we were saying, Jim. I'm sad because of Richard. You see, he's still very ill. In fact, he's undergoing surgery right now. That crushed part of his leg has to come off. I'm driving back to Bath in the morning. I guess I'm going to miss you all.' Not only that, but now he knew what was happening on the home front, he was worried Watson would achieve a complete takeover in his absence. That was something he could not discuss with young Jim.

As soon as they entered the house, Jimmy ran to find his mother, a model of Robert's Daimler tucked under his arm. Charles hurried to his rooms, picked up his phone and rang the hospital. He was told that Richard was still in theatre.

June arrived with a tray. 'I've brought you up some supper.'

'Thanks, I could do with a bite to eat.' He took the tray from her and put it on the table. He took her in his arms. 'I'm so afraid of losing you.'

She rested her head on his shoulder. 'We won't let that happen.'

'I'm sorry, June, I shouldn't be leaving you again. We've had no time together for ages. But Richard needs me, especially now. I'm the closest thing to family that he's had for some years. I don't know how he'll cope. Psychologically, I mean.'

'Of course you must go. My time away has not been for such noble purposes. No, Charlie, don't be sorry, it's my fault we've been parted so long.' She looked up. Longing in her eyes told him what was to follow. 'Can we do a little catching up tonight, or are you too tired?'

Little was said during the following hour. Words were not necessary. The warmth of their love was fuelled by their need for closeness and comfort. Their desire for each other burst into the flames of passion they had shared on the last occasion. Was it only six weeks before? To Charles it seemed so much longer. Before long, something more than lust of the flesh took over: a deeper, earthier intercourse that had more to do with life and death, joy and pain, happiness and sorrow — a release of the anguish and fear lying hidden deep within the human heart. They finally climaxed, collapsed and slept; each with cheeks flushed and damp with raw emotion.

Chapter Twenty-Two

With Rosie catching up on her studies and Charles away in Bath, June was going to have to rely increasingly on her sister's help, especially with Jimmy's comings and goings. Peggy was most agreeable to working extra hours and so gave up her temporary evening job, serving in a pub, to accommodate the new arrangements.

Peggy volunteered to collect Peter and David when their school broke up for the holidays. But that was something June wanted to do herself. It was important to see her boys' teachers and discuss their progress. On the Sunday before Christmas they would all decorate the tree that Peggy was asked to choose and arrange to be delivered. June intended to allow a little shopping time with her boys before the following Thursday — Christmas Day.

She also decided that the boys should have a party to make up for having had a quiet Christmas the previous year. Although she did wonder if the real reason was to make up for her shortcomings as a mother — a constant cause of anxiety. Rosie's eighteenth was just days after, but that was going to be an adult celebration expected by the Rogers clan. The boys deserved to have something of their own where they could let off steam. Peggy agreed to help Annie with the cooking, run the boys around in her car, clean, shop and anything else to ease June's workload over the Christmas break, and to make Rosie's day special.

'You're a precious gem, Peggy,' June said, giving her sister a peck on the cheek. 'I don't know what I would do without you. From what Jimmy's told me, Charlie would be lost too.'

'I can assure you, June, he only gets a massage.' She laughed in her tinkling manner. 'Plenty of slap, but no tickle!'

Having spent longer than intended with Peggy, June arrived late for work. She entered Robert's office flushed and apologetic. He looked up from his desk, sent his secretary off to write letters he'd been dictating, and asked June to sit down. 'So what's the problem? Or have you decided to be mistress of the Old Rectory?' He grinned. 'That would solve all your problems at one stroke.'

June made herself comfortable in the chair already warmed by Judy. She could detect the secretary's perfume and vaguely wondered if Robert had given it to her — for services rendered? Had her perfume scented Robert's bed at his new house?

'I'm sure you're not short of a mistress or two for your new home, Robert,' she said, crossing her legs and straightening the skirt of her olive-green outfit.

He pushed back a heavy lock of hair that had fallen over his forehead, and regarded her closely. His eyes travelled from her legs to her breasts, where they briefly lingered, and finally upwards to take in her eyes. Sitting back in his padded chair, he rubbed a thumb into the hollow of his chin. 'Do I detect a hint of jealousy?'

She shook her head to free her mind of Robert's compelling gaze, and memories of his exhilarating performance on the Old Rectory's kitchen table. It was true: she didn't like to think of him sexually entwined with Judy or romping with any other woman.

'Ridiculous!' she snapped, far more brusquely than intended.

'Oh, really?'

She refused to be baited. 'Did Charles mention he was returning to Bath?' she asked in a businesslike manner.

Robert folded his arms and became more alert. 'As I remember, our conversation was somewhat brief. Returning to Bath? For good?'

June told him what had happened. To her surprise, Robert was remarkably sympathetic. He even had a few pleasant words to say about Charles.

'I have to admire that man's sense of duty towards a wounded fellow officer. To leave you once again for a sick man's bedside is friendship indeed.' He rubbed his thumb into his chin thoughtfully. 'They must be exceedingly close. At a time like this, I guess his friend needs a prop to lean on. Good man Charles. Stalwart and true.'

'I thought you hated him.'

'One has to give credit where credit is due. Charles has made clear his priorities and stuck by them. I admire that in a man.'

Smiling pleasantly, he leaned forward. 'Take it easy this week. There's to be no overtime. And take two full weeks off for the seasonal break.' He raised the palms of his hands. 'Longer if you need it. At the least until your lads are back at school. Isn't that what we agreed?'

Free of anxiety over domestic matters, June settled down to develop ideas she had been working on for the new project. Things were going smoothly with Robert. He was undemanding, kind and considerate. Surely this change in him must be an enlightenment akin to religious conversion? Of course, there was no doubting his exciting sexuality smouldering under the surface — it showed in his eyes and the way he looked at her — but he had it well under control. She was most impressed.

Because of Christmas activities Jimmy had no homework that week, so June took him to the Old Rectory on several evenings to swim and work out in the gymnasium. It gave her time to consult with Robert about a few designs she had developed. At least, that was the excuse she gave. But she was only too aware there was more to her visits than that.

Soon, decisions would have to be made. She needed to be certain that what she would be giving up to marry Charles, was in the best interests of all the family, especially Jimmy's.

Dressed in a turquoise robe over a slinky white swimming costume, she was sitting by the pool discussing a new type of ski suit with Robert when Jimmy came out of the pool to sit at his father's feet.

'Dad, are you coming to see me in the school play tomorrow afternoon?' His voice was a little hesitant as though fearful of disappointment. Clearly, his father's presence meant a lot to him.

But Robert's face lit up with interest. 'You're in a school play? I didn't know that. Your mother must have forgotten to tell me.'

'Didn't I mention it?' Of course she didn't! The implications of Robert turning up at Jimmy's school didn't bear thinking about. 'It must have slipped my mind,' she finished lamely.

'I most certainly will be coming, James,' Rob said, smiling broadly. 'I look forward to seeing you perform.' He put aside the papers he was holding and glanced meaningfully at June. 'It will give me a chance to meet my son's teachers. Time I took an interest in his education.'

She expected it to happen sometime. Jimmy had already been seen with Rob. Soon, the whole neighbourhood would know Robert Watson was Jimmy's father. So be it. Rumours had been circulating about her and Charles too. Hardly surprising since they shared the same house. Charles had not been pushing her into marriage, but perhaps....

'How long will Charles be away?'

Was Rob reading her thoughts again? 'I don't think even *he* knows that,' she answered, picking up a sketch and making a show of studying it.

Would he be away for weeks? Months? How long would it take for Richard to recover? With all of his injuries and operations, the poor man had a mountain of suffering to deal with. She turned to Jimmy. 'We have to go soon. Better get changed.'

When her son was out of the way, June turned to Robert. 'I'd rather you didn't consult Jimmy's teachers. It's just *not done* on those sort of occasions.' She tried to control her nervousness. 'But if you *must* see them, I'll arrange a private interview after the Christmas holidays.'

'Don't distress yourself,' he answered, taking hold of her hand and gently squeezing it. 'I'll just tag along to the concert as a friend of the family. That all right?'

But it turned out far from all right. They went to the school concert in good time and Robert insisted on sitting near the front in a prominent place. Jimmy took the lead in the play, and Robert — dressed casually but smartly in a tweed jacket over a soft jersey — sat looking every bit the proud parent. Obviously, Jimmy was pleased to see both his parents sitting there. June could see him whispering to his pals who were then looking and smiling in their direction. With few fathers being present, Rob — always a powerful presence in any situation — stood out and caused heads to turn. No doubt, mothers and teachers were wondering if he was Arthur's replacement. June caught a whisper from behind her: 'Didn't take her long.'

After the concert, June didn't want to stay around long enough to be questioned, but Rob was in no hurry to go. He was looking at children's work on display and chatting to other parents about how well it had all gone. June was on thorns waiting to hear the question, 'Which one is your child?'

It didn't take long for Jimmy to change and collect the Christmas items he'd made. He came running into the hall with a card in his hand.

'I made this for you, Dad.'

June took hold of Jimmy's arm. 'I'm expecting a phone call, Jimmy. We must be getting home now.' She quickly hurried him away.

Robert walked with them to the Rover. Jimmy clambered into the passenger seat and turned on the radio. Rob put his hand against the driver's door to stop June opening it.

'You know, June, if we got married, you'd be saved all this embarrassment,' he said softly. 'I have the wealth and power to override every kind of prejudice and snobbery.'

June didn't answer him, but she knew he was right.

'A new start for all of you,' he continued. 'Yes, and for me too. You and Jimmy could change my life completely. A happy family life for all of us. No pressure. Just think it over.'

June remained silent. This new Robert was perplexing. He was no longer demanding, but gently persuasive. Yes, a hard businessman, but surely he couldn't be the hard, conniving, unscrupulous bounder that Charles was making him out to be?

He pulled the car door open for her. 'Since you're collecting the other boys tomorrow, I'll come for James and Rosie. I want her to look at her room, and choose furnishings for it. We can go shopping and afterwards return for a swim.' He lightly kissed her cheek. 'Is that all right with you?'

Chapter Twenty-Three

Charles sat patiently waiting for the telephone receiver to be picked up at Bloomfield. He'd already tried to get through a couple of times. Eventually, he put down the phone and bit into the ham sandwich he'd made earlier that day. Sipping at the strong coffee he'd just percolated, he considered what he was going say to June. As usual, he had little to report about his friend, other than that his stump was healing and there'd been a general improvement. Emotionally, progress was almost non-existent, but that was something he preferred to keep to himself. Not wishing to diminish Richard in any way, he alone would share his comrade's heavy burden.

Today he was ringing early, so that after talking to June he could have a long chat with Jimmy. He was missing the boy and secretly hoped that Jim was missing him. Of course, he knew it was most unlikely: Jim had a father now taking considerable interest in him.

Was it genuine affection? Judging from their telephone conversations, June seemed to think so. He wasn't so certain. Watson was probably using the boy as a pawn to overcome June's marriage refusal. Of course, his reluctance to accept Robert's fatherly love for Jim could be plain jealousy. To have a child born of one's own seed was indeed something to be envied. With June so committed to her job, would fatherhood ever happen to him?

He bit savagely into his sandwich and chewed hard. Surely it was time he looked on the positive side of their relationship? He relaxed as he contemplated their good times together.

After several attempts, his phone call was answered. June's voice came down the line. 'Hello, is that you, Charlie?'

He swallowed his mouthful of chewed food. 'It certainly is.'

'Jimmy's here. He wants to talk to you.'

Charles was greatly uplifted. 'Nice to hear you, Jim,' he said as Jimmy's cheerful, 'Hello, Uncle Charlie,' met his ear.

Jimmy was soon talking excitedly about the school concert: 'It was great. I didn't forget my lines but some of the others did. It was ever so funny when the wings dropped off the Angel Gabriel. Some people started giggling but everybody clapped us at the end. I've made you a calendar, Uncle Charlie. I made a card for Richard — a get-well sort of card — and I made a big Christmas card for my dad. Dad said it was the best he's ever had. He came to see me in the play — wasn't that great? We've being seeing him every day — honestly, every day! I've been swimming in his pool while Mum's been working with him.'

'Sounds wonderful, Jim.' He said the words, but his heart was not in them. 'I'm sorry I missed the play. Swimming is good too. I'm glad you're getting plenty of exercise.'

'He's been ever so nice — my Dad, I mean. Rosie is going to choose furnishings for her own room tomorrow. You know, her bedroom at the Old Rectory. My dad says it's really a bedsit. The room's ever so big and she's got her own bathroom that's just like mine. Dad's buying....'

Charles waited for Jim to stop blabbing about Watson. Indigestion was giving him heartburn: his sandwich had been eaten too quickly, his coffee had been too strong, and now bile stimulated by ire and envy was rising in his throat.

'Do you know, Uncle Charlie, Aunt Peggy is getting us a tree? Dad's going to help us decorate it on Sunday. He's bought us lots of decorations. You know... shiny balls and trimmings for the tree, not the stuff you hang from ceilings and walls. Will you be here to help us?'

Charles was completely torn by his desire to be with the woman he adored and her family, and by duty and love for his friend. Would a few days away from Bath matter to Richard?

Maybe not. But he could not desert him at Christmas. Neither did he wish to be Watson's assistant. 'I'll see you all soon,' he said, 'but not in time to help with the tree... at least, I don't think so.'

'That's okay, my dad is helping us. He says he's never ever decorated a tree. Never even had a Christmas tree. Won't it be nice for him to share ours?'

Charles groaned within himself. 'It certainly will,' he lied.

'Hello, Charlie.' June was back on the phone and sounding worried. 'I'll explain everything when we can talk properly. Nothing has changed. It really hasn't. I love you. Only you. And you must stay with Richard as long as he needs you.'

Was June being honest with him? Was Watson taking the opportunity to creep more deeply into her family life? Be a dad to all of her children and a husband to her? Did she really want him back home, or out of the way? No... how could he think such things? Weary with worry over Richard as well as the situation at Bloomfield, he tried to listen more carefully to what June was telling him.

'Rosie has stopped asking after Richard. I guess she's trying hard to forget him. She's been working solidly all week. Jack has been helping her. Going to the Old Rectory tomorrow will be a bit of a day off for both of them.'

'I'm really sorry about Rosie. You know, June, I'm sure Richard is missing her almost as much as his leg. It's all so cruel. But, in the long run, perhaps it's for the best. At least, that's what I keep telling myself.'

Charles kept his unhappiness about Watson's involvement in their lives to himself. After a gentle love talk, followed by a forced jovial chat about Jimmy's concert, he put down the receiver. Sad of heart, he cleared away his unfinished meal, turned down the heating and returned to the hospital for yet more silent heartache.

On arrival at the Royal United, Charles received a message to call at the consultant surgeon's office. Mr Franks greeted him with his usual courtesy and invited him to sit down. While sucking occasionally at an unlit pipe, Franks informed Charles what he knew already: there was a satisfactory improvement in Richard's overall physical condition, but emotionally he was still a broken man.

'Commander Andrews is optimistic enough about adapting to a prosthetic limb, but his self-image has taken a hard knock. Gradual adjustment will take place, and hopefully he will see the amputation not so much in terms of disablement, and loss of manhood, but more as a challenge. That is, a hurdle to be overcome. With the right encouragement, I feel confident that he will regain his zest for adventurous living. After all, a man with his reputation and service record isn't going to allow such a setback to alter his whole way of life. No, there must be something else holding him back. A woman, perhaps?'

'Possibly,' said Charles.

'Mm, yes. I saw a lot of that sort of problem during the war. It works both ways. Women, especially young ones, sometimes find it as hard as the amputee to adjust to the new situation. But then, fear of a woman's rejection, however unfounded, can also be emotionally crippling.'

Charles knew the truth of what he was being told. It seemed to him that much of Richard's depression was due to his breaking off with Rosie. The self-imposed separation was making a void in his life to add to his physical one. Back at Richard's bedside, he decided to bring the situation out into the open.

'Richard, you're a damn fool,' he said forcefully, trying to look him in the eye but not succeeding. 'You have a girl who loves you, and you turn her away.' He threw up his hands despairingly. 'Why won't you reconsider?'

Clearly alarmed by this complete change of bedside manner, Richard stiffened. 'You don't understand.'

'Don't I? You're wrong there. I'm a bloody fool too. I've been allowing another man to steal away the only woman I have ever loved.' He shook his head. 'We're both bloody idiots.'

'Maybe, but what I did is best for Rosie.'

'How can you be certain of that?'

Richard slowly shook his head.

'Speak to Rosie on the phone. Give her a chance to love you, just as you are. The man you have always been — courageous, honest and true. What does it matter if part of you is being replaced? It does not change who, and what, you are.'

Richard looked down at the ungainly stump, misery turning his weathered face into a wrinkled mask. 'I don't want her to be hurt,' he muttered.

Uncomfortable at causing his noble friend further pain, Charles shifted in his chair. 'Neither do I. But I've just realised what *my* motive would be for turning away a young girl like Rosie — sheer panic that she would reject me because I'm not the man I used to be.'

Richard cringed. 'Perhaps you're right.'

'Let her back into your life, man. Give yourself something to hope for... something to get healed for.'

'You don't know what you're saying. She's just a kid. Okay, I'll be fitted up to walk again and I can use my brains and work. I know men with far worse injuries who lead whole lives, but it's not fair to saddle a young girl to an ageing cripple.'

'If you had seen Rosie last Sunday evening, you might question who is being fair.'

'I hear what you're saying,' said Richard, nodding his head. 'But I just don't know. Physically, I feel stronger and more able to cope, but....'

He sighed deeply, his broad shoulders drooping as though too weak for the burden he was bearing. 'Have I hurt her badly?' he asked, his voice full of remorse.

'You have the power to turn her tears to joy,' Charles told him, deliberately avoiding a direct answer. 'Leave it too long and who knows? She may become embittered, and who could blame her? She lost her father just a short while ago, now she has lost you. But, unlike her father who had no choice in the matter, you have turned her away. She feels rejected.'

Richard covered his face with his hands, his fingers taut as though wrestling with contradicting thoughts. After a while, he looked up, his face deeply strained. 'I really do love her. Is it too late to make amends?'

'I hope not, Richard.'

He hesitated, wondering how much to burden his sick friend with. 'Frankly, I don't know what's going on back home. I seem to be getting different messages. Robert Watson gazumped us on the Leisure Centre deal. and now it looks as though he's gazumping me on my own family. He's highly influential and has a great deal to offer. His ability to control people is quite remarkable. At the moment he seems to be acting Mr Nice Guy. I can sense what is happening with June and young Jim, but I don't know how Rosie will behave once she's under the power of Watson's charisma.'

'You must go home, Charles,' Richard said, now in command of himself. 'I'd feel better if you sorted things out. And my Rosebud, find out if she still loves me.'

Go home now? It was only five days to Christmas, a highly emotional time of the year. June would be missing Arthur and all the things they did together as a family. She would be even more vulnerable to Watson's magnetism, especially now he was worming his way into the affections of her family. June might be fooled into thinking Watson had changed, but he himself would take much more convincing. Yes, he needed to be at Bloomfield.

Even so, to leave Richard on his own at Christmas? That seemed like deserting a fallen comrade. He came to a decision. 'I'll go home tomorrow afternoon and see what's happening. I'll have a word with Rosie and see how she feels about you. The sooner you get back together again, the quicker your recovery. But I'll be back within a few days. You can count on it.'

The door opened and Sister Landers came breezing into the room. 'Right, Commander Andrews, time to get you bedded down for the night.'

Charles grinned. 'Bedded down? Now there's an offer you can't refuse!'

Richard smiled. 'You dirty old sea-dog. Shame on you!'

'Dirty?' said Charles, putting on a doleful expression. He turned to Sarah. 'Would you like to give me a bed bath, Sister?'

For the first time since his accident, Richard laughed.

'What a pair!' Sarah exclaimed, beaming with pleasure. 'Clear off, Captain Rogers, before I send for security!'

His heart gladdened, Charles left the hospital full of hope for Richard's complete recovery.

Chapter Twenty-Four

Rosie was pleased to accept Robert Watson's invitation to furnish a room for herself at the Old Rectory. Anything to take her mind off Richard Andrews was to be welcomed, but this was something really exciting: a suite of her own at a beautiful old house tucked away in the country. Somewhere she could go for a break, to swim, to exercise or just relax. A place with staff to cater for her needs. She would be meeting new people, influential friends and business associates of Robert Watson, and that could be good for career prospects. There was even a promise of learning to ride and going out with the local hunt. All this, and room for her family too!

A strange arrangement maybe, but she knew what was behind it. Robert intended marrying her mother, and that they all live happily ever after. Until then the Old Rectory was more of a country retreat, just one of the properties owned by her mother's boss, and no doubt an excellent investment that would accrue a bob or two over the coming years. It seemed to her that business was at the heart of everything that Robert Watson did. And why not? Love and lovers just caused misery. If Robert wanted to encourage and pamper her, she was game.

It was Saturday afternoon and Watson was driving her and Jimmy to the Old Rectory in his Daimler. Rob had sat her next to him and had been talking about the place. Now he was asking her many questions. He seemed to be particularly interested in her schoolwork.

'You seem to be doing rather well, Rosie,' he said, glancing in her direction. 'But designing is your future. I know what you can do, and what you are capable of achieving. How about you work for me after you leave school?'

Rosie was utterly thrilled, but she had no intention of showing it. 'Mum thinks it best if I go to Art College,' she said coolly.

'Maybe, but is that what you want to do? You know, with your talent and the opportunities I can give you, you don't need college. Your mother worked for me when she was just seventeen. Of course she has the gift, but it needed bringing out. Learning on the job is better than airy-fairy theoretical ideas. I taught her everything about fashion and the clothing industry. You don't get that from teachers who have never entered a factory or tried to sell their designs!'

Of course she had heard it all before, but she let him go on, enjoying the attention and the sense of power it engendered over her own destiny. 'I understand what you are saying, Mr Watson,' she said eventually, 'but I'm not sure if I want to follow in my mother's footsteps. I want to be me, and to do my own thing. Quite frankly, I don't like the way my mother works all hours and thinks of nothing but work. I don't want to be like her. After all, there is life beyond the workplace.'

'Call me Rob. Mr Watson is much too formal when we are sort of related.' He turned the car off the road and brought it to a halt, ready to turn into the drive. He let down his window. A touch of a button on a white post and the exquisite wrought-iron gates opened automatically. Robert turned and gave her a broad smile, making him look younger and devilishly handsome in a rugged kind of way. 'I know your mother works hard,' he acknowledged, 'but if all of you moved into this place, things could be easier for her and for all of you.'

He drove on through the gateway and pressed another button to close the gates. Jimmy was on the back seat telling her how it worked, but she had no inclination to listen to his prattling. The Daimler sped up the drive and then round to the garages. A man came running from a back entrance.

'Give her a wash and polish, Frederick,' Watson said, opening the car door. He turned to Rosie. 'You see, my dear, what money and influence can do for you? You are free to do the work you really enjoy. Ambition is a spur to getting on in life — a necessary driving force — but only a fool is enslaved by it.'

Rosie watched Jimmy running inside the house. 'Perhaps you should tell my mother that,' she said, when her brother was out of hearing.

'But June is not a slave to ambition, she is ensnared by conflicting emotions. If she were true to her fondest desires, then her life, and the lives of all of you, would be greatly enhanced.' He looked into her eyes and she felt a shiver of excitement race through her body. 'Not only can I fulfil your mother's ambitions, but I can give her everything — yes, my dear, *everything* — a spirited woman could possibly want and need.'

He shrugged off his statement with an exaggerated sigh, and waved a hand towards the house. 'James will be waiting for us. Come along, let's get inside.'

The pool looked inviting but Rosie, now dressed in a bikini, felt too self-conscious with Watson standing over her, to slip off the bathing robe hanging from her shoulders.

'I'm a bit tired,' she said, her eyes avoiding his almost-naked body. 'I'll just watch you two for a while.'

Jimmy had already jumped into the pool and was shouting for Rob to join him in the water. Robert put a hand on Rosie's shoulder. She felt its warmth connecting with her inner being — most disturbing. 'Drinks are on the trolley by the chairs,' he told her. 'Help yourself. Join us when you feel like it.'

Robert executed a smooth dive into the water and was soon racing with Jimmy, chasing after balls and splashing around. She watched them, struck by the strong resemblance to each other and by the obvious happiness they shared in each other's company.

Jimmy pulled himself out of the water and went off to get changed, saying he was going to use the gym with his dad. Robert swam a couple of lengths, burning up energy with strong strokes to exercise his muscles. Or was he showing off his body? He certainly had a physique to be proud of, especially for a man of his age and occupation. Rosie was most impressed.

Robert swung himself over the edge of the pool and came to join her, sitting in one of the comfortable upholstered loungers by the tropical plants. He gave himself a quick rub on a towel placed over a chair and then poured himself a drink, standing over her while he swallowed it down. He was obviously aroused and didn't mind showing it. She tried to keep her eyes averted.

He stood there until she looked up at him. Their eyes met. She felt drawn as though by a magnet. He put out a hand. She took hold of it and allowed herself to be pulled up. Her robe fell from her shoulders and her body gave a little shiver. He quickly pulled her closer to him. She felt the power of his masculinity brush against her body. Her heart was beating wildly within her breast. She closed her eyes and lifted parted lips in expectation of a kiss.

'Ah, there it is.'

She opened her eyes and saw Robert picking up a spider from a giant leaf just above and behind her.

'Little devil was about to drop on you.'

'Ugh!' She quickly moved sideways, tripping over a plant pot. 'Oh!'

Laughing, Robert caught her and held her to him. 'It can't hurt you.'

She felt more than a little foolish. Did he know what she had been expecting? Well, so what? He was holding her now, for longer than necessary. Mm... he felt pretty manly. In fact, quite impressive.

'Still tired?' he asked, letting go of her. 'Perhaps I should show you up to your room now. Don't forget you have work to do.'

As he released her, she looked up. His smile was enigmatic. Was he mocking her?

Perhaps her imagination had been carrying her into forbidden areas. Maybe he was an arrogant chauvinist, but there was definitely something mysteriously dark and earthy — sexually exciting — about Robert Watson. If she had wondered at her mother's infidelity resulting in the birth of her brother James, she did so no longer. This man could steal a woman's soul as well as her body, of that she was convinced.

Chapter Twenty-Five

After visiting the Royal United Hospital on Sunday morning
— he had to be certain that Richard was still all right to be
left — Charles tried phoning June to say he was returning to
Bloomfield. Since no one answered his call, he decided they
must all be at the church. He rang again before setting off,
but still there was no answer.

He hoped his arrival would be a pleasant surprise. He
most certainly did not want to barge into anything he
was not intended to be part of, nor did he want to witness
something not meant for him to see. A jealous lover
sneaking home was not the impression he desired to give.
Surely Watson would use anything to discredit him.

He quickly harangued himself for having such paranoid
thoughts. 'Get control of yourself, Charles,' he muttered to
himself. 'Didn't June say that nothing has changed? She
loves you, only you.' Ah yes, but....

He turned on the radio. Morning Service from a cathedral
was being broadcast. Mind eased by the choir's singing, he
set off, slipping easily through the gears. With reasonable
weather and little Sunday traffic to slow him down, he
made excellent progress. He saw a public telephone, but it
was occupied and two people were waiting. He drove on,
thinking to phone later. Pulling in at a transport café —
filled with black-leathered bikers smoking cigarettes, and
wolfing down bacon sandwiches with mugs of strong tea —
he tried again to telephone Bloomfield, but the phone was
out of order. He bought a sandwich to eat out, and happily
left the café to the bikers. After stretching his legs and
satisfying his hunger, he headed for home, determined to

phone June when he stopped for petrol. While his tank was being filled, he walked over to a telephone cubicle by the garage toilet.

'No use going there, mate,' said the petrol attendant, 'A gang of youths smashed the money box.'

Determined to let June know of his arrival, Charles stopped the car at the deserted railway station a short distance from Bloomfield. He stepped out of his Mercedes and headed for the red telephone box, diving into his pockets to collect a few coins. Fully prepared, he pulled open the door. A bent coin was jamming the telephone's money slot! Grinning sardonically, he threw up his hands in surrender. 'So be it!'

A few minutes later, he was parking his car on Bloomfield's drive and collecting his bags from the boot. It was late afternoon and light was shining out of a number of upstairs windows, casting shadows from the many trees surrounding the house and adding a frosty sparkle to tips of branches. The curtains were closed downstairs, but through a narrow break he could see a log fire burning in the lounge grate. He breathed in the sweet fresh air, joyful, even if a little apprehensive, to be home and with the woman and children he loved. Watson's car was not in sight, so maybe the tree decorating was finished and his rival had left to catch up on his workload.

Of course, since June's Rover was visible at the side of the house, the Daimler could be parked in one of the garages. But so what? The man would be going home before long. Using his own key, he entered by the front door. Music, laughter and shouts of excited boys met his ears. Home!

He put down his bags by the stairs and threw his coat over the gleaming banister — highly polished by sliding children from generations past and present. Smiling at his memory of hitting his bottom on the ornate newel post at the age of seven, he walked across the hall — decorated with swathes of ivy, holly, baubles and paper garlands —

and peeped around the door into the sitting room. A large Christmas tree was standing in the corner. Jimmy and Peter were sorting out the decorations piled on the cherry three-piece suite and the floor. Christmas cards, some still in their envelopes, were heaped on the glass-topped coffee table. Rosie and David were festooning the tree with a long string of fairy lights. A guarded fire was blazing in the hearth, bringing to life the tinsel and baubles with its flickering flames. It was a homely scene. He recognised Tom Jones singing, 'I'm never gonna fall in love again.' Since Rosie was joining in, he wondered if the record was her choice.

Peter looked up, a silver star in his hand and strings of tinsel hanging from his neck. 'Uncle Charlie!'

Talking all at once, the boys gathered around him. Charles ruffled their hair. 'Hello boys, good to see you again.'

Throughout the chat, some of it requesting news of Richard, he kept glancing at Rosie, trying to get a clue to her present emotional state. She turned her face away at the mention of Richard, but she appeared to be much brighter. How will she react to Richard wanting her back in his life? He decided to have a word with June before saying anything to her daughter.

'Rosie, where's your mother?' Charles asked her.

It was David who answered him. 'We couldn't find the lights we put on the garden tree. Mum went upstairs to look in the attic. I think her boss is with her. He's been helping with the tree.'

He could see Rosie watching to see his reaction. Although his facial muscles tightened, he managed to keep his voice calm. 'That's nice of him, especially since he's a busy man.'

Rosie said, 'He's really nice when you get to know him, and he's great with the boys.'

'Yes he is,' Jimmy piped up.

'We all went to the Old Rectory for lunch today,' continued Rosie, ignoring her brother's efforts to get Charlie's attention. 'We used his pool and gymnasium. The boys loved it.'

Charles had another cause to inwardly groan. Perhaps he should wait until June and Watson came down rather than go looking for them. While he was waiting, he gave a hand putting up trimmings at the top of the tree. After a while he decided to go to his rooms and put his things away.

As he walked up his stairs, he suddenly realised that the attic cupboards where the trimmings were stored, were off his hallway. He hesitated, fearing he would catch June and Watson together in a compromising situation, but then decided to go on and know the worst. The hall light was on, but there was silence and all the doors were closed. He breathed a sigh of relief. Then came a deep sense of guilt over his lack of trust.

After washing and changing, he went downstairs to wait for June to turn up. When he reached the first landing, he looked in the direction of June's bedroom and hesitated. No, he would not pamper to his fears. He ran quickly down the remaining stairs, intending to relax with a cup of tea while he pulled himself together. The door to the kitchen was partly open. June, looking flushed in a white fluffy jumper and blue ski pants, was sitting on a chair by the range. Watson, casually dressed in black cord jeans and roll-neck jumper, was standing behind her. He seemed to be picking bits from off her jumper. He then began massaging her shoulders. It was a cosy, intimate scene.

As Charles walked in, June looked up. Surprised, she rose from her chair to greet him.

'Charlie!' she cried, running to him with open arms. 'I thought you were in Bath.'

'So it seems.' He instantly regretted his petulance. 'Sorry,' he said, embracing her. 'Tiring journey.'

But the damage had been done. He felt June stiffen.

'You being absent,' she said pointedly, 'Robert is helping with the tree.' She moved away from him and grasped the top of her right arm. 'I pulled my shoulder getting the lights from the attic cupboard. Rob wanted to come upstairs to help me, but I didn't think you would want him to enter your space.'

'June, I'm so—'

'If I'd known you were coming home,' June cut in. 'I would have left the tree until tomorrow.'

'I tried phoning several times, but there was no answer.'

'We've all been to Robert's place for lunch. He's been incredibly good to the kids while you've been away. They've had a great time.'

Charles realised he had more to worry him than looking foolish: June's occasional indiscretions were nothing compared with the whole family coming under Watson's spell. It was all happening so quickly — too quickly! He turned to look at Robert, now sitting by the range, casually rubbing his thumb into his chin.

'Sorry I got the wrong impression,' Charles told him. But his apology was entirely for June's benefit.

Watson smiled benignly. 'That's okay, Charles. Quite understandable.'

'Well, that's sorted.' June said happily. 'I must pop upstairs and tidy myself up.'

The men watched her go and then glared at each other.

'Understandable indeed,' said Watson, his eyes narrowing. 'After all, I have made my objectives clear. I intend to be a father to my child, whatever it takes. And June will be my wife.'

'You may gazump me over property,' Charles retorted, 'but June is not a possession to be bought. She alone will decide whom she marries.'

Voices sounded in the hall. 'Come and help us, Uncle Charlie!' Peter was shouting.

'We want to put the lights on the garden tree,' said David, entering the kitchen. 'I can climb the ladder but mum won't let us do it on our own.'

The tense atmosphere was broken. Charles unclenched his fists and relaxed his muscles. 'Glad to give a hand. I know that tree well.'

'I'll help James and Rosie complete the indoor one,' Robert said, getting up. 'It will be my pleasure.'

It took an hour to get the lights sorted, tested, and then hung on the fir that stood close to the house in a corner of the front garden. June suggested they all put on their coats, light the lanterns made by David and Peter, and sing carols under the tree as they'd done when Arthur was still with them.

It was a beautiful, if poignant occasion. June was a little tearful and Charles put his arm around her, mutual grief and renewed love drawing them together. He glanced at Rosie with concern: Robert was taking an opportunity to cuddle her while they shared a carol sheet. Next time he looked at Rosie, she had her head on Rob's shoulder. What now Richard's chances of getting back with his Rosebud? That certainly would not be in Watson's interests.

When Watson announced his departure after hot punch had been served in the hall, Charles was greatly relieved, that is, until Rosie said that she was going with him.

'Robert has asked me to help him. He's planning a party for his staff on Christmas Eve. It's at the Old Rectory. A sort of house-warming party.'

Watson, who was leaning on the newel post of the banister, smiled broadly and waved his empty punch glass. 'It will give Rosie a chance to know me better, and to meet my top staff. Of course, I expect you to come to the party, June.' He turned to Charles. 'If you are not escaping to Bath, you are welcome to join us.' He put down his glass on the hall table. 'Come along, Rosie,' he said, grasping her arm and leading her towards the front door.

'Don't wait up, Mother, I have my key,' Rosie called back, hastily fastening the buttons of her coat.

Watson ushered her out. The outer door closed, snapping the lock shut.

What bothered Charles more than anything was that June did not object to Rosie's close involvement with Watson. When they were alone in the kitchen, preparing supper for them all, he decided to tackle her about her easy-going attitude.

'Knowing him as you do,' he told her, while slicing bread for sandwiches, 'how can you let that man spend so much time with Rosie?'

'He's only taking a fatherly interest in her,' she said, buttering the bread. 'It's remarkable how much he's changed. You don't really know him, Charlie. He's not the man he was.'

It was going to take more than a few days of gentle behaviour towards June and her family to convince Charles. 'I'm sorry, I don't believe it. People like him don't change that easily. He's deceiving you. All of you!'

She looked at him dolefully. 'How can you, of all people, say that?'

A stab of pain shot through his heart. Of course, it was true that he was once a disgrace to his family. Not only that, but, when intoxicated, he had treated June with utter contempt, sexually assaulting her and exposing her to downright humiliation. His father had caught him pinning her down, half-naked, on the sitting room floor. But afterwards, he'd gone through a profound experience — some might call it religious — and his life had never been the same again. As far as he could discern, Robert Watson had not changed inwardly. He was still a cheat and a liar — a positive danger to innocent women. But there was no way he would be able to convince June of his suspicions.

'You are right. I am not in a position to judge anyone,' he answered, picking up two plates of sandwiches and carrying them to the lounge. The boys were watching a quiz programme on a new, expensive colour television, the screen of which was the largest he had ever seen. Bought by Watson? He didn't ask.

It was half-past ten before he went upstairs to his bedroom with June beside him. Rosie was still out and he was worried about her. He wanted to drive over and collect her, but June would not allow it.

'I know what it's like planning things with Rob,' she said, walking over to the bed and stripping off her jumper. 'Anyway, it's good for Rosie to have something to keep her from thinking about Richard.'

Charles pulled off his chunky woolly and unbuckled his belt. 'How's Rosie been? Is she still fretting?'

'As far as I know, she's put him from her mind. Perhaps just as well. Let's face it, they've only known each other a few months. As Richard realised, she's far too young to be tied down. It was a hard choice for him, and painful for both of them, but he made the right decision. He's a lovely man. I hope he'll find someone nearer his own age to love. Rosie mentioned a friend of his. A nurse called Sarah? An old girlfriend, apparently. Rosie seems to think they still cared for each other. Now, being a nurse, she would be an ideal wife for Richard.'

'June, Richard will make a full recovery, he doesn't need a nurse for a wife. Yes, he will have some disablement, but not enough to prevent him leading a normal life. As for him marrying Sarah, forget it. Rosie has got it wrong.'

'Maybe, but it could come to something. She must be of a similar age to Richard.'

Charles was now down to his underwear. This was not the way he wanted to begin their evening together, but he couldn't let the matter drop. 'Why does Richard's age concern you? The difference in age between Rosie and Richard is not as great as it was between you and Arthur.' He thought it better not to remind her that she was twelve years younger than him.

'That's true, but she's over Richard now.' June turned her back to him. 'Undo my bra please, Charlie. My shoulder still hurts.'

'Gladly,' he said, pleased at the intimate contact. But being reminded about her shoulder brought Watson's massaging technique to mind. He struggled to rid himself of the unwanted image.

'Anyway,' she continued, 'Richard made it clear he wanted to end the relationship.'

Pulling off his socks and tossing them into the laundry basket along with his other soiled clothing, Charles told June what had happened, and what Richard had said. 'You see, Richard needs Rosie in his life. Believe me, I've known that young man a long time and I know he's sincere in his intentions.'

June was now completely naked and sitting on the bed. She sighed deeply. 'Rosie has been really hurt by all this. Suppose Richard changes his mind again?'

He moved beside her waiting body. 'Life is about risk,' he told her softly, nuzzling her ear. 'All I ask is that Rosie talks to him. Just to hear her voice would be a tonic.'

She mewed with pleasure as he wrapped his hands around her breasts. 'You can talk to her,' she murmured. 'Can't stop you anyway. But test the ground before you tell her Richard wants to speak to her. I don't want either of them hurt.' She threw herself backwards on the bed. 'Oh Charlie, forget about Richard and Rosie. Let's get on with it.'

He stretched himself beside her. He was ready and his need was great, but he was determined not to rush things. He wanted them both to enjoy every nuance of his love-play.

It was a while before the clock in the downstairs hall began striking twelve. Charles sighed happily. They had come together and June's dramatic climax had matched his own. Not wanting to disturb the precious moment, he relaxed with her straddled across his sweat-drenched body.

Light suddenly moved across the ceiling, and Robert's Daimler could be heard slowing in front of the house.

'Thank God, she's home.'

June rolled over and stretched out on the bed. 'It is late, but she probably had a meal before working. Maybe a swim too. You worry too much, Charlie.'

'It's not just Rosie that's worrying me.' He sat up. 'The truth is, I'm jealous of Rob. I can't help it. He has so much to offer you. He does something for you that's beyond my comprehension.'

'Forget him. Please don't spoil things. It's been wonderful. Now you're dragging Robert into bed with us.'

He lay by her side and pulled her to him. 'Sorry,' he said, rubbing his cheek against her soft, curly hair.

But the irritating doubt scratching at his heart refused to be appeased. Watson was making unbelievable advances. From the moment he knew about Jimmy, he must have been planning the family takeover just as keenly as a highly profitable business transaction, with nothing left to chance. Richard's accident must have been a godsend — no, dammit, the luck of the Devil! Robert Watson's relentless pursuit of his goal would go on, picking up speed as June and her family became dizzy with it all. How long before Jimmy was known as James Watson. And June?

'Come on, Charlie,' she was murmuring, her hand endeavouring to revive his flagging ardour.

It was no use; his body was refusing to cooperate with June's sexual advances. How could it? How could he possibly keep his mind on another romp under the sheets when his whole future happiness was at stake? He had to know where he stood or there would be no peace.

'Marry me, June. Please say you'll marry me. Let's make it soon.'

'Can't we stay as we are, just for a bit longer?'

'I can't go on not knowing any more. I thought I could stand back and wait, but I was wrong. Waiting like this is agony.'

She sighed. 'Our lives are so unsettled.'

Though fearful of the answer, the question had to be asked. 'Do you intend living at the Old Rectory?'

'I'm not planning to. But that's what Robert wants… he's made that clear.'

His arm tightened around her. 'Don't do it, June, please don't do it.'

'I don't want to. But, I must admit, when I see Jimmy and Robert together — they really are close, you know — well, living at the Old Rectory seems the right thing for us to do. I'm just stringing Robert along at present, hoping to see a way ahead.' She rubbed her face against his shoulder. 'Tell me to give up my job and I'll do it, but it won't stop Rob being Jimmy's father. Jimmy needs stability. Robert can give him that, and more, especially if we all live together. He's offered me a large apartment at the Old Rectory. A whole wing. My relationship to Rob doesn't have to be a sexual one. Nothing has happened while you've been away.'

'June, you're kidding yourself,' he told her, angry at her naiveté. 'He's out to get you for his wife. But you can't get saddled to a man because of one mistake. The boy would have been Arthur's if Watson hadn't….'

He hesitated. 'Sorry, I didn't mean to bring that up again. But I'm sure Jim will be just as happy if you marry me. I wouldn't stop him visiting Watson.'

'You have no idea what's happening at the Old Rectory, or you wouldn't treat Jimmy's relationship with Robert so lightly.'

He most certainly was not treating the relationship lightly! He knew exactly what was taking place in the lion's den. But he wanted to hear June's distorted view of the man's intentions. 'Enlighten me, then,' he said.

Wrinkling her brow, June explained Robert's intense fascination with his son. 'And Jimmy is responding as though they had been in close relationship for years, instead of just a few concentrated weeks. It's uncanny, Charlie, it really is. Jimmy is picking up Robert's mannerisms, even that way he has of frowning. You know... sort of narrowing his eyes under those heavy dark brows. The only difference is that Rob uses it to some purpose, Jimmy does it to copycat or impress.' She pointed to her chin. 'Haven't you seen him rubbing at his dimple? I'm sure he wants to make it into a deep hollow just like his father's.'

Charles winced. Jim was slipping away from him, and it hurt badly. 'I suppose wanting to identify with his real father is important to him.'

'Robert is changing too. He's becoming softer, less aggressive... yes, kinder. You would hardly believe it.'

He certainly didn't believe it. Watson may have been better at disguising his leopard spots, but his claws and teeth were not so easily hidden for those with eyes to see.

'He plays with Jimmy like a kid,' she continued. 'And yet, sometimes he talks to him as though he were his most valued apprentice. You know, passing on little gems of knowledge about the business world. How to be successful. He's even bought him his own portfolio of shares so that he can follow the market trends.'

'Good heavens! He really does want an image of himself.'

'You can say that again! James — Robert hates him being called anything different — has become a spur to even greater achievement. Robert sees marriage to me, and James following in his footsteps, as the foundation of a new dynasty. Can't you see, Charlie? His present scheming goes beyond empire building. Power and authority are no longer enough. Robert wants to ensure his own immortality through flesh and blood too. Jimmy has given him a whole new view of life. One that includes genuine affection. Love now has meaning for him. Love can change people. Maybe that is what is happening to Robert.'

Charles then understood how hard the battle was going to be. Watson had convinced June that he was a changed man. The pressure on her would be gentle and subtle, until she fell into his arms without realising what was happening. No doubt, Rob's methods in the bedroom — still an unknown to him — would continue to be part of the man's allure. Not that he thought anything had happened in that department while he'd been away… surely that was part of his cunning too. What a devious devil. But, agony though it may be, he would not give in. Not until June wore the other man's ring.

Chapter Twenty-Six

While June was shopping with her three boys, Charles decided to pack the Christmas presents he'd bought for the family in Bath and put them under the tree. Rosie walked into the dining room with a cup of coffee in her hand.

'Like a coffee, Charlie? Annie's made a fresh pot.'

'Thanks, I'll finish this first. Peggy brought me one ten minutes ago.'

'Doing a good job there,' she said, sitting on an arm of the chair by the fire. 'I like the paper.'

'Bought it in Bath,' he said, tying a fancy bow with red ribbon. 'Just one more and that's it.'

'Very swish!'

'So, you've been helping Watson with his party planning.'

'Robert appreciates it.'

'You get on well with him, I can see that. He doesn't make too many demands on you, does he?'

'Demands? What exactly do you mean by that?'

He looked up and saw that she was blushing. The frown on her face suggested anger but there was embarrassment too, as though being caught out like a naughty child.

'Oh, you know,' he said casually, 'expecting too much of you. After all, you are working hard at your studies.'

'I'm not a kid, Charlie. I enjoy helping Robert. She put her cup down, fell on her knees and gave the fire a poke. Sparks flew up the chimney. 'I'll be eighteen next week.' It was a statement of fact, clearly meant to bolster her right to choose the way she spent her time.

'Indeed. You will come of age, and have the right to vote and to marry without consent.'

She started to poke the fire again. 'Huh! Who wants to be tied down to a man for life? Better to be free.'

'Some might see marriage in a different light. Of course, I know only too well how being tied to the wrong person can be destructive. But surely, with the right partner, it can bring a new kind of freedom and security.'

'Oh, really? And how can you be sure you have found the right partner? You fall in love?' She sat back on her haunches, gazing at the leaping flames. 'Maybe the person you love doesn't love you.'

Charles tied the bow on his last parcel and placed it with the others spread over the dining table. Moving to the fireplace, he picked up the little hearth brush and pan, swept up the dying sparks littering the patterned tiles and tossed them back onto the fire. He then placed the fireguard, which Rosie had removed, back into its rightful place. He sat on the chair by Rosie. 'Do you want to know how Richard is?'

She didn't look up. Her eyes were fixed on the fire as though mesmerised by the flickering of the flames. 'Robert said to forget him. That's best isn't it? He doesn't want me. If he really loved me, he wouldn't have sent me away. Robert said so. I don't care about Richard any more,' she said adamantly, but a tear rolling down her cheek told him otherwise.

'He nearly died, Rosie. He didn't want you to die with him. He loves you too much to ruin your life. He's recovering now and would like to talk to you. If he rang you, would you speak to him?'

'I don't know. Does he really want to talk to me? Does he want me back?' There was a hopeful note in her voice. Then she sighed and a slight tremor crept over her. 'No, Robert was right. I can't let Richard hurt me again. It's over. Too late to start again.'

'Too late? Are you going out with someone else? Perhaps young Jack?'

'No, but I've a new life now. I'm going to live with Robert.' She caught his shocked expression. 'Not what you're thinking. I'm going to live in his house as a sort of daughter. Jimmy goes all the time now. Mother takes Jimmy and sometimes stays to work with Robert. David and Peter like going there, but, as you know, they'll be going back to school in a couple of weeks. I think you should know, Uncle Charlie, I'm finishing with education. Since I'm going to work for Robert, qualifications are not relevant.'

'All rather sudden, isn't it?'

'I guess so. Robert's helped me sort things out. Why struggle with maths and exams when he can teach me the things that really matter? I'll be earning good money too. The prospects are fantastic. Much too good to miss.'

The situation was far worse than Charles had imagined. Not wanting to antagonise Rosie, he decided to discuss the matter with June before saying anything about Robert to her daughter.

'I see,' he said. 'Well, you seem to have made your mind up. I guess the coming year will see a lot of changes. Richard is on the mend now and we can start discussing a joint venture again. Yes, a new life can be quite exciting, even if a little scary.'

Rosie didn't comment. Was she listening?

'Jack Cummings seemed keen on getting you through your exams with flying colours. Does he know of your decision?'

'Not yet.' The words were spoken with a hint of remorse.

'He seems a pleasant young man. Did you say he's going to be a teacher?'

'Yes. He's totally committed. I don't know if he'll want to see me again now I'm giving up school.'

'I'm sure he will. It's good to keep up friendships. How's that Paul guy doing? Oh yes, and Steven Blake. Is that his name?'

'The last time I saw Paul was once too many. As for Steven Blake, I saw him with Robert at the Old Rectory, but he was too busy to speak to me. He's always too busy.'

'I suppose it's the nature of the work, plus his demanding boss. Rob's a bit of a slave driver. Your mother is a good example of being driven.'

'Huh, haven't you noticed? My mother drives herself. She always has done. I know she wasn't far away when I was little, but we didn't see much of her, at least to talk to. Having a nanny somehow distances you from your parents, don't you think?'

'I never had a nanny, so I can't really comment. Arthur used to give me a lot of time when I was young. He understood me.'

Biting her lip, Rosie looked down at her hands. 'My father understood me, too. All of us really, including Mother.' Sniffing, she rubbed under her nose with the back of a hand. 'It's nice when someone understands and cares.'

'I care, Rosie. Not having children of my own, I guess I don't always understand you. But if you give me a chance, I can learn to empathise with your problems. I do love you, you know.'

'I love you too,' she said, fiddling absentmindedly with her bracelet. 'You're like my dad in many ways.'

He took hold of her hands. 'Then I hope you know I have your interests at heart.'

She nodded. A tear streamed down her face.

He pulled a handkerchief from his pocket. 'Here, use this.' He gave her a few moments to regain her composure. 'I guess I was away when you needed a shoulder to cry on,' he said gently. 'I'm sorry about that.'

She nodded and handed him back his hanky. 'Thanks.'

'I wonder how your father would advise you now?'

She dropped her eyes. 'I don't know.'

'Think about it.' He sat back in his chair. 'I'll be seeing Richard again shortly, and I might stay with him for a week or two when he's back home. In any case, I have to visit Bath from time to time.' He put a card in front of Rosie. 'This is Richard's home address and telephone number. The hospital number is there too. The other side gives the details of my flat in Bath. You can always reach me somewhere. I guess I know where to find you.'

Rosie continued to look down — mulling over what he'd told her? Then she suddenly sat up and stuck out a determined chin. 'I'm going to visit Robert's company this afternoon. I'll be helping to entertain his staff at the party.' She spoke with a confidence that didn't ring true.

He smiled at the sudden change. Such guts and determination! 'Quite the lady of the manor.'

Her eyes flashed. 'You're laughing at me!'

'Now why would I do that? No, it's a good thing for you to see Watson's people at work, and at play. They're probably expected to do each just as efficiently. You're doing a good job there, Rosie, but don't work too hard.'

Snatching up the card, Rosie stood up. 'I have a lot to do. I must go to my room,' she said, heading for the door. She stopped and turned to face him. 'Tell Richard....' Her voice was choked with tension. 'I... I....'

Charles rose from his chair, but she turned and ran.

He watched her disappear up the stairs. Without doubt, her feelings for Richard had not gone away. He must give her time. They all needed time to sort out their emotions, but Watson had no intention of giving any of them space for reflection — he was out for the kill! Not only was he taking advantage of the situation regarding Richard, but also, at this most sentimental time of the year, he was increasing the pressure. They were all being swept along on an emotional tide of his scheming. Robert Watson a new man? Never!

When Charles returned upstairs to his rooms, he found Peggy busy cleaning his kitchen. She asked after Richard, showing considerable concern about his amputation.

'I've been thinking about him a lot,' she said. 'Not good to be stuck in hospital at any time, but it always seems worse when folk are enjoying themselves at parties.' She wiped over the table. 'I'll just put the pots away and that's it in here.'

'Have a coffee, Peggy,' he said, collecting two mugs before she returned them to the cupboard.

'Thanks, Charlie, I could do with a sit down. I've been on my pins all morning.'

Charles put the kettle to boil. 'I guess it's a busy time of the year for you and Annie. What with Christmas, Rosie's party, and New Year celebrations.'

'What are you planning, Charlie? Will you be here for the kids' holidays?'

He shrugged his shoulders. 'It depends on what June and her brood are doing. I will be visiting Richard part of the time — that is certain.'

'When he gets home, could he do with a helper about the place? Maybe a bit of massage too? It would help him relax. I'd be pleased to work for him until he's active again.'

'What a grand idea. I'll ask him.' The kettle boiled. Charles made the coffee and passed a mug to Peggy. 'I would feel much better leaving him in safe hands.' He grinned. 'A massage, eh? If you need a bit of practice, I'm game.'

While Peggy was working on his back, relaxing taut muscles, he asked her what she was doing over the Christmas period.

She gave his bottom a squeeze. 'Nothing special, but I'm open to offers.'

'Tempting, but haven't you got things to do here?'

'Not after today: Annie will be here and her granddaughters are coming to help out. June's given me time off for good behaviour.'

'Really?'

'Yes. I was surprised myself. I thought I would be working. That's what we planned. Can't complain, she's paying me full wages.'

'I meant about Annie's granddaughters. I didn't know she had any.'

'Ruth and Lisa. They're her daughter Jenny's girls. The eldest must be about twenty, and I think the younger one is fifteen. They were brought up by their aunt. Jenny was always off with some feller or other. She's living in Spain at present.'

'What about the girls' father?'

'I doubt if even Jenny knows who fathered her children. If you know what I mean. The eldest is a real good-looker — very striking. She's not a bit like her mother.'

'If I remember right, Jenny was a pretty kid.' Charles was thinking back some years to when she had obliged him with a few energetic sessions in the kitchen quarters.

'Knowing you, Charlie, I'm sure your memory will be accurate where pretty blondes are concerned. What I meant was, Ruth is a tall, dark-haired, dark-eyed beauty. Elegant too... does a bit of modelling. Not having a full-time job, she does a bit of all sorts to earn money for clothes and necessities. Anyway, you'll see Ruth yourself tomorrow.'

'I doubt it. I'm going to Bath for a couple of days. Peggy, I was thinking, would you like to come with me and meet Richard? You know, talk to him about what you're proposing. I'll be back Wednesday evening to go carol singing with the kids.'

'Alone with you and your Merc? How can a lady refuse?' she joked. 'Seriously, Charlie, I'd love to. I think Richard is a lovely guy.' She started on his legs, her hands moving in long strokes. 'I had a few dances with him at your party. Hard to think of such an active man losing a limb.'

'Is it going to distress you? I mean, seeing him as he is now?'

'Oh, no. Doesn't make him less of a man. I once went out with an ex-pilot with two stumps for legs — but he sure knew what do with his third one! If Richard's forgotten how, I could extend my massage technique to give him a reminder.'

Charles burst out laughing. 'Peggy you are incorrigible. You'll kill the poor bugger!'

She slipped her hand under Charlie's hips. 'Would you like a demonstration? It is Christmas, and I'm offering.'

He pushed her hand away. 'Nice thought, Peggy. I'm tempted, but no can do.'

By the time Peggy had finished, Charlie was feeling completely calm. He took her out to lunch and made plans for going to Bath early the following day.

Charles dropped Peggy off in town. She said she had shopping to do before returning to Bloomfield. 'You don't have to wait, Charlie,' she said, getting out of the Mercedes, looked on by a young couple admiring the car. 'You can only park here for twenty minutes. Anyway, June might be waiting for you.'

Charles grinned: Peggy was giving the ogling couple a pride-of-ownership smile. But she deserved more than crumbs from her sister's table. As much as he would miss her, working for Richard in Bath might open up better opportunities for a talented, hard-working woman like Peggy.

When he arrived home, the Rover was parked in the drive. As he entered the hall from the porch, he heard June speaking to Helen on the telephone.

'Are you sure, Helen? I'm perfectly happy for Bobby and Michael to come here, you know.' She looked up and gave Charles a little wave. 'All right then, if you insist. He's just walked in. I'll ask him.' She covered the mouthpiece with her hand. 'Charlie, Helen would like you to take the boys over there. I could take them, but she wants to ask you about Richard. Do you mind?'

He did mind, but at least it meant the boys would not be going to the Old Rectory. It was bad enough that Rosie would be there most of the day and night. 'Of course not,' he said. 'I'll take them now.'

When the Mercedes swept into Helen's drive, Michael was waiting by the open front door. The three boys hurried inside, but Charles hung back. Helen appeared, dressed in blue and looking as beautiful as ever. She was wearing tight-fitting ski pants with a clinging jumper, showing off her figure to good advantage. Her make-up was delicately applied and her blonde hair brushed casually over her shoulders. 'Come in, Charlie, I want to know how Richard is doing,' she said, her big violet-blue eyes and innocent smile enticing him as always.

He could hardly discuss his friend's condition on the doorstep. 'Thanks, Helen, but I can't stop more than a few minutes, June will be waiting.'

While he was drinking a cup of tea, he told her about Richard's medical problems. She was sympathetic. 'Poor man, what a terrible thing to happen to such an intrepid adventurer. You know, two years ago I really fell for him. He made himself available while we were on that sailing holiday. But it came to nothing. I still like him a lot, though. How will he manage on his own?'

'He'll get help while he's recuperating, but once he's fitted up he'll be able to do most of what he's always done.'

'Good for him,' Helen said. 'He's a man to be admired.'

'I have to agree with you,' he said, putting down his empty cup. 'Thanks for the tea, but I must be off. Lots to do.'

She stood up with him. 'Well, if you must....'

He came to a sudden decision. 'Helen, there's something that needs to be said.' He sat down again. 'It shouldn't take long.'

'Sounds serious, Charlie.' She sat looking at him with her bright eyes wide open. So childlike!

He did not want to hurt her, but there was no easy way to be honest. 'We've had some good times together,' he said, leaning forward in his chair, 'but it's strictly above board friendship from now on.' He watched her eyes tighten in a hurt expression. 'I'll not be the cause of trouble between you and George.'

'You, Charlie, be the cause? But I told you about—'

'I did not suggest you get a divorce, Helen,' he cut in sharply. 'What's more, I doubt the letter you read was any more than what George told me it was.'

'You men all stick together,' she said angrily. She jumped up and started pacing the floor. 'I would show you the letter if George hadn't put it on the fire. He complains about what I spend, and says I keep him working to pay for everything. But did he tell you that I have money of my own? That's why he doesn't want a divorce. It's nothing to do with the children.'

She sat down again and looked at him accusingly. 'Anyway, why should you concern yourself? You have June back now.' A devilish little smile curled the corners of her mouth. 'Or do you? From what I've heard, she'll be moving in with that rag-trade millionaire, Robert Watson, any time now. It's the hot gossip of the neighbourhood since they went to school together. Not to mention they were seen buying a super-duper bed for the master bedroom! Jimmy was with them. You ask him. Ask him too what else they've been doing. She's practically living with the man already. Now everyone knows that James is Watson's son, and poor Arthur was made a cuckold of. Where does that leave you, Charlie?'

Charles stood up, walked from the room, and to the front door. Helen was racing after him. Without looking back or listening to what she was calling to him, he slipped into his Mercedes and drove back to Bloomfield. It was hard to put Helen's bitter remarks from his mind. Who indeed was at fault in their marriage? Who was telling the lies? Were June and Watson being gossiped about? Both of them being well known, why not?

Watson going to Jim's school had been a master stroke. June was being drawn even more deeply into a relationship already bound by her child and by her work. Helen was right, where did that leave him? Then there was Rosie to think about. Poor child, caught in the middle of an emotional maelstrom. Why, oh why did he encourage June to work with Watson again? But then, with Jimmy involved, a renewed relationship was inevitable. Even if the whole family moved away, with Watson being in the public eye, his striking looks would, sooner or later, have been matched with young Jim's. No, June must have freedom to be herself, and he had to be strong and fight Watson for all their sakes.

He found June in the study, signing cheques. She looked up as he entered. 'You took your time. How's Helen?'

'Can we leave her for a moment? I must talk to you about Rosie.'

'If you think so. We'll go to the sitting room and sit by the fire. Might as well be comfortable.'

Charles told June everything that Rosie had told him about school and working for Rob. 'And she's planning to live at the Old Rectory with him. I somehow don't think Arthur would approve.'

June was shocked. 'I had no idea about her leaving school, she's been working so hard with young Jack. What could have changed her mind? As for living with Rob, what sort of reputation will that give her? What is Robert thinking of to ask a young girl to live alone with him?'

'I could give a few good reasons, and I don't like the one uppermost in my mind.'

'I think you're wrong there. I'm sure he sees her more as a daughter. You know, Jimmy's big sister. Of course, he wants us all there. Perhaps he sees this as a step along the way.'

'And when are you and the rest of your family moving into the Old Rectory? From what I've heard today, the two of you are already doing the "proud parents" thing. Young Jim is just being used and you can't see it.'

'You're wrong. Robert genuinely loves Jimmy. You should see them playing together. If you had a child, you would know how Robert feels for his son. He's just chuffed at suddenly finding himself a family man. Now he's building up a future for himself and James together. It's quite understandable if he wants me with him too. Apart from being the mother of his child, he loves me just as much as you do.'

More excuses for Watson! Why? She of all people must know how devious the man could be. He could only see one answer.

'And do you love him?' he demanded. 'Is that what you're really trying to tell me? You fancy yourself as Robert's wife? No more guilt over your indiscretions? Free to have Rob's lips all over your body with his piledriver at work day and night?'

June's eyes turned wild. 'That's horrid!' she cried. 'How can you say such things? Rob hasn't touched me while you've been away, not that we were short of opportunity. You know I don't love Robert. Nor do I intend to marry him.'

'So you tell me.'

He knew he was being petulant, driven by jealousy. He calmed himself. 'I'm sorry, what I said was unkind. It's just that... never mind.' He flicked his hand as though to brush away the picture — June entwined with Watson — that lingered in his mind. 'But it's Rosie I'm concerned about. Isn't it bad enough *you* being under Watson's spell? I can see the opportunities she will get at the Old Rectory, but what does Watson want in return? Your daughter's body, as well as her soul?'

'You're being ridiculous and you know it. I want Rosie to finish school, but I can't make her if she would rather be independent.'

'She won't be independent under Watson's influence. You know how he is with you. What are you thinking of, June? How long will it be before he gets her into his bed?'

'That's stupid.' She thrust an accusing finger at him. 'Admit it, Charlie, you're jealous of Robert.'

'Do I have something to be jealous about?'

Her eyes flashed. 'I'm tired of your jibes,' she told him, bending forward with hands over her face. 'I'm trying to think things through, and I can do without you getting at me all the time.'

He was overcome with regret. Of course she was right — he was getting at her. He should be easing her burden, not adding to it. He touched her shoulder. 'Sorry,' he apologised. 'It's just that I'm fearful for you and your family.'

'There's no need to be,' she said, speaking from under her hands. 'I have no intention of doing anything in a hurry.'

'Just as well you're getting a break from me for a couple of days. I'm off tomorrow to see Richard. Peggy is coming too.'

June sat up straight. 'Peggy is going with you to Bath?'

'She may be working for Richard when he gets home. She'll do him good.'

June looked at him accusingly. 'And does she do you good, Charlie?'

'Actually, yes she does. She gives me a splendid massage, and makes me laugh. She's good company when you're away. I can assure you, June, that's as far as the attraction goes.'

'Oh really? From what I've heard, Helen and half the women at the badminton club are drooling over you. Sister

Sarah and other old flames are blazing away at Bath. Angela is ready to give you a bit-of-what-you-fancy anytime you're hungry. And my sister is having a pummelling session as soon as I'm out of the way! And I was feeling so bad about me and Robert.'

'Well, perhaps you have something to feel bad about — I don't.' He said the words, but he knew they were not entirely true. It had been difficult to subjugate an uninvited arousal when thoughts of Helen's seduction techniques popped into his mind. Being alone in bed at the time, he had allowed himself the pleasure of reaching a torrid conclusion.

June thrust her fists over her eyes. 'I can't cope with all of this.'

Charles instantly regretted his outburst. He put an arm around her quivering shoulders. 'I'm sorry, June. I guess neither of us is lily-white. And gossips will always see scandal in the most innocent of relationships.'

She pressed her head on his shoulder. 'Yes, you're right. And I'm so tired, which doesn't help. I don't know what's the matter with me. I'm getting so jumpy and irritable. Perhaps I need a tonic.'

He kissed the top of her head. 'You need a rest, and less hassle from me.'

She smiled. 'It's been a busy year for all of us.' She took hold of his hand and held it to her face. 'I'll speak to Rosie, but you know what's she's like. Maybe she's just tired of studying. A complete break over Christmas might bring her back to her senses.'

The afternoon had darkened, but the room was warm and cosy. In the mellow light they sat cuddled on the sofa, watching the flames of the fire.

'I'll be back in time for the carol singing on Christmas Eve.'

'I thought you would be.'

'I take it we'll all be having Christmas dinner here. What have you planned for Boxing Day?'

She told him about a party being organised for the boys and their friends. 'I've hired a local pop group to liven things up a bit.'

'Really?' He laughed. 'That should make the timbers creak!'

'Perhaps I should tell you, Charlie, Rosie will be staying at Robert's on Wednesday night because the staff party will go on late. I know you won't go, so I'm not going either. Anyway, I would rather be home with you to myself.'

He nuzzled her ear. 'I wonder what else you've planned?'

'Come with me,' she said, taking his hand and glancing upwards.

Chapter Twenty-Seven

At eight o'clock the doorbell rang. Charles opened the front door to find a handsome young woman standing outside.

'I'm Ruth Craven,' she said, giving Charles a gorgeous smile. When she saw his puzzlement, she added, 'I'm helping Mrs Rogers this week. She asked me to call this evening. You know, to work out some menus and look around the house to see what needs doing.'

'Oh yes, I'm sorry, I had completely forgotten.' He was thinking that he was not the only one, but then he and June had been somewhat distracted for the last few hours. 'Do come in.' He closed the door behind her. 'It's good to meet you, Miss Craven,' he said, offering to shake her hand. 'I'm Charles Rogers, June's brother-in-law. Do come this way, I'll get June for you.'

Charles was thinking how right Peggy had been in her description of the girl. She was absolutely stunning. He left her sitting in the hall, but turned to look at her again before locating June in the kitchen. There was something about Ruth Craven that both disturbed and excited him.

'The new help has arrived. Ruth, that is, not the other Craven granddaughter. She's waiting in the hall.'

She eyed him quizzically. 'What is it, Charlie? You look strange. Is Ruth Craven an old girlfriend?'

'Too young. But there is something familiar about her. Can't think what.'

'Perhaps you've seen her in town,' June said, taking off her seldom-used apron. 'I'd better go and meet this mysterious lady.'

Ruth Craven stood up as June approached. No doubt about it, even at a distance Ruth was a strikingly beautiful woman — tall and slender, ivory complexion, dark hair bobbed in the latest style, dark eyes, long lashes, perfectly proportioned nose, full mouth that blossomed into a gorgeous smile revealing strong white teeth. Not a bit like her grandmother, or what she could remember of Jenny. Moreover, her dress sense was impeccable and the latest in fashion: black flared-trouser suit with velvet trim on the double-breasted jacket, white blouse with heavy guipure lace inset at the throat, red chunky-soled shoes, and a matching red bag slung over her shoulder. June offered Ruth her hand. The hand that took hers was long and slender; the filbert fingernails clear of varnish but highly polished.

No wonder Charlie was in a tizzy! Being suddenly faced with this beauty was enough to increase any man's blood pressure. Was having her around the house going to be a problem? She instantly dismissed such unworthy thoughts. It was time she trusted Charlie, instead of heeding rumours spread around by Angela and the local gossips.

'With your looks, I'm surprised you want to do this kind of work,' she told her. 'Surely there must be more glamorous jobs than working in a kitchen?'

'Actually, I do engage in a little modelling, but I'm rather choosy. I refuse to do certain jobs,' she added, lowering her eyes. 'I'm waiting for the big break. But I do enjoy cooking.' She delved into the cavernous bag. 'I have a diploma in culinary skills.'

'Please don't bother getting it out, being recommended by your grandmother is enough for me. Come this way.'

June escorted Ruth to the kitchen and explained what was required of her. She was soon impressed by Ruth's willingness to do whatever was needed and more besides. Her availability over the whole holiday period was definitely going to be a boon with Peggy being away. She wondered if Ruth might be able to give Rosie a hand at the Old Rectory.

According to her daughter, a London financier had poached Robert's cook and Rosie had been left to sort out the catering for the party. When asked, Ruth said she would be pleased to help out.

June was delighted. 'That's fantastic. I'll give the Old Rectory a ring and speak to my daughter now.'

It was Rosie who answered the phone. She was pleased at the prospect of having Ruth to help her. 'I'll speak to Robert first. I think he's in the gym. Won't be a minute.' She was soon back on the line. 'Robert would like to have a few words with Miss Craven before he employs her. Can she possibly drive over tonight?'

A mental picture of the twisting lane brought June to a quick decision. 'It's a tricky road even in daylight, and the house is hard to find in the dark. I'll drive her over in my car.'

'If Rob approves, could she start early tomorrow?' Rosie asked. 'I expect you'll need her most of Wednesday, but I could do with her back here Wednesday evening. Is that all right with you?'

'That's fine with me. I do have Annie, and her other granddaughter. Young Lisa will be starting tomorrow. Yes, we can manage. Talk it over with Ruth.'

June was about to leave the house with Ruth when Charles appeared in the hall. He said he wanted a quick word with the new helper.

'I'm driving Miss Craven to Rob's place,' June told him. 'Rosie needs some help with the staff party. Of course, Robert wants to meet Ruth before Rosie can take her on. We won't be long. Talk to her when we get back.'

'I'll take her there. You're busy in the kitchen and I'm free at the moment.' He smiled at Ruth. 'It will give me chance to get to know this young lady.'

Was Charlie afraid of her driving over to Rob's lair? Or was he sexually attracted to this elegant young woman?

Once more, she rebuked herself for having such devious thoughts, and accepted Charlie's offer with grateful thanks.

Once inside the Mercedes, Ruth thanked Charles for the lift. 'So kind of you, Captain Rogers. I hope you won't be kept waiting. I have no idea how long this interview will take.'

'I think you will find Robert Watson brief and brisk. He makes his mind up quickly. Rosie might give you ten minutes, but Watson two — if you're lucky!'

'I guess he must be a busy man.'

'You could say that. He has fingers in all sorts of pies, but his main interest is building up his clothing empire. You'll soon find out.' He quickly glanced in her direction. 'I seem to think we have met before. Tell me about yourself.'

'I suppose you might have seen me around, but we have never actually met. I'm sure I would remember. I've only been in this area a month or so. I'm staying with my grandmother for a while. I was brought up in Rutland by my aunt.' She went on to explain what she had done since leaving school and about her catering course. 'But I really want to be a top model,' she told him wistfully.

'So what made you come here to live?'

'To be quite honest, Captain Rogers, I'm looking for my father.'

'You have lost contact with him? Doesn't your mother know where he is?'

'I never knew my father,' she said, embarrassment creeping into her voice. 'My mother has always refused to say anything about him. She left us — Lisa and me — a long time ago. Went off with some man or other. Maybe Mum doesn't actually know for certain who my father is, or Lisa's for that matter. Evidently, she has a bit of a reputation where men are concerned. My aunt was forever holding her up as a warning to us girls.'

'I'm so sorry. Have you no information at all?'

'Obviously, I know roughly when I must have been conceived. Twenty-one years ago this Christmas. My mother was still at home then. So it's likely he lived in this area. I've asked Gran where Mum was working and where she used to hang out. She says she's forgotten.'

'Twenty-one years ago?' Not a difficult date for Charles to remember: it was a couple of weeks before he returned to active duty in the Navy. A memorable Christmas, when his life had undergone a remarkable change. 'Well I can tell you where your mother was at that time, but I can't tell you all the men she might have been seeing though. You are quite right, Jenny was very flirtatious.'

'You knew my mother?'

Charles stopped the car in a gateway. Ruth was clearly alarmed. 'I'm not my mother's daughter, Captain Rogers. Please don't try any funny business. I've taken lessons in self-defence and you'll be sorry if you do.' She sounded tough and serious.

Charlie laughed. 'I'm pleased to hear that.'

'Very funny,' she said stiffly.

'I'm sorry, I shouldn't be laughing. Insensitive of me. A woman's virtue is a serious matter,' he told her contritely. 'But you're quite safe. I only want to talk to you.'

'As much as I would like to chat, Captain Rogers, I do have an appointment to keep. I've heard enough about my mother's promiscuity to last a lifetime. But if you have something positive to tell me, I would like to hear it.'

'Miss Craven — Ruth — I'm going to be blunt with you. I can't say where Jenny picked up her boyfriends, but I do know where she was working that Christmas. She was employed as a domestic at Bloomfield, assisting her mother. On Christmas Eve, she stayed overnight.'

'Are you sure?'

'Absolutely.'

'How can you be so certain after all this time? Even my gran can't remember.'

'I have good cause to remember.'

'I've heard of your reputation, Captain Rogers.' She sounded a little nervous. 'Are you saying that you were one of her lovers?'

'Only on that one occasion. I'm not proud of it. I should have known better than to have taken advantage of her infatuation—'

'She was held captive under your own roof!'

'Hardly that. Look, Miss Craven, Jenny was—'

'Abandoned when she became pregnant. You bastard!'

'I didn't know anything about it. I don't recall ever seeing her again after that Christmas. Apart from getting married, I was back in the Royal Navy. I certainly didn't know she had a child. I always took precautions, even if your mother didn't. I can't speak for the other men she went with. Sorry, Ruth, but you can't presume to be my daughter until we test it out.'

'You are willing to do that?'

'Nothing would give me greater pleasure than to be a father, but I feel certain that Jenny would have told me about it, even if she had been with others that Christmas. Family honour would not permit desertion. Jenny would know that. Perhaps she thinks your father is someone else.'

'She has always refused to tell me anything.'

She was obviously disappointed. In the light from a passing vehicle, he saw she was looking dejected — eyes glazed and lips unsmiling. He felt a curious warmth towards her, desiring to take her in his arms and tell her what she so much wanted to hear. Was it possible? From the moment he met her there was a certain something that drew her to him.

'You know, when I first saw you,' he said gently, 'you seemed familiar. There is a strong resemblance to what I've always seen in my mirror.' He switched on the engine and prepared to move off, annoyed with himself for going a step too far. 'Anyway, I should be getting you to your destination.'

But while he carefully drove the car along the narrow lane, they continued talking about the possibility of the relationship. He knew they were hoping for something more desired than probable. Remembering Jenny as he did, she was not a girl to struggle on her own unnecessarily. No, she would have been demanding money, or marriage!

On arrival at the Old Rectory, Charles parked the car and then waited while Ruth had her interview. After about thirty minutes — longer than he had anticipated — Ruth came out smiling. She slipped into the passenger seat.

'What do you think?' she said, bubbling with excitement. 'Mr Watson has offered me the cook's job. What's more, since he doesn't need one full-time at the moment, he wants me to model for him as well. I can live-in. My own private quarters with full facilities!' She sighed, exhausted by enthusiasm. 'It seems too good to be true.'

Charles was thinking just that. But he didn't want to deflate Ruth's palpable joy. 'Sounds promising.' He started up the car and moved off. 'If that's what you want.'

'Of course, it's only a start,' she said, settling down in her seat. 'Cooking's all right, but I really want full time modelling. But isn't Robert Watson wonderful? He was so nice to me, he soon put me at ease. Miss Rogers is younger than I expected. Silly really, having met her mother, I should have known better. If I accept, I can move in whenever I want, but I don't start properly until next week. I told Mr Watson I would be working for Mrs Rogers over Christmas, but I'll be there tomorrow to help out.'

'Don't rush into anything, Ruth, especially where Robert Watson is concerned. People aren't always what they seem to be.'

'Don't I know it! That's why I turned down some modelling jobs. But Mr Watson seems all right. He didn't suggest anything improper.'

'He wouldn't with Rosie there, but I doubt that would be his technique. It could be a good opportunity for you, but frankly I don't trust him. I'm not at liberty to discuss my reasons. Anyway, you're a sensible young woman, I'm sure you'll do the right thing. I assume you don't have to give an answer straight away?'

'After Christmas,' she said, almost inaudibly.

Having deflated her enthusiasm, she was quiet for the rest of the short journey. Was she thinking over what he'd said about Watson, or again about her parentage?

Feeling protective towards her, he had his own thoughts to contend with. He would have to talk to Annie Craven, but it would have to wait until he returned from Bath. The possibility of having a child by one of his past sexual partners had never occurred to him. Of course, jonnies were not a hundred percent safe, but his more sophisticated partners usually took precautions themselves. Although the actual bedding was vague within his memory, the event had been noisy enough to draw Arthur's attention. It happened after returning from church, in the servant's room at the back of the kitchen. It was a Christmas he would never forget: the beginning of his redemption. Could he have slipped up?

It made him feel quite strange and somehow elated to think Ruth might be his daughter. He decided not to say anything to June about Ruth — now was not the time to bring up his womanising past. Investigations and explanations must take place after Christmas.

As planned, June crept into Charlie's bed. But she didn't feel like making love and he did not press her, accepting that she was genuinely tired and with a lot on her mind. It wasn't just the decisions that had to be made that bothered her; she was also concerned that her periods were now becoming scanty. The change of life worried her. Apart from the lack of ability to bear a child, might she suddenly become wrinkled and unattractive? Wanting reassurance, she told Charlie of her fears.

'June, with all the work and worry you've had lately — plus your finicky dieting — don't be surprised if your body decides to go on strike!'

'Rubbish! I don't diet, I merely eat the right food.'

He put an arm around her and pulled her close. 'Well, whatever you do, you look fantastic to me, in fact quite blooming.' His hand began gently exploring her body. 'You feel jolly good too.'

Soon, the warmth and thrill of his touch, his tender kisses and soft nuzzling of her breasts, turned her weariness into erotic desire. 'I've changed my mind, Charlie,' she whispered. 'I don't feel tired any more.'

'In that case,' he said, slipping off his shorts, 'let's make a really good effort at procreation.' He slowly removed her nightdress. 'Unattractive? Nonsense, you make me feel incredibly randy.'

Charles began his intensive love-play.

He was always a tender lover: unhurried, sensitive to her responses, and rich in technique. Soon she was lost in hedonistic pleasure that excluded all worldly problems, fear, and guilt. She was Charlie's and he was hers, united in a surge of rapturous ecstasy.

Yes, Charlie was the man she truly loved — and always had — and Charlie was man she would marry.

Chapter Twenty-Eight

Uplifted by a night of love and not in the least bit tired, Charles picked Peggy up early. They set off in the Mercedes, with the prospect of good weather for the drive down.

Peggy was chatting and joking, clearly high with excitement and the expectation of a pleasant episode in her rather dull life.

'I know it isn't going to be a shared bed and romance, but you never know, maybe I'll get my hands on you for a bit of slap and pummel.' She laughed. 'Anyway, I'm really looking forward to seeing Richard again. Does he know I'm coming?'

'I want to surprise him. When I last saw Richard he asked me if I would find a suitable person to assist him when he left the hospital. He wanted someone he could trust. I was going to trawl the agencies and ask around when I was back in Bath. Then you offered. He could not get a better helper in the whole of Britain.' He glanced in her direction. 'I know he will be delighted.'

Peggy was smiling contentedly. 'You really know how to make a woman feel wanted, Charlie.' She settled back and closed her eyes. She sighed audibly. 'What I don't have, I can at least dream about.'

It was early afternoon when they arrived at the hospital. Sister Landers met them in the corridor. 'Commander Andrews is now sitting out of bed for part of the day.' She gave Charles a huge smile, indicating both pleasure and relief. 'I think you will find a big change. I'll leave you to discover why.'

Charles entered Richard's room, leaving Peggy outside. Sun was shining through the window, adding light and life to the sick room. Richard's fair hair was caught in a sunbeam, the halo effect giving him an angelic appearance.

'Hello, Richard. Good to see you looking much better.'

Richard smiled. 'Thanks, Charles, lovely to see you again.' He nodded towards a vase of carnations on the table next to him. 'As you can see, she's been in touch.'

Charles picked up a card by the flowers. The message was simple, telling him to get better soon and to let her know when she could visit him. It was signed 'Love, Rosebud.'

Certainly, the communication was reason enough to lift Richard's spiritual depression. Charles was jubilant, not only because of the flowers, but also because Robert had failed to influence her.

'I'm so pleased, Richard. I wasn't sure how things had gone, but now I know.'

'They came this morning.' Richard's smile turned to an uncertain frown. 'I very much want to see Rosie, as long as it doesn't take her from her studies.'

'I'll telephone her and see what can be arranged.' Surely it was best not to say what was happening in Rosie's life. He moved a chair to Richard's side. 'I brought Rosie's aunt to Bath with me. Do you remember Peggy, June's sister?'

'I could never forget Peggy.' A grin spread across his face. 'We danced together at your party. Had a few laughs, I can tell you. She told me her name was really Margaret Rose. She said it was hard luck on her niece. Comparing pretty Rosie with her namesake was like comparing Beauty with the Beast. Of course, Peggy was quite wrong. That woman has an inner beauty that pulsates with life and joy. I like her. Is she here?' He sounded eager to meet her again.

'She's outside. Do you want to see her?'

'Show her in, don't keep the poor woman waiting.'

'First, I'll tell you why Peggy is here.' Charles leant back in his chair. 'You wanted a cleaner, cook, personal helper and general dogsbody. Peggy is all that, and more. She is a good companion, and skilled in massage to boot. All these accomplishments, I can personally vouch for.'

'Sounds just the right person for me,' said Richard. 'Show her in, man!'

'Before you decide one way or the other, see how you feel about it when you've had her around for a couple of days.'

'A lively housekeeper-companion, plus massage on tap? Can't see me turning that down. For goodness' sake, Charles, get her in before she gets away!'

Charles opened the door. 'Come in, Peggy. Better watch out, Commander Andrews is feeling much better.'

'Hello sailor!' She went straight up to Richard and kissed him on the cheek, the cleavage of her red woollen dress falling open in front of his eyes. Throwing her coat over the chair just vacated, she sat down.

'Looks as though your ship came adrift,' she said, sweeping her eyes over his damaged body. 'Good to see you've made it back to port. I must say, you're looking pretty good. Since you're still afloat, I guess you've lost none of your essential tackle!'

Richard grinned. 'It's good to see you again, Peggy. I really enjoyed our dancing together. Charles had better not leave you alone with me. I'm not sure what might happen.'

'Don't worry, I know how to behave. Charlie can tell you, I haven't laid a finger on him all the way down here. If I get the chance you'll find my massage relaxing, my washing whiter than snow, my cleaning impeccable, and as for my culinary skills… well, my cooking is out of this world.' She laughed. 'Perhaps that's where it ought to be. Is there a fish-and-chip shop near by?'

Charles collected another chair from the corridor. He sat back, enjoying seeing his friend so animated after weeks of pain and sadness. Yes, the gloom had lifted, and Richard was on the road to wholeness.

With Peggy keeping them amused, the afternoon went swiftly by. When she left them — she said for ten minutes — Richard asked Charles to draw closer.

'You know, Charles, apart from yourself, I'm used to visitors coming in with glum faces and expressing their sorrow at my accident. Most do their best to avoid looking at my stump. I can't blame them. But Peggy came in like a fresh summer breeze filling the sails after the doldrums, and putting smiles on all our faces. Most of all, my stump does not embarrass her.' He nodded his head and grinned. 'I think we will get along fine.'

While Richard had his evening meal, Charles took Peggy out to dine. She was quieter than usual. Charles appreciated this serious side of her personality. Clearly she had been touched by Richard's injuries, even though she had made light of them. She said how she hoped that her hands could do him some good, and how much she looked forward to helping him once he was home.

'He's a lovely young man. Mid-thirties?' She sighed. 'I wish I was a bit younger. I really could fall for that guy.'

There was a lot that Richard and Peggy needed to discuss, so Charles left them alone together while he visited old friends and colleagues at his old club, of which he was still a member. When he returned to the hospital, he found the pair drinking tea and happily chatting. They looked up as he entered the room.

'It's all fixed up,' said Richard, smiling happily. 'From tomorrow, Peggy will stay at my flat and get it ready for when I leave here. This kind lady is going to be my personal assistant, gofer, cook and cleaner.'

Charles smiled across as Peggy. She was looking radiant with happiness. 'Looks as if you're going to be busy,' he told her. 'Don't let him turn you into his willing slave.'

Her lips curled into a one-sided smile. 'I can think of worse things.'

'Being able to drive is an added bonus,' said Richard. 'Peggy will be able to take me to Outpatients and anywhere else I need to go. I've heard my Spitfire is a write-off, so I'm getting a new car. Would you go with Peggy tomorrow to choose one? Something large and classy. You know, easy for me to slip in and out without needing a shoehorn. A one-owner used car will do. I will be changing it for something more sporty later on.'

Charles was pleased to hear Richard talk of getting back to normality. It was a splendid idea to get a car for Peggy to drive in the meantime. Obviously the accident had not put him off driving, or being driven. Talking about various makes and models of cars shifted Richard's mind from his hospital room to the world outside. That could only be a good thing.

'We can have a look around in the morning, but being Christmas Eve, not sure how far we'll get,' he told Richard.

Sarah Landers breezed into the room with a wheelchair. 'If you two are stopping the night, I'd better get blankets and cocoa.' Smiling at each of them, she placed the wheelchair by Richard. 'First, I have to take Commander Andrews to the heads. So if you don't mind….'

Saying goodnight to Richard, Charles took the hint and escorted Peggy from the room.

'Heads?' she queried.

He smiled. 'A ship's latrine — lavatory. Sarah was probably being diplomatic.'

'She's a lovely person. She came in a few times while you were absent. I saw the way she looked at Richard. A woman in love?'

'Could be, but realistic with it. You're so right: Sarah is one of the loveliest women I know.'

'Sounds as though you know her intimately. I'm jealous,' Peggy said, her tinkling laughter ringing down the stairway.

'And I'm flattered.' Charles told her, grinning. 'Sarah is an old friend. Let's leave it at that.'

They arrived at the exit. He opened the door for Peggy. Soon they would be heading for his flat. What were her expectations? Better to be open about it.

'Being together in my flat tonight might not be the best thing,' he said, putting a hand on her shoulder and steering her towards the car park. 'Would you rather go to Richard's place tonight?'

'No thanks. You need a shoulder massage and I need the practice.'

'Sounds good.' But, knowing Peggy, was it good to be alone with her in such a compromising situation? He forced a laugh. 'Well, don't get carried away, I might find your methods too hard to resist. As much as I appreciate your willingness, Peggy, there is only one woman for me now.'

'That's not what Angela is saying. I think I should tell you, Charlie, that woman is fishing around and spreading gossip. Not long ago, she came into the Hare and Hounds where I was serving at the bar. She was with an old friend come up from Bath, or so she said. She didn't introduce me: I'm *persona non grata* as far as Angela is concerned. Helen Rogers was there too, with some of her badminton buddies. They got huddled together in a booth. Angela made sure I heard your name mentioned, but the rest of their rumouring was in secret. I wouldn't be surprised if she has spies all over the place.'

'That explains a lot,' Charles said, opening the passenger door of his Mercedes. 'But if Angela's hoping to get me back, she's going a funny way about it.'

Peggy slipped into her seat. 'As far as your ex is concerned, if she can't have you, then no one else will.'

He knew only too well the depths Angela would sink to in order to get what she wanted. She even hired a private detective to spy on him before the divorce settlement. Ironically, he ended up paying the bill!

'She won't succeed, Peggy,' he told her with a confidence he did not feel. With Watson doing more than waiting in the wings, Angela was a potent influence not easily dismissed. 'But enough of that woman. Apart from visiting Richard, you, dear lady, are going to be on your own over Christmas. Instead of the massage, suppose we join the merry throng at my local? I'll introduce you to some of my friends.'

'How thoughtful of you, Charlie.'

'Not really. Sarah Landers is having a Christmas get-together with some of her friends, a few of whom happen to be mine. She suggested we join them. I thought you might be too tired — it's been a long day.'

'Too tired for a knees-up? You must be joking!'

'Not exactly a knees-up, but knowing you, Peggy, I dare say it might end up as one!'

He started the engine, looking forward to a pleasant evening. Even so, with having to find a car for Richard in the morning before driving back to Bloomfield, he was glad they would be thrown out of the pub at closing time. At least the place was only a hundred yards from home. He grinned at his thoughts — if Peggy got sozzled, she wouldn't be the first woman to get carried to his flat.

Chapter Twenty-Nine

It had been a troubled night, made worse by the wretched Angela ringing her up to tell her that Peggy was staying with Charlie in his Bath flat. Of course, she put the receiver down when she realised who was speaking, but the damage was already done. Angela had a way of getting the message across before revealing herself.

June dragged herself out of bed just as the bedside telephone began once more to challenge her frayed nerves. What was wrong with her to let that bitch get at her? She snatched up the phone.

'Who is it?' she snapped.

'June? It's me.'

'Charlie! Thank goodness.'

'You sound distraught. Were you expecting someone else?'

'Not really.' Why worry him about Angela? 'I didn't sleep well. I guess I'm missing you. I thought you would phone me last night. I like to know you get there safely, especially after... well, you know. How's Richard?'

'A lot brighter. Rosie had been in touch. It meant a lot to him.'

'Rosie has been in touch with Richard?' Her daughter was so secretive these days, and it worried her. 'Did she phone him?'

'Sent him flowers and a card. She wants to visit him.'

'Is that wise, Charlie? Oh, never mind, she'll do as she pleases anyway.'

'I guess she will. Wise? Perhaps the affair needs closure one way or another, for both their sakes. Clearly she still has feelings for him. Richard certainly does for her.'

She heaved a deep sigh. 'I hope he doesn't let her down again.'

'Are you all right, June? You sound so weary. Didn't you get any rest?'

'Not much. I got off to sleep about midnight when the phone woke me up again.'

'Who was it?'

'Nobody important. I thought it might be you. You told me you would ring.'

'And I let you down. I'm so sorry.'

'I was waiting for the call.' She knew she was being petulant, but she was too tired to care.

'By the time we were back at the flat, it was a bit late.'

'We? Is Peggy with you? I thought she would be staying at Richard's place.' Angela's mocking words were now ringing in her ears.

'She will be from tonight. His flat will need a bit of airing and heating. Peggy will be staying in Bath for quite a while. She's agreed to look after Richard when he gets home. Perhaps we can get Ruth Craven to take Peggy's place for a while.'

'You know very well that Ruth will be working for Robert.'

'It's certain, then?' He sounded disappointed. Was it because he wanted a potential lover on hand?

Oh, why did she have such unworthy thoughts about Charlie? Of course, it was Angela putting them into her mind. But why did he have to get her sister so deeply involved? Peggy was needed at Bloomfield.

'Perhaps Lisa will help out,' Charlie was telling her.

'I can ask her.' If not Lisa, she could find someone else; Robert would see to that. She was just being ungracious.

Poor Richard must come first. And Peggy? It was obvious that she was in love with Charlie — always had been. Maybe she needed to get away from Bloomfield.

'June, have I upset you? I'll make sure you get the help you need, even if I have to don an apron myself.'

Charlie in a wraparound pinny? She had to smile. 'It won't come to that. I'm sorry for being grumpy. I guess I'm tired and edgy. I suppose Peggy will enjoy being in Bath for a while. I don't begrudge her a bit of happiness — heaven knows, she deserves it.'

'Hardly surprising that you're tired. And I haven't been much help to you, robbing you of your beauty sleep before I left.'

Memories of their love-play brought sweet refreshment to her weary body. 'I'm surprised you had the energy to drive to Bath yesterday. After all, you didn't exactly go to sleep on the job.'

'No, but you gave me pleasant dreams.'

The sound of his lips sending her kisses came down the line. Then came his words of love. She lay back on the bed and drank them in, closing her eyes and feeling his intimate touch. It was not passionate enough to set the telephone wires ablaze, but she felt pleasantly revived.

'Keep your pecker up,' he told her, as he neared the end of the call. 'I'll be home in time for the carol-singing tonight. With Peggy here, I won't need to be worrying about Richard. We'll have more time together from now on... promise.'

Showered and dressed in a mauve chevron-striped outfit, June ran downstairs, her skirt swirling above high white boots. She found the youngsters already busy doing their own thing. Rosie had gone out, but Mrs Craven and Lisa were going to be in the house all day. Ignoring the latest postal delivery on the hall table, mostly Christmas cards reminding her of her bereavement, she left the boys in Annie's care and drove over to the Old Rectory to see Robert.

She found him in the stable yard, walking a handsome black pony. In the far corner, a man and a youth were negotiating a large white horse from a horsebox.

Robert called her over. 'Come and see James's Christmas present.'

'Robert, he's beautiful,' she said, stroking the black pony's silky neck, 'Jimmy will love him.'

'James, June. My son is called James. You gave him that name, please stick to it.' He waved a hand towards the horse. 'Two more will be arriving at the end of the week. I'm employing Bill Smith, an experienced jockey and groom, to look after the horses. A lass will be coming in to muck-out.'

Robert might be a ruthless businessman, but June could not help but admire the way he had advanced during the twenty-plus years she had known him. After all his hard work, long hours, and the risks he'd taken, he deserved his rich rewards. And yes, now the gentler man within him was released, he deserved the love of a wife and family. Even so, she had no intention of obliging him.

After stroking the new horse, Robert led her to the rear entrance. He replaced his outdoor boots with soft leather shoes, and led her through a brightly-lit corridor to the Old Rectory's splendid hall.

'Allow me,' he said, as she slipped off her coat.

She smiled up at him. 'Thanks.'

'I'm sorry you're not coming tonight,' he said, putting an arm around her. 'I was looking forward to us sharing my new bed afterwards.'

She pushed his arm away. 'Sharing your bed was never on the cards, Robert.'

His eyes smiled at her. 'Is that so? I think we both know different.'

Footsteps sounded at the top of the stairs and voices, including Rosie's, were heard coming from a number of directions. The place was like a beehive.

'We'll go to my study,' he said. 'The only place we'll get some privacy.' He took her arm and walked her across the hall. 'Too bad you won't be here.' He closed the door behind them. 'But then, I do have your daughter to compensate my loss.'

She turned swiftly to face him. 'What exactly do you mean by that? For goodness' sake, Rob, she's just a girl.'

'Calm down.' He held her tightly to his chest. 'Rosie is only helping with the party. Don't jump to conclusions.'

'Of course, I'm sorry. I thought—'

'Pretty obvious what you thought,' he cut in, sounding deeply hurt.

He sought her lips and kissed her, his hands tenderly embracing her cheeks.

'Sit down, you look tired,' he said, walking her to the fireplace. 'I'll get you a drink.'

She sat in the proffered armchair by the coal fire. He poured a small measure of golden liquid into a glass from a decanter set on a small cabinet.

'No whisky for me, Robert. Just something light.'

'Of course.' He reached for a bottle and filled a glass with a clear liquid. 'Drink up, you'll like it.'

She did. It was sweet and tasted of oranges. He sat opposite her, his eyes penetrating her mind. Sipping her drink, she turned to look into the dancing flames, trying to get her thoughts together.

Rob broke into her meditations. 'Rosie is quite splendid. Organising parties seems to be her forte.'

'It's about Rosie that I came to see you.' Her voice was shaky. She fought to control it. She swallowed down half of the liquid in her glass. 'What have you been saying to her?'

'You have a lovely, intelligent daughter.' His voice had an unusual softness and she was drawn to look at him. His dark eyes were gently smiling. 'I want to train her, just as

I did you. Her living here will make it easier. She will also be company for James when I have to be away on business.'

'You talk as though Jimmy's going to be living here permanently. I can't let that happen.' She looked at him defiantly. 'I'm not losing my son, Robert.' She emptied her glass.

He lifted his hands in a gesture of surrender. 'Of course not. We'll both be away quite a bit. It makes sense for James to be here with his sister. I don't want my son looked after by hired helpers when he has his family.'

Sitting back in his chair, his thumb began ploughing into the furrow of his chin. 'You're not telling me that Charles is going to be hanging around looking after your kids while you do your own thing with me?' He paused, his eyes holding hers in their mesmerising gaze. 'Or are you?'

June was trying to think through what Rob was saying. How could she expect Charlie, married to her or not, to be her housekeeper and childminder?

'Be reasonable, June, it makes sense for all of you to be living here.'

'Sense? You move too fast, Rob.'

'Rob? Now that sounds more friendly.'

'Nothing is decided. Rosie should finish her studies. You're taking advantage of her recent unhappiness to get her to work for you and to live here.'

'Are you saying you would rather your daughter be unhappy?'

She was beginning to feel light-headed. Little sleep, warm room? 'Of course not. Work is one thing but if you're thinking of something more...'

'Intimate?'

'I won't allow it. She's just a kid.'

He looked hurt. 'Do you think I'm into cradle snatching? My own son's sister?'

She was now feeling foolish. And yet? No, he was a father, and all he wanted was a family life; something he'd never had despite all his accumulated wealth and success. 'I'm sorry, Rob. Put that way... well... silly isn't it? It's just that I know your need for... well, to put it bluntly—'

'Sex?' Rob cut in. It was such a small word, but the way he said it and the way he was devouring her with his eyes thrilled her to the depths of her being. 'If you come to live here, you would provide all my needs.' His hand touched her knee. 'And I yours.'

Erotic sensations added to the growing heat of her body. She wanted to strip off her clothes and lay naked on the rug, free of restraint, free of inhibition. What was wrong with her? She felt quite giddy. She forced herself to look away and stare into the fire. But awareness of his overpowering presence continued to infuse her with desire. Flames were dancing before her eyes. Flames were leaping in her body. She sensed him lean forward and leave his chair. He was standing behind her: hands lifting up her hair, soft moist lips touching her neck.

His voice was soft and cooing: 'Live here with me, we can discuss marriage later. James deserves to be with both his father and his mother. He loves us both. Don't tear him apart by marrying someone else.'

'But Charlie—'

'Give him his freedom. Don't tie him down. He's shown you who's most important in his life. Even his woman comes second to an old friend. Doesn't that tell you something? Face it, June, he could have married you years ago, but he went off to sea. Then he wedded that peachy woman: blonde, sexy Angela. Didn't last long, did it? Do you really think it will last with you?'

It was hard to think. She struggled to find words. 'It will last. We love each other.'

'Love is more than fanciful feelings. We are soul mates, June.' His words were soft in her ear. 'Ask yourself, why did you really come here this morning?'

She felt herself being lifted from her chair.

'Look at me,' he murmured softly.

His eyes were sucking her in. She couldn't hold back. Now he was hard against her, his mouth closing over hers. She let go and breathed his breath. The room swam around her in a magical hazy glow.

A loud knocking and a familiar voice shattered the moment. Muttering, Rob sat her back in the chair and moved towards the door. She saw him turn the key and open the door a mere crack.

'What is it, Rosie?'

That delivery of wine has arrived. You said to—'

'Wait in the hall a moment.' He closed the door and turned.

'I have to see to this. Don't go away, I'll be back soon.'

But June had no intention of staying. What on earth was she doing locked in Robert's study? How far would she have allowed him to go? Feeling dreadfully guilty, dizzy and confused, she grabbed her bag and hurried from the room. Through an open door, she could hear Robert arguing with someone about the wine. Women's voices drifted from the dining room. Before anyone could stop her, she snatched her coat from the chair where Rob had dropped it, left the house and breathed in the cool fresh air.

Her head began to clear. Before getting into her car, she looked up at the beautiful elegant house, with its stables and outbuildings, its gardens, paddock and woods. To be part of this place? A not-so-impossible dream. But to be Mrs Watson? She shook her head, opened the car door, threw in her bag and started on her way home.

Home was Bloomfield, but for how long? She began seriously to consider the question. Charlie would never force her to move, but it would not be fair to expect him to restrict his opportunities. If he started a business elsewhere, would they end up with two homes and lead separate lives? He in a comfortable flat shared with Richard, his business partner? She, where? In a big house hardly occupied except when David and Peter were home?

It seemed certain that Jimmy was likely to be living some of the time at the Old Rectory with his sister. In their holidays, his brothers would likely want to join them. Since Robert was using the Old Rectory for business, she would be spending some of her time there too. Sighing deeply, she slowed down and stopped at a traffic light. A number of times she had been approached by a property developer to sell the house. Technically, she owned it, but she had never thought it was really hers to sell. It had been in the Rogers family since it was built. Now everything seemed to be falling apart. Perhaps it was time to reconsider their offer, and move into a smaller, more manageable, place. The amber lights came on. She made a cautious move forward. Why, oh why, did she feel so nervous and uncertain? A tear trickled down her cheek. She brushed it aside.

'I must talk to Charlie.'

Chapter Thirty

It was five-fifty when Charles entered Bloomfield. The family were practising carols. He could hear Jimmy and Peter singing the words, 'While shepherds washed their socks by night.' Obviously, modern boys were no more reverent during the Christmas festival than when he was a lad. But surely they ought to be able to think up more original words over the years?

He put down his bags at the bottom of the stairs and headed for the kitchen. As he opened the door, delicious smells filled his nostrils. Annie Craven was busy baking. Plump with rosy cheeks and dressed in her usual pinny, she was a constant reminder of days long since. She looked up as he walked in.

'Would you like something to eat, Captain Rogers? The others had something an hour ago.'

He kissed her chubby cheek. 'Thank you, Annie. Just an odd scrap will do. I had a good lunch.'

'Oh Captain Rogers, get away with you,' she said, rubbing her cheek with the back of her floury hand. 'There's a nice bit of pork pie in the fridge. I made it myself. Ruth made some sausage rolls and little puffy things with creamy fillings. They're in the pantry. I'll just get these mince pies in the oven. You can have a couple of those in a few minutes.'

Intending to quiz Annie about her granddaughter before they were disturbed, he sat down in one of the armchairs by the range.

'Great. I'll hang on for one of those.'

'I'll pour you a cup of tea. I've just made it.' She took a pretty china cup with matching saucer from the dresser and picked up a plain pot mug from the draining basket. 'Milk but no sugar?'

He sipped the hot tea from the china cup. 'Great, just what the doctor ordered.' He watched Annie prick the tops of the next batch of pies. 'So, Ruth has been helping in the kitchen. I thought she was working at Watson's place.'

'She's working here a few hours too.'

'Is she going to take up Watson's offer?'

'Don't know. She's a good worker. Makes lovely pastry. I don't know about the modelling stuff she does. Best stick to proper work, I say.'

'Ruth is a beautiful young woman. I'm told she's Jenny's daughter.'

Annie sat down at the table to drink her mug of tea. 'Quite right, she is.'

'She doesn't look much like her. But it must be about twenty-one years since I last saw Jenny. Did she move away?'

'Yes, Mr Charles, she went to live some distance away. She didn't come home for quite some time. Then she was off again.'

'I understand from Ruth that her mother wasn't for settling-down. She liked to move around.'

Annie shrugged her shoulders and huffed. 'If you mean that she was always chasing the men, then that's right. And a lot of good it did her. She left those lovely girls to go off with a man who refused to have them around. Fancy, my own flesh and blood choosing a lousy rogue rather than look after her own children. I'll never understand her.'

'What about the girls' father, didn't he have anything to say about it?'

'I don't know who the fathers are,' Annie said emphatically, lifting up her mug and swallowing down a gulp of tea.

Charles sat back in his chair and smiled. 'She may have been flirtatious, but surely she didn't have that many men?'

'Jenny was headstrong and foolish. Probably still is.' She emptied her mug in the sink and got on with her baking.

Charles watched her tight lips working in rhythm with her hands. Clearly the poor woman was uncomfortable talking about her daughter. But he had no intention of letting his sympathetic heart rule his need to know. 'I would have thought Jenny would have needed financial support from the fathers,' he said, sitting back in his chair and trying to sound casual. 'It must have been hard for a single mother in those days.'

'Jenny got a lot of support when Ruth was born, don't you fret,' Annie told him, clearly agitated. Lifting pastry from the mixing bowl, she formed it on the floured board. She picked up her rolling pin and held it like a weapon of defence. 'I think it best if I say nothing more. I'm sorry, Mr Charles.'

'Ruth was born nine months after Jenny helped out at this house,' Charles persisted. 'Twenty-one years ago this Christmas. Of course, she may have been seeing a number of men, but I know of one in particular who bears a strong resemblance to your granddaughter.' He watched the dear lady's face muscles tighten. 'You know what I'm going to ask you, don't you, Annie?'

'Mr Charles, just let things be.'

He noted that she was addressing him as in former years. Significant?

'Does your granddaughter want to let things be, Annie?'

'I know Ruth wants to know who her father is, but perhaps it's better for her to be kept in ignorance.'

He watched as she stabbed out the rounds of pastry, putting them in patty-tins ready for filling.

'Annie, suppose she met a half-brother who wanted to marry her?'

'That's not possible, her father hasn't got any children.'

'So you do know who her father is?'

Annie turned from the table to inspect the oven. She brought out a tray of mince pies, moved the bottom tray up a shelf, put in another prepared tray and closed the oven door. Tight-lipped, she scooped the tempting pies on to a wire rack and sprinkled them with caster sugar.

'Here you are, Mr Charles, fresh from the oven,' she said, placing two pies on a china plate. 'Just like when you used to come in my kitchen all those years ago.' Her eyes were wet, but her lips were smiling.

'And your baking hasn't changed a bit. These look delicious!' he said, breaking off a corner of a pie, giving it a blow and then nibbling it.

'Thank you, Mr Charles.' She brushed away a tear with the back of her hand and went on filling pastry cases with mincemeat.

Charles licked a trace of fine sugar from his fingers. 'Ruth is a beautiful woman. Maybe her father will meet her one day and ask her to marry him.'

She took pies from the oven and replaced it with others. She stood a moment with her back towards him. 'He has someone already,' she said, her voice trembling.

He rose from his chair and put an arm around her. 'I slept with Jenny that Christmas.' He nodded to the far wall. 'It was in that room next to the kitchen. Afterwards I had a talk with Arthur and he helped straighten my life out. So I have good cause to remember. Please tell me the truth, Annie. If I am Ruth's father, I want to take responsibility for my actions and make amends.'

Tears ran down Annie's hot-looking cheeks. 'I promised your father never to speak of it. Please don't ask me, Mr Charles.'

He nodded. 'Just as I thought. My father was behind the cover-up. He was involved in politics and wouldn't want a scandal. Did he pay her off?'

'It wasn't like that. Jenny thought it might be yours, but she was going out with a redheaded bloke at the time. It was when the baby was born — such a dark-haired beauty — that you seemed more likely to be the father. The resemblance was quite striking. You were married by then, and back on active duty. Colonel Rogers didn't want you to be worried, so he arranged for Jenny to get an allowance for eighteen years, even though he had no proof the baby was yours.'

Charles thought his own version of events more likely, but that was not important. He gave the unhappy woman a hug. 'You're an angel. Don't worry, Annie, you've done the right thing in telling me the truth. The rest is up to me and Ruth.'

He already knew his own blood grouping details. Ruth probably had hers. To get them both checked by experts for a paternity relationship should not take long. Heady with the knowledge of his probable fatherhood, he had another pie and went to join the family. June met him in the hall.

'Charlie! I thought I heard your car ages ago. Where have you been?' She flung her arms around his neck and kissed his lips. 'Don't tell me, I can taste sugar and brandy mincemeat.' She took his arm. 'I see your cases are here. I'll help you take them up. Does this mean you really are home for a while?'

'I am. Richard has Peggy to look after him now.'

A youthful voice yelled across the hall. 'Come on, Mum and Uncle Charlie, we'll be late at the church hall. They'll go without us.'

Charles picked up his coat from the banister. 'We'll talk later.'

By a dying fire in the lounge, Charles helped June make intriguing stocking-filler parcels for her children. It had been a merry band of carollers walking the streets and singing out their Christmas message. The group had eventually split up, with most of them going back to the church hall for mince pies. But they and the boys had gone home. It was obvious to Charles that June was afraid of gossiping tongues. He did not press her to attend Christmas Communion, even though he knew it had been a Rogers tradition for many years. Within his mind, he could see Arthur reading one of the lessons as he had done year after year. For June to face her loss in the presence of holiness could have been a healing thing to do, but wagging tongues and sly looks would have soured the occasion, adding pain and guilt to her natural grief.

After hot drinks all round, the boys were now in bed, tired out with excitement and robust singing. Sitting on the rug before the glowing embers, June was quiet and reflective, tying ribbons with unseeing eyes. Was she thinking of Arthur's last Christmas? He had no desire to intrude on her memories.

Suddenly she turned to face him. 'I can't marry you, Charlie.'

Charles was stunned. 'What's happened? Is it because I took your sister to Bath? I can assure you nothing happened.'

'It has nothing to do with Peggy,' she said, her eyes lowered. 'Our lives are leading along different paths. I'm stifling you. If Arthur hadn't died, you would be running a business with Richard by now, far away from here.'

'Maybe, but Arthur did die.' Even as he said the words, a lump constricted his throat. 'We both know it was his wish for us to marry, even if the words were not actually said.'

'He was asking too much of you. If you want to, we can still be lovers,' she said softly. 'But you must be free to marry someone else. Someone who can bear you children of your own. Then you can forget me, and live as a proper family should. We have no future together. I'm destroying you. You must see that.'

He dropped the Action Man he'd wrapped in Christmas paper, and held her shoulders in a firm grip. She turned her face away.

'Look at me, June,' he demanded, but she continued to stare into the dying fire. 'What has brought you to this conclusion? Have you stopped loving me?'

She shook her head. 'No,' she whispered. 'I could never do that.'

He took hold of her hands. 'Then why won't you marry me? You know I won't stop you working. I'll find something close by.'

'And suffocate like a beached whale?' A tear rolled down her cheek. 'No, Charlie, my mind is made up. Whatever your future enterprise, I want you to be as successful as I am. You can't do that living here. And what about Richard? Sticking here, you would be letting him down.'

'We are both adaptable. We can both wait until the right opportunity presents itself.'

'Wait? For how long? No, Charlie,' she said, shaking her head. 'Look how things have been these past months. You need to work at your own interests.'

'I'll get something to keep me busy.'

'Dancing instructor? Tennis coach? Swimming bath attendant? You're worth more than that. I would be the successful designer, always a busy schedule and frequently absent. And what would happen to you? How soon before you become resentful and suspicious? You would be a prey of bored housewives. Soon you would be the talk of the neighbourhood. Angela would make sure of that. We would constantly quarrel and end up with a love-hate relationship.'

Had Angela been getting at her again? Had Watson been putting ideas into her head? Did she really believe in the pessimistic picture she had painted of their future together? But there was more at stake than the happiness of themselves. 'What about the children? You need someone here for them, and running Bloomfield as a home. They need more than a big empty house to come home to.'

'You, a househusband and caretaker?' She shook her head again. 'No, Charlie, no. It doesn't change what I've said. I don't want you to put your future on hold. Neither can I see things working out if we are living apart. Anyway, I'm going to sell this place. A property developer wants to build prestige flats on the site. I've been offered a considerable sum. It's all very sudden. A letter came by hand this afternoon.'

'Christmas Eve? They must be keen!'

'Actually, I was approached months ago. Several times, in fact. But I had too much on my mind to even consider such a proposition. I threw the papers in the fire. Now they've made this fantastic offer.'

Charles felt a surge of anger welling up within him. 'Let me guess. You're going to move in with Robert Watson. Could he be the dealer who's suddenly appeared to make you an offer too good to refuse?'

'Of course not, why should he?' She frowned.

'Isn't it obvious? This is just one more push to get you living with him. Can't you see that?'

'Frankly, no.' She pulled herself free of his hands. 'You're being paranoid again.'

'Am I? Do you need the money?'

'No, but it seems pointless keeping this huge place on when Jimmy and Rosie will be spending most of their time at the Old Rectory. David and Peter are at school most of the year. With me working as I am doing — at the Old Rectory as well as the Nottingham office, plus travelling all over the place — it makes sense to sell up.'

'Not to me, it doesn't.' He took hold of her hands again and gripped them tightly, fearful she was slipping away from him. 'It's too soon. Too quick.'

'Look, Charlie,' she said, as though explaining simple truths to a slow-witted child. 'You need to be searching the whole of the country to set up in business with Richard. In any case, I can't expect you to be home for my kids.'

'So you keep telling me. How long do I have to change your mind? When are you selling up?'

'Let go of my hands,' she said, squirming, 'you're hurting me.'

'Sorry, so sorry.' He glanced with shame at her red wrists, but, utterly convinced that Watson was behind the house deal, his anger was not abated.

She looked at him with pleading eyes. 'Please don't be angry, Charlie. Try to be reasonable.'

Reasonable? What was reasonable? He found it hard to cope with his tangled emotions. Anger, jealousy, sorrow; but above all — love! He sucked in his breath. 'Where are you going to live?' he asked. Did he really want to know the answer?

'We have to be out of here sometime in January. The boys will be back at school. If I don't find a suitable house straight away, I'll look for somewhere convenient until the future is more settled.'

'The Old Rectory, for instance?' he asked, bristling with ire. 'Now that would be a most convenient lodging place. Everything laid on. Watson's personal service — hot-and-cold-running sex!' He jumped up. 'All this talk of concern for me, when all you really want is an excuse to be in Watson's bed — married or not! Well, I hope you'll be very happy!' He stormed out of room and ran up both flights of stairs.

When he reached his bedroom, he lay on his bed and did his relaxation exercises to help lower his blood pressure and calm his tensed nerves. He then coolly looked at the situation from June's perspective. Why on earth hadn't he listened to her, instead of getting riled up over Robert Watson?

It made good sense for her to get a house more suitable for her changed circumstances. He should have seen that for himself. Of course, it had been convenient for him to be in his old home, living in his comfortable flat, sharing his bed for their mutual pleasure. Yes, June had benefited by his presence there, but then, so had he.

She and her family needed stability, and what alternative could he presently offer? Marriage, yes — if he got her to change her mind — but until he knew what he was doing and where he would be living, June's life and career would be suspended, with Watson pulling her in one direction and he in another. Would she be able to continue with her designing if they moved to another area? Not as she was doing.

If only that Leisure Centre deal hadn't fallen through — the place was within commuting distance. He had to admire his rival's cunning. But Watson hadn't won yet. He stood up and went in search of June. He found her in bed, sobbing, Arthur's photograph on the pillow beside her.

He kissed her wet face. 'I'm sorry. I tell you to make your own decisions and then come down heavy with jealousy. But I beg of you, don't marry the man. At least, not yet. Delay things for a while.'

June looked at him, her eyes red and swollen. 'I don't intend to marry Robert. Oh, Charlie, I feel as though my life is out of control: Rosie, the boys, my job, running this place — even Annie said this evening that she wants to retire. The gardener's never here, the window-cleaner hasn't been for months and now soot's falling down the chimney.' She started laughing hysterically.

Charles wrapped his arms around her and swayed her gently. 'It's my fault, I should have been more understanding. I could have taken care of the house for you. No wonder the offer is so attractive.' He tenderly kissed her cheek.

'And I'm so worried about Rosie. If she lives with Robert, she might become his mistress. It could destroy her life.' She released a deep sigh. 'I feel so sick and weary.'

'I'm not surprised. You're emotionally washed out. You were thinking about Arthur tonight, weren't you? Missing going with him and the kids to Christmas Communion?'

She nodded. 'It was more than just a tradition with him. Me too, I guess. But I couldn't have gone, Charlie. I suppose

I feel too guilty, And tongues would be wagging. I just couldn't go, I really couldn't.'

'I know. And now I've upset you. I'm sorry, my darling.'

'I can't blame you. Everything is so unsettled.'

'We were supposed to be spending this night together in love and relaxation. Forget your problems over the house for now. Nothing can be done over Christmas anyway. I'll see to the maintenance work. I'll ask Ruth to work for you full-time, whether you stay here or move somewhere else.'

'Do you think Ruth would do that? I thought she was going to work for Robert.'

'Over my dead body!'

'Why are you so protective towards that young woman?' There was a hint of suspicion in her voice.

'Ruth being Annie's granddaughter, I feel a certain responsibility towards her. I don't trust Watson with any pretty woman.' Now was not the time to burden her with an untested paternity relationship. 'Working for you need not stop her modelling activities.'

'I suppose you're right. About Robert, I mean.'

'And don't you worry about your daughter. I have an idea Rosie will go back to school when she sees things more clearly. As for my future, I'll let you in on all the options as they come along. You can say what you think. I won't try to push you into anything. I love you. And I think you love me.'

'Yes, Charlie, I do. I really do.'

'Well, don't rush into anything. You are my life now, and I don't want to lose you.'

Tears gathered in her eyes. 'You're so good to me, I don't deserve you.'

'With my reputation, do I deserve you? Look, I'm going this weekend to see Richard. I'll go early and come back the same evening. I want to take Rosie with me. Perhaps you would like to come too? We can make a day of it. We'll stay overnight at one of Bath's grand hotels. I'll ask Ruth to take care of the boys for you.'

'That would be lovely. I really would like to see Richard. What about Rosie? Do you think she will go to see Richard?'

'I feel certain she will. Now go to sleep, my love, we could have a busy beginning to Christmas day. Tell you what, while the kids are busy opening their presents downstairs, suppose we have ours up here?'

Lips and eyes smiled up at him. 'I'd like that very much.'

He slipped off his clothes. 'I'll just lock your door. With Santa on his way, we don't want noisy intruders coming aboard in a few hours time.'

Chapter Thirty-One

Jimmy quickly tore the wrapping paper from his presents. But he found it difficult to get interested in his gifts — cassette player, cassettes, books, puzzles, Action Man, yo-yo and other toys spilling out of a huge red sock onto the floor — because he was waiting to see his pony. He knew he was going to have to wait quite a while and it wasn't easy. Someone had lit a fire and old Annie was busy in the kitchen. She had made him tea and toast because he was too excited to eat a proper breakfast. But his mum was not up yet.

How could she lie in bed on Christmas morning? It would be yonks before he got to see his pony. Waiting was agony, agony, agony. He picked up one of his new books that he'd thrown aside with the puzzles. Books and puzzles were never greatly welcomed and were always looked at after everything else had been explored. He tore off the paper still covering the title. Wow! It was a book about ponies, and how to train and care for them.

'Hi, Jim. Happy Christmas!' Peter had come into the sitting room.

'And you,' said Jimmy, looking up from his book. Grinning, he pointed to the far side of the Christmas tree. 'Yours are over there.'

He knew it was an unnecessary remark. The whole world must know what Peter was getting for Christmas. Anyway, something that big could not be disguised. He watched Peter's eyes light up when he saw what was arranged in the corner of the room. It was always fun to share in someone else's pleasure.

'Fantastic!' yelled Peter. 'I've got that drum kit we saw in Briggs and Maplin. Good old Mum!'

The glistening blue drums, partly covered with sheets of wrapping paper, were already set out ready to play. Jimmy raced to help Peter tear off the pretty pictures of bells and angels to get at the stool and drumsticks. Before long, Peter was doing his own version of *All Shook Up*, tapping at the snare and toms, and occasionally working a foot pedal to clash the high-hat cymbals. Soon his other foot began working the base drum pedal, its deep *boom-boom* reverberating around the room, causing the baubles on the tree to dance and twinkle. Jimmy, who had put his Elvis Presley recording into his player, began joining in the din by singing the words, strumming an invisible guitar, and gyrating his hips in an impersonation of the King himself.

David's voice yelled above the racket: 'Pete, go easy!' But he was soon tearing the paper from the latest ten-speed Raleigh Chopper with Sturmey-Archer hub and high backrest. 'Oh boy!' he howled. Soon he was astride the bike and trying to ride it around the room.

The door opened and Rosie came in. 'What the hell is going on in here?'

'Christmas!' shouted Jimmy. 'And I'm all shook up,' he sang, giving his pelvis another jerk.

On his way to shower and dress, Charles nearly bumped into Ruth. At the sight of her, his heart filled with joy. She was his daughter, a child of his own seed. 'Hello, Ruth. Happy Christmas. Where are you off to?'

'Happy Christmas, Captain Rogers. I've just got back from the Old Rectory with Rosie. We stayed overnight. I was going to help my gran in the kitchen but she told me the bedrooms needed seeing to first.'

'Ruth, I need to speak to you privately. Could you come up to my rooms in about half-an-hour?'

Her eyes glowed with interest. 'Of course. I'll come up when I've tidied the boys' bedrooms.'

Charles performed his usual morning exercises followed by a shower. Part of his mind was on Ruth and how much he was going to tell her, but overriding that concern was his relationship to June. Things had gone well after their making up. To prove the sincerity of his love, he'd given her the diamond ring he'd bought for her before coming to live at Bloomfield.

'Marriage or not, keep it to remind you of me. Wear it on whatever finger you choose, but please wear it.'

The gift had stunned her. 'Charlie, it's beautiful!'

He had left her sitting on the bed looking at the symbolic diamond, a sweet smile curling her lips. Surely that gentle acceptance of his gift augured well for the future?

He was just about to leave his bathroom when Ruth arrived at the top of his staircase. He quickly slipped a robe over his naked body and headed for the bedroom.

'I'll just get changed,' he told her. Daughter or not, it was not appropriate to discuss their relationship with him wrapped in a bathrobe. 'Would you like to wait a minute in the sitting room?'

Ignoring his request, she barred his way. 'Captain Rogers, my grandmother came upstairs to explain things to me. She has told me everything she knows.' Her eyes widened with childlike excitement and wonder. 'You *are* my father.'

He was deeply touched by her joy, but he was also determined to be cautious. 'It certainly looks as if I am, but we must make sure.'

Ruth threw her arms around his neck in wild euphoria. 'I just know it's true. When I saw you, something inside me drew me to you. I've waited so long for this moment.'

As she hugged him tight, a thrill ran through him. His child, his own dear child, here in his arms. He kissed her cheek and ran his fingers through her silky hair. 'Wonderful, isn't it? I never thought it possible.'

A demented shriek rent the air and clawed at his eardrums. Realisation of its source seared into his brain like a streak of lightning. He turned and saw June. Her contorted face was a sickly white, and her eyes were wild and staring. Before he could explain, his ring was flying at his face and June was rushing down the stairs.

'I have to get dressed!' he shouted, as much to himself as at Ruth. He rushed to his bedroom. 'We'll talk later.'

June was not in her bedroom. He raced downstairs. She was nowhere to be seen.

'Mum's taken Jimmy to see his pony,' said Rosie, in answer to his agitated running around. 'What's up, Charlie? You look worse than she does. Had a row?'

He rushed past her to see if her car had gone. Then he walked slowly back inside, worried about June's state of mind. With no chance for him to explain what she had witnessed, her emotions would remain in turmoil. Robert Watson again had the advantage and he would exploit it to the full.

Walking the white horse around the stable yard, Robert was pleasantly surprised to see June's car coming up the drive. He had been expecting James in the afternoon, so what could be the reason for his son being brought so early? James pestering her? Or had she finally realised where she truly belonged? Not only belonged, but where her duty lay?

Without doubt, June was deeply religious at heart. It was partly her upbringing, but also Arthur's influence. She found promiscuity deeply disturbing. Her association with him was a cause of both frustration and guilt — frustration because her inhibitions meant she could not get enough of him, and guilt because her earthy desires were anathema to the wholesome image she held of what a good woman should be. He knew her daughter's outlook on sex worried her, and that she feared that she was to blame. Silly woman! If she wanted peace of mind over her past indiscretion, and wanted to do the right thing by James, she had no choice but to marry the boy's father. Her guilt would then die a natural death. She could abandon herself to sexual pleasure, and go to church with impunity. He might even go with her. The churchgoing family man image would add an air of respectability and trust within the business world and society at large. Home life going smoothly, he and June would work even closer together.

Without doubt, June marrying him was good for business and better for everyone all round. The sooner Charles realised it and cleared off, the happier June and everyone else would be!

Well, whatever the reason for tearing herself away from Charles and the kids, things could not have worked out better for him. After a jolly good party and an exhausting hour in bed with Judy, he was ready for the simple pleasures of filial affection.

'Dad!' Jimmy yelled, running around the house towards the stables.

Robert handed the horse over to Bill Smith. 'Take Lightning to his box and give him a good rub-down. But first, bring the black pony out.'

The following half-an-hour was pure bliss. Apart from his excited son fussing over him and the pony, he had a woman who was giving him the impression that she was on his own wavelength for a change. Having gone through the process of James giving the pony a name and trying a saddle out for size, Robert decided to leave his son in Bill's capable hands and take June inside. Lucy, the stable lass, was given the job of leading the pony around the paddock.

'Take it easy. Let them get to know each other,' he called over his shoulder as he ushered June indoors.

Robert pulled off his highly-polished boots and slipped on the loafers he'd left in the side entrance porch. He led

June through to the hall and across to his study. With a special delivery of furniture and works of art the previous afternoon it was now complete, and he wanted to impress her.

In spite of its size and purpose, the room was warm and cosy. In front of a stoked-up fire was a large deerskin rug. It was set between two soft leather armchairs, chosen for comfort and relaxation. Each chair had its own small table. Impressive-looking books filled the shelves of a tall glass-fronted cabinet. Large, unframed contemporary works of art drew the eye and demanded attention. Two filing cabinets, a large desk with executive chair, and a rectangular table surrounded by high-back chairs — all of light oak and of linear design — revealed the room to be his working area as well as his den. One or two other items of furniture held interesting pieces of sensuous sculpture. The carpet was a deep red, and the curtains of a matching red with fine stripes of gold. Pale-beige leather was used on all the chairs and red leather on his desktop and boardroom table.

With pride of ownership, Rob watched June's eyes admiring his possessions and soaking in the ambience of the room. He poured her a glass of sherry and then sat opposite her, rubbing his thumb into the masculine cleft of his chin. 'I missed you last night. But I'm really pleased to see you this morning. I have something for you.'

He walked over to his desk. Unlocking the top right-hand drawer, he took out a little parcel and handed it to her. 'Happy Christmas.'

He watched her as she carefully untied the bow and tore away the violet tissue paper. When she uncovered the small ornate casket, she hesitated. It could hold a small brooch, earrings or a ring. What was she hoping for?

He was keen to see her reaction. 'Open it, June.'

The urgency in his voice had alerted her. She looked up at him, her eyes questioning. Licking her lips with the tip of her tongue, she pressed a small stud. The lid sprang open.

As she lifted the magnificent solitaire ring from its confining casket, the many facets of the huge diamond caught the light from fire and windows, in snatches of lightning radiance.

She looked up at him, her eyes wide and her face pale. 'Rob, I can't accept this.'

'Can't?' He lifted her left hand and put the ring on the third finger. 'Now it's official.'

He pulled her to her feet and held her close. Pressing his lips to hers, he kissed her with unrestrained passion. Her initial resistance crumbled — as he knew it would — and she hungrily opened up her mouth for more. The first step had been taken. Before long she would be Mrs Robert Watson.

'Now we'll be a complete family,' he told her softly. 'Anything you could possibly want will be yours, and every night will be a night of carnal lust.'

She was trembling in his arms. 'Rob, I can't marry you. Not yet. I need time.'

'You can have it,' he told her, confident they would be married within a month. 'But remember, our son needs his father and mother together. Move in as soon as your boys go back to school. You can start a new life. A secure life. You can be your true self: creative, sensual, passionately alive, and as radiant as that diamond on your finger. No more guilt trips, and struggling with your feelings. No more divided heart. You belong with me, June. You always have. You know it's true.'

'Maybe you're right. I—'

The door burst open. 'Dad, can I—'

'Never come in here without knocking!' Robert bellowed. He saw the look of horror on his son's face. 'Sorry, James, I should have told you,' he said, walking towards him and putting an arm around his son's shoulder. 'It's a rule of this house. My study is sacrosanct. Do you know what that means?'

'Sacred?' James offered nervously.

'Good enough. This room is out of bounds for most people. No one may enter without consent. Always knock on the door and wait until you have my permission to enter. Is that clear?'

'Yes, sir,' James answered.

'Good,' Robert told him, pleased with the touch of respect. 'Now, what is it you wanted, son?'

'Can we can go riding together?' His eyes were big and pleading.

'I'm looking forward to it. But first you need a little practice. I will leave that to Bill and Lucy.'

'But, Dad…'

'Not now, James.'

June intervened. 'We have to go home, Jimmy. We'll be back this afternoon.' She picked up her coat and hurried for the door. 'I'll see you later, Robert.'

He caught her arm. 'Hang on, I'll come outside with you.' He knew she needed time to digest her new status. Showing off the ring would surely cement the engagement. Charles would know the battle was lost and, with luck, clear off to Bath and Richard's bedside.

'Bring the others with you,' he told June, taking her hand and walking beside her. 'Let's be a family. Isn't that what you want?'

A cloud seemed to pass over her face, but it quickly vanished. 'Yes, Robert, that is exactly what I want.'

When they reached her car, James had disappeared. Rob collected him from the stables. 'Come along, James, your mother is waiting for you. You must always do as your parents tell you.'

Jimmy smiled up at him. 'Yes, Dad. We're all going to be living together soon, aren't we? You know, like a proper family?'

'Certainly, that is my intention.'

As James was getting into the Rover, Rob ruffled his hair.

His son turned and threw his arms around him. 'Thanks, Dad, Blackie's the best present ever!'

Robert smiled and turned to June. 'You see, we're a family already. Time to make it legal.'

Charles waited anxiously for June to return home. The irony of what had happened did not escape him. That she should arrive on the scene at a moment of ecstatic rejoicing, only to misjudge the situation was just too cruel for all concerned.

Poor, darling June. What a turn of events. After that bitter quarrel, a night of love and tenderness ending with him giving her a symbolic ring, and now that ring was back in his pocket and the situation was even worse. Having had no chance to explain why Ruth was in his arms was so frustrating. But surely she would understand, maybe even laugh about it, once she knew the facts.

He heard the Rover arrive in the drive. His heartbeat quickened. Pushing aside the pile of Christmas cards he'd been attempting to read, he jumped up from his sofa and hurried down both flights of stairs.

Jimmy came rushing into the hall ahead of his mother.

'Uncle Charlie, Uncle Charlie, you should see my new pony. I've called him Blackie. Will you come with us this afternoon and see me ride him? You will come with us, won't you?' He hung onto Charlie's arm, pulling at him for attention. 'Please, please, please!'

Charles was torn by Jim's pleas, which he found difficult to address at that moment, and wanting to catch June before she disappeared from the hall. 'We'll talk later,' he said, wrenching his arm free.

'But you will come, won't you, Uncle Charlie?'

'We'll see,' he said without conviction. June was making her escape and there was no time to stand arguing with Jim.

'June,' he called, rushing after her. 'I must speak to you.'

She ignored him. He grasped her right arm as she was mounting the stairs. She tried to pull away. 'I've heard enough of your lies,' she told him. 'Keep away from me! Angela was right. You have to sample every woman you meet!'

'That's rubbish! You got it wrong. Let me explain.'

'Let me go!' she yelled angrily, clawing at the hand clutching her arm.

Caught in the light of the hall's chandelier, a diamond sparkled from a ring on her third finger. Little rays of light were flashing the unmistakable message of her engagement. His heart grew heavy in his chest. He looked at her, hoping for a word telling him that his conclusions were wrong. Her head was turned away. He let go her arm. She hurried up the stairs.

Jim was pulling at his arm, but he didn't hear was he was saying. He broke free. 'Not now, Jim. Christmas dinner will be served shortly. Better get yourself washed.'

'Yes, Uncle Charlie,' Jim grunted, and trudged up the stairs.

Charles sighed. What now? Better for everyone if he disappeared. His presence in the house would only be an embarrassment. Just as well he kept his flat in Bath. He made his way upstairs to pack.

So, she had finally decided. Perhaps marriage to Watson was what she had wanted all along. Everything — career, home, husband, family — dressed up in one package. Her future was settled. No more big decisions to make. His living at Bloomfield had simply confused her. All she needed was an excuse to be free of him, and he had given it to her. To explain now would only bring her into confusion again. Better to leave at once before she found out the truth.

The boys, tired by lack of sleep and the morning's activities, were sitting down waiting to pull their crackers. Rosie was filling their wine glasses with orange juice, David complaining that he'd rather have wine.

June had taken off her ring, thinking it better to choose the right moment to announce her engagement to Robert. Thankfully, Jimmy had been too full of his pony to notice the huge diamond on her finger. But now she was back at Bloomfield, she was wondering if it had all been a mistake. Had her acceptance been a reaction to seeing Charlie with Ruth, rather than a considered decision? Of course, it made sense; there could be no disputing the benefits the whole family would gain. Robert was right in just about everything he'd said, and yet....

'Where's Uncle Charlie?' Peter asked, looking at the empty chair his father used to occupy. 'We can't get started without him.'

Just as Ruth was bringing in the turkey, footsteps were heard in the hall. She put down the dish on a heated tray resting on the sideboard, and ran from the room. June heard the front door bang as it closed shut behind her.

June walked to the window and saw Charles put down the bags he was carrying and turn round to speak to Ruth. He took a card and something wrapped in a handkerchief from his breast pocket and gave them to her. They hugged each other briefly and Ruth walked back to the house. As Charles was getting into his car, he turned and saw June standing by the window. With a look of deep sadness, he lifted his hand in farewell.

She stared motionless, grief mingling with anger. She was deeply wounded, but her love for him would not easily diminish. How could he act in such a blatant manner? And to think she had been feeling so bad about her relationship with Robert — the guilt never left her. Charlie had been acting strangely towards Ruth — a mere girl — ever since she arrived on the doorstep. How far would things have gone if she had not turned up? In her own home too, and on the morning of his giving her that symbolic ring. Yes, straight from her bed into the arms of a younger and much lovelier woman. 'Wonderful isn't it? I never thought it possible.' Those were the words he'd used.

She suddenly felt old and ugly, and dreadfully tired. Fighting back tears that threatened to overwhelm her, she closed her eyes to the retreating Mercedes. Determined not to spoil her children's Christmas, she put on a smile. It was enough that Arthur was no longer with them; they must not suffer her absence too. She turned to face the silent dinner table.

'Charlie's left. Silly of me, I forgot he was going to Bath. We had better start the dinner. Pull the crackers!'

After the meal June went up to her room. She could no longer keep up the pretence. She fell on her bed and sobbed bitterly.

There was a knock at the door. 'Mrs Rogers, it's Ruth. Can I speak to you, please?'

June took no notice. She was the last person she wanted to see at that moment. When she did confront her, it would be to tell her to leave.

Ruth persisted. 'I must tell you something, Mrs Rogers. It really is important. You got it wrong.'

June let her in. 'I heard it with my own ears,' she said bitterly

'I'm Charlie's daughter,' she said. 'At least we think so.'

June was stunned. Could it be true? Impossible, Charlie would have told her. 'Oh, really?' she snapped. 'Well, that's a new one! Does your grandmother know?'

'It's true, Mrs Rogers. We've only just found out. You can ask my grandmother, she will tell you the same.'

June dropped onto the bed and sat plucking absent-mindedly at the cover. Was it possible? Charlie a father? Why hadn't he told her? Why did he clear off? Of course, he saw Robert's ring on her finger and guessed correctly.

'How could you think I'm his lover?' Ruth persisted. 'He's about thirty years older than me. Frankly, I'm not that desperate, and I doubt that he is.'

Everything clicked into place. June realised she had made a terrible mistake. Or had she? A relationship had to be founded on trust both ways. But she had not even allowed him an explanation. Anyway, it was too late now — or was it? She asked Ruth where Charles had gone.

'His flat at Bath. He gave me his number, and others that would reach him when he's visiting Commander Andrews. He also gave me this to give to you.' She took a handkerchief from the pocket of her frilly apron and carefully unfolded it. It was the ring June had thrown back at him. 'He said he wanted you to keep it.'

Ruth left her, saying her grandmother needed her help. June looked at the ring. It was not as lavish as Robert's, but she loved it all the more for its simple beauty. She must speak to Charlie and ask his forgiveness. What then? No, she could not think that far ahead. One thing was certain; she could not see Robert that afternoon. She ran down the stairs and sought out Rosie. Her daughter was not difficult to find. Over the top of recorded pop music, and Peter's amateur drumming, her voice could be heard singing along with the Beach Boys. Entering the sitting room, she dragged Rosie out to the hall.

'Take the boys to the Old Rectory, Rosie. Rob is expecting all of us, but I have a headache. Tell him I'll be along sometime this evening.'

'Glad to. A nice quiet swim will be great. By the way, the boys want to know why you haven't opened your presents yet.'

She opened the presents one by one, smiling at her sons' choice of gifts — pretty embroidered handkerchiefs with delicate lace edging, a red umbrella, and a pink silk scarf with horse motifs. Rosie had bought her a red leather handbag, just the sort she would choose for herself.

After the family had gone, June sat looking at the gifts and at Charlie's ring, thinking she must be the luckiest woman alive. As she sat by the fire in the sitting room, memories of her younger days drifted through her mind: Arthur awakening her to romantic love when she was but sixteen, and of her growing affection for Charlie. Always in the shadows of her mind was Robert Watson. Rob who brought her talents to life, and stirred up a hungering for hedonistic pleasure. Yes, such a rich life and so much to be thankful for. Her children's happy faces drifted before her closed eyes. Smiling with contentment, she allowed herself to drift into sleep.

The telephone ringing broke into her dreaming. She pulled herself together and walked over to the phone perched on a corner table. Picking up the receiver, she sat on the floor — the kids had moved the chair elsewhere.

'June, are you all right?'

'Yes, Rob, I'm fine. Just a bit tired.'

'Then why aren't you here? Dammit, it's eight o'clock!'

'I fell asleep. I'll be there soon. I have something to do first.'

Back in her bedroom, she slipped Charlie's ring on the third finger of her left hand. In the light over her dressing table, Robert's ring sparkled its magnificent brilliance as if to compete for her affections. Sighing, she picked it up and returned it to its little casket. 'I'm sorry, Robert,' she practised aloud. 'I can't marry you. I love another man, and always have.'

She sat on her bed, reached for the telephone and dialled the number of Charlie's flat.

A woman's voice came on the phone.

'I'm sorry,' said June, 'I think I may have the wrong number. I wanted to speak to Captain Charles Rogers.'

'He's visiting a friend at the hospital. Can I give him a message for when he gets home?' said the pleasant well-spoken voice.

'To whom am I speaking?'

'Sarah Landers. I don't recognise your voice, would you like to leave your name?'

So that was it. It didn't take him long to find consolation. Sarah Landers had a key to Charlie's flat and was waiting to bind his damaged ego. Angela had warned her about the obliging nurse; now she knew for herself.

June put down the phone. Hot tears were racing her cheeks, but she didn't try to stop them. Slowly, she slipped Charlie's ring from her finger and replaced it with Robert's.

Chapter Thirty-Two

When Charles arrived in Bath he went straight to the hospital. When he opened Richard's door, two nurses came out, giggling. His friend was dressed and sitting in a chair, surrounded by cards, balloons, streamers, a paper hat and a glass of what appeared to be whisky and soda. Richard looked up as Charles walked in.

'Charles! How lovely to see you,' he said, smiling broadly. 'Happy Christmas! But why are you here? You should be with June.'

It was clear to Charles that Richard had just had some therapy not listed on his medical chart. He grinned. 'From that lipstick on your face, I can see your Christmas is not without its jolly moments. In fact, apart from the location, it's business as usual.'

Richard laughed. 'I didn't expect you coming here today. You should be with June and her family. But it's grand to have you again so soon. Bring that chair over and sit down.'

Charles removed a urine bottle — stuffed with a bunch of mistletoe — from the chair. 'I see hospital humour is still alive and kicking.'

Grinning, he lifted the chair closer to Richard. He took off his coat and sat down.

'I thought June needed time alone with her kids during their holidays.' It was not exactly the truth, but it sounded logical. 'David and Peter see little of her for most of the year. Anyway, I had a hankering to be back in Bath for part of the season.' He could see that Richard did not entirely believe him. 'Well, let's say, with Peter getting a set of drums and noisy kids all over the place, a bit of a rest will do me good. An old bachelor like me needs time to get adjusted.'

Richard nodded. 'That sounds more like it.' Obviously not convinced, he looked at him quizzically. 'Is there something you're not telling me?'

Charles shrugged his shoulders. 'What else is there to tell?' We can have a chat about my boring love-life some other time. Now what about you? Sister Landers looking after you properly?'

'As ever.'

Charles nodded at the balloons. 'Trust Sarah to pile on the Christmas cheer.'

Richard picked up a green party blow-out and put it to his lips. A squeal rent the air as it uncurled with a little feather dancing at its tip. He twiddled it in his fingers. 'I've heard from Rosie,' he said softly, his whole demeanour changing from merriment to pensive reflection. 'She says she misses me. So if I'm smiling, you know why.'

'I'm pleased, Richard. Rosie is a bit of a handful, but she's a lovely girl. I'm sure you'll be good for each other. That is, if it goes that far.'

'You know me, Charles, a bit of a handful is what I like!'

Charles laughed. Richard's future being so uncertain meant that nothing could be taken for granted. Better to keep things light where relationships were concerned.

'How are you getting on with Peggy?'

'What a woman!' Richard exclaimed. 'It will be good to have her around until I'm back on my feet — well, foot or whatever. She should be back soon. She's gone to my flat to get some clean pyjamas. I left the place in a hell of a mess. I expect Peggy has been doing some tidying-up.'

'It's Christmas, she can stay at my flat tonight. Not that I'm knocking your place, Richard, but I think the dear lady deserves a little comfort on a night like this. We'll invite some friends and have a glass or two. I'll be glad for her to give me a massage if she can afford the time.'

Richard chuckled. 'Aha! Mutual comfort, methinks.'

'We should all spread a little happiness. And I like Peggy spreading it on my shoulders and back. I can assure you, that is as far as it goes.'

'She loves you, Charles. You do realise that, don't you? Are you sure you ought to encourage her?'

'Come on, Richard, we are both adults, you know. However Peggy may feel about me, she knows the score. Using her skills on me is pleasurable for both of us. Would that all relationships worked so well.'

'You're practically engaged to her sister, doesn't that cause tensions?'

'Why should it?' Charles shifted in his chair. 'Let's talk about you. How are you progressing?'

'As you see,' — he picked up a balloon and patted it to Charles — 'sailing with fair winds on a new adventure.' He looked Charles in the eye. His cheerful face turned serious, causing his weathered skin to age him. 'You mustn't think yourself committed to our ideas for sharing a business venture. Let June come first. Twenty years of frustrated love are punishment enough. Don't lose her now through being tied to a vague business notion.'

'I'll bear that in mind,' Charles told him. 'Actually, marriage is not on the cards at present. Anyway, I have some interesting news for you. It looks as though I may have an offspring.'

Richard's face lit up. 'June's having a baby? That's great news. I'm so pleased for you both. Especially you, Charles. I know how much you—'

Charles put up a hand. 'Stop right there. June is not my child's mother. My daughter is twenty years old.'

Richard's smile changed to a grin. 'So, my friend, your past is catching up with you? Tell me more.'

Charles stretched his legs and then settled back in his chair. He told Richard everything he could about Ruth, and how she came to be conceived. 'But I'm afraid for her. That swine Robert Watson has offered her a job, part of the time modelling and the rest of her hours as his live-in cook.'

'I can see you're worried, what do you propose doing about it?'

'I don't know yet, but since she'll be starting soon, I'll have to think of something quick. Perhaps I could get her to live down here with me for a while. It would give us a chance to get to know one another.'

Richard frowned. 'What about June? Are you leaving her to Robert Watson's mercies while you indulge in newly-gained parenthood?'

Charles looked away, searching for a reasonable answer.

'There's something wrong between you and June, isn't there?' Richard asked him directly. 'You don't have to shelter me from your heartaches, Charles. Our friendship is too strong to have you suffer alone.'

Charles leaned forward; elbows on chair arms, head in hands. He fought to keep his voice steady. Richard listened to his story without interruption.

'But it's not too late,' Richard said, when Charles finally lifted his head with a grim smile to end his tale. 'When she knows the truth she'll regret what she's done. It was only on the spur of the moment.'

'Maybe. But she's been torn apart for ages. Watson's ring was on her finger. Perhaps she now has what she really wants — and needs. I don't want to throw her back into indecision.'

He heaved a deep sigh. 'She can find me if she really wants to. But I shouldn't be bothering you with all this. It certainly was not my intention.' He sat up and straightened his back.

'I'm glad you did. What are friends for? As for sheltering me from such problems, I'd rather be used as a sounding board than sit here like a piece of driftwood.'

The door burst open and Peggy entered, looking like Rudolph with her red nose and sheepskin coat, gloves and boots.

'Couldn't stay away from me after all? Happy Christmas, Charlie!' She gave him a sloppy kiss. 'Sister Sarah told me you were here.'

'Do you have a dose of tonic for me, too?' Richard asked, pursing his lips.

'With that lipstick all over your face, I think you've had enough,' she laughed. 'But, if you insist, how can a girl refuse a handsome sailor?'

Sister Landers came in with a tray. She smiled at Charles. 'Back so soon? Is it the company, or do you like hospital tea? I'll get two more cups.'

'Now there's a lady you can invite to your party,' said Richard as Sarah Landers breezed out of the room. 'I know she has nowhere to go tonight.'

Peggy looked up from the bag she was emptying into Richard's locker. 'A party? You're having a party, Charlie? I hope I'm invited.'

'You certainly are. And you can stay the night.'

'Now there's an offer,' she said, giggling. 'Who else is coming?'

'Don't know yet, but I have a few ideas.'

The tea arrived, complete with Christmas cake.

By seven o'clock, five nurses and two young doctors shortly going off-duty, plus an unspecified number of Charlie's old friends and colleagues, had agreed to join the party. All of them offered to bring a bottle or items of food. It appeared that most of them had received edible Christmas gifts they wished to share, or otherwise dispose of. Sarah said she would go ahead to the flat with Peggy and organise things.

When Richard was put to bed, Charles left his friend to sleep. He drove to his flat determined to put on a good show. Surrounded by a throng of folk in festive mood until the early hours was merely a diversion. A troubled heart was not so easily assuaged.

Chapter Thirty-Three

June woke up on Boxing Day full of apprehension. Bloomfield promised to be somewhat hectic. With the youngsters at home all looking forward to the special party and no Charles to keep control, how on earth was she going to manage? Why had she agreed to it? She knew why — guilt for not giving them the parental attention she thought they deserved.

Feeling nauseated, she struggled out of bed and made her way to her bathroom. She threw up into the toilet pan. Feeling faint, she allowed herself to slip to the floor with her head in her hands. Memories of the night before — enforced jollity, keeping up with the youngsters, being plied with food and drink, Rob's constant pressure to get her agreement for a January wedding — rushed through her brain like a turbulent riptide. She struggled to her feet to vomit once more.

Showered, make-up heavily applied to conceal her weariness, and dressed in a cheerful bright-red trouser suit, she quickly made her way down the stairs. She might just have time for a piece of unbuttered toast and a cup of coffee before Robert was due to collect Jimmy. From the open door of the sitting room came the raucous sounds of squabbling, beating drums and loud music. The boys probably had a couple of friends in. She closed the door to soften the din, and made her way to the kitchen. Mrs Craven was there.

'Sit down, Mrs Rogers, I'll get you some breakfast. You look all-in.'

So much for the work she had done on her face! 'Thanks, Annie. Just plain toast will do.' She sank into a chair by the kitchen range.

The door burst open. 'Robert's here,' said Rosie. 'Where do you want him?'

'We'll go in the lounge,' June told her. 'Will you ask Jimmy to get ready, please, Rosie?'

Robert was pacing the floor — no doubt exercising his brain as well as his legs — when June joined him two minutes later. His restless energy tensed her nerves.

'Sorry to keep you waiting,' she said, putting on a smile.

'What's the racket? Party started already?'

'That's to come. Oh Rob, I can't cope. It's all on top of me.' She threw up her hands in despair. 'Hells bells! I could just scream!'

He put an arm around her shoulders. 'Where's your minder? Keeping out of the way?'

'If you mean Charles — he's gone.'

'Gone? You told me he walked out when he saw my ring. I thought he just wanted to sulk. Well, well, soon gave up, didn't he? That should tell you something. Nice of him to run off just when he's needed. Never mind, I'll take the boys off your hands. Let's see… Frederick, Bill and Lucy are in today. Jane — pretty young thing — started this morning. You've met her mother, Mrs Lindsey. She comes in to clean. I'll take care of James myself. The young lasses will keep the other two occupied.'

He lifted her head and kissed her lips. She found it hard to respond.

'I'm sorry,' she said, dropping her eyes to avoid his. 'I'm not in the mood. I'm so very, very tired.'

'Not surprising with this mob running riot. Perhaps this will convince you to move in with me — sooner, rather than later. It's too much for you. All this strain will ruin your creativity.' He stood up. 'Go and fetch them. I'll bring them back around five. At least you have Rosie and Ruth to assist you at the party. If you want me here, just ask.'

'I am asking, Rob. Please do come, I need a man to handle the boys.'

He seemed pleased. 'Right. I accept your invitation. Casual dress?'

As Rob drove off, June started to feel better about everything. Robert was acting so much the family man that she could see her future as being congenial and ordered, with nothing at all to be feared.

And Charlie? A sudden pain seized her throat, destroying her composure. She must learn to live without him, just as she was learning to live without his brother. A tear ran down her cheek. She hastily brushed it away and hurried to her bedroom to repair her mask.

By five o'clock the pop group had arrived and was busy setting up at the bay window end of the lounge. Lisa was helping Annie in the kitchen and Ruth was assisting Rosie in the dining room. Chairs were moved around the walls to leave plenty of space to collect food from the large dining table and sideboard. Ruth helped Rosie spread white damask cloths and polish up the silver cutlery. Piles of plates and Christmas serviettes were placed at the table ends. An impressive arrangement of white painted twigs, hung with twinkling crystal icicles and shiny red baubles, was placed in the centre of the sideboard. Holly, rich with red berries, ran along the table centre. Rosie said it was to stop greedy kids stretching right across the table and spoiling the food. 'Last year a horrid boy ruined a trifle and a plate of sandwiches by catching his elbow on the cream. And he knocked a pile of iced fancies on the floor.'

'No dog to clean it up?' Ruth asked.

'Not unless you count my greedy brothers!'

They both laughed.

'I think it's time we had a break,' said Rosie. 'I'm whacked!'

It was pleasant drinking tea by the fire, but Ruth felt guilty: she was being paid to work. She stood up, but Rosie told her to sit a while. 'I want to ask you something,' she said, looking towards the door.

'The door is closed, Rosie. Your mother is upstairs and my gran is in the kitchen. But I can't sit here much longer. I've got work to do.'

'There's something going on between you and Charlie. But I don't think that's the only reason why he left. Mum's engagement to Rob did that. His ring came as a surprise to all of us, but it must have been a kick in Charlie's gut. Even so, I'm amazed he deserted Mum just when he was needed. It's not like him. Not like him at all. He's always been the faithful, if ill-fated, lover. He'll be back, you know. He loves her too much to stay away. Unless... well, you tell me, Ruth.'

Ruth felt uncomfortable. 'I suppose it has to come out some time. But say nothing to anyone else yet.' She paused, biting her lip. 'It looks as if Charlie is my father.'

Rosie frowned. 'It had crossed my mind when I saw the two of you together, but I couldn't believe Charlie would not acknowledge his own child.'

'It's not like that.'

'Isn't it? Now he's run away from the situation. What a rotter! No wonder mother is marrying Robert. At least he's owning his child and doing his duty. And I always thought Charlie wanted children. You know, I pitied him because he didn't have any? I can't understand him.'

Ruth was deeply upset by what she was hearing. 'You've got it wrong, Rosie. Charlie isn't like that.' She quickly put her right, telling her the details as far as she knew them. Then she told her how June had caught her embracing Charles. 'To make matters worse, he was only wearing his bathrobe.' She told Rosie about the words June must have heard. 'She probably had the impression that we were about to become lovers.'

'Good heavens!' Rosie exclaimed.

'But how ridiculous! Look at the age difference. If your mother had seen her fiancé kissing you in the kitchen on Christmas Eve, would she have assumed he was having it off with her own daughter? The whole thing is outrageous. But then, I guess your mother isn't thinking straight. Or maybe she's wanted Robert Watson all along.'

Rosie felt naked and ashamed: Ruth's words about Robert kissing her had come like a shock of cold water. Robert had bewitched her the night of the staff party and she knew it, even though she had tried to hide it from herself. Not only had he kissed her, but also — in a devious sort of way — he'd hinted there was more to come. What had he said? 'I look forward to our new close relationship… I'm rather fond of you… but I think you know that already.'

Maybe there was nothing special in those words, but his voice and his look told her something much more explicit. As though in his mind he was already fornicating with her. Not for the first time, she had been utterly thrilled by Robert Watson; a man many years her senior. A shiver ran down her spine.

Ruth was looking at her. 'Are you all right, Rosie? You look quite pale.'

'I'm okay, but poor Uncle Charlie. He must be terribly hurt. First he finds a long-lost daughter, but then loses the woman he's always loved. I wonder if he's gone to see Richard?'

'Richard? Is that Commander Andrews, the friend in hospital?'

'Not only Charlie's friend, but a friend of the family.' Memories of their torrid lovemaking came back to her in a jumble of sound and colour. Her desire to be back in Richard's arms was overwhelming. 'Oh Ruth, Richard is the most daring, most dazzling man alive.'

'And he's only just a friend? Come off it, Rosie, you sound like a woman in love!'

A woman in love? Of course she was. She just had to tell Ruth the story of her love affair; for in the telling was the reliving of a magical romance. Best to start at the beginning. She told Ruth about her relationship with her father and her mother. Tears came to her eyes when she spoke of her father's death. Joy drove away sadness when she recalled Charlie's arrival, and a frown drew her brows together when Robert Watson came on the scene. A frown maybe, but also a lightning thrill which caught her off-guard. That was something best kept to herself. With Ruth sitting quietly listening, she went on to speak of her various boyfriends and how they had let her down, that is, until Richard came on the scene. Pent-up emotions, connected with grief and sorrow, came tumbling out.

'Now Richard wants me back. At first I was afraid of being hurt again, but now I understand why he sent me away and I love him more than ever.'

She threw her arms around Ruth. 'Thank you. You're such a good listener. I wish you had come into our lives long ago. You must be Charlie's daughter, you're so incredibly like him.'

Loud noises were coming from the hall. Guests were arriving and the band was in full swing. June, changed into a glittering dark blue dress, came rushing into the dining room, inspecting the table, sideboard and things in general. She saw the girls sitting by the dying fire and became agitated.

'I knew I shouldn't have been resting. What have you been doing all this time? Half the food is still in the pantry. Can you get on with it, please? Everyone will be here soon and you're both sitting chatting, for goodness' sake!' She rushed out again.

Robert was in the hall, talking to George. Helen was next to them, casting admiring glances at Rob. Lucy, the stable-girl, was talking to David. Peter and Jimmy were running up the stairs, hopefully, to get changed.

June sent David upstairs to get washed and changed too. Michael and Bobby quickly took his place beside Lucy. The doorbell rang again. More guests had arrived. She opened the door and welcomed the neighbours, who had their daughter Emma with them. June made a mental note to keep an eye on her and David. More cars were pulling into the drive. To June's relief, Rosie took over at the door.

Half an hour later, teenage sons and daughters of family friends had filled up the large lounge cleared for dancing. Youngsters were either hovering around listening to the music and singing, or getting stuck into twisting, rocking, shaking and anything else that amused them. The grownups tended to drift into the sitting room.

Robert was being supportive by keeping the party going in an orderly fashion. June was both surprised and grateful. She left Rob twisting to the music with Lucy, and walked to the sitting room to mingle with the adults. Most of them had seen Robert's ring glittering on her finger and had been pressing her for explanations.

The room was buzzing with talk. A blonde in a long white and gold-thread dress had her back to her. June was astonished. Surely it wasn't Angela? The woman turned. It was Angela!

'Hello, June darling,' she said, smiling like a cat fed on tinned salmon with cream for afters. 'I heard it was open house, so here I am to celebrate your engagement.' She lifted June's hand to view the ring. 'What a beauty!'

June was baffled. 'How did you know?'

'About the engagement? I didn't until I got here. Now, of course, everyone is talking about it. What have you done with Charlie? I must give him my commiserations.'

'Yes, where is Charlie?' Helen butted in.

The chatter in the room had ceased and all eyes were on June.

'He's visiting a sick friend,' she said, furious that Angela abetted by Helen were stirring things. She took hold of Angela's arm and led her to the hall. 'This is a not an engagement celebration, Angela. We are having a party for youngsters and their parents. Please will you leave?'

'But, darling, Helen said it was a family party. We are sisters-in-law, are we not? I divorced Charlie, not you.' She smiled triumphantly. 'I'll get back to the others. Helen and I need to catch up on gossip.'

June grasped Angela's arm so tightly that she let out a little squeal. 'You are doing no such thing, Angela,' she said angrily. 'Get your things and go!'

'I'll see this lady out,' said an authoritative voice. 'Please get your coat, madam.'

Angela's eyes flashed with anger. Then she turned and saw Robert Watson heading straight for her. 'Gladly,' she said, giving him a sweet smile. She picked up a white fur coat thrown over the banister. 'Would you care to drive me home?'

She posed by the newel post, showing off her figure in its clinging, deep-plunge, side-split dress. Robert's lips twisted into an enigmatic smile. 'This way,' he said, with a sweep of a hand.

He took her arm and led her across the hall, through the open inner door to the outer one. With a flourish, he invited her outside. 'Thank you, madam, if I want an experienced prostitute, I know where to find one.' He closed the door. Even the music from the lounge failed to drown Angela's screams of fury.

June smiled at Robert in gratitude. 'What a relief!'

He gave a little bow and offered her an arm. 'Well, June dear, shall we join the party? I don't think Charlie's cast-off will be bothering you again. That fool was too soft with the woman.'

June, with Robert by her side, became the centre of attention in the sitting room. Everyone wanted to gaze at the ring and offer his or her congratulations. Robert was smooth and friendly, easy to talk to and showing none of the arrogance that was so much part of his personality. June marvelled at how well he fitted in. By now they must all know that he was Jimmy's father, but it seemed to be accepted. Perhaps their getting married had something to do with it, but she knew full well that personality, wealth and power helped ease the way.

After the party, Robert took Lucy home. He returned to Bloomfield to sleep with June. She knew he would. Tired though she was, he would soon breathe new life into her. But one thing she could not do: let him into the bed she had shared with Arthur and then with Charlie. Apart from which, the large guest room, being at the end of the rear extension, was more private and secluded. Once Robert was asleep, she would slip back to her own room.

In the morning, June watched Robert leave for home with Jimmy sitting beside him. Tomorrow was their son's birthday, and they would all be spending most of the day at the Old Rectory. She sighed: how quickly everything had happened. Part of her accepted the new situation, but she ached for Charlie. Dear Charlie, what was he doing now? Was he living with Sarah Landers? Did it matter? Surely he was entitled to a little happiness. She sighed even more heavily.

As she closed the door, Rosie came up behind her. 'That's a big sigh, Mother. Regretting accepting Rob's ring? Why don't you get in touch with Charlie and ask him back? We're all going to miss him dreadfully, not just you. How long do you think Rob is going to play the caring father once you're married? He's married to his job. We both know that.'

'You're wrong, Rosie. Robert has changed. He loves Jimmy and me, and wants to lead a more homely life with all of us. Rob's never known what it's like to have real family affection. He's a new man. You saw how he was yesterday.'

'A flash in the pan. Back at work he'll be the big chief again. No time for play... at home or anywhere else. You'll be his full-time slave.'

June took Rosie's arm. 'Come into the lounge. It's more private.'

'Why have you turned against Rob?' she said, when they were sitting down. 'I thought you wanted to work for him yourself. Have you changed your mind?'

'Yes. I'm going to see Jack this afternoon to see about teacher-training college. I don't want to be like you, Mother. I want a life of my own.'

'Are you upset because Charlie's gone? He always did make a big fuss of you.... I expect you'll see him occasionally, you know.... But I can't ask him back, Rosie... he has a life of his own. I don't want to spoil his plans.'

'If you won't, then I will! I've seen the two of you together. That's love, Mother — real love — not whatever is going on with you and Robert.'

'What do you know about it?'

'More than you think. There's something about Robert that's irresistible.'

'Rosie, has Rob—'

'No! At least, not what you're thinking. But it could have been heading that way. I don't want to live in Robert Watson's house. I want to live with you and Charlie. I'll find out where he is. Maybe he'll come back to us.'

Before June could say anything, Rosie was on her way out. June sighed wearily; her daughter had always been impetuous. Now Peter was practising on his drums! She put her hands to her head and screamed.

Ruth appeared in the room, her handsome face looking most concerned. 'What is it, Mrs Rogers? Can I help you?'

'Just letting off steam. Don't worry, I'm not ill, or hurt. I'll go to my room.' She turned at the door. Ruth was picking up ashtrays and bits of rubbish from the night before. 'Don't put the ashtrays out again, Ruth. Since Arthur's death, I won't allow smoking in the house. I didn't like it before, and I won't have it now.'

'I'm sorry, Mrs Rogers, I didn't know. Someone asked for one last night, so I put one in each room.'

'I expect it was Angela,' June said, thinking how that woman polluted everything around her.

'Before you go, Mrs Rogers,' said Ruth. 'Do you want me to change the sheets and tidy the guest room?'

'I'll do that myself.'

Panicking at the thought of someone entering the room she had shared with Robert, June hurried up the stairs and along the corridor to the back of the house. Once inside the guest room, with its unmade bed and her clothes — shoes, stockings, torn dress, knickers, bra — strewn around in a whirlwind mess, she sat down and wept.

Chapter Thirty-Four

Saturday afternoon, Charles drove Peggy around Bath to find the right car for her to drive. Due to early closing, they had not been successful on Christmas Eve. An eager salesman, telling them a sob story about his need to secure his Christmas bonus for the benefit of his sick wife and new baby, had almost sold Peggy an old taxi. Then a brassy-haired woman, with a youngster in tow, had turned up wanting to know why he hadn't arrived home. Evidently they were due to go to her mother's house for Christmas. Through the noise of battle, Peggy told the salesman she liked the idea of a roomy taxi but had no confidence in its supposed good condition.

As far as Charles was concerned, it had been a good decision. Peggy deserved something better to drive. The ideal car had just arrived at a garage on the edge of the city. It was a well-maintained, elderly Rolls Royce that Richard would be able to get in and out of without much difficulty. Peggy was ecstatic at the prospect of driving such a princely automobile. 'Golly, after all my old bangers, whoever thought that one day I would be sitting in one of these, let alone driving one!'

They took the car for a test drive and Peggy was for taking it there and then. The garage owner told them of a few small problems that needed fixing, but the car could be ready, washed and polished, for the following day.

'Oh Charlie, I can hardly wait. What with living in Bath, looking after a handsome naval officer, and driving a Buckingham Palace-on-wheels, I'll think I'm in heaven!'

They returned to his flat with two bags of groceries. Peggy set about preparing them omelettes. He was making them coffee when the phone rang. It was June.

A trembling voice whispered, 'Charlie, is that you?'

'Hello, June, can you speak up, I can hardly hear you.' His yearning for her had not diminished and it pained him that he was not there to give her the comfort she obviously needed.

'I'm so sorry, Charlie.' She was speaking louder, but the tremor in her voice was increasing. 'I know I've hurt you. It was all a big misunderstanding. Ruth explained things.'

'I'm glad about that. I should have told you myself. I'm sorry.'

'I guess you have Sarah Landers to keep you company now.'

'Sarah Landers? Oh, were you the lady who called Christmas evening? Sarah was helping to prepare an impromptu party. Surely you didn't think...?'

He was deeply hurt. 'You must think my love is very shallow, June.'

Peggy called to him. 'Ready, Charlie.' She muttered something about omelettes turning to leather. 'Don't keep a lady waiting!' she yelled, her tinkling laughter drifting from the kitchen.

'Is that Peggy I can hear?' June asked.

'Yes, do you want to speak to her?'

'Not really.' She hesitated. 'Will you be coming to Rosie's party on Tuesday? Peggy too, if she can get away. Rosie will be very sad if you don't come. You know how much she loves you. She told me today she wants to be with you, not living with Rob and me.'

'I thought Rosie was keen on Robert. Has she seen him in his true colours at last?'

'Please don't be bitter. Robert has been really helpful with the boys, and marvellous at organising the kids at last night's party.' She sounded too enthusiastic. 'Rosie says she wants to do her own thing and be a teacher.'

'Good for her. I can't promise to come to her party. I'm not sure if I can stand being in the same room as Watson, but I'll give it some thought. Don't worry about Rosie, she just thinks she wants to live with me. She'll stay with you, you'll see.'

'I'm pleased you have a daughter. Ruth is a lovely girl. She told me all about it and how I got things wrong. Sorry, Charlie.'

'So you said.' What did June want of him? Absolution for the sin of jumping to conclusions? In her position he would have done the same. 'Perhaps it's worked out for the best. Helped you make up your mind. That can't be bad.' A lump was forming in his throat. He must not let her know how wretched he felt. His misery would only make her more anxious. 'Look, I have to go now. I'll be seeing you soon. Take care.'

Before June could reply, he put down the receiver and covered his face with his hands.

He felt a hand touching his taut shoulders. He took hold of it and pressed it to his haggard face. 'I have to let her go,' he said. 'But it's so hard to do.'

'Can I help you? I really do understand,' Peggy said gently.

He turned his head to look at her, forcing himself to smile. 'How about one of your deep muscle massages?'

'Are you sure that's all you want?'

'Yes, Peggy, that is all. Nothing more'

Peggy bent over and kissed his cheek. 'I know I'm not much to look at, but there's not much wrong with my sparking plugs. They just need a bit of use occasionally. Always remember, Charlie, you can get my engine running any time. And it will be my pleasure to take you wherever you want to go.'

In spite of his unhappiness, he had to smile. 'Peggy, you are as handsome and reliable as that majestic Rolls Royce. What would I do without you?'

It was early evening when they arrived at the hospital. Peggy went off to get them a drink, leaving Charles to tell Richard about the car.

'That sounds great. Just the thing! Now what about payment and insurance?'

The details were soon sorted.

'What else have you been up to, Charles? 'You're looking a bit strained. Is all this running around on my behalf getting you down?'

Charles shifted uneasily in his chair. 'Well, I might as well tell you. June rang. She apologised about the misunderstanding. Ruth told her about our probable relationship. And I've been invited to Rosie's party.'

'Please go, Charles. I know it will be painful for you, but Rosie loves you and needs you there. After all, you were her father's closest brother. Not only that, but I would like you to take her a present from me.'

'All right, I'll go. I suppose I did rather leave June in the lurch. I should have sorted things out before leaving. I guess I owe her something. I'll talk to Rosie too. Poor girl doesn't know what she wants.'

He told Richard about Rosie's present plans for the future. 'Maybe teaching is the right thing for her. At least she'll be away from Watson's influence.'

Richard nodded. 'I'm sure Rosie will enjoy that sort of work, and her creativity will come in useful.'

Peggy came in with cups of tea on a tray.

'You're looking lovely tonight, Peggy,' said Richard. 'The Bath air must agree with you.'

'There certainly is something bracing about this place,' she said, smiling at both of them. 'Not sure it's the air, though.'

'I've heard other women say the same sort of thing after they've met Richard,' joked Charles.

Richard shook his head and grinned.

Chapter Thirty-Five

Rosie left June playing table-tennis with Peter. Of course, the game wouldn't last long: Robert Watson was looking for her mother. That man always insisted on getting his own way. He wanted them all to stand watching Jimmy riding Blackie so he could take photographs. Well, it was *not* going to happen. They had already obliged him by acting the fool while he directed a home movie with Jimmy in the starring role. She'd had enough of Robert fussing over her brother. Huh! It was for sure she wasn't going to call him James just because Rob said so.

Having come prepared for a swim, she was off to the conservatory pool. She smiled at her thoughts. She wasn't the only escapee: David had been seen slipping off with young Lucy. Robert Watson would have to get his family photos some other time, if ever. She agreed with her mother: young Jim, even if it was his birthday, was getting far too much attention.

But why should she hate Robert Watson, apart, that is, from stealing her mother and changing everybody's lives? She had enjoyed him fussing over her: inviting her to stay, giving her a capacious en-suite room of her own and freedom to roam. But she didn't trust him. Was she jealous? No, she was fearful. Yes, that was it — fearful. Not just of the break-up of her family, but of Robert himself. He had mesmerising powers. She could not trust herself when alone with him, and that made him a dangerous man. A *very* dangerous man indeed.

Familiar voices sounded somewhere close. Robert appeared, dragging her mother off to the stables. 'You should be concentrating on James today, not Peter.'

Rosie kept herself hidden behind a potted tree fern in the conservatory until they were out of sight. She took the opportunity to slip off her clothes down to the pink bikini she was wearing in readiness for a lonesome swim. There was something tranquil and relaxing about having the pool to herself. At least that was one uncluttered benefit that came out of her mother's relationship with Watson.

'Hello, Rosie.' It was Steven Blake. He was sitting in a lounger by the pool, dressed in a shiny costume that barely covered his manhood. 'I thought I would find you here,' he said, smiling broadly. 'Mind if I join you in the pool?'

The rotter! He'd been sitting there all along. She threw her clothes over a cane armchair and stood in front of him, hands on hips. 'What are you doing here?'

'The boss told me to call in today. He said he had work for me to do. He's told me to have a swim while I'm waiting.'

'Oh really?'

'It's good to see you, Rosie. You haven't answered any of my calls.'

'No need. And if you're going to be here with Robert Watson, I'm off.'

'He only said to wait here. I think he's busy at present.'

'He's busy, all right. Now I wonder why he told you to come here? Could it be because he knew I would be coming for a swim?'

'I doubt it. Why should he?'

'Huh! Do you lick his riding boots clean every morning? Wimp!'

She jumped into the water and started swimming. He jumped in and waited for her to return across the pool. He gripped her arm.

'I'm really sorry I wasn't able to make it that night. Won't you let me make it up to you?'

'I don't want someone who thinks more of his job than he does of me.' She drew up her legs and kicked him away with her feet. 'Clear off. I don't want you here.' She swam to the other side and gripped the rail, waiting for him to go.

He swam across to her. 'But we'll be working together soon. Best to be on good terms.'

She tossed her head. 'Afraid not. I'm staying at school to do my A levels. Then I'm going on to college.'

He came closer, holding on to the rail and letting his legs float. Rosie refused to look at his bulging crotch. He was not going to lure her that way!

'Robert's expecting you to start work in a week's time,' he said, wriggling his toes and lifting his hips. 'He won't be pleased.'

'Too bad.' She put on an angry mask. 'If you're going to stay in here fouling up the water, I'm getting out.'

She swam to the steps and heaved herself out of the water. Steven quickly followed, grasping her arms to pull her to him. She tried to knee him in his groin, but he was too quick for her. With an adroit movement, he dragged her on to a lounger and tried to kiss her. She turned her head to bite his ear, but the lounger suddenly tipped over and he landed on top of her. Furious, she tried to push him away.

'Get off!' she yelled.

'Come on, Rosie. You know you like me.'

She struggled to free herself. But he was gripping her wrists tightly, and the weight of his body made her immobile.

'Get off! Get off!' She spit out the words through clenched teeth.

'I guess I really disappointed you. But we can make up for that right now. Come on, darling, stop struggling.'

'Get off me, you swine!'

'Let's do it the way we planned.' Holding both her wrists with one hand, he pulled her bikini top upwards and sucked her nipples with his wet lips.

'Get off!' she yelled, trying to get her knee to his groin.

'You wanted your wrists tying to the bedposts.' He tightly wrapped her bikini top around her wrists. 'Sorry, there's no bed.'

She couldn't reply: his sloppy wet mouth was soon covering hers, and he was thrusting his tongue as he'd done many times before. She used to welcome his love-play, but not now. She belonged to Richard. Belonged to Richard? Yes! Now she was certain. With all of her heart, she belonged to her buccaneer.

She felt Steven's knees parting her legs. Surely he wouldn't….

'Get off our Rosie! Leave her alone, or I'll kill you!'

Rosie glanced sideways and saw Peter standing red-faced with fury, his fists clenched and poised for a fight.

'We're just having a game,' Steven shouted. 'Clear off!'

'Stay here, Peter, until I get changed,' Rosie said, trying to speak normally. 'Steven's stupid game is over. I don't like his rules, and I don't like him!'

Steven stood up, picked up his towel and ran off towards the changing room. He stopped and turned. 'Rosie, I'm sorry, I didn't intend—'

'I don't want to hear your lies,' she yelled at him, trying at the same time to free her hands and cover her breasts. 'Get out of my sight or I'll let Peter deal with you!'

'But, Rosie—'

'Go!'

She watched him disappear through the door of the short passage leading to the changing room facilities, and beyond to the house. 'Don't come back!' she shouted vehemently. 'Peter's got a black belt, and he's the school's boxing champion too!'

Peter was agog. 'I've only just started doing judo at school. I'm not much good at boxing either,' he confessed, freeing her hands while trying to look the other way. 'I only know a few things Uncle Charlie taught me.' He passed her a towel from the back of a chair.

'So what?' she said, drying her legs. 'You've got a black belt holding your trousers up — you could have belted him with it!'

Peter laughed. 'Oh Rosie, you are funny.'

She didn't feel humorous. What on earth had happened to Steven? He had never treated her like that before. How far had he intended going? Rape? Surely not!

She slipped on her jersey top and gave Peter a hug. 'You are my hero, Peter. You saved me from a fate worse than death.' She pushed him away. 'Now clear off while I get my clothes on.'

She watched him leave by the door Steven had used, and hoped he wouldn't have a go at punching him up. Dear Peter, everyone underestimated that young man.

Having dressed, she sat by the pool, towelling her hair, and thinking about what had happened. If Peter had not arrived on the scene….

Her thoughts were interrupted by the sound of the outside door of the conservatory sliding open. She turned ready to thump Steven, if he came anywhere near her.

'Rosie, Rosie, I've got something to tell you!'

'Peter! Shut that door quick, there's a heck of a draught.' She slipped her leather jacket over her shoulders. 'Come and sit by me.'

'I followed Steven and what do you think?' he said excitedly, sitting on the edge of the proffered chair.

Rosie put a comb through her hair, pressing in a wave with the help of her fingers. 'I'm sure you're going to tell me, so get on with it.'

'He went straight to Robert Watson and told him what had happened. I was hiding behind a wall. Mum was with Jimmy and didn't hear what was going on. But I did. I heard every word. Steven sounded ever so nervous.'

'I bet he did,' Rosie said, thinking she had been right.

'Mr Watson was furious. He called Steven an idiot. He said he'd told him to seduce you, not rape you. Actually, he said lots of juicy swear words, but I'm not allowed to speak them.'

'Right, that's it!' Rosie said, getting up and pulling on her boots. 'You keep out of the way, Peter,' she called from over her shoulder. 'I'll deal with this.'

She found Robert changing his footwear in the side entrance porch. 'How dare you instruct your lackey to seduce me?' she bellowed.

He laughed. 'What are you talking about, Rosie?'

'Don't deny it.' She lifted her head triumphantly. 'You were overheard!'

'I thought I saw a scraggy figure running off. Your sneaky brother, I presume? What do you expect from Peter? He's jealous of James and will do anything to get attention. I should give him a damn good hiding. As for Steven? Yes, he told me what happened before you had a chance to complain. He was supposed to persuade you to take up my offer of working for me. He may have been a little overzealous. But then, you two were once rather close. Or so I was led to believe. In fact, didn't you complain when he let you down over a hotel bedroom assignation? But if he overstepped the mark, then he's out — finished! Does that make you any happier?'

'But Peter told me—'

'I don't give a damn what that stupid boy told you. I'll have a word with your mother about that little liar.' He walked along to the hall, calling to Mrs Lindsey to clean the mud from the side entrance.

Rosie hurried away to find her mother. She was in the stable yard with Jimmy, holding out a carrot to Blackie.

'Give it him on the flat of your hand, Mum,' he was instructing her.

'You do it, Jimmy,' Rosie told him. 'I need to speak to Mother.'

'Will you come over here a minute?' she whispered, taking hold of June's arm. 'I have something to tell you.' She moved her to a corner of the yard out of Jimmy's hearing.

'What is it, Rosie? Make it quick, I'm getting jolly cold out here.' She turned up the collar of her coat. 'Jane has already called us in for tea. Can't we go inside and talk?'

'No, we'll be overheard.' Glancing around her, she told her mother what had happened. 'If it hadn't been for Peter, he would have raped me. Mind you, I was putting up a damned good fight. But I'm sure he thought I was enjoying it. Anyway, Rob is the one telling lies, not Peter.'

'But could Peter have misheard what was said, Rosie? You weren't there. Obviously Steven was in the wrong, but surely Robert is not implicated? He gave you a perfectly feasible explanation. I know he's keen to have you working for him. Surely he wouldn't do anything to wreck his chances? Steven was probably being overzealous. Did he hurt you?'

'Well, not really.'

'Was he exposed? Did he try to… you know?'

'No to both questions, but only because Peter arrived.' She looked at her mother angrily. 'You think I'm lying because Steven let me down that night. Is that it?'

'Of course not, but you were once very close. Maybe he misread the signals.'

'He tied my wrists together with my bikini top,' she said, fury rising in her breast. 'That is hardly compliance on my part!'

'No, of course not. But whatever Steven intended, I'm sure Robert had nothing to do with it.' Her expression told Rosie that she was by no means certain of any such thing.

'You refuse to believe Peter, then?' Rosie persisted.

'I'm sure Peter thought he heard what he said he did.'

'I don't see why Steven should get away with attempted rape!'

'That would be hard to prove. If you made allegations, just think about the consequences. You know what will be said.'

'That I enjoy kinky sex? That Peter caught us at it, and I'm trying to make out I'm a victim rather than a willing participant? Or is it that I'm trying to get revenge? What do you believe, Mother?'

'Of course, I believe what you say happened, Rosie. Robert is sacking him — his personal assistant — isn't that enough?'

'And you'll let Peter be called a liar?'

'No, of course not. I'll have a word with Peter. Maybe he did get things wrong, but I'll not let Robert abuse him in any way, you can be sure of that.'

'Really? It seems to me that once you marry Robert Watson, you'll have no say in the matter. Watson is only interested in his own son, not yours.' The sting of her remarks showed in her mother's eyes. She was looking harrowed, cold and incredibly weary. 'I'm sorry, Mum,' she said, putting an arm around her. 'I don't want to hurt you, but neither do I want Robert making your life a misery... or ours!'

Chapter Thirty-Six

On Monday morning, June was waiting to see her doctor. She glanced at the other patients seated in the comfortable armchairs of the waiting area. One patient looked really ill: his face pale and drawn and body hunched with coughing. A mother sat with a sleeping infant on her knees, and a teenage girl was keeping her head down, ostensibly looking at an old magazine but never turning its pages. Since this was a private practice with an appointments system, normally there would be no waiting to see her doctor, but Dr Wilson's colleague had been taken ill — so his nurse had informed her — and there were extra patients that had to be fitted in.

She sighed. It was her turn next, but why was she bothering her doctor at this busy time of the year? Of course, she knew why. It wasn't that she was ill as such, but for a few weeks she had been feeling tired and irritable, sometimes nauseous and, more recently, depressed. To be able to cope with the pressure she was under, she needed help. Maybe a tonic. Her present circumstances were affecting her health, and vice-versa. If she had been fully herself, maybe she would have acted more reasonably when she had caught Ruth kissing Charlie. But no, something within her had snapped. Too late for regrets.

Admitting the need for professional help did not come easily. The depression she had suffered after Peter's birth still haunted her like a spectre. She didn't want sedatives to dull her brain, didn't want to be labelled, didn't want to be thought of as sick! Maybe she was going through an early menopause. It was a horrible thought, but hormone medication might help. Better to know the problem than imagine the worst.

A voice broke into her consciousness. 'Mrs Rogers? Dr Wilson will see you now.'

The nurse ushered her into the well-equipped, light and airy consulting room.

'Good morning, Mrs Rogers,' Dr Wilson began, standing up and offering her the chair by his desk. 'What's the problem?'

June told him her symptoms and confided her innermost fears. He was a good listener: nodding his head in understanding when she hesitated, and urging her to go on until her stream of woes dried up.

'More than anything, you need a good rest,' he told her, levering his huge frame out of his seat. 'But I think it would be as well if I gave you a thorough examination. We'll do a few blood and urine tests too, just in case you have an underlying problem. If you would like to undress behind the screen? Just to your underwear will be sufficient. I'll get Nurse Jones to join us.' He lumbered to the door of the surgery dispensary. 'Bring the blood test tray in, please, Nancy,' he called in his pleasant, mellow voice.

Dr Wilson was thorough in his examination. 'You may get dressed now.' He turned to Nurse Jones. 'Assist Mrs Rogers then leave us, Nancy.'

'Well, Mrs Rogers,' he said, when they were alone, 'I hope your fiancé will be pleased to know you have a child on the way. How do you feel about it?'

June was astounded. 'I'm pregnant? Surely that's not possible? I know my periods have been scanty, but I can't be having a baby.' She shook her head. 'No, definitely not. I've had four and I know the signs.'

'You are at least three months pregnant. No mistake about it. The urine test will confirm it, but there's no doubt in my mind. If you think carefully about your symptoms you will realise the obvious. True, according to my notes, your previous pregnancies have been a little different: heavy sickness and fainting in the first week or so, no bleeding whatsoever and blooming health from then on.' He looked up from her file. 'But I can assure you, Mrs Rogers, you *are* having a baby.'

He began giving her advice on taking care of herself, but she was only half-listening. It couldn't be Rob's child, the doctor was certain about the timing. It had to be Charlie's. The thought thrilled her and yet....

Dizziness was overtaking her. She bent over with her head in her hands. Dr Wilson led her to a side room so she could lie down. 'Rest until you feel stronger. You must not drive home. Have you someone who will collect you?'

Rosie entered the room where her mother was resting. 'What's the matter, Mother? Are you ill?'

Nurse Jones answered her question. 'Just a little faint. Doctor says she'll be fine soon. Make sure your mother gets some rest.'

While they were on their way home, Rosie was talking about calling off the party. 'I'm sorry, Mum, I didn't realise what all the extra work is doing to you.'

'Don't worry, Rosie, I'll be fine by tomorrow. No need to cancel anything. Others can do the preparation. When we get home, I'll have an hour or two on my bed. Dr Wilson says I just need to take things easy for a while. I'll let you organise getting my car back to Bloomfield. Can't leave it there overnight.'

Back home, Rosie took charge of the household. She insisted her mother stay in her room for the rest of the day, threatening the boys with banishment from her party if they made any noise. Apart from preparing lunch and washing up, Annie Craven and Lisa were to sort out the laundry before going home early afternoon, and Ruth was to bake for the party. Mid afternoon, Rosie made sure things were progressing in the kitchen.

Working alongside Ruth, she told her what lay heavily on her mind: 'Peggy and Charlie should be coming to my party. I'll miss them. Richard should be here too,' she added wistfully.

Ruth was sympathetic. 'What a shame things didn't work out,' she said, cracking some eggs into a basin. 'You really love that Richard, don't you? Tell me more about him. The boys talk as though he's some sort of buccaneer.'

Rosie laughed. 'I suppose he is quite a character. He looks every bit a romantic adventurer, with his hair bleached by the sun, and his face tanned and chiselled by the weather. In a way, he's quite handsome, and very strong. You should see his muscles!'

She knew she was talking like a starry-eyed fool, but that was how she saw Richard, and always had. She put the kettle on to make coffee and continued to talk about him in glowing terms.

Ruth was grinning.

'What's so funny?'

'I guess you'll have to marry the guy. What a man! He must be out of this world.'

'He is, he really is.' She sat down at the table, greasing patty tins ready for Ruth's little almond tarts. 'When Mum's better, I'm going down to see him. Looks like I'll have to wait until the boys go back after this weekend. Robert Watson is having a big do for New Year's Eve. With Mum not well, I suppose I'd better help out. Could you stay here until she's better?'

'I guess so. I haven't agreed any commitments yet.'

June was lying on her bed, but doing very little resting. Her whole situation had changed. Rob might accept the baby if he thought it was his, but would he accept Charlie's child? Surely not! She was going to have to tell him and she dreaded it.

Of course, Charlie must be told too. But when? Perhaps she should leave telling either of them until the boys were back at school. Maybe wait until the baby began to show? No, for peace of mind she had to have closure, whatever the cost.

She rang Rob's home number, but was told he was at his office and wouldn't be home until late. She decided to leave it until after Rosie's party. But she had a deep feeling of dread and knew it was going to stay with her until the truth was out.

Rosie was not looking forward to her party, but she was prepared to put on a smile and make sure the guests were given a good time. The house seemed to be filled with inescapable noise. Jack had come early to shift furniture and prepare quizzes and games. He was going around whistling. David and Jimmy were blowing up balloons and deliberately bursting some of them. Someone had put on the Rolling Stones recording of *Honky-Tonk Woman*. Peter was tapping at his drums, and making such a racket that he was distorting the music and drowning out the lyrics. It had to stop!

'Stop that, you monsters!' Rosie screamed at her brothers. 'David, they'll be no balloons left to hang up. Peter, go help Ruth.' The tapping continued. 'Now!' she yelled, dragging him away from his drums.

She stood in the hall, looking fierce, making sure Peter went off to the kitchen. She closed the lounge door to soften the rest of the noise and breathed a sigh of relief.

'Sounds as though you could do with a hand, Rosie.'

'Charlie, you've come back!'

Rosie ran to him, throwing her arms around his neck. 'Thank God, you've come home.' Tears were streaming down her face.

'What a welcome!' he said, kissing the top of her head and rubbing his cheek against her hair. 'Happy birthday, darling girl.'

He unwrapped her arms from his neck and kissed her cheek. 'I'll take my things upstairs out of your way,' he said, picking up his bags and coat from the floor.

'I'm so pleased you've come,' she said, taking his coat. 'The boys are playing me up, things need doing and Mum's not well. You will stay, won't you? She really does love you, whatever you think. Don't let her marry Robert Watson.'

If only it were that easy. 'It must be your mother's decision, Rosie.'

'Then why are you here? You must love her.'

'It's you I've come to see,' he told her, walking up the stairs with her close behind him. 'I have presents for you, and a letter.'

He stopped at the first landing. 'I'm not sure if June wants me here. I'm sorry she's not well. Perhaps I can help, but I don't want to get in her way or spoil things for her.'

'She's in her room,' Rosie said, grasping his arm. 'Talk to her. Make her see sense.'

'Your mother made a decision. It wasn't easy for her. It would be wrong to upset her again.'

'She can't marry Robert. He hates Peter. I know he does. Peter looks like you and that's enough for him. I don't think he cares much for David either.'

'Watson isn't used to having teenagers around. He'll get used to the boys.' He said the words but he wished he could believe them. 'Maybe June will let me stay for a while, at least until the boys are back at school.'

'But Charlie—'

'Please, Rosie, not now,' he cut in quickly as June opened her bedroom door. 'Here, take these.' He handed her a bag with presents, cards and a letter. 'We'll talk later.'

June was standing by her door, staring at him in shocked silence. He put aside his bags and rushed over to her. She avoided his embrace by opening her door and beckoning him inside.

'Better talk in private,' she said softly, offering him one of the chairs by the table in the window.

Charles was shocked to see how tired she looked. Even the make-up failed to cover up the weariness she must be feeling. The red and black lurex dress she was wearing looked good on her figure, but the red brought out the pinkness of her eyes.

'I'm sorry you aren't well, June. I shouldn't have rushed off and left you in the lurch.' His whole desire was to take her into his arms and somehow make her better. Anything rather than sit there, divided by a table and making polite apologies. 'I should have been happy for you, not behaving like a jealous kid. Can you forgive me?'

'There's nothing to forgive. I'm the one who's in the wrong. We've all missed you. Are you here for the day or are you stopping?'

'I really would like to stay until things are going more smoothly for you. Is that all right with you?'

The doorbell sounded. Guests were arriving. She burst into tears. He jumped from his chair and drew her to her feet, holding her in his arms to comfort her. 'What is it, June? Have I upset you by coming back unannounced?'

'No, of course not. It's so good to have you here with me. But what about Peggy? Will she mind you being here?'

'Peggy? Why should Peggy mind?'

'I thought... I'm sorry, forget I said it. How's Richard?'

'Don't change the subject. You really think I'm having an affair with your sister? Oh, June. First Sarah, now Peggy. You know Peggy is only in Bath to care for Richard.'

'Charlie, please don't be cross. It's just that....'

Loud voices were heard in the hall. June rushed to her dressing table mirror and dabbed at her face with a tissue. 'Guests are arriving. I should be downstairs.'

Suddenly the door burst open and in walked Robert Watson. 'Ah, the runaway has returned,' he said. 'I thought it was your Mercedes in the drive.'

'Robert, I've been trying to phone you,' June said, a worried frown making her look even more weary.

'So I was told,' he answered, his narrowed eyes observing her closely. 'Well, I'm here now. Has Charlie been worrying you, sweetheart? Shame on him! I'll see him out of your bedroom. You tidy up and come downstairs.'

While June meekly disappeared into her bathroom, Charles stood his ground. There were words he intended saying, even if he kept his fists to himself.

Robert turned to him, malice distorting his face. 'You have no place in my fiancée's bedroom.' He nodded towards the door. 'Do you mind?'

Their eyes clashed. Afraid that things might get out of hand, Charles bit back the words he had ready and headed for the door.

'I do hope you had a happy Christmas with those tarts of yours,' Watson said, as he was seeing him out. 'We had a great time. My fiancée had something really big in her Christmas stocking.'

So Watson was again showing his true colours. A reformed character? Never! Charles was not going to allow him to drive him away as long as June needed him. He made his way to his rooms and quietly meditated for ten minutes to cool his anger.

Showered, shaved and changed into evening wear, he eventually made his way downstairs and mingled with the guests. Music was playing in all the reception rooms. Laughter and chatter were drowning out the words of the singers. A sure sign of a successful party in progress.

There was no need to search for Rosie. With her glossy, dark-chestnut hair swept up in a bouffant arrangement encircled by a tiara, she stood out like a princess amongst mere commoners. Charles quickly took in the simple-cut white satin dress with its deeply scooped neckline and tight bodice encrusted with embroidery, rhinestones and twinkling diamanté — showing off those alluring, rounded breasts to perfection. Clearly, it wasn't just her birthday that was making her the centre of attraction.

He was taken back twenty years. The girl in a white dress then was Rosie's mother, and soon to wear Arthur's engagement ring. His heart was stabbed by painful longing for the woman he had lost yet again. When June married Arthur she had chosen the better man and it was something he could live with, but how could he possibly accept her engagement to Robert Watson? And yet, to fight against the marriage would only cause June to have to choose between them, suffering yet more pain of indecision.

Ignoring the young men around her, Rosie came forward and greeted him warmly, thanking him for his lovely present of an antique gold-and-pearl brooch.

'Its fabulous, Uncle Charlie,' she said, throwing her arms around his neck and kissing his cheek. 'I really love it!' She let him loose. 'Peggy has sent me a pretty scarf.'

Her face creased into a puzzled frown. 'But Richard has sent me a little empty box. How odd. In his letter he says I will have to get its contents when I visit him. I must drive down this week.' Her eyes betrayed her excitement at the prospect of seeing Richard again.

'No, Rosie, I'll take you down. We can go at the weekend if you like. Will your mother be able to spare you on Sunday? I could have you back by late evening.'

'I should think so. Ruth has agreed to stay. She's sleeping here as long as we need her. I expect Jimmy will be going to Robert's at the weekend. David too. He's fallen for Rob's mucker-outer.' She chuckled light-heartedly. 'Puppy love!'

Charles smiled, remembering his own youthful love affairs. 'Don't knock it, Rosie. Puppies are loveable creatures!'

'Peter's been playing up, and I don't mean with his drums. He's refusing to go to the Old Rectory again. At least, when Robert's in residence. I don't blame him.' She glanced furtively around her. 'Come over here, Charlie,' she said, taking his arm and leading him out of earshot of others.

Charles listened to the story of the incident with Steven, and of Peter's alleged fibbing to get attention.

'But, I have to admit,' she continued, 'his behaviour can be quite disruptive.' She frowned in the manner of a strict schoolmistress. 'I don't go in for this "boys will be boys" nonsense.'

'I've been worried about Peter,' Charles confessed. 'I don't think he's happy at school. And now that he's home, his little brother is getting most of the attention. As for the Steven incident, I'm more inclined to believe Peter's version of what Watson said.' Out of the corner of his eye he saw Jack Cummings hovering around. 'I'll have a chat with Peter,' he said, moving aside. 'I'll leave you to your guests.'

Charles moved across the busy hall just as the inner entrance door was opening. He walked over to greet his brother and Helen. Their two sons had already run off, each clinging to a gaily-wrapped parcel.

'Nice to see you both,' he said to Helen and George. 'I'll take your coats.'

'Thanks, Charlie,' Helen said, her violet-blue eyes seducing him from under their long lashes. 'Nice to see you again.' She was wearing a deep-blue miniskirt dress with fringes that shimmered as she walked, her shapely legs descending into high-heeled sequinned shoes — very sexy!

Charles tore his eyes away from her. 'Everything okay?' he asked George.

George merely grunted, but Helen said: 'I thought you'd gone away for good. You must come round sometime.' George glared at her and moved off. 'As you see,' she continued, staring after her husband, 'things are as normal. From what I've heard, you could do with a bit of what I'm missing.' Her lips curled up into that familiar beckoning smile.

'Sorry, Helen,' he said quickly, looking across the hall to avoid her gaze, 'there's something I have to attend to. No doubt I'll see you later.'

'You can bet on it,' she said as he hurried away.

Charles deposited their coats in the cloakroom, noticing that George's Burberry was frayed at the edges, while Helen's fur appeared to be straight out of a Bond Street store. Feeling sorry for his brother, he started looking for Peter. After searching all the rooms where the party was in full swing, he found him sulking in the study.

'What's up, Peter? It's not like you to miss out on a party. Has someone upset you?'

'Huh! Mr Watson told me to come in here because I was playing my drums. I don't care. I'll play them tonight when he's in bed with Mum. I know he's going to sleep with her after the party. I heard him telling Lucy that she will have to go home with someone else. Uncle George, I think. He didn't know I was listening.' He rubbed his nose with the back of his hand. 'I don't care if he hits me. I hate him!'

'Has Watson ever hit you?'

'He's threatened to,' he muttered. 'But it's just like school, nobody believes anything I say.'

'Sounds as if you've been having a tough time. Do you want to talk about it?'

Peter started with the bullying he was getting at Plowden. Apparently it had not stopped, despite the talk with the headmaster. Then he told Charles about the incident at the pool, and overhearing what Robert had said to Steven.

'He did say it, Uncle Charlie. I'm not daft. But no one believes me. I don't think even Rosie does now. She keeps shouting at me. Everyone shouts at me. David goes off with

Lucy and Jimmy's got his pony. I might as well be back at school!'

'Hold on, shipmate, things at home can't be that bad. I'll see what I can do. And you're not going back to school until the bullying gets sorted out. I'll talk to your mother about it. But whatever else you do, don't do anything to antagonise Mr Watson. It will make my task more difficult and it won't do you any good either. Agreed?'

'Yes, Uncle Charlie. Thanks. You're the only one who listens to me.' His face brightened up. 'I'm glad you're back. Are you staying now?'

'I'll be here a little while before returning to Bath. You'll be able to phone me there.'

'Can I come and live with you? I thought it was going to be nice at Mr Watson's place, but he doesn't like me. I hate it there.'

That wasn't difficult for Charles to understand. 'I'll have a chat with your mother and see what's happening. We'll talk again sometime. Now you come with me, and stick close by so you don't get into trouble.'

As they left the study, Robert was going through the hall to the dining room. He saw Peter and gave him one of his harsh glares.

'If you so much as touch my nephew, you'll have me to reckon with,' said Charles.

Robert merely grinned. 'Now that is an interesting proposition.'

By midnight the guests began drifting away, and by two the party was over. June told Ruth to leave the clearing away until morning and almost staggered up the stairs to her bedroom, satisfied that things had gone so well. With the more energetic guests taking over the cleared floor of the lounge, music and dancing had gone with a swing. Jack Cummings had produced his party games to howls of laughter. As for Rosie, she had looked incredibly lovely, and happier than she had seen her for ages.

Yes, thanks to her helpers, the guests had gone home happy and satisfied. But what now?

The guest room was occupied by family from London. Robert was staying the night, but she did not want him sharing her bed. There were too many memories of a different life that Robert was not part of. What's more, knowing Charlie's baby to be in her womb, it seemed a sacrilege to have Robert penetrating her body. In fact, now she was so closely linked to the man she really loved, to still be engaged to Robert — however right it had seemed at the time — must surely be wrong. And yet....

She heard men's voices on the landing. 'I'll leave you to lock up, Charles.' It was her brother-in-law, Frank. 'We're off at six-thirty, so I don't suppose we'll see you again for a while. Come and see us when you're in London.'

'Will do. Goodnight, Frank.'

The front door bell sounded.

'That will be Watson,' said Charles. 'I think he was driving Helen home. George took their boys and Lucy ages ago, but he didn't come back.'

'Leave the bugger out. June's your woman, Charles. Arthur would turn in his grave if he knew what's going on.'

Charles replied, but she couldn't hear what he said. There were heated voices in the hall. A few moments later, Robert entered her room.

The house was quiet again. It was getting on for seven in the morning and the relatives from London had gone. As June sat by the warm kitchen range drinking hot tea, she was trying to work out how to tell Robert about the baby, and how he would react. It would be so easy to let him think it was his. Of course, the child would not look like James, but maybe it would have her features. Surely he would be delighted to have another child — or would he?

But why even think such thoughts? She would not want to deny Charles knowledge of his child, nor did she want to live a lie. No, what her heart told her was something quite different. Had not this baby been planned out of love and desire? It was hers and Charlie's. Surely there could be only one outcome. She had to talk to Charlie as soon as possible.

June poured herself more tea. It had not been difficult to keep Robert out of her bed. She relived the scene: when he came into her room, she had rushed into the bathroom to vomit, telling him that she had a dose of sickness and diarrhoea. She smiled at her thoughts. Well, at least the nausea was genuine, and for good reason! The moaning and flushing of the toilet had been a good piece of acting. He left, saying he was off to London first thing in the morning, but would call in to see how she was. He must be arriving any minute.

Sighing, she sipped her tea, thoughts and ideas going through her brain like a never-ending loop of recorded tape. Break the engagement and marry Charlie. Give up her job? Then what? Robert could make things difficult for her. He would get at her through Jimmy, and use dirty tricks to stop her working for others. Anything to get her back or destroy her future. He had the power to block almost anything she might try on her own. She only functioned at her best through him anyway. But surely Robert had changed? Or had he?

The doorbell rang. At seven in the morning, it could only be Rob. Maybe now would be a good time to either break off the engagement, or tell him about Charlie's baby and let him do it himself.

She stood up and quickly walked to the front door before he rang again.

'Come in, Rob. Early as usual,' she said, smiling as he walked inside. 'I'm drinking tea in the kitchen. Do you want a cup?'

'Had coffee before I left,' he said, following her across the hall. 'I only called to see how you are.'

'Tired, but okay,' she told him, sitting by the kitchen range in the expectation that he would sit there with her. 'Nice of you to pop in.'

'I see you're better now.'

He seemed restless to be on his way. Of course, now he knew there was no need to worry about her, his mind would be on the business ahead. This was good; he would not be in a mood to argue. She came to a decision.

'Robert, I want to break the engagement,' she said, beginning to remove his ring from her finger. 'I can't marry you. It's too soon after Arthur's death.'

Robert pushed the ring back on. 'You're just tired,' he said in a perfunctory manner. 'I was expecting it. What with the parties and trying to manage here on your own, what do you expect? Those boys of yours need a firm hand. Just as well they'll soon be back at school.'

'It has nothing to do with the boys. Rob, I—'

'Good heavens, woman!' Robert cut in. 'You were ill last night, and here you are a few hours later planning today's lunch! Go and get some sleep. We'll talk when I get back.'

He stood up. 'Must dash. I've got meetings all day and it's the management dinner this evening. I'm meeting with the sales team tomorrow morning and I'm off to Paris in the afternoon.' He kissed her cheek. 'I'll be back Sunday evening. Pity you can't come with me.' He headed for the hall. 'When I return, we'll discuss latest developments and see where we're heading.' He suddenly stopped and took hold of her shoulders. 'This is exciting stuff, June. For both of us. But we need to be fully focussed. Get some rest.'

'Robert, please—'

'Do as I say,' he demanded, looking deep into her eyes.

'But Rob—'

He silenced her with a kiss. Sliding a hand inside her housecoat, he lingered with his fondling. As always, she succumbed to his touch and hated herself for doing so.

'Now go to bed and think of me,' he told her softly, pulling up the zip of her housecoat. 'When I return next week, we'll sort out your domestic and business arrangements. The sooner you leave this place the better. Bloomfield belongs to your past. You and your family have a splendid future ahead of you.'

'But, Robert—'

'No more buts!' he called from over his shoulder, as he hurried across the hall.

She followed after him. 'Rob, I can't just....'

He turned by the open door. 'You most certainly can. There's a rewarding time ahead for both of us. We're breaking new ground and need to be on our toes.' He reached his Daimler. 'Get some rest. We'll talk Sunday evening.'

She watched him slip into the driver's seat. The car door shut with a soft thud. A moment later he was gone.

A fine vapour trail from the Daimler's exhaust was caught in the light from the open door. It lingered in the cold, frosty air, and mingled with her panting breath. She wrapped her arms around her and ran inside, snapping the door closed. The loop of recorded tape started once more on its relentless course within her brain. Pressing her hands against her temples, she ran to the cloakroom. She threw up bile mingled with undigested tea.

Chapter Thirty-Seven

It was with a sinking heart that Charles, from the landing above the hall, witnessed the amorous scene between June and Robert Watson. Erotically kissing was bad enough, but to see his hand fondling her breasts sickened him. And to hear Watson's words concerning Bloomfield and June's future was simply heartrending. He'd had to walk away, deeply ashamed of his voyeurism. Now he was wondering how far she had gone along with his proposals. Was she handing over every part of her life for him to deal with? Since they were engaged it would be natural enough. What right had he, merely her brother-in-law, to interfere?

Having heard the Daimler drive away, he decided to go downstairs and clear away the party debris. Furniture needed shifting too. Since Annie and Lisa were having the rest of the week off, Ruth could do with a bit of help. As he reached the hall, he heard someone retching in the cloakroom. June? He grimaced: that viper's kisses were enough to make any woman sick. At least he had not spent the night with her. There was no mistaking the Daimler's engine, even if he had been too late to see it leave. It certainly was not in the drive when he'd looked out of his bedroom window. He had hoped that she had finished with him. Obviously not, so why did he go home?

He collected a sack from the scullery cupboard and took it to the lounge. Pulling back the curtains, his eyes registered an untidy mess: wrapping paper, streamers festooning the furniture, paper hats, party toys, balloons in various stages of deflation, plates with half-eaten items of food, empty and partly-full glasses, crumbs and cake all over the carpet, a sandwich half-stuffed behind a radiator! Trying not to think about what he had witnessed, he set about his self-imposed task with gusto. He cleared a table and collected Rosie's birthday cards and presents together for her to sort out. Rubbish was stuffed straight into the huge sack.

More sacks would be needed for the other rooms, plus a bucket for ashes from the spent fires. The symbolism did not escape him. What was he to do with the ashes from a spent love affair? Trouble was, the heat of desire refused to cool and continued to burn within his heart. Sighing deeply, he made his way to the kitchen. June was there, still wearing her housecoat, and sitting by the range with a cup in her hand. She looked up, a wan smile creasing her weary face.

'Hello, Charlie. Thanks for locking up and making sure everything was safe last night... or rather, this morning.'

He put down the sack of rubbish and sat by her.

'I'm pleased to be useful,' he said, trying to rid himself of the image of Watson's hand unzipping that pretty flowered housecoat. 'You look as if you've been awake all night. Are you ill?'

'Charlie, I'm...' She turned away her eyes. 'No, I'm not ill. Just exhausted.'

What was she going to tell him? That she was selling up? His heart went out to her. 'Get back to bed, June. Leave me to take over while you rest.'

'Charlie, have you made any new plans yet? You know, what you are going to do next, and where?' She sounded worried. Sorry that she was going to have to kick him out?

'Richard has been told of possibilities of openings up north. Something we can both look at. Don't you worry about me, June, you have your own future to think about.'

She kept her eyes lowered. 'Yes, things will have to change. How far up north?'

'Two hundred miles or so. But its just a vague possibility at the moment.'

'I see. A long way. Anything else you're looking at?'

'Yes, but that's even more uncertain.'

'Oh.' She hesitated. 'Charlie, will you…?' The question hung in the air.

'Keep in touch? Of course. With you, *and* the kids.'

She nodded. 'Suppose we were to…?'

'Move in with Robert now? I'll stay around until something is settled with Richard.'

'That isn't what I was going to ask, but thanks anyway.' She glanced up at him. Her eyes were pink beneath their dark, puffy lids. She quickly looked down, as though to hide the tell-tale signs of stress. 'I have something to tell you, Charlie.'

He watched her wringing her hands and twisting Watson's engagement ring as if the stone was burning her finger. Was she having second thoughts about marrying Watson? Now was not the time to push her. He could bide his time.

'We can talk later. Let me help you, June. You're not well. Please go to bed and rest. I saw Watson's Daimler leave. I assume he's working today?'

'He'll be away until Sunday evening.'

'Good, he's not around to disturb you. I'll keep the kids occupied so they don't bother you.'

She smiled up at him. 'Thank you, Charlie, I will go to bed.'

For the rest of that day and most of the next, June spent a lot of time in bed resting. Charles kept the place running smoothly, happy to be of service and praying that June would delay making irrevocable decisions until she became stronger. He realised that once Watson returned, the pressure would be on for her to sell out and move into the Old Rectory. She needed time and space for quiet reflection. He sent Rosie upstairs with her meals, but June seemed to be eating very little and this worried him. He tried once to get her to see her doctor, but she was quite adamant that he was not needed.

'I'm just tired, Charlie,' she said, giving him a confident smile as if she had some secret knowledge.

Maybe she had. What did he know about women's problems? When he thought about it, he remembered his mother going through a difficult period. It was never talked about, but the family had assumed it was to do with her depleting hormones.

On Friday, Charles managed to get a cancellation for a box at the theatre. It was for the Christmas pantomime. According to Jim, Robert Watson had refused to even consider going. 'Pantomimes are rubbish to amuse idiots,' is what his father had told him. 'We can find better things for you to do.'

To see June and her children laughing and playing the fool gladdened his heart. It took Charles back many years to when, as Arthur's stand-in, he had taken June to the Royal as a surprise. They had pretended to be kids again, shouting and laughing at the antics of the players. What a magical night that had been. To be young and in love had blinded him to the futility of the longings of his heart. It was no different now. Or was it?

She turned to him, a wistful look in her eyes. 'Do you remember, Charlie?' she said softly. His heart leaped with renewed hope. Surely his love would win through, in spite of Watson and that glittering rock. He glanced at June's finger. The ring was not there. Significant? Best not to ask.

That night, he heard someone coming up his stairs. The door opened and June came in. She slipped into bed beside him, like a worried child seeking the safety of a parent's presence.

'Can I stay, Charlie?' she whispered. 'I don't want to be alone.'

He turned out the light, put his arm around her and let her rest.

In the morning, he woke at his usual time but did not want to disturb June. He so much wanted to know what was troubling her, but he knew sleep would be doing its healing work. He carefully slipped out of bed, did his exercises in another room, showered, and dressed in his jogging gear.

The dawn of a bright frosty morning was only just lifting the darkness of the winter's night as he opened the back door to set out for a brisk run.

'Can I come with you?' shouted Peter's voice from the window above. 'I'm a good runner. I won't hold you up, Uncle Charlie.'

Five minutes later they both set off. Charles was pleased to have his troubled nephew by his side. He had been quiet since Rosie's birthday: well behaved, but withdrawn. The boy slipped on ice a few times, but Charles made certain to be ready with a steadying hand. Yes, what the lad needed in his young life was a supportive father figure. He most certainly would not get that from Watson. Whatever the future might have in store, somehow he would have to keep in touch with his nephews — he owed that to Arthur.

By the time they returned home, the sky to the north was a slate grey, but the morning sun was shining brightly across the shadow-streaked garden. The cold frost on the trees and grass sparkled in its golden radiance. The strong contrast of dark and light held a kind of magic. With his hand on Peter's shoulder, he breathed in deeply, gazing at sky and garden. 'Always look on the bright side of life, Peter. What a beautiful morning!'

Instead of going straight to his rooms, Charles walked to the kitchen with Peter. Not only did he want to eat with him, he thought it would be a good time for a friendly chat — one-to-one. But Rosie, David and Jimmy were already there, sitting at the table and eating porridge.

Rosie jumped up and filled two more dishes.

'Here, eat this,' she said to Charles. 'It will put hairs on your chest.'

'How?' asked Jimmy.

'It fertilises the roots,' said Rosie with a straight face.

'Like horse manure?'

They all laughed.

Ruth came into the room, carrying a bucket of ashes in one hand and a letter in the other. She was laughing too. 'I heard that,' she said. 'I had porridge for breakfast. Now I really am worried!' She put the letter in front of Charles. 'That's just come. It's for you, Captain Rogers,' she said, carrying the bucket through to the back door.

Charles smiled at the formal way she addressed him in front of the others. He had an idea this letter was going to change all that. He opened the envelope and read the contents. Smiling, he waited for Ruth to return. 'Please stay, this concerns you as well as me.'

In fact, he wanted to talk to them all. Just then, June, dressed casually in a pale pink jumper and plaid sunray skirt, entered the kitchen.

'What's this?' she asked, smiling. 'A family conference?'

Charles grinned. 'I guess so,' he said. 'Here, come and sit in my chair. I have an announcement to make.'

He stood up with the letter in his hand.

'I've only just found out for certain. I want you all to know that Ruth is my daughter. My own flesh and blood. There can be no doubt about it. I hope you will welcome her into the family.'

Ruth's eyes lit up with joy. 'Oh Charlie, I'm so happy!' She wrapped her arms around his neck and kissed his cheek.

The disastrous incident that took place on Christmas morning flashed through his mind. The horror of betrayal written across June's face was impossible to forget. It constantly invaded his thoughts and hindered the pleasure he knew he should be feeling at that moment. But when he glanced at June he was relieved to see her nodding and smiling. It was a strange sort of knowing smile, which he found hard to fathom. Clearly, that particular misunderstanding could now be put to rest. If only what followed — her engagement to Watson — could just as easily be erased.

June stood up and embraced Ruth. 'Welcome to the Rogers family, Ruth.'

The rest joined in, hugging Ruth with a babble of welcoming chatter, and the inevitable questioning.

Beneath the happy din, Charles heard a whispered query concerning Ruth's mother. He saw David give Jim a dig in the ribs to keep him quiet. He realised a bit of explaining was due some time, but that could wait.

'I'll make some coffee,' he said, loud enough to make himself heard. 'I think this meeting will be going on for quite a while yet. No one leave the room, we have things to discuss.'

'Sounds intriguing,' said Rosie, getting mugs and glasses from the drainer, and orange juice from the fridge.

'Now let's have some order,' Charles said loudly, clearing away used dishes from the table. 'I would like us all to sit down and give a listening ear to anyone with a problem. If I remember correctly, it's what your father had you do at the beginning of each new year.'

There was no objection. The two armchairs by the range were brought over to the large kitchen table so all seven of them could sit down together. Ruth poured out the coffee and handed it to those who wanted it. The rest had orange juice.

Charles looked around the table and saw eager faces looking to him for direction. His heart swelled with love. Arthur's family and Ruth were together as one. And June, her eyes bright, was gazing at him as though in adoration. What was going through her mind? He jerked himself free of speculation and concentrated his mind on the fatherless youngsters. He looked at Peter.

'Peter, would you like to share your problems with us?'

Peter hung his head and muttered something unintelligible.

'Come on, Pete,' said David, 'we're all listening.'

Before long, words came spilling out of Peter's mouth. Hints of good times mingling with unhappy ones. Inner loneliness was only too apparent.

Rosie, sitting next to him, put an arm around him saying she was sorry for not being a proper sister. June took over from Rosie and held him to her bosom. Jimmy said he was sorry for telling him to clear off when he'd asked for a ride on his pony. David said he was sorry for ignoring him during the holiday, and for being too busy at school to keep an eye on him as he said he would.

Peter, looking more cheerful, said that he was sorry for playing up and acting like a stupid kid. 'But it's true what I told Rosie. Mr Watson did say those things. And he's always horrible to me — always!'

Eyes turned to June.

'I believe you, Peter,' she said, giving him a smile of reassurance. 'Robert can be difficult. Of course, he's not used to having young people around. But, don't worry, it won't happen again.'

Charles picked up his cup and swallowed down the coffee, suppressing the words that came into his mind concerning Watson's character.

'He's my dad,' said Jimmy, frowning at Peter. 'But I guess he hasn't been very nice to you, Pete. Like Mum says, he's not used to being a dad. He does let you and David use the pool and everything.'

Charles thought it best to move things on. 'Does anyone else have anything to say before we get ready to go to skating?'

'Skating? Great!' yelled Jim and Peter together.

Rosie laughed. 'I guess I'd better volunteer to help with taxiing. Even a Merc would be hard pressed to accommodate a coach-load!'

Following the visit to the ice rink, fish and chips were consumed and then on to a football match at Meadow Lane. The evening was spent playing Monopoly. To see the family so happy and united gave Charles hope for the future. Maybe he could not be their stepfather, but at least he could exercise his duty as godfather to each of them. But why be pessimistic? June was not married to Watson yet, and certain signs should be giving him cause for hope.

Once again, she crept into his bed. He made no attempt to make love to her. Somehow they had an unspoken understanding that she just wanted his company, nothing more.

She snuggled up to him, her face resting on his chest. 'Charlie, I have something to tell you.'

'I'm listening?'

'I… I think you should know….' She bit at her thumb as if to plug her mouth.

He was intrigued. What did she want to tell him that was so hard to put into words?

'June, what is it? I know something has been on your mind since I returned.'

He sat up with his arm on the pillow, and looked at her keenly. But she averted her eyes.

She began tracing a finger through the hairs of his chest. 'How soon will you be moving up north?'

'I told you, it's just a vague possibility at present. It partly depends on Richard.'

She nodded her head in understanding.

'But that can't be the problem,' he said, picking up the restless hand and pressing it to his lips. 'Are you about to throw me out? Look, if you want to get rid of this place, don't worry about me. I can rent a flat in Nottingham. I'll stay around until you settle elsewhere.'

A tear rolled down her cheek. 'It has nothing to do with Bloomfield,' she whispered.

He kissed away the tear, tasting the salt on his lips. The proximity of her swelling nipples beneath her flimsy nightdress pulled at him like a magnet, but he was determined not to take advantage of her vulnerability. If she wanted him to make love to her he knew the signals, and none of them was forthcoming.

She was silent for a few moments. Her eyes told him she was somewhere else. She blinked and her lips curled into a little smile. 'I do love you, Charlie. Please believe that.'

'But you love Watson and your career more?'

He regretted the words as soon as he'd said them. Why did he have to bring that man into bed with them? But, of course, he knew why. The image of the two of them kissing in the hall had been hovering like a spectre, ready to pounce at unguarded moments.

She closed her eyes and rolled over with her back pressed up to him. 'I'll talk to you after I've seen Robert,' she said softly. 'There is something I must do first.'

Chapter Thirty-Eight

June seemed more at peace with herself in the morning. He watched her sleeping for a while, love gnawing at his heart but glad to have been of comfort to her.

He performed his exercises, thinking about what had been said the previous evening. What was it that she intended discussing with Watson? That she was ending their engagement? Nice thought, but not likely. Terms of employment? She wanted more time with her family and to be a better mother to them; that much he did know. She'd told Peter that if he wanted to leave Plowden Manor College, then he could go to a local day school where she could keep a personal eye on him. As it so happened, Peter had decided to face up to things and go back with David. Even so, the gesture showed that her children's happiness was important to her.

Charles showered and returned to his bedroom. June was out of bed.

'I need to use my own bathroom,' she said, quickly leaving the room. 'I'll see you downstairs, Charlie.'

Ruth was preparing them all a fried breakfast when he arrived in the kitchen. He asked her if she would go with June when she took the boys back to school later that morning. 'Let her think you offered, Ruth. I don't want her to think I'm interfering, but I am worried about her.'

'I'd love to go,' Ruth said, turning the bacon in the frying pan. 'I've always wondered what these posh schools are like.'

Hurried footsteps told Charles that the boys had got a whiff of the frying bacon, and were ready to eat.

Jim came in first, closely followed by his brothers. 'Goody!' exclaimed Jimmy. 'Fried bread, bacon and eggs. Are you doing sausages as well?'

'Greedy guts,' said David, under his breath.

'What are you doing today, Jim?' Charles asked, passing him the tomato ketchup. 'Rosie is coming with me to Bath. Are you going with your mother to Plowden?'

'I'm riding Blackie,' Jimmy said, thumping the bottom of the bottle. 'Lucy is expecting me.' Tomato ketchup shot over his breakfast and onto the table.

'All right, Jimmy,' said June, coming into the kitchen. 'You can go, but don't make a nuisance of yourself. I'll collect you late afternoon. And get a cloth to wipe that mess up!'

'Mother is going to break off her engagement. We aren't going to move into the Old Rectory, and she's hanging on to Bloomfield,' Rosie said as they drove along the A4 towards Bath. 'We had a chat this morning. I wanted to know what's going on. Ever since her visit to the doctor, she's been odd. I know she's run-down, but it's more than that. I was really worried. I thought she might have something seriously wrong. You know, the big C.'

Charles was shocked. That June could have cancer had never entered his head. And yet, there were certain significant signs. With his mind distracted, he nearly missed the junction and had to brake suddenly. Rosie jerked forward.

'Sorry, Rosie, are you all right?'

'Yes,' she said, settling back into her seat. 'I sort of saw it coming.'

'I must get seat belts fitted. No point in waiting until I get the new car in September.'

Charles collected his wits together, taking note of the road ahead of him and glancing in the mirror to see what was coming up behind. Being Sunday there was little traffic, but motorcyclists sometimes came roaring past at high speed to quickly disappear from sight. He guessed they saw a Mercedes ahead of them as a bit of a challenge. Bends in the road merely added to the excitement. He slowed to let a string of them go honking past. Shaking his head at their foolish behaviour, he picked up speed again. His thoughts turned to June.

'What's wrong with your mother, Rosie?'

'She wants to tell you herself.'

Now he was truly worried. 'Is it serious?'

'I guess for her it is. I don't know what she's doing about her job. I don't think she knows herself. But she's stopped wearing that monster diamond, and it's not because she's doing the washing-up. If Rob's back from his business trip, he'll be getting it back today. He won't be pleased. He's not used to rejection.'

'Rosie, will you go home by train if necessary? I'll pay for the ticket. I must get back this afternoon.'

'I thought you might,' she said, looking straight ahead and smiling.

The last few miles to the Royal United was driven in silence. Charles was thinking back to things June had said, and began worrying about the things she had kept to herself. Peggy had told him about their mother suffering from dementia. Was June worried that she was going the same way? That was enough to make any sane person concerned for the future. He remembered her being worried about her periods. Was she having serious problems in that direction? Maybe she needed a hysterectomy like his mother had done? 'Oh June, why wouldn't you tell me? I would have understood,' he thought aloud.

'What was that, Charlie?' Rosie asked him.

'Just talking to myself,' he said. He turned the car into the hospital parking area. 'Here we are. Let's see how the invalid is doing. I hope there's room for all these presents we're taking.'

The walk to Richard's unit was quickly covered. Sister Landers was sitting by her tidy desk. She looked up and gave them a broad smile.

'Go straight in, Captain Rogers. I'll let Commander Andrews tell you himself how he's doing.'

Peggy emerged from Richard's room.

'Hello, Charlie.' She gave him a peck on his cheek. 'And Rosie, too,' she said, turning to put an arm around her niece's shoulders. 'Richard's done nothing but talk about you since Charlie phoned to say you were coming.'

'In that case,' said Charles, 'I'll take you for a quick lunch while Rosie and Richard get reacquainted.'

He popped his head around Richard's door. 'See you later, pal.' He threw the presents on the bed. 'Santa got the address mixed up. Or maybe the reindeer ran out of hay.' He didn't wait for a reply — Rosie had walked in behind him and was getting Richard's full attention.

'I've had a sandwich already, Charlie,' said Peggy as they made their way to the car. 'But I'm happy to have a tasty pudding and watch you eat steak.'

'Nonsense, Peggy. We both eat Sunday lunch, and I know where to get the best.'

As they ate their meal, Peggy brought him up to date with Richard's condition.

'So you see, he's going home sometime this week. Continued progress is expected and he'll soon be fitted up with a prosthetic limb. Now, tell me how things are going back home.'

Not wanting to alarm her about her sister, Charles gave a guarded report.

'June should be marrying you, we all know that. What does she see in that guy with the bedroom eyes?'

She let out a tinkling laugh. 'I guess I've answered my own question.' Her face became serious. 'You go and sweep her off her feet, Charlie. Make her see sense. That man has a hold over her. You have to break her free.' She stabbed at her meat. Bloody gravy ran out. She forked a chunk into her mouth. 'He's a devil, so give him hell, Charlie — give him bloody-hell!'

When Charles and Peggy returned to Richard's room they found the couple holding hands. They were as close as it was possible to get in separate chairs. Rosie showed them a ring on the third finger of her left hand.

'It was Richard's mother's ring. Isn't it wonderful? We're going to be married as soon as Richard is back on his feet.' Her cheeks turned pink. 'That is….'

Richard laughed away her embarrassment. 'It's all right, Rosie. When I have that new foot it will be entirely mine.' He grinned mischievously. 'If I start running after other women, you'll know what to do — hide it!'

His laughter was infectious. Charles knew for certain that he was free to leave the three of them and get back to Bloomfield. June's need was now the greater.

After expressing his delight at their engagement, Charles said that he must get back.

Richard looked at him, his face lined with concern. 'We'll be thinking of you, Charles.'

Charles gripped the proffered hand. The warmth of Richard's friendship passed into him, as it had done on many other occasions when faced with uncertainty. 'Thank you, Richard. Goodbye for now.' He turned to the women. 'Look after the old sea-dog, ladies.'

As Charles was leaving, Richard called after him, 'Thank everyone for their presents and cards. Young Jim's is brilliant. I love the pirates visiting Baby Jesus!'

The way things were going, Charles wondered if next Christmas, Jim's card would have a financier mounted on a black pony and taking gifts of company shares!

Chapter Thirty-Nine

It was with trepidation that June approached the Old Rectory. Rob had not returned when she had collected Jimmy, but Jane Lindsey, who was now in residence, had told her that he was expected home at any time. Yes, there was his Daimler parked by the garages, its gold paintwork dull with miles of travelling. Not that it mattered; Frederick would soon restore it to mint condition. Rob's words rang in her brain: 'You see, my dear, what money and influence can do for you? You are free to do the work you really enjoy.'

And she did enjoy her work. But for how much longer?

She drove up to the front entrance. Forcing her mind to be strong and unyielding, she stepped out of the Rover and approached the house. The door opened before she pressed the bell. Robert greeted her in his white velour bathrobe.

'Saw you through the window. I'm about to have a swim. Come and join me.' He set off towards the back of the hall.

'No, Rob,' she said, holding her ground. 'We have to talk.'

He stopped in his tracks. 'Sounds serious,' he said, turning round. 'All right, come into the kitchen. Jane made a pot of coffee a few minutes ago. I'll have another cup myself.'

She followed him to the back of the house, pleased that she wasn't alone in the building with Rob, but nervous that she was entering the setting of his previous erotic love-play. He switched on the spotlights above the central table, and pressed a button that automatically let down the window blinds. The stage was set before her. She tried to keep the image of their writhing bodies from her mind but it was impossible, her automatic responses were coming into play. She felt flushed and moist.

'Jane's just gone off to see her mother until morning,' he said, observing her closely. 'So we have the house to ourselves.' He poured coffee into two cups. 'You look warm. Take your jacket off.'

She stood her ground. 'Robert, we have to talk.'

'So you said. But you might as well be comfortable while we do so.' He stepped behind her and pulled off her jacket. 'That's better. Now take a seat.'

He indicated one of the high stools by the worktop, but she shook her head. He brought the coffee tray to the table and offered to pour her a cup.

'No, thank you.'

He looked at her intensely. His dark eyes moved from her face to the raised nipples showing through her cashmere jumper. He leaned against the table, smiling and stabbing his thumb into his chin.

'That's what I like to see, ready and eager.'

Blushing, she wrapped her arms across her breasts. 'I haven't come here to be admired, Robert. There is something I have to tell you.'

'You don't sound very pleased to see me. What's the problem?' he asked, eyes narrowing. 'Charlie Boy been getting at you? I can soon make you forget him.' He took hold of her arm. 'Come on, if you don't fancy it here, we'll go upstairs.'

She pulled her arm from his grasp. 'I can't marry you. I love someone else.'

Sighing deeply, he shook his head. 'Love? Why did you marry Arthur if you loved his brother? No, June, we've been over that already. You know what you really want.'

He grabbed her to him. 'So stop playing these silly games. I've had a long, tiring day. We both know what you've really come for.'

His mouth covered hers, his tongue seeking her throat. A hand was inside her jumper, pulling down a bra strap. As he thrust his tongue he gripped her swelling nipple. She opened her mouth wider with the thrilling shock, and was forced to suck in his breath. She stopped struggling as a soft mist enveloped her. A hand was moving up her skirt, sending shocks of delicious expectation to her brain. No, no, it must not happen. She dug her nails into his hand.

'You little bitch,' he muttered between his teeth, his eyes dancing with hedonistic pleasure. 'So you want it really rough, do you?'

The moving hand tore at her pantyhose. She screamed and clawed at the fingers now invading her body.

'Don't hurt me, I'm pregnant!' she yelled, tears streaming down her face.

Robert stepped back, a puzzled expression replacing the ruggedness of lustful intent. 'Pregnant?' A glimmer of delight passed over his eyes, to be replaced by a thundercloud. 'I hope you're going to tell me that *I'm* the father.'

She dropped her eyes to avoid his gaze, but they came to rest on the blood oozing from his hand. Her whole body began trembling. 'I'm over three months' pregnant. Work it out for yourself.'

Rob's face tightened. He walked in a small circle, his thumb worrying the cleft in his chin. He stopped in front of her.

'I can't allow you to have someone else's child.'

'You have no say in the matter,' she said, straightening her clothing. 'We can't get married now. I'm sorry, Robert, really sorry.'

She picked up her jacket, fished his ring from the pocket and put it on the table. 'This is yours.'

He grabbed her arm. 'No, my love, you keep the ring. You get rid of the baby.'

'I will not! And you can't make me.'

Robert grasped her shoulders and shook her violently. 'You will do as I say,' he demanded through gritted teeth. 'We belong together.'

She squirmed under his grip. 'Let me go!'

His eyes flashed. 'Can't you understand, woman? You can't be sentimental about this. Too much is at stake.'

Throwing aside his robe, he pulled her, struggling, to the floor. 'I've left you alone too long. You've forgotten how good sex can be.'

The trouble was that she had not forgotten, and it was taking considerable willpower not to give in. 'Don't do this, Rob, I really don't want you to. It could hurt my baby.'

'Exactly!'

She clawed at his face. He pulled back his head to protect his eyes, but her nails caught his cheek. He jumped up and stood looking down at her, a curious, benign expression on his damaged face. A little blood was trickling down to the corner of his mouth. He licked it away with the tip of his tongue. Practically naked, with muscles flexed, he looked incredibly virile. She knew he was playing on his sexual attraction.

Damn him! She tore her eyes away from his powerful masculinity and tried to calm her carnal craving. She lay panting, fearful of what he might do next. To her surprise, he gently assisted her to her feet.

'So, you're bearing Charlie's child,' he said smiling. 'Well, maybe I can handle it. We'll work something out.'

'Rob, I....'

But she could not find the words. She knew how much he had invested in their coming together, both in business and in married life. Just saying that she was sorry for ruining his plans would be totally inadequate.

'I'll go home now,' she whispered, turning to pick up her jacket. 'I won't hold you to my contract. I think it would be better if we parted company.'

There, she had said it. She could not envisage a future devoid of all the recent creative activity, nor a life without the excitement of Robert to stimulate and satisfy that darker side of her personality. He kindled desires best buried. Well, she had risen above them, and now she was free to marry Charlie.

'Have you any idea how much is invested in our present enterprise?' His voice rumbled like thunder before an oncoming storm. 'Millions are about to go up the spout because you want to play this stupid game. You must have known you were bloody pregnant weeks ago. What sort of fool do you take me for?'

His eyes flashed. Suddenly the tempest within him broke free. He swung his arm angrily across the table, sweeping china, coffee, cream, sugar crystals, biscuits, juice, glasses, a bowl of fruit and various dishes of salad to the floor. A bottle of olive oil went flying from the table to smash against the edge of the marble worktop behind him. It crashed in pieces to the floor, spreading its contents over the tiles.

She had never seen him so angry. Terrified, she threw out a hand and grasped the neck of a wine bottle teetering on the edge of the table.

'Keep away from me!' she yelled.

Rob's eyes flashed and a great roar exploded from his throat. As she backed away, his hands reached out to grab her. She swung the bottle at his head. He gripped her wrist. There was no contest. The bottle crashed to the floor.

He stood back with hands on hips, and roared with laughter.

Seized by fury, she swung her foot into his groin. He folded, his face twisted with pain. Then, slowly, he straightened up, grim determination twitching at the corners of his mouth. His eyes were looking straight into hers. An uncontrollable shiver ran through her body. She was in the grip of intense fear. Like a frightened rabbit she became immobile — trapped against the table.

He grasped her by the waist and threw her, front first, over the edge of the table. She struggled to get free, but his hand was weighing down the small of her back.

'So, that's the way you want it. Fine by me. The rougher, the better.'

'Let me go! You're hurting me!' she yelled.

'Then don't struggle.' He threw up her skirt. 'Unless, of course, you want it really rough!'

'No, Rob. Please, no....' Her sobs turned to whimpers.

Ashamed of her submission, she closed her eyes. He was pulling at her pantyhose and briefs. Mixed emotions and sensations were tearing her apart. She must keep calm and do nothing to harm her baby. Trembling, she waited for him to grip her thighs and....

It did not come: her legs were suddenly released. Rob yelled out. She turned. Like a film in slow motion, she saw his arms flaying the air as he fell backwards, hitting his head on the worktop before reaching the shards of glass littering the floor.

She carefully stood up. Leaning on the table for support, she looked down at Robert. He was too still. A growing pool of blood began swirling with oil and wine around his body and soaking into the white bathrobe on the floor.

She started to back away. Enveloped in misty nothingness, from far away she heard herself scream....

Chapter Forty

A white-coated doctor came out of the emergency room and addressed Charles.

'Mr Rogers?'

Charles stood up and nodded. 'Yes. How is she, doctor?'

'Your wife is fully conscious. She has no serious injuries but we are keeping her overnight. You'll be pleased to know her pregnancy is not affected. She's a healthy woman, but make sure she gets plenty of rest for a few weeks.' He nodded towards the open door. 'You can see her now.'

Charles did not correct the doctor concerning his relationship with June. He was too stunned on hearing of the pregnancy. Was that why she had accepted Watson's ring? Once more he had an attack of jealousy. As to what had happened in the Old Rectory kitchen he could only guess at, but what he had met there told him that things were far from harmonious. The engagement ring was sparkling from a mix of coffee dregs and smashed china.

He was about to go in to see her when another doctor came to tell him that Mr Watson wanted to see him urgently.

'He's conscious at the moment, but that could change any time. Don't stay too long. He's a sick man.'

'How bad is he?'

'Possibly a fractured skull. He'll be going to x-ray shortly. He may still have some glass in his body that will need surgery. One or two of his wounds are quite deep and he's lost a lot of blood.' He looked at Charlie's bloodstained jumper and trousers. 'I guess you know that already.'

Charles walked to the cubicle indicated. He had no doubt that Watson wanted to taunt him about the baby. Better to get the unpleasant business over with before seeing June.

Rob was lying on a trolley with a nurse beside him. His skin looked pallid and his eyes half-glazed.

'Mr Watson's waiting to be taken to the x-ray department,' she told him. She nodded at the equipment next to the trolley. 'He's getting a blood transfusion. He's weak and needs to rest. Don't stay too long. I'll leave you alone for two minutes.' She left, pulling a curtain across to give them privacy.

Robert gave Charles a crooked smile. 'It seems I have to thank you,' he said weakly 'I might be dead on the kitchen floor if you hadn't staunched the bleeding and called an ambulance.'

Charles nodded. 'My concern was for June, not you.'

'Now she's having your child, I suppose you'll marry her.' Watson smiled ruefully. 'But I warn you, Captain Charles Rogers, she'll be forever restless until she's back with me. You know that. So does she.'

Charles was stunned. The baby was his?

Watson grinned, wincing with pain as he did so. 'She hasn't told you?' His eyes slowly closed as his voice drifted away: 'I wonder why....'

Charles left the cubicle, telling the doctor that Watson had lost consciousness. But his mind was on June. Indeed, why hadn't she told him about the baby? He put on a mask of tranquillity, and walked into the room where she was resting.

A bandage covered part of her right arm, and a butterfly stitch held together a small wound on her forehead. She seemed to be asleep. A nurse was about to leave. She pointed to a hospital refuse bag standing on a chair in the corner. A rolled-up bundle of clothes stuffed inside it gave off an aroma of wine, olives and blood. 'Would you like to take your wife's clothes home, Mr Rogers? She will need clean ones to go home in.' She didn't wait for an answer.

Now alone with June, Charles approached the bed, uncertain what to say to her. She was dressed in a hospital gown and her head was resting on banked-up pillows. A faded pink cotton blanket covered her tummy and legs. The nurse's voice must have alerted her to his presence. Her eyes opened and her lips creased into a smile.

'Hello, Charlie. I have something to tell you.'

'You mean about our baby?' he said, kissing her cheek. 'I heard about it from the doctor. It's fantastic. I couldn't be more pleased. But why didn't you tell me? I would have looked after you better. You shouldn't have been bearing it alone.'

'I didn't know myself until a week ago. I tried to tell you a couple of times, but I didn't want to upset your plans with Richard. And I...'

'My plans? There is nothing definite. Nothing that can't be changed. You are more important to me.'

'Maybe, but I had a lot of things to sort out in my mind. I decided to tell you tonight. That is, after breaking my engagement to Robert. I didn't know how he would react. Our futures were so bound together. He was furious. I decided to break with him altogether. Now everything is in shreds.' A tear glistened on her cheek.

Charles sat on the edge of the bed and held her hand. 'Has this baby ruined everything for you?'

A wan smile told him more than words alone could. She shook her head. 'Just changed things, that's all.'

'I guess I don't have to ask how Watson took the news. I mean about the baby.'

'First of all, I told him I loved another man and handed back his ring. He wouldn't accept it. He came on to me. So I told him about the baby. He was furious and said I had to get rid of it. I refused. He tried to force me to... to... you know. I wouldn't give in to him. Then all at once, he said that he could handle it. Me, having your baby that is. But I didn't trust him. You and our baby are more important than my job, Charlie. I told him I wouldn't hold him to our contract. And that it was time to part company.'

'That must have been a shock to Watson,' he said, stunned by the revelation.

'You could say that! We sort of had a fight. He was going to...' She hesitated, biting her lip, '...persuade me. Anyway, he slipped on all that mess.' Her expression suddenly changed to one of deep concern. 'Oh Charlie, is Robert all right? There was so much blood. I know it was an accident, but I feel it was *my* fault. His hopes for the future are ruined. Of course, his sport and leisure business will go ahead. And once he's back on his feet, the new designs will be developed by a string of designers anxious to work for him. But his personal life is in tatters. He really does love me and—'

'Stop it, June. Rob will be fine. He's a survivor. He turns setbacks around to his own advantage. He would never have accepted another man's child. We both know that. He still has Jim. I would say that makes him a very lucky man.'

She slowly nodded her head. 'Yes, you're right, Charlie.' Wincing, she put a hand to the wound on her head.

Her pain touched him too. 'Does it hurt?'

'A bit,' she said. Her eyes narrowed in concentration. 'I've been trying to work out what happened after I fainted. How did you suddenly appear in the kitchen, Charlie? I know the doors were locked and we were alone in the house.'

'When Rosie told me what you intended doing that evening, I came back early from Bath. I knew Watson was not going to be pleased about getting his ring back. Ruth told me where you were. I jumped back in the Merc and drove straight to the Old Rectory. Not sure what I was going to do... have a showdown with Watson?' He shrugged. 'Maybe, but I knew I had to get you out of there. I drove up to the front entrance. Before I reached the door, a girl was leaving the house in a hurry. She said she was late for something-or-other. I asked her if you were inside. She looked a bit embarrassed and said you were in the kitchen with Watson. I drew my own conclusions. We both heard you scream. I told the girl — I think she said her name was Jane — to wait in the hall while I went to investigate. You had fainted on top of Watson. I asked Jane to phone for an ambulance and then find me clean towels and blankets. Meanwhile, I gave you both first-aid. Of course, I had to move you away from Rob and tidy you up a bit.'

'I have a vague memory of that,' she said, smiling. 'I couldn't get my head together. I thought I must be dreaming.'

'Hardly surprising; you probably thought I was still in Bath. Well, after carrying you to the hall, I asked Jane to stay with you. I thought it best not to move Robert. I returned to the kitchen until the ambulance men arrived.'

She looked worried. 'What did they think happened, Charlie?'

'I told them it looked like Watson had been swimming. He, or maybe both of you were about to have coffee or a meal. The bottle of oil must have been dropped accidentally and Robert slipped on the contents. Probably, he stretched out a hand to steady himself and accidentally swept all that stuff off the table. With all that blood and the shock of what happened, you obviously fainted. It was not for me to conjecture more sinister happenings.'

She smiled wryly. 'Did they accept your version of events?'

'It seems that is what the ambulance men told the doctors here. When the medics asked me, I repeated the story. Unless you want to make a complaint, I doubt things will go further.'

'No, I don't. Definitely not! Please don't get the police involved. I couldn't bear it!'

He gently squeezed her hand. 'Whatever you say.'

Clearly, the engagement was over and, from what she had been saying, she had given up her job as well. What a sacrifice for love of him and their child! But could she live without the adrenaline that Watson and her work continually pumped through her veins? How could he make it up to her? Where did he stand now? Dare he ask her to marry him yet again?

He took her hand in his, and gently kissed it. 'June, will—'

She put two fingers over his lips. 'Don't say it, Charlie.'

He nodded. Rejection came hard. He dropped his eyes so she would not see the hurt.

'Don't be sad,' she said, 'We're going to have a baby that will be ours… just ours… yours and mine.'

A wonderful glow welled up within him. He remembered the child's conception. Yes, the timing was exactly right. 'Adam, you said we would call him Adam.'

She put his hand on her tummy. 'Yes… a child of our love.' She pulled herself to a sitting position. 'There's something I've been wanting to ask you.'

'What is it?'

'Marry me, Charlie. Soon, very soon.'

Epilogue

August 1970

As the Daimler wound its way along the country roads, Rob's thoughts were not on the magnificent scenery surrounding him, but rather on the business potential of the area. With the Motorway being extended northwards, the lakes and mountains were going to become easily accessible to thousands of day-trippers as well as tourists. Opportunities abounded for country clothes, leisure casuals, and sportswear. It might be a good idea to open a small chain of boutiques specialising in eye-catching day and evening clothes, maybe combined with quality leather goods and accessories. He made a mental note to get a feasibility study done. A heavy investment in property — holiday apartments, marinas, whatever tourism demanded — was already taking place. A few million in profit could be expected within a decade. Handy cash, but not as inspiring as putting clothes on female backs! Buzzing in his brain was a property, already viewed, as being a local centre for his businesses in the Lake District area.

Robert Watson believed every defeat should be used as a spur to future success. He smiled contentedly: James was his future too. As for June? She could never give up her designing...or him. He laughed derisively.

'When she gets tired of playing mummies and daddies, she'll be back!'

Rosie nursed tiny Adam and looked up at Richard. Their eyes met and he smiled at her knowingly.

June nudged Charles. 'Isn't it lovely to see Rosie looking so happy, and Richard the man he was before the accident?'

'They make a handsome couple,' Charles agreed.

June felt pleased that her daughter was settling into their new home, ready and eager to start at the area's teacher-training college. She smiled at baby Adam, pink and podgy in his grandfather's christening robe, and then looked across at her three older sons, each of them handsome and loveable. How greatly blessed her life was now. She looked up at the pretty church with its little bell tower. It was good to be part of the Church again. Churchgoing had been a weekly event when Arthur was alive. Now married to Charles, she felt comfortable and spiritually at ease sitting beside him. Only the months of a divided heart and her lusty need of Rob had made it difficult for her to attend services. She frowned at the thought of young Jimmy being picked up by his father that afternoon to spend three weeks with him, but she would not deny Robert access to his son.

Breathing deeply to take in the wonderful fresh country air, June's eyes swept over the surrounding fells and mountains. She had been feeling relaxed and at peace since moving there after their marriage. In her mind's eye she could see the next watercolour she would paint: the lovely old slate church set amongst yews and native deciduous trees in their summer glory. Or maybe she would wait for the golden tints of autumn. Why not paint both? Yes, spring and winter too. From different angles maybe? Quite symbolic really, from every perspective: life itself was ever changing and yet familiar. New birth and decay... light and shade... joy and sorrow.

Unexpectedly, a sudden yearning tugged at her heart. Painting wasn't enough for the creative urges that welled up within her and she knew it. But she was determined not to give in to the unwelcome inner clamouring to be back in the swim of things. She must think positive. Explore the Windermere boutique project suggested by Charlie?

Dear Charlie. The four months since their marriage had flown by. He was already settled in his own new job, managing a new commercial submersible project in a not-too-distant coastal town. It suited him very well. Of course, his satisfaction was enhanced because Richard was his team leader: they worked so well together.

The voice of her sister Peggy drifted to her ears: 'Being a daddy suits him. He's still as handsome as when he used to call for our Junie all those years ago.'

June smiled. She knew Peggy was talking about Charlie. Thinking about Peggy's situation, living under the same roof as Charlie must put her under a bit of a strain. And will she get the opportunity to lead a rich full life of her own?

And what of Ruth? She certainly seems happy chatting with family members she hadn't met before. What a surprise the Rogers clan had when they discovered Charlie's well-endowed skeleton that had been hidden in the family cupboard for twenty years! She looked so lovely in her softly flowing floral dress, but she had the figure to make even a sack look elegant.

'Mum, come and hold Adam,' David called. 'Everyone will think he's Rosie's baby!'

Eventually, family and friends filled their cars and made their way along the country lane to the big house overlooking the lake. June swept her eyes around the property. It was a healthy place to live with so many opportunities for outdoor activities. A wonderful area for bringing up a large family too. Maybe next year, they would have a brother or sister for Adam?

At five o'clock, Jimmy was waiting in joyful expectation for his father to come for him. Although he could go horse riding locally, he missed his pony Blackie. But most of all, he enjoyed being with his father. He received a lot of attention and, young as he was, he enjoyed visiting where his father worked. It made him feel important to see how his dad was respected and obeyed. The women staff made a fuss of him, calling him 'Mr James' and he liked that very much.

The Daimler arrived and Jimmy ran outside to greet his father.

'Dad, My baby brother's been christened. Do you want to see him?'

'Your father is waiting to be off, Jim,' said Charles carrying a case and a couple of duffle bags to the car.

'My son is called James,' said Robert Watson, putting the luggage in the boot of the Daimler. 'Please remember that, Captain Rogers.'

Watson reached into the car and brought out an envelope from the back seat. 'Take this to your mother, James.'

'No, Jim, give it to me. I'll give it to her.'

Jim saw his father give his uncle a piercing look.

'I don't mind being called Jim,' he said, afraid of trouble between the two men he loved. 'But I like being called James too, and Jimmy.'

He jumped into the passenger seat. 'Bye, Uncle Charlie.'

Smiling at Jim's diplomacy, Charles watched Watson drive away. He knew June would be watching from the window and his heart went out to her. Had he done the right thing by bringing her away from Watson and his hypnotic influence, but also far from friends and family? Certainly, she had been in full agreement, saying she could think of no better place to live. The joys of motherhood probably dulled the pain of what she had lost, but sometimes he caught a faraway look in her eyes. Maybe she would turn again to freelance designing, or perhaps open up a boutique selling exclusive designs.

Back in the house, he took June to the study where they could be alone, and handed her the envelope. 'Watson left this for you.'

She frowned and pushed it away. 'Burn it in the grate.'

'A bit drastic,' he said, wondering if she would later regret such a hasty action. 'It could contain anything: legal documents; enlarged photographs of Jim; something irreplaceable.'

'Then *you* look inside, Charlie.'

He went over to the desk and slipped out most of the envelope's contents. They were glossy pictures of top models wearing June's designs for sport and leisure clothing. All of them had come from leading magazines and each had her name printed somewhere prominent. They were impressive. He was about to push them back into the envelope when he became aware of June standing behind him. She was smiling with pleasure.

'A good job all round. Nice to see my work reach fruition.'

She eagerly shook out the rest of the envelope's contents. A piece of paper came adrift and fell to the floor. She picked it up and read aloud the message.

'The door is still open.'

Charles was struck with a horrible feeling of déjà vu.

Gladys Hobson lives in England. She is married with three sons and six grandchildren.

Mrs Hobson worked in the fashion industry, education, and in pastoral ministry before taking up full time creative writing.

Her works include:

When Angels Lie, all hell is let loose and demons fly! (as Richard L Gray)

Blazing Embers (as Angela Ashley)

The Trilogy:

Awakening Love

Seduction By Design

Checkmate

When Phones Were Immobile and Lived in Red Boxes.

Still Waters Run Deep, stories of hidden depths

When Angels Lie and Blazing Embers are published in the USA in own name.

The trilogy is published in the USA where Awakening Love is known as Desire.

REVIEWS

Seduction by Design

Here's a book that carries the reader right along in a smooth, continuous delight of romance, erotic adventure and well woven suspense. Author Gladys Hobson kicks right off with a bang, introducing us to the sensual June Rogers. A fashion designer by trade, June is grieving the death of her husband, Arthur, and begins to take readers on a tangled journey of love and hate with the attractive Charles and the ever despicable Robert--and is he ever!

Trite as that might sound, Hobson truly brings these three main characters (and a surrounding cast of delightful cast members) to vivid life in her "Seduction by Design." This book keeps the reader on one's toes as misfortunes lead to twisted plots and motives, and then to one misunderstanding after another that almost lead to tragedy and final heartbreak and yet, in the end -- well, the writer sums it up best as, "Deja vu," which you will have to find out by reading this delightful piece of work!

Gladys Hobson is a well practiced writer, spinning a tale smoothly and naturally. She is economical and yet she is capable of painting entire scenes and montages with dialogue, a quick glance, the sparkle of an eye or the dart of a smile so quickly that a reader doesn't even know it's happening. This is a rare talent and a delight.

"Seduction by Design" is good reading. It's flat-out entertaining, suspenseful, erotic, fun, and heartwarming!

Andrew O'Hara (editor of The Jimston Journal, author of prize-winning The Swan, Tales of the Sacramento Valley) lives in the USA and now runs the Badge Of Life.

I was keen to sink my teeth into this novel, 'Seduction by Design' because she had me hooked with her 'Desire' (known in the UK as Awakening Love).

These are no ordinary romance novels. They are written by a mature age author, whose abundance of wisdom invests the chapters with a fragrance rare. A young person simply could not achieve this, and the gems of insight Ms Hobson scatters throughout her story delighted me.

It is the early seventies, the setting having jumped a couple of decades from that of 'Desire', and my word how well Ms Hobson has integrated the plot from that instalment!

The thermostat regarding eroticism has been turned up a few notches in 'Seduction...', and that's saying something, and yet, as with her first, there is nothing dirty or obscene in her explicit portrayals, and I tip my hat to her for this achievement: sexually charged encounters aplenty, without impurity – trashy romance writers take notice!

Something rare for me: I was actually mesmerised in places as I consumed this believable story involving an assortment of characters that would exist in any big town and city. And as in my previous review, let me reiterate that, as a writer, I continued to be informed and educated regarding effective technique to convey and captivate.

Well done Ms Hobson, and when is the final novel, 'Checkmate', going to be finished for me to learn what happens to these characters, who have become such a part of my imagination?

Payton L. Inkletter (writer, thinker, humorist)